Baugh, Laura VanArendonk, author.
Shard & shield

2019
33305243636168
sa   02/25/20

SHARD & SHIELD

The Shard of Elan, Book 1

Laura VanArendonk Baugh

Æclipse Press
Indianapolis, IN

Copyright 2019 Laura VanArendonk Baugh

Cover design by Damonza

ISBN 978-1-63165-021-5
www.Aeclipse.com

All rights reserved. This book or any portion thereof
may not be reproduced or used in any manner without
the express written permission of the publisher, except
for the use of brief quotations as in a book review.

For Alena,
who bore with me and all our terrible jokes.

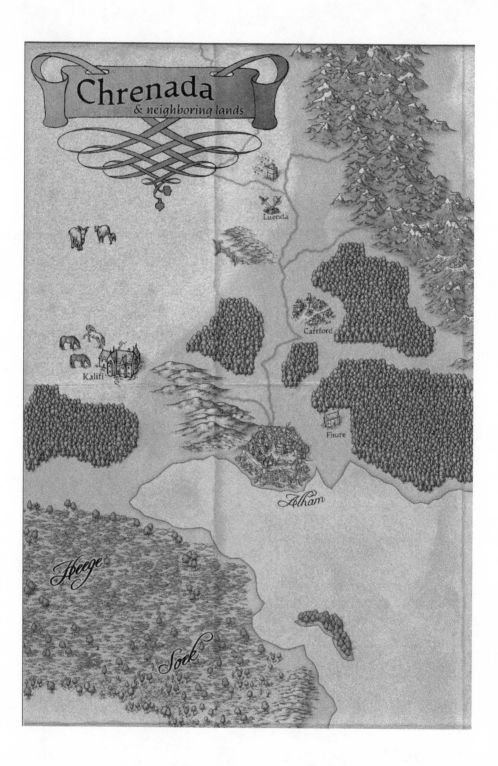

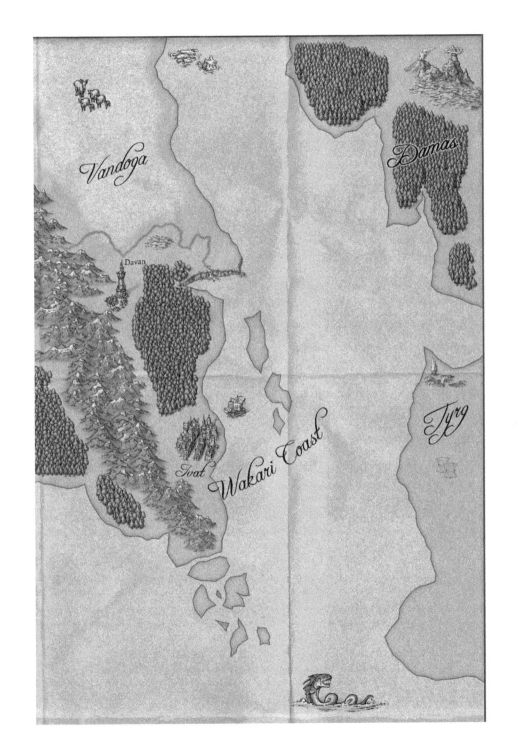

CHAPTER 1

Ariana spotted Shianan Becknam in the traffic almost immediately, but she pretended to search a moment longer. It was a guilty opportunity to study his features for telltale characteristics.

Beside her, young Tam pointed too helpfully. "He's there, near the soldiers."

Ariana crossed the road to the bench outside the public house, untangling a few dark strands of hair from her pack strap. Becknam gestured to waiting ales. "Was the market worthwhile?"

"I bought some chocolate."

Becknam gave her a flat glance. "Only a few bites, I hope."

Tam led the way inside and crouched to tuck their packs beneath a table. Ariana shook her head. "Not much."

Not much for Becknam to carry, anyway, as the packet was in her bag. She probably shouldn't have purchased the chocolate, as every pound would matter in the mountains. It would make a nice treat one night, though. She wanted something for Tam as well; he had not yet complained despite the difficult journey.

She glanced sidelong at Becknam. He, too, had made no complaint, but that was to be expected.

A smiling, stout man emerged from the kitchen, a child toddling curiously behind him. "Welcome! Suppers for all? Mutton and herbed roots tonight. Sing out if you find the bottom of your cup."

Ariana began to reclaim her windblown hair into a braid. Watching Becknam across the table, she thought the line of his jaw was reminiscent of the king's. She wondered if he had considered a beard to conceal that, or if he preferred the resemblance to be seen. She wondered if everyone wondered such things as they looked at him.

The room was filling with locals, and soon they were sharing their table and benches. Ariana sipped at her drink and traced a finger through its condensation on the table, drawing loose geometric designs. Idly she asked, "Did you know some ancient art includes winged men as icons of beauty? Not quite Ryuven, but wings, anyway."

"Then it was ancient art indeed," said Becknam, "from well before the Ryuven. Those monsters aren't winged men, and they

7

aren't beautiful." He cast a suspicious eye toward her. "If my lady had seen—"

"I am quite aware of what the Ryuven can do. I only—it's odd that we should have imagined men with wings, don't you think?"

"Artists have more imagination than sense, and more sense than usefulness."

Ariana drew a bolder design on the table.

Tam shifted the ales to make room for cold mutton and warm turnips and parsnips, sprinkled with shredded herbs and chunks of butter. The landlord beamed at Ariana's praise for the food and retreated to the kitchen, shooing the child ahead of him.

The man to her right was intent on a story for his other tablemates. "And so there was Sergeant Vanguilder, pulling his last arrow, and then out of the sky comes this Ryuven—"

"The Ryuven in front of him?" asked another.

"No, another Ryuven, come from above. And he strikes the sergeant like a lightning bolt and he goes face down—the sergeant—and I don't have to say the arrow goes wide, and the Ryuven—the first one, now, the one on the ground—jumps for him like a terrier on a rat."

One of the listeners rolled his eyes. "Maybe a stunted terrier. On a fat rat."

"Eh? The sergeant ain't fat."

"Or maybe if the rat had a bow and a pike, and the terrier had a mace and magic."

"What's that supposed to mean?" the storyteller demanded. "Stupidest thing I ever heard."

"Well, that's a stupid way to describe it, terrier and rat. You ever seen a Ryuven shake a soldier by the spine? Say plainly he went for the sergeant with his hammer or whatever he had. He didn't use magic, I'll guess, or you wouldn't go on about terriers."

"You done for a bit? Can I tell on?"

Ariana hid her smile behind her hand.

"So I use my sword and I cut a steak out of this Ryuven, and then over us comes this shadow, and—"

"And it's Pairvyn ni Ai himself, right? Only he sees you and he runs for his life? And then King Jerome comes and says he wants you in his personal guard—" The rest of the listener's heckling was drowned in a chorus of mocking laughter.

"Shuddup!"

"It wasn't yet that the king asked him," protested someone

else, laughing hard enough to muddy his words. "He had to go and save His Majesty's life first, right?"

"Shuddup," repeated the storyteller, sullen. "I did so guard the king at Ason Field."

"Right you are! Wait, I thought you said it was at Scout's End?"

Ariana glanced at Tam with a conspiratorial smile and whispered, "The king wasn't even at Scout's End."

Tam pursed his lips. "Was so."

"How would you know?"

"Same as you—I've listened to your father's stories."

"And my father said the king wasn't at Scout's End!" Ariana laughed.

Tam's grin vanished and he started up from the bench. Ariana caught a flash of movement and then the storyteller's hand twisted into her shirt collar, pulling her off-balance. "You calling me a liar, girl?"

She blinked and struggled to find words. "No! No, I wasn't even—"

The storyteller curled his lip, glad to vent his frustration. "We fought and bled and died there, and you got no call to be mocking those men who—"

"I'm sorry." Ariana gathered power into her palm, just enough to knock him off his feet if necessary. "I didn't mean to offend you. I have only the highest respect for—"

Becknam appeared beside them, his eyes on the soldier. "Let her be."

"I won't be mocked by a piptit not old enough to—"

Becknam's hand rested lightly on Ariana's shoulder, very near the soldier's. "Let her be."

For response, the man released Ariana and pivoted, driving a fist toward Becknam. Ariana ducked and Tam seized her, pulling her into a stumble.

Becknam parried the fist outward with his left hand as his right jabbed the end of Ariana's wooden spoon deep into the attacker's bicep. The man's fist recoiled, and Becknam slid the spoon beneath the storyteller's upper arm and over the wrist, pressing his arm back. The storyteller stuttered back a few steps but could not reclaim his balance, and Shianan eased him backward to the floor, pinned by the spoon on his wrist and a knee on his chest.

The room went quiet.

9

"Now, she's said she was sorry and wished no harm," Becknam said, "and I'm sure you mean the same, so let's all be neighborly." He rose and offered the man a hand.

The soldier frowned and didn't take the hand. "That was too slick to be farm work."

Becknam shrugged. "Farms need defending."

"You're in?"

Becknam nodded, and Ariana caught her breath. But he added casually, "I'm posted at Stoneship, on leave to visit home."

"Stoneship?" The soldier held out a hand, and Becknam pulled him to his feet. "That's where I did two years."

"No joking?"

"And Edgar was there, too. Hear that, Edgar?" The soldier slapped Shianan's shoulder. "That was a slick turn, but you're lucky I didn't see it coming."

Becknam laughed and turned into the group, nodding and smiling and clasping wrists like old friends.

Ariana sighed and sank down on the bench. "I could have defended myself," she murmured to Tam. "I was ready."

Tam was irritatingly practical. "Magic would have been harder to explain than fisticuffs, and less soothing than trading soldier stories."

"Maybe. But I was ready."

Tam scooted onto the bench beside her, watching Becknam accept an ale. "It was Steward's End."

"What?"

"The king went back to Alham before Steward's End, not Scout's End."

Ariana clenched her jaw; her history error had nearly cost a great deal. "You'd better not let his lordship hear you correcting your betters so lightly."

Tam barely suppressed his usual grin. "Right, my lady."

The landlord appeared beside her. "You're all right, I think?" he asked with concern. "They're not an unfriendly bunch, though they can be loud." He nodded toward the group, still exchanging eager anecdotes with Becknam. "But your friend seems to know his way around old soldiers."

She nodded. "Did he say we wanted two rooms for the night?"

"I told him I've only the one. We don't see much traffic here. The merchants mostly use the south pass, it being open all the year."

"One room," Ariana repeated. She couldn't expect the Count of Bailaha to sleep in a public room, even if they were traveling covertly.

"It has two beds," the landlord offered, though his face betrayed surprise at her hesitation.

"That will be fine," Becknam said, returning.

Ariana nodded. They would do without social niceties like walls once they were beyond inns.

"I'll just take up fresh bedding after I get ales around, then, if you'll wait a bit. Or send the boy back with me now, and I'll send him up with the linens."

Tam followed the landlord to the kitchen, and Becknam leaned an elbow on the table. "You trust him to run about on his own?"

"What?"

"Will he talk?"

"Tam's a model of discretion." Ariana nodded toward the kitchen door. "He's a servant of the White Mage—a famulus, even. There isn't much Father's hidden from him."

"So I saw when I met with your father." He gestured. "I just don't feel settled."

That was understandable. It had happened so fast once her father had announced his discovery. He had introduced Ariana to Commander Shianan Becknam, Count of Bailaha, a man she had always heard of and never known, and barely a day later, they had set out to retrieve the Shard.

The landlord passed again, trading a folded blanket for Ariana's empty plate. "Your boy's gone up now, so whenever you're ready. Here's an extra blanket I found. You'll want breakfast?"

"Early, if you please," Becknam answered. "We don't want to lose daylight."

The guest room was small but comfortably heated by the kitchen chimney. Becknam dropped the blanket on the sheets Tam was tucking into place. "Extra bedding for you tonight."

"How nice." Tam pulled a sheet tight. "I carried his lordship's bedding, and he carried mine."

Becknam stiffened. "Few would confuse a commander with a slave."

Tam shrugged. "You take orders just as I do."

"I give them as well."

"Tam!" Ariana said. "That's enough. I'm sorry, your lordship."

Becknam shook his head and sat on the other bed, his muscular

11

frame making the ropes creak. Tam looked away.

It was not like him to be rude. Ariana took his wrist, the metal cuff cool against her fingers, and drew him to the other side of the too-small room. "You were out of place," she warned softly. "Think on what you say."

"But he shouldn't—a prince might become a slave. It's happened, it's in stories. And a slave might be—"

"You are not a prince!" She checked herself. "Tam, you know better than to fixate on stories, and saying such things could get us all into trouble. You would reflect badly on Father, and someone might demand you be punished. Do you understand?"

Something unreadable crossed Tam's face. "Yes, mistress."

She sighed. "Don't be like that, Tam. I'm saying this for your own good."

Tam was an intelligent boy, too old to imagine himself a lost prince. She sighed. They were both on edge, nervous around Becknam and the enormity of their task. It had been a long time since she'd exchanged a joke with the boy.

She watched Tam finish the bed. If their journey tired her, what strain must it be on him? That might have been weariness speaking.

The room was too quiet. "I should confess," Ariana offered, "I'm excited to reach the citadel. This is an adventure of sorts. So many tales start with a quest for a wondrous artifact: Kalen and the Forgotten Diamond Diadem, Gabriev and the Sword of Light...."

Becknam gave her a flat look. "Think less of stories and more of duty, my lady. There's little connecting a taproom tale and a true battle."

Ariana stiffened, but her eye caught Tam's before she could retort. *Stories*, he mouthed.

She fluffed her pillow.

Becknam lay back and turned to face the wall. Tam made a nest of blankets beside their beds and curled into them like an animal, leaving only his blond hair visible.

Ariana considered Tam's choice. There was space between the foot of her bed and the wall, where he could have slept without danger of being trod upon. Yet Tam always slept between her and Becknam—did he think to protect Ariana from dangerous intentions? The thought made her stifle a giggle. Becknam might be a commander and now a count, but Ariana was the daughter of the White Mage Ewan Hazelrig. And as a grey mage, she could defend herself. And Tam was a mere boy—how could he hope to stop a soldier?

Still, there was something endearing about the gesture. And Tam would soon relax. They couldn't afford suspicion or friction if they were to travel efficiently and quietly.

"Wake, Tam. Time to go." Ariana frowned at the curled drape of blankets on the floor. "Tam?" She flipped the end she guessed covered his head, ruffling his fair hair, and he protested inarticulately. "Tam, up. Now."

The boy shielded his eyes. "Morning?"

"Morning," she confirmed. "His lordship woke early," she added, trying not to sound as resentful as she felt. "As always."

Across the room, the commander's mouth quirked upward. "I had an effective education—each dawn, my mattress inverted. I learned to wake in the dark."

Ariana was not sure how to respond. "That's not...."

He looked away. "I'm sorry. It was an awkward thing to mention to a lady."

"I am not so naïve as that, my lord."

"I wasn't *my lord* then."

His embarrassment embarrassed her, and now Tam sat smugly concealing his smile at the two of them embarrassing themselves before a slave boy.

Becknam pointed at Tam. "Up and ready," he said gruffly. "We're losing daylight."

After a quick breakfast they were on the road again. "No more inns," Becknam said as he shouldered his pack. "We'll sleep under the stars tonight."

"We always sleep beneath the stars," Tam offered. "Whether we have a roof makes no difference to their place."

Ariana stifled her chuckle when Becknam frowned. *Stick-in-the-mud.*

The mountain terrain, just beginning to green, dazzled Ariana's urban eyes. Spring melts had filled every rivulet to a run, and they never escaped the plashy sound of running or falling water. The air took on a tang of spicy cold which had nothing to do with the temperature, energizing Ariana. "I never knew mountains were like this! It's—amazing."

"You're not properly in the mountains yet," called Becknam

13

from his place at the front. The brown hair bound in a tail down his back was not so dark as the king's. "These are just foothills; there are still some farms and holdings along here."

"What's the difference?"

Becknam glanced over his shoulder. "A mountain is taller."

"No, between a farm and a holding?"

"A farm is a thin hide of arable land and a few hills of goats, and a holding is the shale ledge from which the farmer is trying to keep from falling."

Ariana frowned at his back. "I have either misheard or misjudged your lordship. Was that a joke?"

He grinned over his shoulder, and the expression looked out of place on his face. "I may be out of practice."

The road narrowed to a cart track, still smooth but more flexible as it ascended the hills. They would leave it soon. Becknam knew a quicker route for those without wagons, and speed mattered during the Migrations.

Ariana paused and turned, but the twisting road did not permit a view of the plain beyond. Would there be a clear sky for stargazing tonight? As Tam passed she started uphill again, muscles protesting. Or perhaps she would be too tired for stars.

Ahead on the road, Becknam halted, extending one arm as if to block their progress. Tam stopped instantly, and Ariana glanced at him before looking back to Becknam and coming to a slow halt. "What?"

He slid his pack to the road, slipping a sword from its wrapping as he straightened. "Wait here."

Ariana looked past him and saw a shape near the next curve, a dark mass lying at the edge of the road. Her arms tingled with sudden gooseflesh. "Is that...?"

Becknam didn't go to the body directly, but circled it, his eyes scanning the brush and the sky. After a moment, he knelt beside it. "Magic and mace," he reported. "If this isn't Ryuven, it's meant to look like it."

Tam edged forward. Ariana moved with him. "Here? On the road? But there's no reason...."

Becknam shook his head as he rose. "A farmer, by the look of him. Probably had a place near here. He was trying to get out, for help or maybe just to run." He sighed. "I suppose we ought to look. There are usually survivors."

14

Ariana kept her eyes on Becknam and away from the mass between them. "Survivors?"

Becknam nodded, turning to look up the road. "The Ryuven are butchers, but they're not stupid. You kill a farm's people, you get one harvest. Raid and run, without killing more than you can help, you get a harvest once or maybe twice a year."

The body stank. Ariana glanced down, unable to stop herself, and stared in mute horrified fascination. The man lay face-down, for which she was grateful—she didn't want nightmares of gaping mouth and dried-out eyes. His shoulder and back had been crushed with heavy blows, and magic had scorched his torso. He smelled of old blood and feces and flyblown meat.

Tam reached for her hand, and she took it and squeezed reassuringly. She had to be strong for the boy.

"Here," called Becknam, ahead on the road. "Here's the track to his place. Tam, bring my pack."

The turn-off led downhill, toward a natural basin where warmth might linger in the hills. Becknam kept his sword in his hand. "Stay behind me," he warned. "That was a good two days ago, but we don't want to startle anyone. Even farmers have weapons."

"And you have a mage." *A Mage of the Circle*, she should have been able to say. "If they have arrows, I can shield us."

"Heh."

"What?"

"Mages aren't so free with their shields in battle," he said gruffly. "Soldiers die by Ryuven magic while our mages stand on a hillside and watch."

"No!"

He glanced back. "Do you contradict me on battle experience?"

"No, of course not," she amended. "But you have it all wrong. First, that's an energy well, not a shield, and—"

"I don't care what—"

"And the dissipation efficiency decreases with reach," she continued over him, "putting the caster at increased risk, so a mage cannot hope to sufficiently cover a group of soldiers at a range of—"

"Quiet!" Becknam snapped. "We're close."

The track dipped toward a compact, well-tended homestead. The tidy image of a stone home with an attached stock shed was destroyed by the presence of two more corpses lying before the door. Becknam swore.

Ariana caught her breath and stumbled; the chickens had been at one body. The other lay near a tethered brown and cream goat, which bleated anxiously at their approach.

"No survivors," Becknam muttered. "Not this."

The body near the goat was a child, younger than Tam. Ariana stopped. "What—what do we do now?"

"Look for the survivors we know aren't here," Becknam answered wearily, "and bury these. We'll tell the village on our way back, after we have the Shard, if no one's noticed by then." He nodded to Tam. "Turn the goat loose, and I hear sheep around back. They can fend for themselves until someone comes for them. And keep an eye for a shovel."

"I'll get the sheep," Ariana said quickly, wanting to be away from the dead.

The outlying shed was open and empty of stores but for a few small burlap bags, a barrel, and two crates. The door creaked as it shifted in the breeze. Tam moved to unknot the goat's rope.

Ariana set down her pack and started around the house. Her heart jumped as she saw more bodies. One was a dead man, a slave by his wrist cuffs. The other was a dead Ryuven.

Ariana crept forward, drawn by a morbid fascination. She had never seen a Ryuven before, alive or dead—not in person. She stepped around the slave and looked at the monster.

It was almost less horrible because of its strangeness. Its shape was similar to a man's, but leaner and lighter, as if made of birds' bones. A pitchfork protruded from its chest, and dark blood stained its light leather armor around the puncture wounds. On either side lay crumpled membranous wings, set into the widened torso like a second set of shoulders.

"Lady Ariana?" It was Tam's voice, worried.

"I'm all right," she called. "But there are more dead."

Becknam came into view, holding a pick, and swore tiredly. "And one of the monsters, too. Well, no time to waste. Tam's got a shovel; free the sheep and let's get to work."

Ariana nodded and looked at the dead Ryuven again. Its face was the most unnerving aspect, narrow and fine and nearly human. It had died grimacing, pulling at the pitchfork.

Ariana tore her eyes away and went to the sheep pen. Sheep skittered around and circled back, calling worriedly, and bunched together before bolting free of the pen and dashing across the yard,

16

splitting neatly around the dead slave and Ryuven.

Becknam looked down at the packed earth, tamped solid by generations of stock. "There's not a chance of digging here," he observed. "I'll try the far side."

Tam came from behind the house and looked at the new bodies with wide eyes. He had likely never seen a Ryuven either, Ariana reflected. He approached with an awkward, jerking gait and squatted to peer at the dead thing.

"Good strike," he said softly, reaching out to touch the pitchfork. "Right through the heart. He never had a chance to heal that wound."

Ariana nodded. Ryuven could not regenerate something so devastating as a severed limb, but with enough time they usually could repair a cut or crushing blow—though not all, as human armies had learned and as this farm slave had demonstrated.

Tam left the pitchfork and crouched nearer the Ryuven's head. He seemed peculiarly still, as if the rigidity of death had spread to him.

"Tam!" Becknam barked. "Stop poking at dead things and come dig. Lady Ariana, are you able to bring the ones out front?"

Her stomach heaved, and she squeezed her eyes shut. "Yes," she managed, worried more syllables might betray her. She opened her eyes, keeping her gaze above the bodies, and took a breath of death-flavored air.

Tam rose and looked at her worriedly. "My lady...."

"I'll be fine," she said more quickly than necessary.

He nodded. "There will be blankets in the house."

She hadn't thought of that and gave him a grateful nod. "You'd better go help his lordship."

Fortunately, the little house held no further gruesome discoveries. The tidy home felt suspended, between breaths, so oddly interrupted mid-routine. The fire had gone out beneath a pot, and a single chicken which followed her in pecked enthusiastically at a ball of over-risen dough. She snatched the chicken and left with the blankets, closing the door behind her.

The goat pushed close, bleating insistently. She needed milking. Ariana didn't know how to milk and shoved the goat aside.

Metal chinked against rocky earth at the far side of the basin; Becknam's guess about suitable ground had been good. Ariana held one blanket before her, high to shield her vision, and started toward the chicken-pecked corpse. The buzzing of flies told her when she was near, and she dropped the blanket over the upper half of the body. Somewhat protected, she steeled herself to roll the corpse into a concealing bundle. It had been a woman, stout and strong with work. Ariana flipped the body one more time over the goat's tether and tied it tightly.

The smaller body was easier to handle, if she kept herself from thinking of a little girl. Becknam had said the raids killed few, and there could be no advantage to killing a child. Had she fought? Had these Ryuven been particularly bloodthirsty?

It wasn't too difficult to lift the girl, and she carried the body to the pit the others were digging. They were making surprisingly good progress; the narrow hole was already knee-deep. "Here's the first."

The goat butted her from behind, sending her stumbling toward the grave. She caught herself and whirled to shove it away. "Shoo!"

Becknam threw a clod of dirt which struck the cream-colored flank. The goat tossed her horns and trotted away, bleating reproachfully.

"She needs milking," Ariana said unhappily.

"These need burying." Becknam rubbed sweat from his forehead.

A fly buzzed around the blanket, seeking the dead girl's face. Ariana's stomach heaved and she twisted away, fighting the burning at the back of her throat. She folded her arms tightly to her abdomen and tried to force slow breaths.

"Keep moving, keep breathing," Becknam suggested dryly. He dropped the pick. "Here, Tam, take this. My lady, use his shovel to clear what we break out. I'll bring the other bodies, including that fellow from the road."

Tam traded tools, and Ariana began clearing the loosened dirt, ashamed. A Mage of the Circle would need a stronger stomach.

By the time Becknam had returned with both the man and woman, Tam was panting behind the pick. The commander motioned him out and took the pick himself. Tam stood at the edge for a moment, breathing hard, and then moved away.

"He'd better not think he's done here," Becknam growled.

But a moment later, Tam reappeared, dragging the dead slave. He paused a moment, panting, and then started off again.

"Wait." Becknam straightened. "We'll bury the slave, but don't you dare to bring that monster."

Tam hesitated. "But—"

"No. We'll not take time to dig for him, too. He invaded, he died, he has no right to expect us to do for him. Let the beasts have him."

Tam's mouth twitched, but he said nothing. Becknam turned and tore into the earth.

Ariana didn't know how long they worked, she and Tam taking turns while Becknam opened the ground. It became harder and harder to toss the dirt out as the hole deepened. "Can't get too deep," Becknam observed. "Still frost here."

When it was her turn again, Tam disappeared. Ariana thought he had just gone to the farm's privy, but he didn't return. "What's taking him so long?"

Becknam, now down to his shirt, straightened and shrugged. "He's tired, he's lazy, he's gone back to peer at the dead Ryuven. I'll help clear; this is nearly finished anyway."

They cleared most of the loose dirt and then Ariana tried to climb out of the pit. Her trembling arms wouldn't hold her weight, and she slid down twice. Becknam bent and extended an arm. "Come on, then."

His arm was damp with sweat, but he pulled her steadily upward and she was able to scrabble over the edge. She dropped to the ground, breathing hard, and didn't realize for a moment she was sitting beside the bodies.

"Where is that boy?" Becknam moved to the other side of the bodies. "Let's get these in. Drop them straight, or they won't all fit."

Ariana took the feet, and they swung in the bodies one by one. Becknam handed her the pick. "Rake what you can; I'll shovel."

Ariana looked down at the tangled limbs. "What about end-rites?"

"Wouldn't do much for them." Becknam kept working. "What do the priests say of it?"

"They say the dead made their choices in life, and the rites comfort the living."

"So, then."

Ariana swallowed. "I'm one of the living."

Becknam's rhythmic motion slowed, and after a moment he straightened. He didn't look at Ariana, but he held his right hand over the open grave, palm down, and closed his eyes. "You have fought well and done well, and your trouble here is ended. May the Holy One remember all that was sacrificed for you, and may you be welcomed into your eternal reward. May you be remembered and honored for all you have done."

It was the shortest end-rite Ariana had heard, efficient and military, but it seemed appropriate and familiar in Becknam's voice. She wondered how often he had recited it.

He began shoveling again, and Ariana joined him.

Finally the dirt was mounded over the crude grave, and Ariana dropped the pick in relief. "Thank the Holy One that's done. I don't think I could move any more dirt."

Becknam smiled tiredly. "Not so squeamish now? That's what happens, burns it right out of you." He collected both tools, a soldier's habit to be careful of his gear, and turned toward the stone house. "Where's that boy? If he's been hiding to shirk—"

But Tam was coming around the house now, dirt-stained and slumped with weariness. They must all look so, Ariana guessed.

"Where have you been?" demanded Becknam.

Tam's eyes shifted. "Digging."

Becknam scowled. "You buried the Ryuven? You left us to bury the farm folk while you wasted time on that monster?"

Tam's jaw protruded slightly. "He was just as dead."

"Through his own bloody actions." Becknam blew out his breath sharply. "If you were mine and I had the strength left.... Put these away and get the packs. There's still an hour or more of daylight."

Ariana's heart sank. "More climbing?"

"We could stay the night here," he allowed, "but we've lost much of the day already, and we've had ample reminder of the urgency of our errand."

It was hard to counter his argument. Becknam went back for his tunic as Tam headed to replace the tools. Ariana started toward the packs.

Near where they had entered was a steep embankment of eroded earth, now with a fresh mound at its base. Tam had set the Ryuven in the eroded trough and torn down the exposed dirt as cover. It wasn't so safe a grave as that given the farmers, but it was some protection from the scavengers.

Becknam returned, fully-clothed, and shouldered his pack, the sword safely wrapped once more but convenient at the side of the pack. His eyes flicked over the makeshift grave and then to Ariana.

"Let's go."

"Tam's still coming."

"It's a clear road. He'll catch up."

CHAPTER 2

They'd made good progress despite their weariness and the time lost to the slave boy's digression, Shianan Becknam decided. He chose an open place and halted. "Here for tonight," he said, sliding his pack from his shoulders.

"What I'd give for a hot bath." Lady Ariana dropped to the ground, her face flushed, and stretched her legs before her. "Enough of climbing. I'll be glad to be into the pass."

"We'll have other worries there. Supper?"

Tam was already bending over his pack. "It's coming."

"I'm not worried about the pass," Ariana said.

Shianan looked at her. "Not worried about the pass? The Migrations?"

Though this pass was easier than the steeper one to the south, none but the desperate or foolhardy crossed here during the Migrations. The great beasts which had long retreated into the mountains were rarely encountered these days except by foolhardy hunters in search of hides and tusks to bring riches. But during the seasonal Migrations, the beasts used the northern pass.

Ariana shrugged. "We'll be careful, and if we meet something I can defend against it."

Shianan shook his head. *Another gentle-born know-nothing mage, and mine to bear on this fetch-and-carry.* "If I may say so, Lady Ariana, I think you're overconfident. We must take all precautions."

"I'm only saying it won't be as dangerous to us as to merchants or farmers."

"And I'm saying I saw twenty men die in this pass!"

Ariana blinked and twisted her raw fingers into the short growth under her. "Those men—those men had no mage."

"I beg your pardon, but they did. He slowed one beast for a moment as it savaged him."

"But surely that was not a skilled mage—not one highly trained."

He set his jaw. "With respect, Lady Ariana, you failed your entrance to the Circle."

Ariana twitched. For a long moment she did not speak. Finally

23

she forced, "That is the reason I am here now. Excuse me, please." She rose and made her way into the brush.

Shianan watched her go, unable to call her back. Heat burned his face. He had not meant to speak so harshly—but he had been a sergeant then, too young for the post, and felt keenly his responsibility to those who died. Still, there must have been a gentler way to remind her of the risk. He squeezed his fists.

It was difficult enough being a royal bastard by birth. He didn't have to make himself one by deed as well.

Tam cleared his throat behind Shianan. "She was very disappointed to have been denied."

Shianan ground his teeth. "I know that."

But Tam spoke again, his tone reproachful. "You should not have—"

Shianan whirled and struck at the boy. "I know that!"

He froze, already regretting his loss of control. Tam had ducked the blow incompletely, and Shianan's knuckles stung where they had skimmed the boy's skull. Tam stared back at him, more startled than frightened. His expression was one of cold outrage.

That pricked Shianan more. He should not have struck the boy—should not have lost his temper, should not have insulted the mage in the first place—but he was well within his rights to rebuke an insubordinate slave. He set his jaw. "What about supper?"

"It's ready. If there's nothing else you need, my lord, I'll be excused."

Shianan watched as the boy started away, uncertain if he'd been carefully disdained. Lady Ariana, returning to the circle of firelight, stopped to speak to the boy. "Tam?"

"The supper is ready," Tam said a little more naturally. "Is there anything else you'll need of me?" She shook her head. "Then may I be excused for a bit?"

"Certainly." He slipped past her into the darkness, and she came to the fire. "I wonder what that was about," she mused, ladling food into a shallow bowl.

Shianan shrugged. Should he apologize, or let his words lie?

She didn't give him time to decide. "We'll be careful in the pass, your lordship." She took a bite without looking at him. "I know I am young, both in years and in experience. Please tell me if something worries you." She paused and turned to meet his eyes. "But I am as capable as any mage. My father said as much after my examination."

24

Shianan nodded. "I did not mean to disparage your abilities." She was not incompetent, or she would not be here with him.

She shook her head. "You said nothing inaccurate. I did fail—something I mean to rectify when we return." She looked around them. "Tam didn't take anything with him, did he? To eat?"

"No, he didn't. But... I know he's not my watch, but he could go without a meal or two if it would tighten his tongue."

Ariana winced. "Did he say something inappropriate?"

"Not exactly—no, he didn't." The boy had only defended his mistress; he wouldn't see him chastised for that. "And we're all a bit short after today." He avoided her eyes. "But he generally—that is, he isn't over-courteous."

"Tam has been with us for years," Ariana said, a little defensive. "He's practically family. We've found little fault with him."

Shianan clenched his jaw, frustrated with himself and the conversation. "The boy likes you," he said uncomfortably. "Not as a slave should feel toward his mistress."

She failed to suppress her smile. "Oh, please!"

"Even boys can have ambitions."

"Not Tam. He's been a perfect servant. We couldn't ask for better."

Shianan laughed. "No one's that good, and certainly not a boy of—what is he, twelve?"

"Older, I think, but—" she glanced over her shoulder—"he's never really matured physically. And no, I mean it. He's different—odd, even. He never went out with other children, even when he was small. He hardly even played with me when we were younger. Always inside with my father, always in the workroom."

Shianan frowned. "Always locked away with your father?"

"As a famulus, an assistant." Ariana regarded him warily, ready to be outraged. "What are you suggesting?"

"Why does your father have a slave?" He held up a hand to forestall her until he could explain. "During the arguments over the Furmelle prisoners, I ended up reading much of the debates of twenty years ago. Your father was already White Mage, and the archives show quite a lot of his opinions."

"What of it?"

"Twenty years ago, your father was one of slavery's most vehement opponents. He wanted stringent reforms and a contracted term of servitude rather than an indefinite condition. The details

25

aren't important now, but the point remains—how did such a vocal reformist come to keep a slave?"

Ariana waved a hand. "I suspect Father felt sorry for him. He brought him back from the Luenda battles. There were a lot of orphans, and it was probably easier to make him a slave in a benevolent household than to—"

"The Luenda battles?" Shianan repeated. An owl hooted from the dark trees.

She nodded. "As White Mage, my father was in the front lines." Her voice gained a note of pride. "He drove more Ryuven back to their own world than any other—"

"Wait a moment. Lady Ariana, Luenda was fifteen years ago."

Her brow furrowed. "But that can't be right."

"It is. I was young to be sent, even in that desperate need." Shianan carefully modulated his tone. "You might be remembering some other time your father was away."

Ariana shook her head. "No, Pairvyn ni'Ai was still fighting. It was Luenda."

"Then why does Tam look so young?"

"I don't know!" Ariana snapped. "I don't know. He's always been Tam—just Tam. I said he was underdeveloped. Would you hold that against him?"

Shianan frowned. It was possible Tam was cursed with bad blood, a heritage of poor development so he looked forever under-aged. It would be easy to underestimate such a slave.

Ariana was trying to peer about the darkness. "It's late. Should we look for him?"

If Tam were older, his ill-conceived infatuation for Ariana might be dangerously real, and his recalcitrance a sign of greater trouble to come. "He'll find his way back. Let's get some sleep before the pass tomorrow."

Was it his imagination that Lady Ariana turned away too quickly, dismissing the curious riddle too easily? Whatever Tam was, he wasn't the cheeky but harmless boy he seemed. Shianan would keep an eye on him.

CHAPTER 3

They descended toward Davan, a scrubby town dominated by the weathered citadel left from centuries past. The citadel was maintained now by the Gehrn, a faction which clung to the idea that ancient wars had been prophetic warnings of greater wars to come. Ariana had never understood exactly what else the Gehrn beliefs included, as the predominant idea seemed always to be preparation for unceasing war, and her whirlwind study prior to departure hadn't clarified their views. They tended to cloister themselves in remote strongholds, and this was their center.

Somewhere inside the citadel rested the Shard of Elan, a relic handed down through history and owned by any number of kings and leaders and revolutionaries. Some had attributed religious significance to it, some magical, some cultural. The Gehrn had it now.

The three were noted immediately as they entered Davan; travelers were rare here during the Migrations. Becknam kept his eyes forward as he strode ahead, ignoring the curious glances they received. Ariana wanted to look around but found herself quickening her stride to keep pace. *They always stare at home*, she realized. He had learned to outpace rude eyes.

Becknam turned on Tam. "You," he said, "will be absolutely silent. Do not speak. Nor will you even move. You will simply follow us and stand like a rock. Do you understand?"

Tam blinked. "I am to be still."

"No insolence."

"I understand," Tam said a little petulantly.

"My lord!" Ariana protested.

Becknam seemed to catch himself, and he glanced from Tam to her and then away. "I'm sorry," he said. "I only wanted.... Let's go."

The citadel had a long ramp beginning in the center of town and leading to the high gate. It was a gradual, weaving climb but narrow, designed to slow charging armies. At the top they had a chance to catch their breath while the gatekeeper sent word of their request for an audience.

They were led to an austere chamber, and shortly a man in layered blue garments entered. "I am Manceps Ande, Flamen here.

27

You asked for me?"

Becknam bowed. "Shianan Becknam, Count of Bailaha and commander in the king's army. This is the mage Lady Ariana Hazelrig."

Ande bowed slightly. Very slightly. "Ah, we expected you. Please, sit."

Tam remained by the wall. Becknam looked a little uncomfortable in the chair; he was likely used to standing. "We have come representing the council and the Great Circle."

Ande glanced again at Ariana, assessing her plain travel clothes. "I did not realize my lady mage was of the Circle."

Ariana's cheeks warmed. "I am not. Not yet."

"Hm." Ande leaned back in his chair. "Do you know what the Shard of Elan is?"

Ariana did know. Only recently the Great Circle, studying a fragment broken away from the Shard centuries before and newly rediscovered in a dusty archive, had discerned the Shard's actual nature. It seemed to be a piece of starry ether, a condensed chunk of the vaporous substance which made up the streaming light of the night sky.

But that was unlikely to be the answer Flamen Ande sought.

Ande looked from Becknam to Ariana. "It is the symbol of our obligation," he said. "The Shard must be defended at all costs. It is sacred to us."

"The Shard is not to be defended," Ariana amended. "It is the key to defense. With the Shard we can erect a barrier against the Ryuven and end the raids."

"The message said you would take it from here."

"You say the site where the Shard rests must be protected," Ariana said. "But it is not of this world. Its presence here may be a sign that it is this world which must be protected, using the gift of the Shard."

Becknam raised an eyebrow appreciatively.

Ande frowned. "And why must the Shard leave this place?"

"Such magic will require regular maintenance," Ariana said. "It will be far easier for the Great Circle to perpetuate the shield with the Shard within Alham."

"We know how important the Shard is to you," Becknam said. "But we ask it only for the greater good of the kingdom—of our world. We offer the Gehrn a chance to protect us all."

Ande, unimpressed, eyed them coolly. "One might think that were the Shard so critical, they might have sent someone greater than a mere commander. Could not a general be found to explain the urgency? Surely if this were the answer to save the kingdom, a prince would come?"

Becknam's wince was barely perceptible.

"And a common grey mage.... You have just explained this is the most valuable artifact in the whole of the world, and yet I see here a girl, hardly even a woman, and certainly no mage of the Great Circle."

Ariana bristled. "His lordship and I were selected personally for this task. The Circle believes me capable of seeing the Shard safely to Alham." She took a sharp breath. "My name, as we've said, is Ariana Hazelrig. My father is Ewan Hazelrig, the White Mage. That I am not yet ranked within the Circle is irrelevant—I was sent for the Shard and I—"

"The council believed," Becknam cut in, "the Shard's safety was paramount. We could not risk its loss to bandits or Ryuven." He faltered.

But his interruption had given Ariana time to recover. "Exactly. While the Shard deserves the highest respect and honor, none of the personages you mention could safely travel from Alham without attracting undue attention. If it were known, for example, that the White Mage and the prince-heir had come to Davan, who would not think there must be a great treasure to draw them? And if the Ryuven were to attack this impressive procession, all might be lost."

Becknam gave her another appreciative glance, and she recognized the telltale look of Tam suppressing a smile.

Ande frowned. "I see." He looked between them. "Still, I have nothing but your word as to who you are."

"As to that...." Becknam withdrew a packet. The waxed outer layers protected the heavy inner parchment with its broad, deeply-embossed closure. "The royal seal, of course. Inside you will find descriptions of my lady and myself, with attestations of our commission."

Ande broke the thick seal and scanned the letter, his eyes flicking from the page to each of them in turn. "I see," he conceded at last.

"I regret we are not the notable persons you mentioned," Becknam said, "but for the safety of the Shard and the kingdom, they

29

could not have come personally. You see, though, how closely they take an interest in your assistance."

Ande drummed his fingers on the tabletop. "This is a weighty decision for us." He stood, and they rose with him. "Will you wait here, so you may answer our concerns as necessary?"

"Of course," Becknam said with a slight bow. "We await your need."

The flamen left without glancing at Tam by the door, and Ariana sank back into a chair. She looked at Becknam. She had expected a man of the court to be more confident in his negotiations. "I thought it would be settled already."

"It seems not." Becknam frowned. "They want something."

CHAPTER 4

Shianan Becknam crossed his arms and sat rigid in the chair, determined not to fidget. Flamen Ande would return to find him calm and expectant. If Ande thought a barb or two would win leverage in new negotiations, he would find the opposite.

As if either of the princes could have been sent. Alasdair was only twelve, too preoccupied with royal hunts and private tutors to be sent across country. Shianan's lip curled; he had spent his own twelfth birthday digging a fresh privy. And Soren....

The king had sired an heir and then a second son, well and good for Chrenada's succession. But between them he had spawned a bastard. King Jerome had tried to conceal the mistake at first, sending the boy to be raised in a remote barracks, but as Shianan grew older the king had become convinced it was safer to keep him within easy watch, and he'd brought him to the capital.

Last year Shianan had been called to court, where the king had bestowed upon him a title and a bit of land. It was a concession to public, if unrecorded, knowledge. It was also, Shianan thought, a gesture from one who wished to be a truer father to his son. At least, that was what he hoped. Many days he believed it.

But Shianan had been sent to retrieve the Shard. Soren, the prince-heir, could not be risked crossing the mountains during the Migrations. Shianan could.

Lady Ariana was looking at him, and he realized he was scowling. *We're here because I'm expendable and she's a failure.*

Ariana glanced away, touching her hair. He sighed; it was hardly her fault; they were both victims of their birth. Only, she could study harder and train more and try again to enter the Circle, if she wanted, while he could never outpace his bastardy.

Enough. He rose and began to pace. Tam ducked out of his path and circled behind his abandoned chair at the table.

Lady Ariana laced her fingers and pushed back against her chair. "They're just being selfish. The Shard isn't exactly vital to their practice; they only acquired it themselves a dozen years ago or so."

Becknam gave her a dubious glance. "Flamen Ande certainly seems attached to it."

31

She shrugged. "He wants it because it's unique, and because we want it. And he wants something for it."

Becknam turned away. "Don't I know it."

Ariana stared across the room and wondered for the eleventh time how long they had waited and whether she looked impatient to Becknam.

Tam had no such worries. He flopped into a chair at the table, arms folded in irritable boredom. "Why don't we just steal the Shard?"

"Don't think I haven't considered it," Becknam said. "But we don't know anything of the citadel or where the Shard is kept. And while I could fight my way out, if necessary...."

Ariana raised her chin. "I wouldn't slow you down."

"King's oats, I hope it doesn't come to that," Becknam muttered. "The crown couldn't—but whatever it takes for this—magic shell...."

"Shield." Tam's voice was nearly hidden as he hastily dropped his chin onto his folded arms.

"Shield?"

"It will be a shield, technically speaking," Ariana supplied before Becknam could respond to Tam's correction. "That is, magic to physically repel, in this case to repel a Ryuven. More specifically, the organs of a Ryuven—heart, lungs, liver...."

"Just the organs?"

Ariana wrinkled her nose. "I wasn't too fond of the picture, either. But it's war, they say."

"So it is." Becknam gave Tam a disapproving look.

Ariana quickly continued, "A shield blocks physical intrusion, like a sword cut. A well absorbs a magical attack."

He raised a skeptical eyebrow. "A cistern, defeating magic."

She laughed. "An inversion well, I meant. The offensive energy is dissipated through the caster—much like a rod takes lightning, if that helps. Stand close to the mage; it's safer to throw a well over someone nearby."

"Not easier, but safer, you say."

She nodded. "That's what I was trying to explain the other day, at the—farm. The dissipation efficiency decreases with distance. And since the residual energy reaches the caster...."

He frowned thoughtfully, and then he shrugged and offered a

half-smile. "I always thought mages did not protect ordinary soldiers because they were too busy protecting mages."

"No! No, it's not—it's not like that at all. Trying to cast an inversion well over so many people would—the mages would die. And soldiers are in less danger from magical attack, anyway."

Becknam's expression closed again. "My men are in very real danger on the battlefield, my lady."

Tam drummed his heels against the legs of his chair and stared at the table.

Ariana nodded. "I didn't mean they weren't. It's... Those without mage-skill are less susceptible to magic. A magical bolt that would kill a mage might only wound a soldier." She leaned forward. "So a mage might die to spare a soldier a clout on the head. Do you see?"

"I know the mages are more susceptible to magic. I meant the soldiers are not un-susceptible." He scowled. "All we're told is that the greater mages are there to fight and the lesser mages are there to protect the greater mages."

She shook her head. "The Ryuven have the same trouble; they are strong in magic but physically weak. So soldiers can fight them with material weapons, while the mages blunt their magic."

Now Becknam grinned. "Thank you, my lady, for your lesson in battlefield tactics. I'll remember that the next time I take soldiers out to fight."

"I didn't...." Ariana flushed hot.

"It's all right. And now I know the difference between a shield and a—a well...."

"An inversion well. The well is like a heat-sink or a lightning rod, and 'inversion' refers to the elemental draw and dissipation of the primary energy while secondary reactive energy is routed—"

"Stop! No more. Not unless you're willing to sit through a return lecture on the anatomical mechanics of a throat strike." He smiled at Ariana's disgust. "I beg your pardon, my lady, but you mages are the ones separating out organs from their torsos."

"I suppose. Tam, sit properly." The boy had curled into his chair, his knees drawn to his chin. At her gentle reproof, he slid reluctantly upright.

He does age, she thought, watching him unfold. Every year, he was a quarter-inch taller, a bit lankier, a bit older. *He does age. Just— not as quickly as he should.* Was it an illness? An effect of bad breeding?

33

She'd heard ailments and disfigurements could appear in remote villages where the blood pooled....

The door opened to a young man with a tray. The iron bands on his wrists had larger rings than Tam's slim cuffs. "The high priest thanks you for your patience," he said softly, "and offers you this meal."

He set only two places. Ariana threw a quick glance at Tam, whose face fell a little. He pushed himself from the table and went to stand against the wall.

Becknam returned and sat, looking over the table—bread and a tumble of root vegetables with bits of roast pork, all in gravy. The Gehrn's slave poured watered wine for each of them, and then he retreated two steps from the table and knelt.

Ariana kept her eyes on the table. She and her father rarely ate with full service, and she had never seen a slave kneel while serving; this must be local custom, or something of the Gehrn.

Becknam was already eating appreciatively. Ariana followed his example, finding the meal delicious. She glanced at Tam. If they were dining with Flamen Ande there would be nothing she could do, but Ande couldn't be offended by what he didn't know. She laid pork over bread and held it out. "Here."

Tam accepted it silently, and Ariana saw the Gehrn's slave watching before averting his eyes again. He had thick black hair which hung to his shoulders. It would need to be cut or bound soon. He was not handsome but had strong features, a good face for a servitor. She could glimpse something occasionally beneath the black hair, but she couldn't get a clear view.

She finished her wine, and the slave rose to pour. As he replaced the pitcher Becknam's hand moved to catch his shoulder. The slave froze, and Becknam reached for his neck and rolled the chain there in his fingers. "You were one of the Furmelle prisoners."

"Yes, my lord," came the quiet, uneasy answer.

Ariana leaned forward to look. A chain of about a finger's thickness lay across the back of the slave's neck, ending in two rings. Through those rings was another linking chain which slid freely and ended in larger rings. The design was clear enough; tension on either or both large rings would tighten the chain about the neck. "That's from Furmelle?"

"Those who fought in the revolt were executed or returned to slavery. Captives were fitted with this collar during transport. It helped to pacify those who thought it dangerous to leave the rebels alive." He picked up his wine. "It was my understanding most had the collars cut off by their masters or when they were sold. Obviously a few kept theirs, though." He frowned. "Bend lower."

The slave obeyed stiffly, and Ariana watched as Becknam shifted the chain to reveal a blotched purple trail around the throat. "You've been giving them trouble?"

The slave licked his lips. "I try to give good service, my lord."

Becknam waved him away, and he backed his two steps. Becknam focused on his plate and did not meet Ariana's gaze.

When at last they finished, the slave rose to gather the empty dishes before bowing over the tray and exiting.

Ariana leaned over the table and looked directly at Becknam. "That was bruising from the collar? They choke him?"

"That is one possibility," he admitted. "Or it could have been restraint when needed. Or it might have simply caught on something. We don't know."

Ariana set her jaw. "Those collars—"

"Were used only on those who had fought us, and were mostly removed."

"This one should have been. Even if that bruising were accidental, it shouldn't be allowed to happen. And if they are using it—"

"It is no different than a quick cut of the switch," Becknam broke in again. "Perhaps even preferable, who knows? You must remember, my lady, not all slaves are treated so well as your own. Tam is quite pampered by most standards."

"I know that! But there may be a difference between what I know to be true and what I know should be true." She stopped, angry at both the slave's treatment and her inability to express herself.

Becknam softened. "I am sorry, Lady Ariana. But you must remember, I saw these same slaves trying very hard to kill my soldiers. Many of them succeeded. The collars, though not my idea, seemed a better alternative than allowing them to try again."

"Force begets force."

"What?"

"It is a precept of magic. Force begets more force, usually a resisting force."

"The force began with their rebellion." He gestured to the room and the citadel about them. "The Gehrn are a militaristic cult; they

35

respect force. That slave fought us once. Would you have him executed, or collared?"

What he said made some sense, and yet.... Ariana crossed her arms. Any apprentice mage knew it was difficult and wearying to counter force directly. Channeling power was far more efficient than resisting it. Any novice knew that.

And yet that was how she had failed her examination for the Circle.

The door to their stark room opened and Flamen Ande entered. "I trust you have not been too inconvenienced?"

"The meal was wonderful," Ariana said. "Thank you."

"And the service?"

"Very good," Becknam answered.

"I am pleased." He seated himself at the table. "Now, to the matter at hand. If we were to allow its use—and I ask only in hypothesis—would the Shard be kept intact?"

Ariana's heart quickened. "Yes, it will not be harmed. We will only use the quality of the ether to resonate a refractive energy—"

Ande lifted a hand. "Your rituals are of a different variety than our own, my lady; your explanation will mean little to me. I am satisfied to know there will be no harm to our Shard." He folded his hands. "Alham is a fine city, well-protected by sea and rock. Your lordship no doubt recognizes its many advantages. We have often admired it as we've thought of expanding our ring of preparation to the west."

Becknam's throat worked. "We will of course welcome your visits to the city."

Ande's mouth thinned. "I have always thought I should like to visit Alham one day." He sighed and turned back toward the door. "I should return to the elders; a few are much disgruntled with the very question and have threatened to leave the table altogether."

Ariana's stomach lurched. They were losing the Shard.

"Wait," she burst. "Flamen Ande... If you can't help us, then let us help you." She threw a quick, pleading glance toward Becknam. "My lord, couldn't we find a place in Alham? A building somewhere, to be a hold for the Gehrn?"

A muscle twitched in Becknam's face.

Ande smiled on her. "Thank you, my lady, it's very kind of you to think of it. It is most unfortunate that we cannot presently lend our strength for the coming wars of prophecy to fair Alham. As a soldier of some experience, commander, you must know one cannot hold ground without an entrenched defense. We of course would prefer to be of every use, were it possible."

"I see," answered Becknam flatly.

"It is most unfortunate you cannot send to ask the council. The Migrations make things so difficult. Perhaps in the next few days you might think over the city for a suitable place for us, some disused gatehouse or other facility? And we shall discuss our Shard."

"A few days?" Ariana repeated.

Becknam pushed a hand through his hair and exhaled.

"It will be so distressing to be parted from the Shard, even with your promises.... A noble cause, but you understand we sacrifice a great deal if our Shard goes over the mountains."

Becknam swallowed visibly. "I have a small townhouse in Alham. It is hardly your usual stronghold, but it is a worthwhile property, and furnished after a fashion. I will sign it to the Gehrn, to be your seat in Alham so long as the crown and council hold the Shard."

Ariana turned in surprise.

"You are most understanding." Ande smiled agreeably. "Your own house? I thank you, commander and Count of Bailaha. And as we will be so near, we would be pleased to share the Shard of Elan with others in need. We have agreed your interpretation of our sacred duty may be valid—if the Shard will protect a greater part of our world, that is what we must allow it to do."

"Oh, thank you!" Ariana breathed.

"But," he continued, "we still have incumbent duties. To that end, I or another priest must perform our annual high rites."

"We welcome your assistance," Becknam told him. "The council will be happy to accommodate your obligations."

"Thank you." Ande sat back in his chair. "I understand the Circle is probably quite anxious, or they would not have sent you during the Migrations."

Anxious enough, Ariana realized, that Ande had anticipated he could extort a townhouse from Commander Becknam. And she had aided him with her too-eager words.

Ande was still speaking. "I trust you have some assurance the Shard will travel safely across the mountains?"

Ariana's throat closed at this fresh aspersion, but Becknam answered readily, "We chose our route most carefully and, being a small party, were able to avoid most dangers."

"You will take with you copies of our rituals. Now, excuse me. It will take some time to prepare the Shard appropriately; please be patient once more." He left the room.

Becknam raked his fingers through his hair and cursed. Ariana looked at his back. "Isn't it finished, now?" She paused. "That was a great thing, giving up your townhouse."

"Heh. I've barely been in the place, and I've never stayed a night; it's no loss to me. But the signing of it... King's oats, what have I done?"

Ariana frowned, not understanding.

They were each occupied in private thoughts when the black-haired slave entered again. Ariana's curiosity was piqued. "Surely the citadel does not receive enough visitors to require a dedicated servitor. What are your other duties?"

He poured wine. "I serve the high priest, my lady."

"I didn't think the Gehrn kept personal servants," Becknam said.

"Only the high priest, my lord." The slave retreated two steps and knelt.

Ariana frowned uncomfortably and turned to Becknam, who gave a slight shrug. Then he looked at the paper and ink the slave had set before him, and with a grimace he began to write.

The door opened again and Flamen Ande swept past the slave scrambling to his feet. "The Shard has been prepared with proper ceremony," he said, taking a chair, "and copies are being gathered of our most important rites." Ande paused and looked at Tam, who had risen to stand against the wall.

Shianan Becknam rose and stepped between them. "We are most grateful for your help. Please share a drink with us, in token of our new cooperation—the Gehrn and the council." He gestured the priest toward the table.

"I will," said the flamen. "Luca, bring another cup."

The slave returned and began to pour. The first drip was accidental, but in his haste to recover he jostled the cup, spilling wine across the table.

"Clumsy dog!" Ande seized the document with one hand and with the other snatched the chain at the shrinking Luca's throat and jerked savagely. The slave was forced nearly to his knees before Ande shoved him away. The cup and the pitcher rolled in a dark puddle on the floor.

Becknam started forward and froze, his jaw clenched. Ariana stared and could not move.

"Clean this mess," Ande snapped, "and bring more wine."

Luca's hand was on his throat and his mouth worked once or twice without sound. "Yes, master," he finally croaked, and he fled through the door.

Tam was staring. "I will clean—"

"Be still, Tam." Becknam's fingers had closed on Ariana's wrist, silencing her unspoken protest and stilling the furious tremor of her arm.

Ande began to speak, more calmly. "I will come for our annual rite in the summer." He lifted the paper still in his hand. "Is this our surety? May I read it?"

Luca returned more slowly, carrying a fresh pitcher of wine and a pile of towels. Without speaking Tam left the wall to help sponge up the spill.

Ariana tore her eyes from them as a tap came at the door. "Flamen, everything is prepared."

Ariana had seen the broken bit upon which the Circle had experimented, but the actual Shard was far more striking—a jagged chunk of dark crystalline stone, about the length of Becknam's forearm and twice as wide. The high priest touched it reverently and then drew up the quilted bag in which it sat. "I trust you will be careful of it."

"We shall take every precaution," Ariana assured him. "It is as precious to us as to you." She took the rolled parchments offered, copies of the Gehrn rites.

Becknam lifted the padded Shard, his face betraying surprise at its weight. He clutched it close to his chest and bowed to the high priest. "On behalf of the King's Council, I thank you."

Ande smiled. "And I thank you. I will come in two months' time."

CHAPTER 5

The journey back into the mountains was less fascinating this time, with the steep climb unmitigated by novelty. Becknam was stern and unsmiling, but he and Tam seemed to have declared an unspoken truce, which relieved Ariana; mediating between them was too wearying while climbing and worrying over the Migrations. In the center of the pass they were threatened briefly by a leucrocuta, but it was young and solitary and quickly deterred by Ariana's repeated light stinging blasts. Unharmed—they were tough creatures, like toothy oversized pig-dogs—it snorted and retreated into the trees and rocks.

Ariana watched it disappear, feeling pleased, and turned to see Becknam with his sword too tight in his hands. He took a deliberate breath, perhaps his first in a while, and forced an embarrassed smile. "They were leucrocutas which killed my men here before."

"The twenty?"

He nodded, sheathing the sword. "They were not truly my men; I was only a sergeant. But I was responsible for them."

Ariana wasn't sure how to respond. "It's gone, now. We should move on."

Becknam started forward without speaking. Behind him Tam watched for a few steps and then started after him.

That night Tam worked quietly and efficiently, likely sensing the commander's frayed temper. Becknam carried the most weight as they traveled, the Shard as well as gear, and he did not share the load.

Despite her fatigue, Ariana did not fall asleep. Her restless mind wandered over the Gehrn fortress, the high priest, the gasping slave, her stifled protest. *Force begets force.* And then, for perhaps the hundredth time, her examination replayed in her mind.

She knew them, of course, the mages who would test her for the entrance rank of Black Mage, but the examination's formality kept her from greeting them as she might another day. Her father, highest in the Circle, would arbitrate. The five others faced her in a semi-circle and, upon his signal, brought their hands into position.

She deflected the first attack easily; it was a simple bolt. The next came hard on its heels and was not much more difficult. The third was a favorite of hers, and she not only blocked it but reversed it upon its caster. There was no damage, of course; these mages were not of a level to be harmed so easily.

The fourth and fifth came together, catching her off-guard. Still she was able to respond competently. She looked at them all then and smiled, confident she had passed. She had already submitted an impressive paper on the proper use of energies for maximum conservation; there seemed to be nothing left. She turned away from the five to look at her father. "Is—"

Power shifted without warning, and Ariana spun back to see all five mages casting together. For one eternal second she watched them, stunned, and at the last possible instant she reacted, flinging up a desperate shield in the palms of her outstretched hands. The invisible bolt struck and burst into sparkling rays which scattered across the room. The six mages easily absorbed the rebounding magic and then stood silently, staring at her.

Ariana licked her lips and turned to her father. "I blocked it," she said, hating the plaintiveness in her voice.

The White Mage sighed. "So you did. Barely. I'm sorry, but that is not enough."

"Not enough? But I did stop every—"

"You hesitated too long at the last, and so your defense was...inelegant. The Great Circle is charged with protecting the kingdom. There is no room for hesitation or error on the battlefield."

The examination had ended, and she had failed. In the weeks since, she had thought of a dozen strategies and responses, but in the critical moment, she had failed.

Force begets force. Her shield, however strong, had merely resisted the mages' magic without altering it. She sighed and thumped her head on her pillowing arm, as if that would shift the memory.

Magic could be redirected and grounded. She could change things if she acted, rather than reacted. She should have protested the slave's treatment, despite Becknam. Becknam and Tam were grating at one another, generating ever more friction; she could try to smooth their interaction, grounding the force. Magic was like anything else: if she only remembered to act, rather than react, it might—well, no, it wouldn't have been worth the failure. But she wouldn't discard the lesson, at least.

It was nearing midday when they first heard the strange, heavy whuffling sound. Ariana looked up the long slide of old scree above the trail and saw a massive dirty white shape moving, browsing for growth among the loose rocks. Her heart froze—a catoblepas! Fiercely territorial as well as enormous. What if it charged them?

By all that was holy, what if she hesitated as she had in the Circle examination?

Shianan Becknam appeared beside her. "Back away, before it scents us. Tam, behind me, now."

But the creature's whuffling changed in rhythm and it turned to face them. She caught her breath. The catoblepas snorted and tossed its heavy head, displaying tusks each as thick as Ariana's waist.

"Too late." Becknam drew his sword.

It stamped a foreleg, shaking its tusks again. Ariana braced herself and concentrated power into a ball balanced in her palms. The catoblepas roared and bolted down the slope, slipping on the scree. Its dark eyes fixed on her.

"Now, my lady!"

It was near enough now that she could see the coarse bristles covering its body. She flung her arms before her and channeled power toward the beast.

The bolt struck it fully, staggering it in its charge, but it did not stop. A sting was not enough. She gathered another, stronger blast. "Get clear! Get out of the way!"

Becknam was man enough to recognize he would be little help. He retreated, leaving her to repel the beast. Was he taking Tam?

She threw the second bolt and felt its impact at the monster's feet. The ground gave way beneath the catoblepas and it fell, roaring. Loose scree ran downhill before it as the creature rolled.

"Lady Ariana!" Becknam shouted. "Run!"

The catoblepas tumbled toward her, propelled by its own momentum and the collapsing slide of debris. Panic struck her and she turned toward Becknam and Tam.

The ground was already shifting beneath her feet. Pebbles and rocks and gravel gave way, sucking her down the slope. She stumbled and went down, flailing her arms in a vain attempt to find a foothold. The catoblepas roared above her.

She saw Becknam and Tam gaping in horror as she swept past. Tam chased after her toward the edge where rocks and dirt spilled into air. She twisted and found herself staring at the panicked catoblepas.

43

Tam's voice shrieked after her.

She clawed at the slide, but it was all gravel and rolling scree and then nothing at all as her momentum flung her clear of the cliffs. The wind burned her face and tears whipped upward from her eyes.

She fell.

Something struck her from behind, thrusting her from the rain of gravel. Had one of the larger rocks hit her?

An abrupt pressure squeezed painfully about her torso. She gasped and the world spun sideways. The cliff wall slowed its frantic race past her and the rocks flew by more quickly. Then she was moving away from the rockfall, into open air, away from the cliff face.

Someone's arms were around her.

She dug her fingers into the arms, terrified to let them slip. The jagged walls spun away. They were flying.

Ariana had no breath to scream; what little was left after the fall had been crushed from her. She dared not move in those impossible arms—lean arms, too lightly muscled....

Terror rose anew, even more gripping. Ryuven—! She would rather have died in the fall. Had Becknam seen? Would he escape to warn her father?

She kicked, but the arms around her were tight. They flew free of the narrow rocky slopes, sinking all the while. The Ryuven could not wholly compensate for her weight and they jolted hard to the ground.

Ariana jerked free and spun with her heart in her throat, ready to face—

Tam.

She froze. No, it wasn't Tam, not quite. He was taller than she was, older, his face not entirely that of the boy she knew. On either side rose the great membranous wings of the Ryuven. She stepped back, unable to speak.

He looked at her, his expression anxious and pleading and relieved all at once. "Lady Ariana?"

It was Tam's voice, aged years. Ariana shook her head. "Tam," she managed, her voice no more than a whisper. "Tam, how...."

He looked upward sharply, his wings jerking behind him. "Hide," he snapped. He shoved her into a jumble of rocks. "Whatever happens, stay hidden. No matter what you see. Stay there."

"Tam!" she called, but he was already moving away. The air changed around her.

Ryuven.

They came into her world with little puffs of air, a whisper of sound announcing the enemy. The first arrived about fifteen feet above the ground, his wings spread fully, and four more appeared as he circled. He eyed Tam. "We'd supposed you dead."

Tam stood still. "I will not return with you."

"No need. The price is for your head, with the rest of you or no." He folded his wings and dove.

Tam flung up his arms to ward off the blow but stumbled backward. Magic scorched through the air. The others swept down on him, battering with hammer and mace. Not killing—they were toying with him, five cats with a single mouse. They came at him from all sides, striking from every angle and throwing him from one to another.

Ariana shrank behind her rock, her breath burning in her throat. She could not move. She dared not move. She could not challenge five Ryuven, not alone. The moment she gathered power they would sense her and turn on her, kill her as they were slowly killing Tam, or whoever this was.

The air shifted again, and another Ryuven appeared in the air. The five paused in their gleeful attack, watching the impressive figure settling toward them. Released, Tam collapsed to his knees, weaving unsteadily. The new Ryuven made a somber gesture, and the others backed away from Tam.

"We found him, Oniwe'aru," one said. "We found him as you asked."

The Ryuven stared down at Tam for a moment. "Leave us."

They disappeared in little puffs of air. The tall Ryuven sank to the ground and stood still, and Tam rose unsteadily and stumbled forward a few steps to drop and bow limply over his knee. His wings hung unevenly, ripped and gouged. One of his arms dangled loosely from its shattered shoulder. Ariana bit down fiercely on her fist, blinking to clear her eyes.

The tall Ryuven spoke first. "You have hidden all these years?"

Tam's voice was torn and ragged as well. "I knew I could not return."

"It was your choice to make it so." The Ryuven frowned at Tam's bowed head. "I will not have you killed by che."

Tam's head sank lower. "Thank you, Oniwe'aru."

The Ryuven stretched one hand over Tam and spread his fingers. Ariana gasped, but the sound was lost in the sudden burst of

45

power. Tam went violently rigid, arcing his spine and crying one final time, and then he collapsed backward, his legs sprawling as he fell across his loose arm. He did not move again.

Ariana could not control the quick sobbing breaths that shook her, but the Ryuven did not hear. He looked down at Tam's still form. "I am sorry it came to this." He turned away and disappeared into his own world.

Ariana's fist was bleeding from her teeth. Tam was a Ryuven. And now he was dead. She had fallen, she would have died, he had saved her, and now he was dead. She gulped and tried to slow her frantic breathing.

A small sound froze her. Another Ryuven had come, one more. She shrank back behind her rock and shivered.

This Ryuven came to earth and stood very still, looking down at Tam's broken body. "Ryl. Essence and flame, Ryl'sho, I'm sorry." He took a slow step forward and knelt over Tam.

Tam's lips moved. "Maru?" His voice was barely audible.

"Ryl!"

Ariana choked on her breath. Tam was still alive? Then this Ryuven would not have him! This was only one Ryuven; she would fight.

She pushed free of the rocks as the Ryuven reached toward Tam, power already coursing through her. "Leave him!" she ordered, braver than she felt. "Step back!"

The Ryuven leapt backward as if stung and stared at her. "Rika." His face hardened. "You won't have him. Not while I stand." He raised his arms in readiness.

Ariana hesitated. "You are defending him?"

His voice was taut. "As long as I last."

Ariana let the throbbing of her power ease a bit. "I, too, mean to defend him."

The Ryuven looked at her a long moment and then sagged. "Can you imagine, rika, how relieved I am to hear that?"

Ariana edged toward Tam. "Others came to attack him."

The Ryuven crouched beside Tam, now silent once more. "He has nothing. He cannot heal."

Ariana nodded. The final attacker had simply drained Tam's energy, leaving him to die of his considerable injuries. "Is there... is there anything we can do?"

The Ryuven nodded. "I can help him a little. It will not be much, but it may be enough." He spread his hand over Tam's face and closed his eyes.

Ariana felt a shift around her, as power ebbed from one to the other. "How are you doing that?"

"What?"

"You're transferring...." She didn't know how to frame the question.

Too quickly the Ryuven stopped and opened his eyes. "That is all I can do. But it is just enough to sustain him." He began to straighten Tam's limbs, moving the shattered bones so very carefully, his eyes on Tam's face as he worked.

Ariana stared numbly. In the house of the White Mage, the Grand Mage of the Great Circle, a Ryuven had sheltered and hidden himself, disguised as a human boy who did not age as he should.

Her father must have known.

She shoved away the prickly thought. "Shouldn't we do something more? He's bleeding.... What about his shoulder?" How was she talking with a Ryuven, asking him to help Tam?

"That will stop in a moment. Beyond that, I haven't the skills or strength to treat him." The Ryuven looked at Ariana. "Rika, do you have any sweet food? Honey?"

Ariana's mind spun, and she upturned her half-spilled pack. "Here," she said, holding out the chocolate. "Sweet food."

The Ryuven stared at it. "Ryl'sho, a delicacy." He broke the chocolate into pieces and pressed one into Tam's mouth. "Eat this."

Tam looked a little better, Ariana thought. He wasn't so ashen as before and his posture seemed a little more natural. The other Ryuven, though, looked pale. "Are you all right?" she heard herself ask.

He nodded. "I gave him as much as I could. I'll be fine."

"Maybe you'd better have a piece yourself." What was she saying?

The Ryuven hesitated, looking at the chocolate, and then took one. "Oh." He closed his eyes. "Very good."

Ariana took a small piece for herself. "What about a blanket?" she asked, indicating the spill of meager supplies. She should have been fighting with this strange Ryuven, not offering him comforts, but she should have been dead and Tam should have been a boy.

They spread a blanket over Tam and each took another. The Ryuven curled his wings about himself. "May I know the rika who is

47

helping Ryl'sho?"

"I'm Ariana Hazelrig," she answered. Belatedly she hoped he would not recognize her father's name. Was he as infamous among the Ryuven as Pairvyn ni'Ai was in Chrenada? "And you are?"

"Maru," he said, and she remembered Tam recognizing him before slipping away again. "Ariana'rika, I do not know how you came to help Ryl'sho, but thank you."

"I thought I knew him, but... he was someone else entirely. What do you call him—Ryl'sho? What is that? I called him Tam."

"Tamaryl," Maru said. "That is his name."

It was a strange name. Ariana shivered. "Do we need a fire?"

"I'll make one."

Ariana bent closer to look at Tam—Tamaryl. A Ryuven name. He looked better, though still terribly wounded. As she watched, he opened his eyes. "My lady?"

"Tam—I mean, Tam. I didn't know—you were—how do you feel?"

His face changed. "Maru! Was Maru here?"

"Ryl!" Maru lunged to his side. He moved as if he wanted to embrace Tam but dared not touch his broken bones.

"Essence and all, it's good to see you." Tam sobered. "If Oniwe'aru finds you've come...."

Maru swallowed. "He won't learn. No one will know. Neither of you will report me, after all."

"Someone will ask where you've been."

"I will not say. Whatever comes for refusing to answer will be better than seeing you die."

Tamaryl smiled, though it was nearly a grimace. "Maru, it's—too long. Far too long."

Ariana did not want to interrupt, but there was too much unexplained. "Wait, who are you? Why did those others...?"

Tamaryl took the chocolate Maru offered. "That is a long night of talking. In short, Maru is my oldest friend, whom I had to leave behind."

This was still too much. "You're...."

Tam understood. He made his voice very gentle, even beneath the pain. "I am Ryuven." His throat worked. "I'm sorry. You should have been told."

Ariana stared at him.

"I left. I no longer agreed with Oniwe'aru. He considered it a

48

betrayal, and I suppose it was."

"So Ryl could not stay," Maru supplied.

"Your father offered another way." Tamaryl raised a hand weakly, displaying his silver-grey slave cuff. It was cracked from wrist to forearm. "An artifact to house the binding that made me Tam the slave boy. I did not know if I could break it alone, but...."

"But that betrayed him," Maru said. "With that kind of energy—he was no longer hidden." He hesitated. "I came as quickly as I could, Ryl, I'm sorry...."

Tamaryl shook his head. "If you had arrived any sooner, Maru, you would have watched them kill me. No, you came at exactly the time to help most." He struggled with the next words. "But you can't stay. You will be missed."

"Ryl, I have only just—I never thought to see—"

"If they seek you, we are both lost. Go back, Maru."

"They won't know you've survived, not for a while. You're weak. I can hardly recognize you from here."

"We can't risk it. Go, please." Tam tried another tactic. "If they come upon me again...."

Maru plainly wanted to argue but did not. "I will, Ryl'sho. But I will watch for another time." He gripped Tam's good arm for a long moment. Then he stepped backward, dropping the blanket, and disappeared with a small disturbance of air. Tamaryl closed his eyes and swallowed.

Ariana felt disoriented, as if she were still falling. She stared at Tamaryl. "I cannot believe... you are my—" She caught herself. *My slave*, she thought. Their household servant was a Ryuven. It was something like keeping a wyvern as a pet.

Tamaryl looked contrite. "I am sorry, Lady Ariana. It was not my intent to deceive you. But you were far too young to be trusted when your father first brought me to your home, and later.... Well, there never seemed a time fit to tell you I wasn't the boy you thought."

Ariana swallowed hard, fighting irrational tears. Her father had kept a secret from her, a dangerous secret. He had conspired with a slave without her—conspired with a Ryuven.

"But we fight the Ryuven," she said feebly. "That's why we're here, so the Ryuven cannot come again."

"I know." He sighed and looked at the chocolate. "Would you hand me another piece, my lady?"

Ariana did. Tamaryl shivered and then flinched. He was not

healed enough for movement, not yet. Ariana gave him the blanket Maru had left.

Tamaryl finished the last of the chocolate. "Thank you. It helps."

"It was his idea," Ariana said.

Tamaryl looked at her. "Are you all right, Lady Ariana? The fall—there wasn't time to ask...."

She shook her head. "I'm fine. And thank you—for saving me." For shedding his secure human guise to save her life.

His eyes were closing. She pulled the blankets more closely around him, careful of his crushed shoulder.

He slept almost immediately. Ariana looked at him, seeing vestiges of the boy Tam in his face. So many things jostled to her mind—Tam's calm maturity, even as a boy; his reluctance to play with other children when his duties were finished; his long hours assisting her father with his magical work. Of course her father would value a Ryuven for that.

Even his appearance was explained. One always remembered another person as he had been. Gradual changes were rarely noticed—or missed. Ariana had hardly thought on how slowly Tam had changed, nor had anyone else of the few who even noticed him. A young slave had been the perfect disguise.

She wrapped her own cloak and blanket around her and lay down a little distance from him. She should not sleep tonight, not so near a Ryuven, but she was exhausted.... And it wasn't a Ryuven—it was Tam, her own Tam, Tam who had been trusted in her home for fifteen years. Tam, who had deceived her, who was a Ryuven. Who was regaining strength with every moment which passed.

Some very powerful Ryuven were able to heal minor injuries within minutes, but Tamaryl had been near death even before his power had been drained. From what Ariana knew of their processes, he was most likely gathering energy as it returned and focusing it on healing small portions at a time. The crushed bone looked as if it had only just been stabilized, but the muscle and other tissues were still weak.

He was not healed, not yet, and he was only one. She could defeat him if the need arose. She huddled beneath her blanket and stared into the darkness.

CHAPTER 6

"Ariana!"

No voice returned except Shianan's own, reflected from rock walls and debris.

"Lady Ariana!"

If he returned without Ewan Hazelrig's daughter.... Better to fling himself off the nearest ledge and save the time and pain. Mage Hazelrig's own daughter....

When had the switch happened? Surely the White Mage would have noticed a Ryuven in his own household. But this explained Tam's inconsistent aging, if a Ryuven had killed him and taken his place. He must have deceived the mage somehow. How long? What had he learned, and what had he passed back to the others?

Shianan had descended all through the night, feeling his way down tracks and ledges he should have hesitated to try by daylight, hoping he might reach them in time. The Ryuven could not carry Lady Ariana out of the valley; Ryuven could glide somewhat with additional weight but certainly couldn't lift a human out of the mountains. If he had wanted Ariana dead, he could have let her die in the landslide, so that meant he wanted her for information or as a hostage. Shianan had to reach them before he had won whatever information kept Ariana useful and alive.

Or, if he had taken her across the between-worlds—

Shianan stopped and called again, turning to send his voice in all directions. "Lady Ariana Hazelrig!"

"I'm here!"

Shianan whipped around, straining his ears. "My lady?"

"Here!"

"Stay where you are! I'm coming!"

Her voice had been tight and worried. He drew his sword and ran.

It took him several minutes, and he lost time pushing through rocky, brushy tangle, but at last he could see her standing. She looked unharmed but nervous. Behind her lay the Ryuven, sprawled as if sleeping. Shianan scanned the area for other threats as he approached. "Are you hurt?"

She shook her head. "No."

"Has he done anything to you? What does he want?"

She took an uncertain breath. "He's hurt. Pretty badly, but he's recovering."

Shianan nodded. "In the fall? They can't handle human weight well. At least you're safe."

Lady Ariana only nodded.

That had saved her, then, if the monster were not strong enough to carry her across with him. The Ryuven sometimes took mages back to their own world, mostly grey mages captured on the battlefield. None had ever returned.

"He hasn't harmed me," Ariana said. "He saved my life."

"For what purpose? Do you realize what a prize the White Mage's daughter could be?"

Ariana stilled. Had she not thought of that?

"How long has he posed as your slave—how many years has he waited, observing and spying and plotting? That is why your Tam stopped aging, my lady. This Ryuven killed him and took his place."

Her eyes widened in slow horror.

If the Ryuven were injured, he might be a good source of information himself. "Can you Subdue him?" Shianan asked.

She stared at him, surprised. "I—I suppose. But why?"

He stared back at her. "We have a Ryuven on our hands. Injured or no, do you want him unrestrained?"

Ariana hesitated, and Shianan wondered if she lacked the power and training.

Then the Ryuven moved, and they both turned to look. Tam— or whatever his real name was—got awkwardly to his feet, his eerily familiar face disturbing in the Ryuven shape. He held one hand near a crushed and mangled shoulder which would never have worked again, were he human. His face was wary. He held no weapon, but a Ryuven would not need one.

Shianan's fingers flexed on his sword's grip, but he did not raise it. "Why are you here?"

The thing that was Tam spoke slowly, as if afraid to startle the commander. "I've been with you all this time, and you've never had cause to fear me. Nor now."

"That's not an answer." Shianan's voice neared a growl.

"I've served Mage Hazelrig for the last fifteen years," the monster answered. "He and I made a pact, and I still hold to it.

Question him if you like, but know I am still bound to him."

Shianan's stomach lurched. Was the White Mage a traitor? But that was unthinkable. Yet what else could this Ryuven mean—unless he was here against his will, saving the mage's daughter by magical compulsion instead of by his own scheming. "A slave in truth, then?"

"Near enough."

Shianan blew out his breath sharply. "King's sweet oats," he muttered, pushed his hand back through his hair. "This just can't be."

Ariana cleared her throat. "Ryuven can modify their appearance to a mild degree—"

"I don't mean that!" snapped Shianan. "I mean there's a double-dyed Ryuven standing in front of us! That the White Mage of the Great Council, charged particularly with protecting the kingdom from Ryuven, sent him in disguise in seeming full knowledge on what was supposed to be a secret task." He shook his head. "Or is this even your Tam? Maybe this one did take his place and is lying about your father's complicity. Maybe killing him would be best after all."

"He just saved my life!"

"Because if you died, he might lose his position in the White Mage's household and that would be the end of his spying."

"But to save me he had to reveal himself, so that doesn't even make sense."

"What part of this looks like it should make sense?" Sweet oats, there was no way clear of this. Either he killed the White Mage's slave in front of his daughter or he let a Ryuven invader live.

Ariana took a breath and pitched her words in a controlled voice. "I don't understand it myself—I don't know anything about it. But I trust my father. You know he would not risk harm to the kingdom, and I know he would not risk harm to me. If he sent Tam with us—if he let Tam stay with us at all—there must be a reason, and there must be a safeguard."

"A safeguard," repeated Becknam flatly. He raked loose hair back from his forehead again with a savage, frustrated gesture.

She held out a hand. "This isn't a battlefield. He's not threatened either of us. He saved me."

"We don't know why, and I for one am reluctant to trust a Ryuven's altruistic impulses."

Tam removed his hand from his wounded shoulder and met Becknam's eyes. "I oppose the repeated attacks on your world. They are devastating to your people, of course, and do limited and

53

unsustainable good for my own. Many are merely Ryuven political battles for favor upon your ground. Even the raids...." He shook his head. "They must be stopped."

Becknam frowned. Court politics could explain many inexplicable situations. "You wish to bar the Ryuven from our world? To serve your political ends?"

"If it pleases you to say it in that language, then yes. But does it not also serve your purpose?"

"What is your political end?" Ariana asked.

One corner of the Ryuven's mouth twitched upward. "I have no ambition but to see fewer Ryuven die and unworthy lords cease to win power merely for killing humans. They are too often incompetent at managing their newly-won lands and all suffer."

"How high-minded," Shianan observed dryly. "And you wish no place for yourself?"

"I was born to a high position."

"But you lost it to a warrior," Shianan concluded pointedly.

The monster looked uncomfortable. "No. I was a warrior myself."

Shianan grunted. "But you lost your taste for battle, and so you want us to use the Shard."

"I do."

"And the White Mage—who has committed several varieties of treason by keeping you hidden—trusts you to assist us."

"My father is no traitor!" Ariana cried. "You know that!"

"I know that," Shiannn said, "or thought I did. But what I believe is irrelevant. It is the Court of the High Star which will judge him if this is discovered."

"Then we won't tell anyone."

"My lady!" Shianan turned toward her in frank disbelief.

"You don't have to say anything!" she pleaded. "Nothing's changed, has it? He's been here all my life and he's done nothing. My father would not have endangered the kingdom, you know that. You can't send him to the Court of the High Star!"

Shianan hesitated. "You ask me to betray my—"

"I ask you to betray no one! Just speak with my father first, please. Talk with him before you accuse him."

"I never said I would accuse him," Shianan said defensively.

"Talk with him. Please, my lord, speak with him first."

Shianan turned hard eyes on the imposter. "I could not accuse him if there were no Ryuven."

Ariana's voice changed as her fear coalesced into anger. "You can't kill my servant in cold blood. If I told—"

"He's not a servant boy!" snapped Shianan. Sweet oats, could she not see beyond her family?

But when they looked, it was Tam again, short, blond, a little under-sized for his supposed age. His boyish face was frightened but steady.

Shianan's lip curled. "You forget, I was at Furmelle. Killing a slave would give me no pause at all." But he did not move.

He heard Ariana's breath catch, and when he looked he saw how frightened she was—not of Tam, not of the Ryuven, but that Shianan would kill him.

It must have been terrifying, first the fall and then the sight of a Ryuven and then the realization that her boy Tam was nothing like he seemed. And while his other injuries might have been suffered in landing with additional human weight, the Ryuven's shoulder hadn't been crushed in landing. It didn't look like magic, but Lady Ariana must have snatched up one of the stones and bashed him off her. And now Shianan had cast suspicion upon her revered father. She was inexperienced and frightened and confused, and she would defend what was known and dear to her, even her slave boy Tam.

And Shianan could not raise a hand against her, not without clear evidence of her treachery. Besides, she may have failed her entrance to the Circle, but she was Mage Hazelrig's daughter and charged with the Shard's mission, and he was not keen to pit himself against her in battle even without a Ryuven standing spectator ready to pounce upon the victor.

King's sweet oats. Shianan sighed and chose his next words. "Our first priority is the Shard. Then we can think of what to do with him."

The Ryuven, once more in his natural form, frowned. "There is little need to do anything with me. I will return to Mage Hazelrig as before."

Shianan grunted and turned to Ariana. "We can't have him traveling like that," he said, gesturing at the tall, lean body and membranous wings. "Can you disguise and bind him as your father did?"

Lady Ariana hesitated. "I do not know exactly how my father accomplished it," she said. "To conceal his true essence, that is unusual—completely different from anything I've done. And his cuffs are broken; they housed the work. We would need something similar to seal him."

"My lady," the Ryuven said, "I will help you to perform the binding."

Shianan was surprised and suspicious. "Why would you submit to that?"

"I helped Mage Hazelrig then," the Ryuven said mildly. "It was the only way for me to remain here."

"Or the mages would note you," Shianan said. He shook his head; nothing mattered more than convincing Lady Ariana to bind the Ryuven again. "We'll ask Mage Hazelrig about him. Keep him secure until then. Lock him back in whatever keeps him a boy, and make sure he can't get out of it." He turned on Tam. "And if you so much as speak out of turn, I will push your false face through the back of your fragile Ryuven skull. Is that clear?"

"He won't," Lady Ariana said quickly. "He won't be any trouble. Come here, Tam...aryl."

Shianan heard the strung-out word and wondered if it were the Ryuven's true name. It did not matter. He looked hard at the Ryuven.

The monster nodded to Shianan. "I understand." Then he walked to Ariana's outstretched hand.

"You can Subdue him?" Shianan confirmed.

The Ryuven gave her a quick, shuttered look. Ariana seemed to consider and then nodded. "I can, yes."

"How long will it take?"

She shook her head. "I can't be sure. A few minutes."

"Good. I'll pack while you work." Shianan started on their blankets and food with an unkind energy.

CHAPTER 7

Ariana led Tamaryl a little further away. "He thinks you were hurt in the fall."

"Good. That's simple enough. You know this won't be a true Subduing."

"The commander won't know the difference. How does it feel?"

Tamaryl started to shift his shoulder and aborted the attempt. "It will heal in time."

"That's good." She hesitated. "And, er, how does it feel to be... another shape?"

"Oh." He considered. "You know when you have to hold a smile you don't mean, for a long while? It's a bit like that, only over the whole body." He gave a small shrug with his intact shoulder. "Many Ryuven do it regularly, just as you might use colors and dyes, but those are small modifications. Holding something so encompassing for more than a breath or two is nigh impossible, even when hale and hearty."

She frowned. "Then how did you?"

He held out his wrists to display the slave cuffs with their small, integral rings. A hairline crack ran down each. "There's enough of a reservoir yet to let me shift for a moment. Your father and I made it together."

She touched it gingerly. "Together?"

"It took some craft, I'll admit. But our magics blended and synthesized far better than we expected. Another question on his list, but one we haven't had liberty to explore in my time here."

Ariana nodded without understanding; there was too much to think on, and she had a daunting task before her. "We'd better get started." She took a deep breath to steady herself; she needed to be calm and centered to work the binding. She shoved aside her worry over her father and Becknam. "What must I do?"

Tamaryl settled on his knees, his back to Becknam. "The cuffs can be repaired; you will not have to create it completely anew."

Ariana swallowed. "How?"

Tamaryl smiled a little, almost shyly. "You are your father's daughter and skilled in his training. Look, and I think you will see it."

He nodded toward his wrists. "You must start by diverting all of my own power and drawing it from me."

"Like a Subduing?" Ariana asked before thinking.

He hesitated only an instant. "Yes, that is the beginning. Then you must compress it as if you would store it away in the metal housing."

"The reservoir."

"Exactly. Only instead of saving this for later use, we are sealing it. I will do my best not to resist and you will be able to draw more than mere power. It is my essence..."

"Something of your soul," Ariana supplied quietly.

He nodded. "That must be sealed as well. It will conceal me."

"And make the binding strong and resistant to you." She glanced at his wrists. "It must have been nearly impossible to get free of it."

"I helped your father to create the cuffs, but the magic must be your doing. I cannot seal myself." He paused. "It will hurt a little," he said quietly. "Hurt me, I mean. Don't think about that. Just recreate the binding."

Ariana inhaled and exhaled once more. "All right, let's begin."

Tamaryl extended his hands to her, palm up. He looked pale. She wrapped her fingers around the cracked cuffs and he clasped her wrists. "Your lordship," she called to Becknam, "I know you are aware, but please do not interrupt us. This will be difficult."

Becknam was staring. He was used to the sight of mages, but of course he had never seen one work magic in alliance with a Ryuven.

Ariana closed her eyes and began to explore the metal wristbands. They were very well crafted; there was no outward sign of their true purpose, no telltale aura of power that bespoke a magicked item. Another mage could stand beside or perhaps even handle these without recognizing them.

She began to pick apart the exterior camouflage, uncovering the binding within.

Mages perceived magic distorted though one of the five usual senses. Ariana was a seer, one who visualized magic as she worked. Powerful sources might appear as bright lights, if she concentrated with her mind's eye, and she often visualized functional magic as gears, hooks, arrows.

This was a tapestry of overlapping strands—threads, cables, chains, all glowing in the darkness. She picked through them, noting which were strong and intact and which were severed. The chains were solid, which relieved her; she didn't think she could have repaired them. She picked out the broken threads and the lighter cables, working them gently. A frayed thread became a light hook; one cable was unraveled, ready to be woven again with another.

It was startling how much of the binding remained. He had burst just enough of the seal to be able to take his natural form, but he had still been mostly restrained. Something in that worried her, but she could not dwell on it as she worked.

The binding was at last remade; it needed only sealing. She waited, knowing he would be able to sense when she had finished. A heartbeat later, she felt a soft pull as he drew power, absorbing it and making it his own. It was an odd, ticklish sensation, as if someone were inhaling from her lungs. The wristbands shifted slightly in her hands. She would have liked to watch him change form, but she kept her eyes closed; the real task lay ahead and she could not afford distraction.

The draw stopped, and she could not sense any air of illusion. He had truly shifted. Now she must close the binding and seal him. This time she quested into him and found his power, bleeding it from him.

He gave the power freely, and it poured from him first like water and then like blood. She took more and more, visualizing a deepening puddle into which she collected his energy. She felt him falter; magic was a Ryuven's natural strength and without it they were far weaker than a human.

She must take it all. As the flow ebbed, she delved deeper, seeking where the shining power puddled within him in tiny reservoirs. She squeezed him, pressing power from him like oil. He began to fight her, an involuntary resistance to protect himself, but she had taken so much that he could hardly withstand her, and she crushed his feeble defenses and scraped him dry, leaving nothing of his inborn ability.

When he was completely empty, bled out, she needed yet more. This would be difficult for them both. She took a moment to gather herself and went further.

She could sense his struggle, feel him trying to suppress the natural desperate need to fight what she did. It was like a drowning man trying not to breathe air. But he was empty of power and unable to block her. She plunged into him and seized him.

He recoiled, straining backward although his physical body

hardly moved. His wrists trembled in her grip. She tightened her mind's grasp on his very self and began to tear it away.

There was a long shriek somewhere far away, but Ariana did not allow distraction. She pulled and twisted at him until a piece ripped free, quivering in her mental hold. Immediately she turned her attention to the tapestry of the binding. The power she poured into it easily, just as if creating a battery of energy for later use, and then she wove the living soul through the threads and ropes and chains, the warp and woof of the binding, and with every movement it cried in her grip, shrinking as if the strands burned it, writhing so that it was hard to keep hold of it. But she persisted, and at last it was firmly ensnared in the careful layers. She began to close the broken bits, weaving the cables together and setting the hooks firmly into the screaming bit of his self.

When it was fully bound she reached for the final seal, the great lock that held every thread and cable and chain together. As she clasped it she felt the key burn across her mind: *Tamaryl.* His name, his true name, would release him, if spoken with intent by the mages who closed this lock.

She had finished, and she withdrew into herself, releasing the metal wristbands and letting the mental picture fade away. Sound assaulted her and she opened her eyes, disoriented.

The boy Tam lay on the ground before her, gasping and clutching his chest. She stared for a moment at his panting, sweating form. "Tam!"

Becknam was on his feet beside them. "Is that right?"

She seized the boy's shoulders, trying to steady him against the ground. "Tam, can you hear me?"

"Don't," he gasped. "Don't touch." He squeezed his eyes tightly closed, his fingers spasming against his chest as if trying to reach his heart. "Just—wait."

"He was screaming. It didn't seem like you heard him." Becknam looked at her. "I don't—did you hear him? Did you keep on through that?"

Guilty horror washed over Ariana. "I didn't, not really. I was concentrating."

Tam's panting slowed, and his rigid form relaxed a little bit. Ariana looked at him. "We don't have any more chocolate."

Tam's hands left his chest to wrap around his torso. "Wouldn't—help. It helps—power." And of course he could not gather power now.

Becknam leaned over the boy. "He sounds a little better."

Tam opened his eyes. "I—I will be all right." He swallowed. "Need time."

Ariana bit her lip. "What did I do wrong?" she asked.

His eyes found hers and he shook his head slowly, his cheek brushing the ground. "You executed everything perfectly. Your father would be proud."

"But—you said it would hurt a little!"

He gave her a small, grim smile. "If I had told you what to expect, would you have done it so readily?" His eyes closed again.

Ariana felt angry and relieved and horrified together. She sat back, slumping as she realized how tired she was. The binding had been difficult.

Becknam sighed, relieved. "It looks like we'll be here for a while at least. We'd better make ourselves comfortable."

"No," Tam said. "Only a few minutes more." He pushed himself up, crossing his arms over his chest. "It passes quickly."

Becknam looked at him critically and then shrugged. "Then we'll go." He nodded toward Ariana's bag. "Much of the slide went over the edge, but it looked passable. We'll have to backtrack and try again."

Ariana looked at him. "Again?"

"We can't get through down here." He jerked a pack cord tight. "Pray we don't meet another catoblepas."

Tam opened his eyes and breathed deep, as if testing his lungs. "All right."

"Good. On your feet."

Ariana began to protest, but Tam shifted his weight and rose, mostly steady. Ariana looked at him and then stood herself, hoisting her pack to her shoulders.

Becknam stepped toward Tam and held out a pack. "This is yours."

Tam looked at the pack and then raised his eyes to return Becknam's gaze evenly. Though the pack sank as he took its weight, he did not drop his eyes.

Becknam turned away and slung his own burden onto his back. Tam hesitated before finally heaving his onto his shoulders, wincing.

Ariana looked at him, remembering his injuries. "You can't carry that," she said.

Becknam turned, and Tam clenched his jaw. "My lady, I can."

He would not back down before the commander. She hesitated, and Becknam gave the order. "Move out."

Ariana started after him, watching Tam. But the boy moved forward determinedly, as if nothing were wrong. She looked at Becknam's stiff posture; there would be no talking with him now.

She was already weary from the binding. She thought of nothing at all as Becknam led them around and up the mountain once more. Ariana kept her eyes on his pack as they climbed, her lungs straining as they ascended. Her mind was empty of everything but following, breathing. Finally they reached a level place and she paused. "Please," she panted, "let's rest a moment."

Becknam nodded without speaking, and she saw he was winded as well. She sat against a rock, stretching her legs before her, and then jerked upright as she realized Tam was not with them. "Where is he?"

Becknam, drinking from his leather bag, gestured down the trail behind them. "He's coming."

She turned to look, and indeed after a moment she could pick him out, head bowed as he struggled up the rocky slope. "But he's so far behind!"

"He'll catch up," Becknam said darkly. "I carry the food and water."

She looked at him hard. "What?"

He looked at her. "Prisoners of war carry no rations or tools." He held out the water to her. "He'll have plenty with us tonight, of course."

"He's not a prisoner!"

"What is he, then? He is either a Ryuven in our hands, stripped of power by your own magic—our prisoner—or he is your slave. I think you'll agree it's hard to think of him as only the latter."

"He is on our side."

"So he says. I might even believe him, after I learn more about it; there are always turncoats and opportunists. But it's also possible he was only biding his time to some purpose, and now that we know what he is he might act more precipitously." He proffered the water again. "Want a drink?"

Ariana took it. "He's no threat now. That binding is strong."

"He broke it once before."

"Incompletely," she said. "Most of it was still in place. He was helpless." She looked back, seeing Tam a little closer. He was climbing the steeper parts on hands and feet, pulling himself up.

Becknam sighed. "I leave it to you, my lady. He is no proven ally. Is he to be a prisoner or a slave?"

Ariana looked at the recently-ennobled count, more the military commander to which he'd been trained, and the indecision behind his eyes. He didn't know what to make of Tam—how could he?—and so he treated him with the caution of one who had been raised to fight the Ryuven. She tried to soften her angry tone. "He is my servant."

Becknam gave her a formal nod. "Then we will treat him as such. He is your servant." He reached for the water and took a final drink. "Are you ready to move on?"

"But he—"

"He will find us tonight; the way is clear enough. Or is my lady in the habit of waiting upon slaves?"

All sympathy vanished. She glared at him and was rewarded by his flinch. He opened his mouth, hesitated, and then spoke. "We're losing daylight." He shifted his pack and turned away, tackling the next slope. Ariana followed, glancing back once more at Tam's distant form.

CHAPTER 8

Shianan Becknam slowed in the city traffic and came to a halt, shifting the pack with the Shard on his shoulders. "I need to take this into the Naziar," he said.

Ariana gestured. "Our house is just a bit—"

"I will not take the Shard into the house of a possible traitor," Becknam said flatly.

Ariana resisted the urge to roll her eyes. "Would that be the same possible traitor who helped determine the Shard's potential and who sent you to bring it for the kingdom's benefit?"

Becknam's lips thinned. "I will deliver the Shard for safekeeping," he said. "And then I will come to Mage Hazelrig's house to discuss his... unorthodox choice in slaves."

Ariana's heart quickened. "He will have an explanation for you."

"I am certain he will. The question is whether his explanation will be acceptable to the Wheel and the council."

Ariana's stomach twisted. Becknam turned away toward the gates to the palace-fortress of Naziar. Ariana saw the guards step forward to challenge him and then snap to attention as they recognized the commander-count. He spoke to them and went inside without looking back.

"If we—"

"Quiet," she said more sharply than she'd meant. She was angry with Tam, she realized, and it was because she was afraid and it was his fault. She swallowed. "We should hurry."

"That's what I was going to say," he responded, his voice faintly petulant. He could be such a twelve-year-old boy, and it disturbed her how easily she might have slipped into believing again.

She did not answer, only started into the heavy afternoon traffic again.

The White Mage's townhouse was on a high street overlooking the marketplace a quarter-mile below, an easy walk from the Naziar. From the front step one could just see the slow river which bisected the city en route to the nearby sea. Between the street, from which it was walled, and the welcoming entrance, it boasted a tiny garden in which were set a variety of flowering plants and two small fruit trees, somewhat overgrown.

Ariana pushed open the ornamental iron gate and went directly to the front door. "Father! Are you here?" Tam came behind her, already reaching for the straps on his pack.

"Ariana!" Ewan Hazelrig hurried around the corner into the elegant entry, his arms outstretched. "Safely home!" He crushed her in a welcoming hug. "Oh, here, darling, slip your pack. Everything went well, I expect? How well you look! I half-expected you to have withered away with travel. Tam, welcome back."

Ariana clung to her father, uncertain of how even to begin. She stepped back and tripped on her discarded pack. "Tam! Take this away."

"Let it wait a moment," her father said, smiling. "It's not urgent, and he's likely as weary as you are."

"Not Tam," Ariana intoned, turning to look at the boy, who hesitated. "He's capable of all sorts of surprising things."

Ewan raised his eyebrows. "Tam, you seem to have gotten on the wrong side of your mistress."

"Let us say rather," amended Ariana, "he has gotten on the wrong side of the between-worlds."

Ewan went still. Tam, his eyes on the far wall, held out one arm to Ewan. The mage glanced at him and then touched the wrist cuff lightly. His eyes widened, and he looked at Ariana.

"How could you have kept this from me?" she burst. "Do you know what this means? By all that's holy, Father, why?"

Her father looked suddenly tired. "Sit down, Ariana. I'll try to explain."

"We don't have time for you to explain—not like you should. Commander Becknam will be here as soon as he's delivered the Shard, and he thinks you're a traitor. And I know you can't be, it makes no sense for a traitor to want the Shard to defend the kingdom, but all he can see is that you've disguised a Ryuven. And—and that's what I see, too." She stared at him, willing him to somehow laugh and declare it all a fantastic joke, though that was wholly impossible.

Ewan Hazelrig rubbed a hand across his face. "Let me say first, it was not for lack of trust in you. But you were too young to be given such a secret for a long time, and... by then, I think it had become habit." He turned and went into the sitting room, taking his favorite chair and lacing his fingers together. Ariana and Tam followed, and

Ariana took another padded chair.

Her father took a breath. "How did Becknam learn the truth?"

Ariana's stomach clenched. "I—we were—we were attacked by a catoblepas, and—I fell. I would have died."

Her father stared. "What?"

"There was a rockslide into the ravine, and—Tam saved me." She looked at the boy standing between them, and her throat tightened as she recalled the rush of wind past her face. "He saved my life."

Ewan exhaled. "Then no matter what comes, it will have been worthwhile." He looked at Tam. "How can I thank you?"

Tam shook his head. "There is no need. I did only what I was sworn to do—what I wanted to do."

Ewan braced his hands on his legs. "You broke the binding yourself?"

"Only just enough to take my own form."

"We didn't think you would be able."

Tam looked at his feet. "I was so afraid I wouldn't."

"But that should have been enough...."

"Enough to be noted, yes." Tam glanced at Ariana. "I told her to hide when they came. Afterward, the commander found us and—"

"No!" Ariana interrupted. "No, he's leaving it out. They came for him, six of them."

"Six," Ewan repeated. "And the binding was not shattered?"

Tam shook his head. "They—were killing me."

Ariana wondered for the first time what it must have been for him—not only the physical brutality which had horrified her, but seeing his own kind for the first time in so many years and nearly dying at their hands.

"But then," Tam said, "Oniwe'aru came."

Ewan caught his breath. "Oniwe'aru?"

"Wait—that was Oniwe?" repeated Ariana, stunned. She had not fully grasped the name until hearing it in her father's voice.

"The aru is the ruler of the Ai," Tam told her. "So he is Oniwe'aru."

"I didn't know aru, but I know Oniwe and the Ai." The Ai was the most powerful clan of the Ryuven. "Why should Oniwe himself bother with you?"

Tam wet his lips and kept his voice low. "We share a mother."

Ariana's jaw dropped. "You...." She shook her head

67

incredulously. "A half-dozen Ryuven, a secret friend, Oniwe himself as your brother.... King's sweet oats, it's a streetside melodrama."

Surprisingly, her father did not correct her language. "This melodrama, as you call it, is a very real concern for us now. Let's focus on a solution. But first, tell me of Oniwe'aru. What happened then?"

"He stopped them." Tam would not meet their eyes. "He granted that I would not be killed by che, and he—he drained me himself."

"Knowing you would not heal from your injuries," Ewan said softly. Ariana noted he did not have to ask what the che were. "Could he not bring himself to...?"

Tam swallowed. "Or it may be that a traitor does not deserve a clean, painless death."

This talk was disturbing. "Then another one came," Ariana began, and briefly related her exchange with Maru.

"And so I healed, at least enough, and then my lady renewed the binding."

Ewan nodded to Ariana. "That would have been a difficult thing to repair; I am proud. It proves again your talent and skill."

Is that why I failed the Black examination? Ariana wanted to demand, but they did not have time for other topics. Becknam was no doubt already on his way.

Ewan looked back at Tam. "So they think you dead?"

"All but Maru," said Tam, "and he will say nothing."

"Why do they want you anyway?" demanded Ariana. "What's to kill for after fifteen years? It just doesn't make sense."

Tam's eyes flicked to her father's. Neither answered.

Insight came to her. "Tam's very powerful—aren't you? That is why they could sense you though the binding was only cracked, why—that's why you were able to break the binding!"

"It was meant more to conceal than to permanently disable."

"Still." She shook her head. "I didn't know there were many Ryuven like that," she said in a little awe. "I mean, to work at all through that seal, you'd have to be—really frightening, to be honest. The stuff of stories to scare naughty children. Pairvyn ni'Ai, returned." She looked at Tam. "So they wanted you to fight for them, to be their champion."

Ewan wrapped his fingers deliberately about the arms of the chair. "He wanted a choice."

"You realize what this means, don't you?" Ariana looked

between them.

"I will have lived fifteen years more," Tam said.

"But what about my father?" she demanded. "What about you? Bailaha is coming here right now. Do you know what the council will do if they discover you've harbored a Ryuven all this time? Or the Court of the High Star?"

"I did the right thing," Ewan said. "He did not want to fight. I did not want to kill him unresisting." He paused. "I do not think you would have wanted me to, or that you would have done so yourself."

Ariana looked at Tam, his serious eyes in his boy's face, and shook her head slowly. "No, I hope I wouldn't. But I don't know what we'll do now. If Shianan Becknam tells...."

"King's oats." Her father looked at Tam. "He has not killed you, obviously."

"He considered it. But my lady argued you were to be trusted even if I were not. He has withheld judgment for the moment, but he wants to speak with you."

"He knows the kingdom needs you," Ariana tried. "He knows no one else has seen anything. He doesn't know Tam's connected to Oniwe. If we can just convince him Tam is harmless—"

Tam chuckled, his expression oddly inconsistent with his adolescent face. "Harmless?"

"No," Ewan said, "think. Shianan Becknam, of all people, cannot afford to overlook a Ryuven. His own position is too... insecure."

"Might there be something to justify a mage privately keeping a Ryuven for interrogation or experimentation?" Tam asked, his voice remarkably even.

Ariana repeated, "Experimentation?"

"Tam has provided both information and assistance in magical research during his time here," her father said with a grim smile. "It would be an accurate claim. However, I'm afraid it's very clear; all Ryuven prisoners are the property of the crown. The crown alone can dispose of them in interrogation, experimentation, or enslavement."

"Enslave a Ryuven?"

"I doubt it's ever been done—really, I mean, not like our situation. But allowance was made. It would be quite impressive, for example, to host Wakari ambassadors at a feast served by trained Ryuven." He sighed. "None of this is to our point, though."

"You said his lordship's position is insecure," Tam said.

"Perhaps that is the hinge to our argument."

A knock sounded at the front door.

Ariana twitched in her chair, looking guiltily toward the entry. She fought the clench in her stomach as Tam went to answer it. "Please enter, your lordship."

Ariana swallowed and looked at her father, who rose from his chair. She nodded; they would show a perfect hospitality to this commander-count bastard who threatened her family.

Becknam came inside, pulling his eyes stiffly from the boy to bow to Ewan Hazelrig. "My lord mage. And my lady," he added, bowing again to Ariana.

"Your lordship," Ewan replied with a small bow of his own. "Please come and sit, and we can talk. I am delighted to hear your journey went well. I trust the Shard is safely delivered?"

Ariana sat, staring at her father's easy manner.

"It is," Becknam answered. "The Circle may begin their work as soon as you like." He paused, looking rather, Ariana thought spitefully, as if he'd swallowed a fruit pit. "Let's be frank, if we may, Mage Hazelrig. I have been a soldier longer than a count, and I prefer blunt speech. During our travel it became apparent your servant is actually a concealed Ryuven. I withheld my sword at your daughter's request, and—"

"Cheese?" Tam proffered a tray. He had been lightning-fast in the kitchen, and Ariana had not even noticed his reappearance.

Becknam faltered, open-mouthed. Ariana was too nervous to smile. "No," Becknam said sharply. "Er—Mage Hazelrig, you can see my position. I am sworn to defend against the Ryuven."

"And so you should," Ewan agreed. "By all means, block any Ryuven threat, and I will be first beside you. But I think you must agree, Tam has posed no threat."

"I am not certain the king will see it in the same light."

"I have served this kingdom for more than twenty years as elected White Mage by the Circle, and in lower capacities before that. My service and my word have gone unquestioned in that time. I tell you now, your lordship, Tam is no threat."

"Your word is not for me to judge," Becknam answered. "It may be that the Court of the High Star will believe you. But that is their decision."

"No!" Ariana cried. "You know what that would be—please consider this!"

Becknam looked at her. "There is no choice for me. You ask that I refrain for your sake?"

"No," Ewan answered before she could. "No, we ask no favors of you, my lord."

Becknam looked at him and his expression shifted into a grim, hard smile. "Of course not. No one would entangle himself in obligation to Bailaha; it is perhaps as dangerous as keeping a Ryuven." He let out a little breath. "I did say we should speak frankly."

"I would not have put it so coldly," Ewan said quietly. Tam set the cheese tray on a table behind him.

"But we understand one another." Becknam shifted in his seat. "Then I have no choice but to—"

Tam darted close and snatched at the knife Becknam wore. He jerked it free and reversed the blade, throwing himself backward from Becknam's reach as he drove the knife toward his torso—

Something slammed invisibly into him, lifting him bodily and flinging him to the side. His arms and legs careened as he tried to catch himself before falling hard on the polished floor. The shock of his impact rattled the floor but he had kept his hold on the dagger, and as he tried to lift it Ariana struck him herself, sending a measured bolt of power to knock his hand aside. By then her father had reached him and he tore the blade away, standing over the sprawled boy. "No!"

"I must," Tam panted, winded from the arcane blows. "You must let me. The binding will last after my death, I'll be just a dead slave, and he will have no proof—"

"Let us all decide that!" Ewan snapped. "At the least I would give you a quick and painless departure, if we even allow you to sacrifice yourself."

Becknam was on his feet. "What is he doing?"

"If I am dead," Tam said, his eyes wet and blazing, "then it will be only the bastard's word against that of the White Mage." He glared a challenge.

Ariana breathed deep to recover from the quick magic and looked between them.

Ewan Hazelrig passed the dagger to Becknam. "Keep this safe, if you please." He sighed and looked from Tam to Becknam. "The binding, as he says, will last through death. With his Ryuven spirit gone, he'll be just a dead boy. Nothing more."

Becknam turned to Tam. "You would kill yourself to protect him?"

71

"I would not see him suffer for protecting me," Tam answered raggedly.

"Then you have me." Becknam slammed his dagger into its place. "If this is not a puppet show for my benefit, he has no far-reaching scheme, not if he is willing to die now. And I am not fool enough to accuse the White Mage without evidence."

Relief rolled dizzyingly through Ariana. "Oh, thank you! I—"

He put up a hand to cut her off. "Do not thank me; it is not my decision." His voice was thick and bitter.

But, Ariana thought, he also looked faintly relieved. He had not wanted to stand against the White Mage, respected and popular while Becknam was neither.

Becknam looked hard at Tam, still winded on the floor. His jaw worked. "But I may confess now—I am glad he was with us, when you fell. I never thought I would be grateful for a Ryuven."

Tam got to his feet and limped from the room without speaking. Ariana watched him go and then looked at the commander-count. "I am glad too, of course."

Ewan returned to his chair. "It was no puppet show, as you say, your lordship. Tam was quite correct in his assessment. I hadn't expected him to attempt such a thing here and now, though."

Becknam shook his head. "He will not interfere in the shield?"

"My lord, Tam wants the shield nearly as much as you do."

Becknam nodded grudgingly. "I have no choice but to accept your assurance," he said, "but I do believe you." He looked toward Ariana.

"Aside from this unfortunate incident," Ewan Hazelrig began bravely, "how did it go? There were no troubles with the Gehrn?"

"No," Ariana said. "They gave it to us with the condition that the high priest perform their yearly rites. And they want a temple-fortress."

"I promised them my townhouse," Becknam said, his voice subdued.

Ariana's father looked at him. "I see."

Ariana returned to her chair, suddenly exhausted with fear and relief. "I don't like the Gehrn much."

Ewan gave a sardonic half-smile. "I didn't think you would."

"They had a slave to serve us," Ariana said, tightening at the memory. "I did not like to see it."

"From the Furmelle revolt," Becknam supplied.

Ewan nodded. "They would be strict."

Ariana shook her head. "They *choked* him, Father. It was something they used at Furmelle, his lordship said. It was awful."

Ewan sighed. "We have asked for laws, but there is worry profits would suffer...." He rapped his knuckles against the arm of his chair. "While a hundred men may be bought for the price of a horse, there will be slavery, and while men remain men, there will be cruelty."

Becknam cleared his throat. "On another subject entirely... My lady, His Majesty has called us tomorrow for personal thanks for our efforts on behalf of the kingdom. Your own invitation should arrive shortly." He took a breath. "It will look best if.... May I, despite all this recent exchange, escort you to court?"

She could hardly refuse him now, not when so much depended upon his agreed silence. For all his reluctant cooperation, he had only to convince another mage of the Circle to help uncover Tam. That would be difficult, both in argument and in discovery, but it was a risk to manage. "Yes, of course."

Becknam again looked faintly relieved. "Thank you. I will come at half past three." He bowed. "And now I will beg to excuse myself."

"Thank you for your service to the kingdom," Ewan Hazelrig said, bowing in return.

Shianan Becknam did not answer, only went to the door and let himself out. Tam had not reappeared.

Hazelrig sank into his chair. "'Soats, that was trying," He glanced at Ariana. "Honest fellow, that one. Says what he thinks, or would like to."

Ariana frowned. "His lordship doubted my abilities. Because I failed the examination."

Ewan shifted. "I want you to take it again."

"Of course. But how can I prepare better?"

"My darling Ariana," Ewan said, "you need only do again what you did before. Had you been anyone else, you would have made Black Mage the first time."

Ariana stared, incredulous. "But—but—Father!"

"I'm sorry," he confessed. "But there were two pressing reasons why I could not allow you entrance last time."

"Two reasons." Ariana sat forward. "Tell me."

"The first is that you are my daughter, and naturally there is suspicion of preference, a certain advantage. There were some who believed you would be admitted even if your work were inferior. I wanted them to respect you, to believe you had earned your place rather than being granted it."

"You failed me for nepotism?"

"Those who tested you were able to speak of your ability and yet knew I considered you capable of better."

Ariana considered the cutting compliment. "And the other?"

"I needed you to retrieve the Shard." He turned his palms up. "I did not trust an unqualified mage to go with the commander, and once you were admitted to the Circle you could not leave without drawing undue attention." He paused. "I have already announced you will be undertaking the examination again next month. I am sorry. I did not wish to make you doubt yourself. But it was for the best."

"But won't everyone say now that I needed two attempts to enter the Circle?"

Ewan chuckled. "Most need two attempts, many need more. It is nothing."

Ariana wasn't sure what she thought of this. "And if Tam decides to test for the Circle? Would a slave boy with arcane power pass the first time?"

"Now you're being petty." Her father looked at her. "And you're wrong. The binding limits him to that form precisely; as a boy he is no more than he should be. Only a boy, but one which happens to have the mind and memories of Tamaryl."

"And how did that happen?"

He shook his head. "It is as simple as we've said. We met at Luenda, and he did not wish to fight. I did not wish to kill someone who did not wish to fight. We determined that if he were hidden here, he could help me to seek an alternate path for our conflict."

"I wish... I wish he'd just gone home."

Her father looked at her. "They would have killed him."

She shook her head. "You know I didn't mean that." She sighed and then yawned. "I need sleep."

"It's not too early. You look tired, and you should be fresh for court tomorrow."

It would be her first court appearance. "Don't think I've forgotten that you failed me even though I deserved better." She rose and kissed him on the cheek. "But I forgive you for saving Tam's life and keeping him a secret. I think."

"I'll take that for a start," he said with a smile. "Good night."

CHAPTER 9

The market was thick with morning traffic. Ariana passed flower sellers, vegetable hawkers, fruit vendors, butchers with cuts of meat hanging from their carts. Imprisoned ducks and chickens and geese protested from their crates. A slave ran after an escaped lamb; at least the meat was fresh and healthy. Most carts had a slave or two working beside them until it was time to pull the carts home. One had a tacked notice advertising the slave was for sale as well as the vegetables.

Ariana moved through the crowd, pressed against a pile of gourds while a litter edged by her, and passed into the next section of the market. Here were spices of all varieties and perfumes, oils, infusions, medicines, mingling to confuse the nose. If she continued straight she would find cloth and clothing and then gems and smithing, but she turned to the paper merchants' row.

Past the booksellers and stationers stood a shop with a sign in the shape of an open book. The bell over the door jingled as Ariana entered. "Hello, Vaya."

The bookbinder tapped at her block to straighten pages and gave a welcoming smile. "Hello, Ariana." Long friendship had eroded formalities. "Here for business, or to see Ranne?"

"Just Ranne today, thanks."

"Go on back, she's unpacking. Lady Bethia's here, too."

Ranne was sorting colored papers into a wall of nooks. "Ariana!" She leapt up to greet her. "You're back! Well, obviously." She laughed and tucked curly red hair behind her ear.

"I am. We arrived late yesterday."

Lady Bethia waved a greeting from her chair. "Just in time, I suppose?"

Ranne hopped onto a stool, cradling a sheaf of emerald stock. "So, where were you?"

Ariana slid onto a scarred wooden counter to face them. "I was on a secret mission, an agent of the kingdom." She grinned.

Ranne rolled her eyes.

"Well, I was an emissary of the council and Circle. I went with Commander Becknam. Bailaha."

"Ew." Bethia screwed up her fine features.

Ranne gave Ariana a skeptical look. "You were a rogue adventurer with the king's bastard? Off across the kingdoms to thieve rare gems from the Wakari Coast and inspire ballads in taverns everywhere?"

"Oh, don't be so dramatic. It would be wrong to steal. We wheedled." She laughed. "We did, actually. For an article which should help against the Ryuven. It's not a secret anymore."

"Rogue adventurer *and* heroine," teased Ranne.

"That will look good for your examination," Bethia said. "I suppose that means no more studying?"

"Don't be absurd! I want all the help I can get." Ariana looked at Bethia. "Unless—did you test while I was gone?"

Bethia shook her head. "No, they've been putting me off. Ridiculous excuses. They're waiting on you, you know." She smiled crookedly.

Ariana didn't have an answer for that.

"Oh!" Ranne slid off the stool and went to a work table where several half-finished projects were laid out. "Speaking of the Circle.... Customer brought a book for binding, and I thought your father might want to know of it." She found the title page and held it up for Ariana: *An Accurate Account of the Battle of Pradina and the Repulsion of the Ryuven.* "Do you think he'd be interested?"

"Hm, probably not. Pradina wasn't that long ago, comparatively, and he's mostly looking for ancient histories. First sightings and such."

"Okay, then. And, I don't suppose you'd mind taking one back to the Wheel with you?"

"Sure. What is it?"

Ranne displayed a finished book with the emerald-toned cover open to show the title, *Arcane Botanies of the Continent.*

Ariana hesitated. "Er...."

Ranne laughed. "It's okay. I don't think he's paid yet, so I suppose I can't send it with you. Maybe I can arrange to be busy so Mama has to deal with him."

Ariana nodded. "He is a bit...."

"Creepy. That's the word you're looking for." Ranne mimed a shudder. "They should have passed you into the Circle just to move him to a different color. That man doesn't need black robes for effect."

Ariana made a show of setting her jaw determinedly. "I'll push him to Indigo yet."

"Good! I know you'll make it this time."

Bethia spoke up. "I could take it to the Wheel, Ranne. It's not out of my way, either."

Ranne gave her an apologetic look. "I just thought, you know, Ariana might be going to see her father."

Ariana stepped in quickly. "Are we still on for studying, then?"

"Certainly," Bethia answered.

"Good." Ariana paused. "Um, I'm appearing in court this afternoon. What would be most appropriate to wear?"

Bethia pursed her lips. "Pastels are very fashionable at the moment, but I don't think they suit you that well. Something else will." She rose and took a few papers from Ranne's stock, holding one after the other beside Ariana's jaw. "Color is more important than cut, for a day audience...." Bethia had flawless skin like dark honey, with thick dark hair to frame her face, and privately Ariana thought her the most beautiful girl she knew. As a duke's daughter she had ample practice in dressing for it.

Ranne extended the emerald paper. "Can she wear a dark green?"

"Oh, that's nice." Bethia held the paper beside Ariana and assessed her. "Do you have anything like this color? Neckline not too low?"

"I have one very close to that shade, hitting about here." Ariana drew a line across her collarbone.

"Perfect. Put a ribbon at your throat, to set off your neck, and you're all set."

"Thanks." Ariana smiled, embarrassed. "It's my first audience. I know it's not so much to you, but—"

"Don't be silly. When is it not important to dress well for meeting the king?" Bethia pinched the green endpaper and waved it cheerily. "You'll do fine."

Ariana stole another glance at the commander's impeccable uniform and smoothed self-consciously at her own gown. She had dressed well, thanks to Bethia's advice, but seeing his brushed, stiff appearance had made her worry anew. He looked very little like the rugged soldier she'd known on the road.

He led her through the palace of Naziar to a well-appointed

anteroom, where several brilliantly-dressed persons waited about the room. Becknam gestured for her to sit on a padded couch and then went to speak with a secretary. He returned and stood beside her. "It will be some time; it always is."

She nodded. After a moment she gave a small start. "Oh! I'm sorry. Please sit. I'd forgotten, I was so accustomed...."

He sat at the other end of her bench and gave her a small, tight smile. "No matter. I tend to be more aware of my manners here."

"I'm a little nervous," Ariana confessed. "I have seen him before, of course, but from a distance."

"Just curtsey at the appropriate moments and smile prettily. You'll do very well." He caught himself, started to speak, and then flushed. "I didn't mean your smiling, I meant—never mind."

Ariana blinked. Was he—was he flirting with her? It was... awkward, if real, and wholly out of place. Or perhaps he was only unsettled.

He stood suddenly and began pacing the length of her couch. Someone else came into the room and spoke with the secretary before taking a seat elsewhere. Ariana noticed several of the courtiers glancing surreptitiously toward Becknam, avoiding eye contact. The door to the next room opened at irregular intervals, allowing another secretary to talk with this one and occasionally admitting or discharging courtiers.

The inner door opened again, and the secretary called for Commander Shianan Becknam, Count of Bailaha and Lady Ariana Hazelrig. Becknam straightened and looked to Ariana. "This way, my lady."

It was a smaller room than Ariana had expected, but richly decorated. There were a number of men standing around the room, a few of whom looked familiar but none she knew. In the center, just rising from a desk while speaking with someone else, was King Jerome. She caught her breath. Beside her Becknam took three more steps and then knelt. Quickly Ariana dropped into her best curtsey.

"What have we here?" The king moved toward her. "Rise, sweet lady. No one with a face such as yours should be suffered to avert it for long."

Ariana blushed. "Your Majesty."

"You are the mage who brought the Shard?"

"With the commander's help, of course, Your Majesty," said Ariana. She should have called Becknam *his lordship*, she realized belatedly, but King Jerome did not seem to notice.

"We owe your effort a great deal," he said. "When the Circle completes the shield, our kingdom will be protected as never before. Thank you, Lady Ariana Hazelrig."

Ariana curtsied again, feeling warm. Beside her Becknam was on one knee, his head bowed. She watched the king's eyes shift. "Bailaha."

"Your Majesty," Becknam said, still kneeling.

"Rise."

Becknam did, as if his joints were too tight.

"We are pleased you completed the task we set you," the king said. "Well done."

The door opened, admitting a handsome man. The courtiers around them gave quick little bows, and Ariana, startled, accordingly sank into another curtsy. Becknam bowed this time.

"I'm sorry for interrupting, my lords," the newcomer said, "but we need a final resolution on the tariffs before the Migrations end. I've been asked for our decision today." He looked at Ariana. "Forgive me, my lady."

"Thank you, Soren," the king said. He turned away from Becknam and held out a hand to the elder prince. "Let's see what you have thus far." He gestured for a few of the courtiers to come nearer, and they began poring over a sheaf of papers Prince Soren had carried. After a moment the secretary looked sternly at Becknam.

"Back away," Becknam whispered. He bowed again toward the king's back, held the door as Ariana curtsied and exited, and closed the door firmly behind them.

Ariana felt a curious conflict of elation and cutting disappointment. "I thought—"

But Becknam was not listening as he went ahead with a long stride. Ariana followed him from the antechamber. "My lord?"

A boy of Tam's age—apparent age—was coming toward them in the wide corridor. Becknam moved stiffly to one side, and Ariana saw the commander's jaw tighten as he bowed. "Your Highness."

The younger prince raised his eyebrows in exaggerated surprise. "What? Did this wing become an army barracks? What are you doing here?"

"I had an audience with the king."

"Did you? That was good of him. And what a relief to know the army is still outside." Prince Alasdair looked at Ariana, who bobbed hastily. "My lady. Good day." He walked on, leaving them behind.

Ariana looked after him—she had never seen the princes so near, either, and she was stunned by the childish, stinging remarks—and then looked back, but again Becknam was already striding down the corridor. Ariana followed at a distance.

Abruptly he stopped and turned to face her. "I am sorry, my lady," he said stiffly. "I did not mean to be rude and leave you behind."

She wanted to say something, but acknowledging she had witnessed the barbs would be cruel. "It is only that I need you to show me the way out."

Becknam sighed. "I'm sorry. I am not usually the best of company afterward." He gestured. "This way, my lady. Mind the steps."

He walked her home in silence.

CHAPTER 10

Ariana stood against the wall, looking across the wide room. The unpolished stonework reflected little light. Beneath the Wheel of the Circle was an ideal location for the shield's epicenter, but the converted cellar was purely utilitarian.

Beside her Tam stood still, trying not to attract attention. He was present nominally in case the White Mage should need to send him for something. The majority of spectators were mages waiting for their chance at the Great Circle and members of the council or military. Ariana adjusted her colorless grey robes against the stony chill.

Near the door, Elysia Parma approached Ariana's father, confirming something in the mages' array. Even conferring, the Silver Mage exuded amiable confidence.

Only the Grand Mage of the Circle was elected to his white robes. All others were ranked by seniority, advancing through the colors as new mages were admitted. Elysia Parma had been a Mage of the Circle as long as Ewan Hazelrig, despite having come to magic later. Ariana admired and respected the Silver Mage, who had reportedly arrived in Alham as a lone farm girl determined to develop her magical gift. Lacking funds to purchase traditional training and an apprenticeship, she had at last done *something* unorthodox and impressive enough to earn tutelage with a respected practitioner. What exactly that had been, however, Ariana had never been able to discover.

Ariana regarded her wistfully. Silver robes were not so different than grey, it might seem, and yet there was a vast chasm between them.

Mage Parma finished speaking with the White Mage and came across the room to Ariana. "I haven't thanked you myself for helping bring this to pass."

"I was only an errand girl," Ariana answered with a little laugh.

"Nonetheless, it was an important errand. Keep close attention today; you'll be assisting in the first renewal, I've no doubt." Mage Parma smiled as if a bit proud of Ariana's achievement already.

"I hope to undertake the entrance exam again very soon."

"I'm looking forward to it." The Silver Mage gave a quick smile to Tam before she moved on. Ariana, pleased, watched as she took up a vial beside the Shard and thumbed it open.

"My lady." Becknam arrived beside her. "Today it ends—the war, your place, and mine."

"My lord?"

"We'll still have the southern warlords, but without the Ryuven threat, it will be interesting to see what becomes of the army and the Circle." His eyes shifted to Tam beside her. "He came to watch?"

"It's only fitting," she said a little coolly. "It is his world we are walling away."

"Quiet!" Becknam snapped, his eyes flicking about them.

Ariana bristled at the rebuke. She wouldn't betray Tam.

The fourteen mages of the Circle took their places—one color to fill—and the room fell silent. They raised their hands, each taking a different position in their colored robes, and then began to move, weaving overlapping magics. Arms rose and fell irregularly, flashing sleeves of deep green, navy, orange, scarlet, yellow, violet. Ariana found the figure in white and watched as her father worked his part of the great spell, weaving together the overarching shield.

She glanced at Tam beside her and saw him very still, lamplight reflecting in the damp trace on his cheeks. She rested her hand on his shoulder, squeezing lightly. She took a quick look toward Becknam, but he had eyes only for the shield-making.

And then she sensed the first effects of the mages' work, a shift in the air around them. In the center of the room the Shard began to glow, spilling a deep indigo light that hardly seemed light at all. The mages continued around it, and she felt a vibration deep within her. Tam twitched beneath her hand. The vibration increased, becoming a heavy throbbing pulsing through the room and through her, and the indigo light spread.

Tam jerked and gasped.

Ariana looked at him and saw him pale, his arms crossing as if to shield his torso. The throbbing increased again and Tam stiffened against the wall. His wide eyes rolled toward her. "Help."

"Tam!" She seized him. The throbbing was audible now, a heavy booming of power that filled the room.

Becknam turned toward them. "What's going on?" She could barely hear him over the throbbing.

Tam winced as the vibration cut through him. "It's affecting him," Ariana said. "It's—"

Becknam swore and pulled Tam from her. "This will reveal him!" He wrapped his arms tightly around Tam and clamped a hand over his mouth.

The indigo light was thickening now, forming a layer of iridescence at its outer rim and shaping slowly into a hemisphere over the working mages. It was of course a full sphere about the Shard, but only the portion above the floor was visible. The sound was deafening. "Stand in front of us!" shouted Becknam. Ariana did, hiding Tam behind her grey robes.

Then the mages began to move in unison, and the iridescent layer solidified, obscuring them. The room seemed to crack with power and the hemisphere suddenly expanded, bursting through Ariana and the observers and speeding on. Beneath the deep boom Tam cried and his body spasmed against her back.

And then it was over, and the room fell silent, the contrast almost painful. The Shard stood ordinary and empty of light, stably supporting the shield. There was movement at Ariana's back. Then someone cheered, and the room erupted into happy celebration.

Ariana spun. Becknam still held Tam, who was resisting weakly. His hand was pressed over Tam's face, pinching off air. "Let him breathe!" Ariana grasped Tam's shoulders. "It's all right, now, let him breathe."

Becknam dropped his hand. "I couldn't during the quiet," he said gruffly. "He was gasping too loudly."

"Tam, are you all right? Tam?" Tam hung limply in Becknam's grip, panting for air. She bent and held his face, damp beneath her fingers. "Tam?"

"Lady," he breathed. "Right. All—right." He swallowed. "Can't stand."

"What's this?" Ewan Hazelrig leaned beside them. "Why are— oh, no."

"The shield hurt him," Ariana said.

"Take him to my office," her father instructed. "I'll meet you there shortly." He turned back and intercepted an approaching mage.

"Hurry, before anyone else sees," Becknam said. He lifted Tam and rushed to the nearby stairs.

Ariana pointed. "This way."

"I know where the White Mage's office is."

They wound their way from the cellar to the upper levels of the
Great Circle's administrative building. It was round, befitting the
Great Circle, and they had to travel a quarter of the Wheel before
reaching the White Mage's office. Ariana led Becknam directly to the
rear workshop and cleared a table of books and equipment. "Put him
here."

Tam was pale. He lay on the table, looking very frail in his
boyish form. "What did it do to him?" Becknam asked.

"I don't know," Ariana said. "The shield is designed to resist
Ryuven passing through it, and it passed through him. We didn't
think—his body is supposed to be human. It shouldn't have affected
him like this. I don't know what it did."

"His body is human," Ewan said, closing the door behind him,
"but his essence is Ryuven. We didn't think that would be critical, but
obviously it is. It would have killed him already if he were wholly
Ryuven. As it is, I don't know what it's done internally. Tam?"

Tam's voice was hoarse. "Everything hurts—inside. Burnt
from within. Hurts to breathe. It hurts when my heart beats."

Ewan frowned. "Let's see if anything is still happening. Take
his shirt, please." He took a jar of yellowish ointment from a shelf and
rubbed it over his hands. Becknam lifted Tam and stripped the loose
shirt, making him wince with the motion, and then lowered him again.

Ewan gingerly placed his fingertips on Tam's sternum. Tam
flinched. "It's hot."

"It will be. The ointment responds to magical injury, and you've
been exposed to very strong magic." He drew his fingers apart and
began tracing over Tam's chest, pressing his palms against the ribs,
traveling more cautiously over the abdomen. Finally he returned to
the chest and lingered there. "There was something here," he said,
"but it's fading now. The effects will pass." He straightened and
Ariana handed him a towel to wipe his hands clean. "You should sleep,
if you can. That will help." He paused, watching Tam's shallow, pained
breaths. "We'll give you something to help you sleep."

"I'll make it," Ariana said, turning to the other table.

"Herbal only, nothing magical," Ewan warned. "He doesn't
need any more conflicting influences."

Becknam let out his breath. "Did anyone see?"

"I don't think so," Ewan said.

Tam shifted his eyes toward Becknam. "Thank you for hiding
me."

84

Becknam shook his head. "That would have been spectacularly poor timing."

Ariana tipped the pestle and brushed crushed leaves into a cup. She added water, warmed over the brazier she'd magically hurried, and brought it to the table. "Here, Tam, drink this."

Ewan pulled a white cloak from a peg to spread over him. "Sleep as long as you can."

Tam tried to smile. "A Ryuven beneath the cloak of the White Mage." His eyes closed, and a moment later his quick, shallow breathing slowed a little.

Becknam pushed a chair toward Ariana without speaking. Ewan's shoulders dropped. "He'll be all right. He just needs time to recover. It was fading quickly, unable to hold to his human body."

"This is too much risk for you," Becknam said curtly. "You should have let him take his chances with his own kind."

Ewan shook his head. "I promised him shelter. He gave me his service and assistance—you've seen how much progress we have made in our research? He was free to return if he wished, but he did not want to risk all of us."

"All of us?"

"If he were released here, they might have come here. He did not want to risk the Shard."

Becknam clenched his fists as he leaned on the table. "Now the shield is up and he is trapped here," he said after a moment. He straightened. "Hide him well." He turned and left.

CHAPTER 11

Captain Torg desultorily eyed the stack of waiting messages on his desk. Rain hummed outside, masking the noise of work in other rooms. He pushed aside the first; that hand belonged to someone in supply, and he would deal with it later. The second was a letter detailing the new troops he could expect. The third—the third was from Alham and addressed in a handwriting Torg had not thought to see again.

He held it for a moment, dreading what it might contain. He had always cursed the unlucky star which had landed the bastard at his barracks. The day the boy arrived Torg had known his fate was sealed, known he would never leave this hinterland outpost. No one associated with the bastard could rise.

But he had done as well as he could, faithfully following his instructions. The boy had learned to wield a weapon, to read and write. He had been raised and toughened with the men Torg commanded. But more orders came....

The rain continued, hard rain without thunder to break its monotony. Torg returned to another rainy evening, when he'd sat at this same desk before a warm brazier. A soldier had brought the boy as Torg read the day's messages. "He was found sleeping on his watch, sir."

Torg frowned deeply. The boy was young and, truth be told, overworked, but this could not be permitted. "Sleeping on your watch?"

Shianan Becknam looked at him with an odd mixture of regret and defiance. "I'm sorry, sir. But it's not as if anything is coming anyway. There hasn't been an attack here in over a year."

"Not as if anything is coming? If you're able to predict the Ryuven, boy, you should have said so. It would save us all so much time and effort."

"What do you want done with him?" the soldier asked. The boy received no special allowance, that was common knowledge. He did the same weapons drills, ran the same conditioning distances, performed the same chores. Sometimes the men thought Torg was too hard on him, but they didn't know the truth.

Torg tightened his fist, crumpling the letter he held. "I think," he said, forcing his voice steady, "we will see he does not sleep on his next watch. Tonight he'll have the northwest walk. And to be sure he doesn't fail, we'll chain him to his post."

Two pairs of eyes blinked back at him. The soldier spoke first. "Sir, tonight that walk will be—"

"I know what it will be," Torg cut him off. "Take him there."

Torg himself went to choose the shackles, selecting chain long enough for his purpose. He did not allow himself to think beyond the night, beyond what he must do.

He climbed the steep stairs to the northwest tower and went out onto the walk, where soldier and boy waited. The wind cut across the plain and through his cloak; the temperature was already falling. Rain sliced the air around them. Torg looped a length of chain around the crenelations on either side of the walk and pulled them snug.

"Between them?" the soldier said, one hand holding Shianan's shoulder. "Not against the wall?"

"He can't keep a good watch with his back to the wall, can he?" Torg asked. "He needs to be able to see." And there would be a modicum of shelter against the wall.

He tested the chains and gestured for the boy to be brought. He fastened the shackles himself and stepped back. The boy's arms were outstretched to the sides, though not tightly, which pushed his heavy winter cloak over his back. Torg moved forward again and unfastened the cloak, dragging it over his wet head.

"Hey!" The boy moved against the chains, breaking the surly dignity he'd tried to maintain. "I'll freeze!"

Torg made his voice steel. "Then you won't sleep, will you?" He turned away, attaching the key to his own belt. He eyed the soldier until the man moved away, and then he strode toward the tower without looking back. The rain fell coldly around them.

Torg worked a little longer at his desk and then retired early, leaving a sergeant to see to the usual posts—of which the northwest walk was not one. His fire could not completely hold back the damp chill. He looked out the window at the paved courtyard and saw a glassy sheen to the rain-slick stones. It was becoming one of those icy storms the north dreaded.

So much the better.

Sometime past midnight he rose and cloaked himself against the storm, going by protected ways to the northwest tower. He opened the top door carefully, hoping the sound would be lost in the storm.

The boy was hunched against the rain, his face turned downwind. His wet winter clothing was plastered to his body, sculpted into stiff wrinkles. He was shivering violently, Torg saw, arms shaking against the chains.

Torg watched him for a while, but little happened. Once or twice the boy shifted, probably trying to ease the strain on his shoulders, and once during a lull after a gust of wind Torg heard him moan as he shivered. Finally Torg returned to his own room, warming himself beside the fire before going to bed.

In the morning he rose early, well before the sentries would be recalled from their posts. Only a hint of light in the east foretold the winter dawn. Torg took the confiscated cloak and went to the northwest tower, keeping to interior walks where the ice had not reached.

The rain had mostly ceased, and only icy drops fell, freezing upon impact. Torg opened the tower door and eased out onto the slick walk. He slid once and caught himself against the crenelated wall. He stepped cautiously toward the limp body and lifted his shaded lantern.

Ice was crusted over the shackles and pointed icicles hung from the chains. The boy's clothing was frozen, frosty ice bleaching the colors. His wet hair had frozen into stiff chunks around his pale face. He had sunk onto his knees finally and hung by his arms. It was a horrific sight.

Torg's breath blew away in a little crystalline cloud as he looked at the boy. He had not wanted to do this, but now it was done. There was nothing left but to take the body. That would be simpler when the ice had melted, but he did not want anyone else finding him first. He bent to examine the ice-covered lock.

A gleam of white moved at the edge of his vision, and he looked sharply toward the boy. No, he had not moved. That was impossible. But he frowned and moved closer; after years of battle against the Ryuven, corpses held no horror for him. He watched the boy for a moment and saw no movement in the pale face, no flicker of the frosted eyelashes.

And then there was a puff, a tiny puff, of vapor, easing from the blue lips. Torg reached quickly to the boy's neck and felt for the throbbing pulse of life. Yes—yes, it was there, slow, weak, but there.

The boy was yet alive.

Torg cursed. It shouldn't be so. Now he must—

Yet if he were yet alive, Torg would not throw back that gift. He opened the shielded lantern and held the key over the flame for a moment before pushing it through the ice and into the frozen lock. The arm dropped heavily, lifelessly, and Torg almost expected it to shatter. Shianan swung unresisting toward the remaining arm and Torg caught him. He reheated the key and unlocked the other shackle, then he threw the cloak around him and tried to lift.

The boy did not rise, impossibly heavy. Torg looked down and saw his legs had frozen to the stones. He lowered the boy and worked at the legs, pushing the lantern close until he could peel them away with chunks of ice clinging to the fabric. He moved carefully, carefully across the ice and into the tower, where he began the cautious descent down the steep stairs.

The boy was deadweight on his shoulder. It might be too late; Torg might lose him anyway. He carried him to his own quarters and settled him before the fireplace, adding two logs to build up the flame. "First order, let's get these clothes off you," he said aloud, hoping his voice might somehow reach the frozen mind. "Jacket first, let's go."

The outer jacket was stiff with ice, and Torg's heart sank. But the next woolen was a little less so, and the woven inner shirt was cold and wet but without ice. The boy's bare skin felt like steel on a winter day, though.

"Boots next." He stripped the boy and left him naked before the fire. Passing into the third of his rooms—being an officer had some compensation—he opened the tap into the small wooden tub. He started the fire beneath and built it larger than was wise, hoping to warm the water quickly.

He returned and set a kettle at the fire's edge. Then he scooped up the boy, carrying him in the damp cloak to the partially-filled tub and dropped him into the water. The boy jerked, moving for the first time, and Torg felt his heart jump. "That's right." He splashed him. "That's right, fight it. Come on, boy."

The water struck his face, and Shianan moved again. He moaned without opening his eyes and then, most gratifying to Torg, began to shiver.

"Yes! Good." He stopped the water at the boy's neck; with his legs folded against his torso more of Shianan fit into the tub than when Torg used it. He added more fuel to the warming fire and then took a rough scrubbing rag to the boy's arms and back, trying to rub

90

circulation back into them.

Shianan whimpered. "Hurts."

"You're speaking!" Torg rubbed harder. "It's going to hurt, boy."

"S'ot."

The water was fresh from the tank Torg and the kitchen shared, and the fire had made it only tepid thus far. "It's not hot, boy, that's just you. You'll be warm soon enough. Move your legs, boy. Wiggle your toes." He began to rub the other arm.

Shianan only slouched shivering in the tub. His shaking was uncontrollable, his teeth chattering violently, but Torg was happy to see it. Shivering meant his body had recognized cold again and had strength yet to fight it.

Encrusted ice melted and ran into the tub, leaving heavy wet sections of hair across Shianan's face and shoulders. "Stay a moment," Torg said, although he didn't think Shianan needed the instruction. He was hardly sure Shianan heard him. "I'll bring you something to drink."

The kettle was hot, and he poured it over a handful of tea leaves. He thought briefly of adding something more but decided against it. While alcohol might make the boy feel warmer, it would actually inhibit the warming of his body. He carried the brewing tea into the bathroom and lifted it to the boy's face. "Drink."

Shianan's lips might have moved, but it was hard to be sure with the shivering. Torg drew his head back and poured the tea into him, supporting Shianan as he swallowed reflexively and coughed. "More," he said, pouring another cup and raising it.

By the time he had emptied the kettle, the water in the tub was warm. Someone knocked at the outer door, and Torg left the boy in the tub to answer it. "Yes?"

"Morning, sir. I just checked the northwest walk, sir, and the boy's not there."

"I have him," Torg said. "I released him this morning."

"Ah, yes, sir." The soldier's eyes asked what he could not ask aloud.

Torg was not obligated to answer his questions, spoken or unspoken. "He's relieved of his duties for the day."

"Yes, sir."

Torg closed the door and exhaled. They would not like this.

He went back to the tub. Shianan blinked at him, his eyes

focusing for the first time. "Sir?"

"Rub your legs with this," Torg ordered, dropping the cloth on his bare knee. "Rub hard." The boy had to move, had to stir his own blood.

Shianan moved his arm jerkily, still shivering. His fingers could not grasp the cloth. "I—I want...."

"What do you want? Rub harder, boy! Put some muscle into it!"

Shianan tried, straining silently. *He always tries*, Torg thought. *He always tries.*

Torg went into his sleeping room and collected the discarded clothing, now fully melted and sopping wet. He hung them before the fire to dry, regretting that the room would smell of hot wet wool.

He then went into his office, the outer room, and gathered paperwork. Later he would have to write a very carefully-worded letter, but that would wait. He worked for an hour or so, glancing periodically toward the bathroom, and then returned.

Shianan was drowsing, his head sagging toward the water. "Wake up! You'll drown yourself." Torg tested the water, comfortably hot. "You've stopped shivering," he observed. Was that a good sign, or was the boy simply too exhausted to continue? "Let's get some warm food into you and then let you sleep. Holy One knows you've earned it."

He went for the boy's under-braies, the only item that had dried, and tossed it beside the tub. "Let me help you out," he said. "You're likely to spill yourself all over." He gripped the boy under the arms and lifted him half-clear of the tub. Shianan tried to lift his legs but they dragged over the edge. Torg deposited him on the floor. "Dry yourself and get into that."

Back in the office, he opened the door and summoned the man who stood nearby. "I need a bowl of hot soup and some watered ale," he said, "and my own breakfast."

"Yes, sir."

Shianan was rubbing his limbs dry with slow and exaggerated movements. It didn't seem he had full control of his body yet. He crawled to his feet, steadying himself against the wall. "In here," Torg said with a nod of his head. "You'll eat before the fire."

Shianan attacked the soup, fumbling with the spoon. Before he had finished the ale, though, he was nodding, and Torg looked up from his work as he dropped the cup, spilling what was left over himself and the chair before the fire. Shianan looked alarmed. "I—I'm sorry...."

"Never mind that," Torg said, "you need sleep." He gestured toward his own bed. "Go."

"But...."

"Into bed, now." Torg followed the boy and helped him with the heavy blankets. "You'll be warmer here than in your own place, and the barracks are probably being swept now anyway. Rest."

Shianan lay absolutely still. Torg thought he was already asleep when a small voice stopped him. "Captain?"

"What?"

"I'm sorry, sir. I won't—I won't sleep on watch again."

Torg's stomach clenched. He thought it had all been a punishment, an unusually harsh penalty. But how could he know more?

Torg left him sleeping and went out to face the cold stares of his men. They knew what Shianan was, but they did not know the contents of the letters Torg received. They resented their captain now, disapproved of the brutal punishment. Torg knew the word would have gone around that their commanding officer had spent the morning trying to save the life of the boy he had nearly killed. They did not know he had been ordered to kill him.

Torg sighed and pulled himself away from the unforgiving memories. The boy was grown, now, and probably unforgiving as well. He did not know that Torg's first instructions had been to raise the boy without being too careful of him; he would not, veiled language implied, be regretted if he were to die in an accident. But no fatal accidents had befallen him, and finally Torg had received the order to arrange a death. That too had failed. Shianan had survived that night in the ice storm, and Torg did not take his life in the morning.

He had sent a letter, his sixteenth draft, relating that Shianan had suffered a terrible night in a storm but his training and natural strength (of good stock, his letter implied without saying anything too openly dangerous) had carried him through. There had been no more letters regarding Shianan for a year, and the next had carried a different tone altogether.

Eventually, Shianan had been made a sergeant at only nineteen and sent into the mountains. He had returned a year later, forged even harder, and remained under Torg only a few months before being called to the capital of Alham—for service, the letter said, but Torg knew of half a dozen who might have qualified for the position. No, Shianan had fared too well fighting the Ryuven and had to be kept under closer watch.

And now Shianan Becknam was a commander—and a count, too, the news said. He'd proven himself unambitious toward the throne, Torg supposed, or else the king had ennobled him to keep him under surveillance in Alham. It was possible he had learned to use his position to advance himself, but that didn't fit with the boy Torg had known. Regardless, somehow he'd become a person of some position and authority, minor as it might be beside his royal half-brothers.

And he had just written to Torg for the first time since leaving his command.

There was no point to delaying. It would read the same tomorrow as today, only weighted with a day's worth of agony. Torg broke the seal, fingering the two pages, and began to read.

Captain Torg, it began, *it has been a long time. I hope you will forgive the personal tone of this letter; it is not yet a military dispatch.*

It could be the opening of anything. Torg forced himself to breathe and read on.

As you may have heard, my commandery is in Alham, where I serve under General Septime. Our Captain Wheate has fallen ill and has asked to retire from service. It is my responsibility to fill that position and rather than promoting one of the men here, most of whom I feel are already serving to the best of their abilities in their present positions, I am writing to ask if you would be willing to take Wheate's place.

There was an ink blotch before the next line, as if the pen had hesitated an instant too long before beginning the sentence. *I know there might be some difficulty in coming at this time; I understand the situation is tense. I refer to the testing of the new shield, of course, and our vigilance as we wait to see whether it will hold. If you feel you cannot leave your post in other hands, I would be happy to hear your recommendation for another suitable candidate or even your brief statement that you are not available. If you are amenable, on the other hand, you will find enclosed authorization to instate a temporary commanding officer for your outpost and to travel to Alham to take up your new position.*

Torg stared at it, re-reading and re-reading. There should be more, something unseen. He would have thought it only Becknam's late-coming revenge, summoning his former captain to his own command where he could torment him at leisure or arrange for something more. But he had been given the option of refusing, and that didn't seem right for entrapment.

In fact, Becknam even acknowledged that Torg might have

reasons for avoiding him. It was nominally concealed within worry over the Ryuven—Becknam was so much more the soldier than the diplomat—but it seemed as much of an honest option as could be conveyed in such a letter.

Torg set his chin in his hand and thought back to the young Shianan he knew. Certainly there had been disagreements, fights, rivalries among the men in his command, but they had all passed. He could not recall Shianan holding a serious grudge.

Torg sighed. Perhaps he should speak with Becknam before deciding. Surely Becknam would agree to that. He took a pen. *I am curious as to the nature of the duties in Alham, and so I will come to discuss....*

CHAPTER 12

Ariana stretched and reached for her cup of tea. It was cool; she had been studying a long time. But she could not afford many breaks. Her assessment was fast approaching, and she would not miss this second chance at earning a place in the Circle.

Sounds came from the entry, and she glanced up as Bethia entered the sitting room, Tam trailing behind. "Oh, hello."

"I see you've started already."

Ariana glanced at the books opened about her. "I think I started years ago. This latest bout started this morning, though. I was reading by eight."

"Half past seven, my lady," Tam offered. "I brought you oat cakes and honey at eight."

Ariana gave him a smile. "So you did."

"I brought you something." Bethia set on the table a tiny rosewood box with a small brass latch.

Ariana opened it to reveal a comb, carved of catoblepas ivory and set with a dozen black pearls. "Bethia!"

"It's only a comb. Not a very large piece." She flipped glossy-dark hair over one shoulder and smiled. "Black pearls, for the Black Mage."

"I hope so." She looked at Bethia. "That is...."

"It's only a matter of time." Bethia smiled again, but it didn't reach her eyes.

Ariana fingered the delicate comb. It was no one's fault that Bethia simply couldn't make the Circle, even if she refused to admit it. "It is beautiful," she said. "Thank you."

"These pearls are a specialty of Soek," Bethia said, leaning forward to look at the comb. "They're found only in the inland sea there." She sat back and drew a book near. "I wouldn't mind a bite myself," she said, flipping pages. "Inversion wells?"

"I know the easy material," Ariana protested. "I'm wrestling with amplification right now." She glanced at Tam. "Please bring Lady Bethia a tray."

"Those were the last of the oat cakes, my lady."

"Then find something else, please? Thanks."

Tam turned to go, and Bethia made a sound of amusement. "Twice."

"Twice what?"

"Twice you said please. Sweet all, Ariana, he's a slave, and a boy even."

Ariana bristled. "He's a nice boy. He's been with us for years, and I rather like him. What's wrong with being pleasant?"

"He'll get above himself."

Ariana stifled an inappropriate giggle. "I don't think so."

"That's just it, you're not thinking. Think of the slave revolts. And think how it looks to others, speaking to a slave as if he were your equal. Do you want to be seen as a slave's equal?" Bethia leaned forward. "And not just the slave, either. I can help you shed the bastard."

"Shianan Becknam?"

"I've seen how he speaks to you. He walks right up as if entitled, as if he has a special claim on your friendship. It's humiliating; I'd be tearing my clothes."

"You overreact. He doesn't mean anything by it. We worked together, of course we know one another."

"Ugh! How casually you say that. You can't let him attach himself to you."

Ariana wanted to roll her eyes. "I hardly think talking to Shianan Becknam will poison my life in Alham."

"Maybe not your life, but your prospects at court, certainly."

Ariana set her jaw. "I choose my friends by my own preferences, not those of some prissy-panted court sycophant. And I think I rather like Shianan Becknam." She did, too, more in that moment than ever.

"If you say so. Your prospects, not mine. Let's leave this and you can tell me about casting through a medium despite refraction." Bethia tapped the book pointedly.

Ariana drummed her fingers. She had no particular regard for Shianan Becknam; in fact, she was a bit afraid of his incriminating knowledge. No doubt Bethia, the duke's daughter, knew best—but she irritated Ariana.

But Bethia had her volume on casting through impediments, and Ariana could not afford to lose a study partner so near her coming assessment. She took a slow breath. "Casting through any medium with a refractive index greater than that of air will require the mage to calculate the refractive angle to direct the energy accurately. To calculate the refractive angle we must first know the incident angle...."

CHAPTER 13

Ariana stepped out of the Wheel, the early autumn sunlight bright against her face after the dim stone building, and clenched her fists in suppressed excitement. She wanted to squeal or dance with giddy happiness, but that was hardly admissible on the very threshold of the dignified Great Circle.

Soldiers, tradesmen, grey mages, and palace servants crossed the yard before her, none paying her any heed—none but one, who hesitated and turned toward her. "My lady?" Shianan Becknam called. "Well? I heard it was today...."

Ariana beamed. "I passed! I am now the Black Mage."

"I was certain you would."

She grinned. "I was nervous anyway."

"Of course you were." He took a quick breath. "May I help you celebrate?"

"How?"

"However you like! If there's something you—" He faltered.

Ariana tipped her head to look at him. "My lord?"

His eyes slid to the side. "It was only an idea. You might have other friends waiting to treat you."

People of influence did not keep the bastard's company, lest they lose that influence. *You can't let him attach himself to you like that.*

Under the weight of her hesitation, Becknam began to excuse her. "But no doubt your father has—"

"Yes," Ariana interrupted, "I would like to celebrate." She held his eyes.

He smiled, almost shyly. "Of course, my lady," he said.

"Your lordship!" A page jogged toward them, winded. "I've been looking everywhere for your lordship. His Majesty calls for you."

Becknam went still. "Where is he?"

"In his accounting room, my lord."

"Go on, then; I'll go to him." Becknam turned slowly back to Ariana. "I'm sorry, but—"

"I'll come along and wait for you."

"My lady...."

She smiled brightly at him. "I have no pressing affairs, now my examination's done. I will wait until you have finished your business. I don't mind." She remembered his mood after seeing the king the last time; he might well forget her.

Why had he offered to celebrate with her? Ariana and her father seemed the last people he should seek out. But they shared secrets, and perhaps that was enough.

They walked together deeper into the Naziar palace, climbing to a higher level and a dimmer, narrower wing. This was not where the king received courtiers and ambassadors or held policy meetings; this was the palace behind the palace, where ledgers were kept and hushed conferences were held. Becknam opened a door and went into a small anteroom, empty but for a few chairs, a desk, and two deep alcoves with stone seats where petitioners would have waited long ago, before the newer wings of the palace were built.

Becknam faced her. "Wait outside, please. I will join you afterward." He turned and passed through the heavy curtain which separated the antechamber from the accounting room beyond. The curtain hung partly open, and she could see him pause inside the door to await acknowledgment.

She turned toward the alcoves. There were faces on either side of the entrances, quite detailed in their differences; probably they were meant to depict real kings. Inside above the benches were other faces, becoming less detailed and more iconic as they stretched back into time. Ariana moved into the alcove to examine them.

A muffled voice from beyond the curtain said something, and someone else spoke sharply. A moment later the curtain opened and three men exited. Ariana drew back, suddenly afraid she shouldn't be here, but they only muttered among themselves and exited, never glancing toward her alcove.

Had they just been dismissed? Was King Jerome seeing Becknam alone? She felt a little shiver of excitement. Perhaps there was a secret acknowledgment there—cold before the court, but privately....

She left the alcove and moved toward the curtain, guiltily curious. *Just one peek*, she told herself, and then she would leave them to themselves.

There were places where the heavy curtains did not hang together; she chose a gap where the curtain didn't quite meet the doorway and leaned close to glimpse through it. Instead of the two men facing one another as she had imagined, she saw Becknam kneeling as he had before, bent low over his right knee, his head toward the floor. The king was pacing, saying something Ariana couldn't hear.

She shrank back, ashamed. Why was Becknam still kneeling?

"And the Gehrn!" King Jerome's voice came sharply through the curtain. Ariana cringed. Becknam was being chastised; no wonder the others had been dismissed. No wonder he had not wanted to bring her.

She could not go after the men who had left, not now, or they would see she had stayed behind and accuse her of eavesdropping. Only Becknam knew she was here. She would wait.

She heard Becknam's voice next, the words soft and unclear but unmistakably his tone. She swallowed her guilt and leaned her ear near the curtain, sacrificing sight for sound. "...the best way to obtain the Shard without—"

"Enough!" King Jerome snapped. There was a dull thud and a soft grunt. Ariana jerked to peer through the hole and saw the king draw back his leg and kick Becknam again, catching him in the left side just below the ribs. Becknam grunted again but made no move to evade. Ariana caught her breath, staring in disbelief, her whole body flinching.

The king turned toward the curtain. "There is more, of course. Besides bringing the Gehrn right to Alham's heart, you..." He turned back and the sound faded. Ariana strained to hear. "...filling posts!"

Becknam did not move.

The king faced Becknam again and sighed. "I brought you to this court to better gauge you. Last year I raised you to the nobility, thinking it would be a reward for service to this crown and it might further inspire your loyalty with gratitude." He looked at Becknam. "I thought I had done well. I thought you would serve me well. And I gave you this vital task for your own success and glory." He stepped back, frowning. "But instead I see you inviting militaristic cults to our capital, into our very Circle, and bringing men loyal to you into the army here."

Becknam's voice was flat and neutral. "Sire, when you charged me with this task you allowed me the authority to treat with the Gehrn if necessary. Though militaristic, they do not seek to conquer and will not threaten us here. I submitted a full report at the time I brought the Shard."

"I did not realize their rites were perpetual. And a Gehrn

holding here within the city...." He sighed. "Always you bring me partial triumphs. You bring me the Shard, but with the Gehrn. You defeat the Ryuven, but with heavy losses." He looked at Becknam again. "Must I purchase your loyalty?"

"No, Your Majesty." Becknam's voice was hardly audible.

"I have no use for men who must be bought," the king said. "I must have men who are proven." He paused. "If the shield holds, we will at last have the resources to deal with the treacherous warlords, and we will move to reclaim our borderlands south of Heege. You must win that for me, cleanly."

"Yes, sire."

"You will serve under General Kannan when that time comes."

"Sire, General Kannan is a man of the east and does not know Heege. Heege is heavy terrain and will be difficult to—"

King Jerome kicked him again, making Ariana jump. "Do not make excuses to me!" He stopped and closed his eyes, seeming to argue with himself. "You are above excuses. You have more within you than that. You could be as worthy as my Soren, if you tried." He looked at Becknam's bowed head and it looked as if he wanted to say more, though in the end he said only, "You—may go." But the king himself started toward the curtain, leaving Becknam on the carpet behind him.

Ariana shrank back and threw herself deep into the alcove. King Jerome shoved back the curtain and passed without noticing her, and she barely breathed relief. Now Becknam would exit, and he would expect her to be in the corridor beyond. But she dared not rush out on the heels of the king—

Becknam came through the curtain, holding his side, and Ariana jumped in surprise. He looked toward her sharply and suddenly his hand was only brushing a bit of dust from his tunic. "My lady."

He did not want her to know. She could not humiliate him with her knowledge. She smiled, hoping it looked sincere. "I was just coming for you."

He looked at her for an eternal moment and then relaxed marginally. "I'm finished here."

"Then you owe me a walk." She gestured to the carved faces. "I was looking at these kings. I confess I don't recognize most of them."

"Nor I," he said, relaxing a little more. "Let's go outside, if you don't mind? We can walk along the green."

"Sounds fine."

They walked in silence out of the palace, away from the Wheel of the Circle and the king's home and the crush of people. Ariana let him set the pace, in case he was in pain, but he betrayed no sign of discomfort. There was a small gate in the wall and Becknam led her out onto the green—once the fortress's grazing ground, centuries ago, but now a strip of grass kept primarily for tradition. A little distance away a girl tended a flock of geese.

Becknam's eyes were unseeing, focused on the ground a little distance ahead of them. Ariana cleared her throat. "It's more enjoyable if we also speak, my lord."

He seemed to startle. "I'm sorry, my lady. I'm not much company now. If you want talk, you'll have to begin it."

"I had hoped we wouldn't be reduced to talking about the weather. Do you think the rains will come early this autumn?"

"I hope not."

"You don't like rain? Maybe not to walk in, but its sound on the roof can be so cozy at night."

He shook his head. "Not even the sound of it. Build a roaring fire loud enough to drown it out."

"What would you prefer?"

"Our nights can be quite different," he reminded her. "If we're out, I like to hear the sentries calling back and forth at night. I know then all is well. And—" He stopped abruptly and scowled. "It's a foolish question."

"Then you should have offered me better conversation."

"Then answer yourself," he returned. "What pleases you, besides being drenched by rain?"

"I must be easily pleased, as I enjoy so many things." She smiled and ticked them off on her fingers. "Study with my father, performing difficult magic well, sunshine on flowers, chocolate, seeing horses—"

"Horses?"

"I think they're beautiful creatures. So exotic. I wish there were more of them."

He nodded. "I suppose I like them, too."

"Ah, something we share. And I like to hear when I've done well, mastered a particularly difficult challenge."

He eyed her skeptically. "Praise."

"Don't mock me! I'm sure you appreciate it, too. Even Tam is glad of a word of thanks—as are most slaves, I think."

"How is Tam, anyway?"

She noted the change in subject, but followed it. "He's recovered completely. He slept the day through in Father's office, and then we kept him quiet at home another day, but he shows no ill effects now."

"If you will forgive me, at least it is proof the shield works."

"True—if he had been fully Ryuven, it would have shredded his heart." She sighed. "He is unhappy though, I think. There was a good friend he left, who risked his life to help Tam. Tam worries over him."

"Slaves everywhere are unhappy," Becknam said curtly. "Freemen are unhappy. Why should Tam be different?"

Ariana looked at him, stung.

Becknam seemed to realize his mistake. "I'm sorry, my lady. It's only—I should not have said it that way."

Ariana exhaled slowly. "Tam was outcast by his brother—his half-brother, maybe. When he did not die in battle, a price was placed on his head. But he wanted to be reconciled. I think he would have done almost anything."

Becknam regarded her warily. "Why are you telling me this?"

Tread carefully. "I only meant to explain why he is unhappy."

Becknam nodded slowly. "Then I have something in common with the Ryuven slave after all; my half-brothers hate me too."

It was the first time he'd alluded to his forbidden parentage. "Why?" she asked, since he'd broached the subject himself.

He shrugged. "Why not? I am a political tool and a constant reminder that their father is imperfect, that the king erred. And their mother...."

Ariana swallowed. "The queen dislikes you."

"The queen will not be satisfied while I breathe," Becknam said darkly. "You have seen how she has stayed in Kalifi rather than the Naziar these recent years?"

"For her health. The air and water are beneficial there."

"Nothing like," Becknam snapped. "She said she would not set foot in Alham while I am here. She has come sometimes while I was away fighting, but she has kept her word."

"My lord, I—"

"Don't," he said, turning his face away. "I have spoken more freely with you than anyone, and we've traveled together as comrades. I would very much like one person to call me by name—

please." He looked a little wild, his expression earnest. "Is that too forward, too impolite for the White Mage's daughter?"

She shook her head. "No. Not at all."

He smiled, embarrassed. "Forgive me—it is the Black Mage now, isn't it?"

"So it is. And don't forget it."

He sighed. "I am sorry for saying so much. I shouldn't have. It's only, after meeting him...."

"But I asked you to talk," she reminded him. "And after all, you have a secret of mine as well." She started walking again, so he had to follow. "In truth, this is what I wanted, to hear you speaking as yourself."

"Do I speak as someone else?"

"I haven't seen enough of the count to be certain. But I think you speak as the commander at times."

"I was raised a soldier."

"But you say what you think one should, even if unconvinced yourself. That is why you felt you should report Tam even—"

He stopped and faced her. "My lady, listen to me. If Tam is ever discovered, if anyone believes I knew about him, I will be dead before he will. He will at least be worth something, for interrogation or barter. As far as I am concerned, it will only be a long-awaited excuse to dispose of an inconvenient mistake."

She stared at him, shaking her head. "Surely...."

Becknam smiled grimly. "It's poor form to slaughter one's own blood without at least an ostensible cause. But I am a potential figurehead, and if there is a hint of treason and I can be attached to it in any fashion, that will be proof enough." He shook his head. "I do believe your father, I think. But guard Tam well, my lady, please, for if he is revealed it may be that of us all only you survive, and that is not certain." He moved aside abruptly, putting space between them. "I'm sorry, my lady. I shouldn't have frightened you."

"Sweet Holy One," breathed Ariana. She swallowed and looked away. "How could he?"

Becknam shook his head. "Do not speak ill of the king. Especially not so near to me."

"My—Shianan," she amended, trying his name. "Come with me." They left the green and she led him toward her house, away from the palace.

He made a valiant effort to recover the conversation. "So, what

107

of you? Now that you're the Black Mage?"

"Now I'm part of the Circle, I may practice my own research." She executed a little swagger. "And I shall become the greatest and most famous mage of my day, of course."

"Going to replace your father, eh?"

"He'd be proud." She pretended to frown. "But there's Mage Parma to consider.... Perhaps she can have the white robes, and I'll settle for silver."

"What, can't you take her in a fair fight?"

Ariana barked a little laugh. "Doubtful. Father says he's the White only because she doesn't want the paperwork, and I'm never quite sure if he's joking."

They skirted the overflowing market, ignoring playing children and vendors' booths until a voice came out of the crowd. "You, sir! Yes, you, my lord! You look like a man of skill. Win your lady a prize!"

Shianan looked at the game, a simple enough challenge of throwing weighted balls into stacked cans. Then he looked at Ariana, who smiled encouragingly. "Why not?"

Shianan turned back and placed a copper coin on the gamer's table in exchange for three balls. Shianan hoisted the first and then set it gently on the table, catching it as it rolled. "The weight is uneven."

The gamer grinned. "If you know that, nothing's unfair. You seem a man with enough skill to compensate."

Shianan eyed the first trio of cans and threw the ball. The stack wobbled but did not spill. "A little more the next time," said the gamer.

Shianan threw again. This time two of the cans fell; the third rocked but remained upright. "Almost," said the gamer. "But you have to take down the full trio at once to win a prize."

"Hmm." Shianan nodded toward the next stack. "Then I'll turn my attention there." He measured the distance with his eyes and then threw hard. The three cans toppled noisily.

"There you go!" the gamer said.

Ariana clapped. "Yes! Well done!"

Shianan gave her a sharp look, and she faltered. The gamer produced a flower, only a little wilted. "One stack earns a flower. Three stacks earn a silver coin in return for your copper. Try again?"

"No, thank you," Shianan said. He turned and proffered the flower to Ariana with a tiny bow. "Sunshine on flowers," he said.

"Thank you," she said, taking it. "But, when I said—I wasn't trying to—"

"I know," he said, walking without looking at her. "You said it in the same way you thank Tam for serving and compliment a landlord on his food." He paused. "Where are we going?"

"My home," she said. "I thought you could stay for supper. Mother Harriet always has more than enough."

"Anything prepared by a Mother Harriet must be better than what will be served to the soldiers," he said. "Yes, thank you."

CHAPTER 14

Ranne opened the door before Ariana could knock. "Well?" she pressed, grasping for Ariana's hands. "How did it go?"

Ariana shook out the bundle under her arm, and the black robe draped to the floor. "Black Mage!"

Ranne squealed and flung her arms about Ariana. "I knew it! I knew you would make it! Come in. Bethia's not here yet."

Ariana wasn't surprised Bethia was late. With Ariana's appointment, the Circle was full, and Bethia would not be able to test.

"You know she tried for the Circle?" Ranne nearly whispered.

Ariana hadn't. "No, I didn't."

"She didn't want to tell you she'd failed. I only know because she told me she had gotten a hearing for her attempt."

"And it didn't go well?"

"She didn't want to talk about it."

Ariana's chest tightened. "Maybe I shouldn't...."

"Yes, you should," Ranne interrupted. "You worked hard and you earned this. She's your friend, and she'll be happy for you."

Ariana wasn't so sure.

Ranne must have seen it on her face. "You'd be happy for her, wouldn't you?"

"Of course I would! I was happy for her, when she became a grey mage before I did!"

"See?"

There was a knock at the door behind them, and Ranne turned back to open it to Bethia. She stood on the threshold and extended an armful of flowers to Ariana. "These are for you," she said. "I thought they could be congratulatory if you passed and conciliatory if you didn't. But given the glee on Ranne's face, I suppose you passed. Congratulations."

"Thank you," Ariana said. "Come in, come in! Ranne made us cheese and onion soup."

Ranne looked at her. "That was supposed to be a surprise!"

Ariana grinned. "Then you should have kept the scent in the kitchen."

They ate with Ranne's mother Vaya, who enthusiastically

111

praised Ariana's achievement, and then settled about the fire with a bowlful of nuts and a nutcracker. "I'm sorry for these," Ranne said, scowling at the nuts. "It's too early in the season still. If you'd tested two or three weeks later, I could have bought some decent ones in the market and candied them."

Ariana laughed. "I don't think I could have waited another two weeks. I was nearly frantic as it was."

"And now you can relax and enjoy your success!"

"Oh, no." Ariana shook her head and drew her feet up on the cushion. "These mages are so talented, so far ahead of me.... Some of them fought at Luenda. How can I work alongside them? What if we go to battle and I can't hold up my magic alongside theirs? What must they think of me?"

"Well, obviously some of them think you should be part of the Circle," Ranne answered patiently. "Which is why they invited you to join."

"But what happens when they find out I'm not extraordinary like them? That I'm just me?"

Bethia laughed. "You're worrying over nothing. Your father is one of them."

Ariana gave her a level stare. "My father fought at Luenda with some of these people. My father is the White Mage of the Great Circle. That's not helping me to feel any less pressure." She gestured in frustration. "And the Silver Mage? Elysia Parma? You can't say you wouldn't be intimidated at the possibility of letting her down."

Bethia nodded seriously. "Yes, I'll grant you that one. Forget the rest of the Circle, *she's* intense."

"And the Indigo," Ranne said. "Forget the rest of the Circle, he's enough to terrify me."

"Unfortunately, I can't forget the rest of them," Ariana said. "I have to work with them, Silver and Indigo and everyone in between. I'm going to gnaw all the nails off my fingers."

"Well, it seems like a nice problem to have," Bethia said, reaching for the bowl of nuts and the cracker.

The words pierced Ariana. "I'm sorry," she said, and she meant it. She hadn't meant to leave her friend behind. But at the same time, she was hurt. Yes, her worries came out of achievement, but they were still worries, and she wanted her friends' support.

Ranne sat forward, catching Ariana's eye. "We're both very proud of you. You worked hard for this."

Bethia glanced at Ariana and then back at the nuts.

"Thanks," Ariana said. "But we don't have to talk about me all night."

"Then I have a change of topic." Bethia rose and retrieved a paper package tied up with string. "I have something to share as well," she said, setting it on a table, "and I brought cakes to celebrate." She pulled apart the string and revealed a cluster of fried dough balls, glazed in honey.

"Oh, I love these!" exclaimed Ranne. "What's the cause?"

Bethia leaned forward, looking between them. "You're the first to hear," she said. "It has to stay a secret for now."

"Of course," Ariana said, propping her elbows on her knees to listen. "Our secret."

Bethia bit her lip, grinning giddily wide, and stretched her hands to each of them. "I'm going to marry Prince Soren."

Ariana's jaw dropped. "What? Really?"

Bethia nodded. "They've been negotiating with my parents. We're not to announce it yet, but of course I had to tell the two of you. But remember, you're sworn to secrecy!"

Ranne leapt up and embraced Bethia. "Oh, I'm so happy for you! A princess, a real princess!"

"Mother thinks they want to dangle the prince-heir as bait for a treaty with the Wakari Coast, but of course they won't make any promises there. He's going to wed me. Perhaps as soon as next year, if all goes well!"

They tore apart the honeyed dough.

"And when will we have news about you and young Kudo?" Bethia asked, eying Ranne pointedly.

"Shh!" Ranne made a flattening motion with her hands. "You can't talk about him!"

"I know how to keep a secret," Bethia assured her. "Even a juicy one like a baron's son going down to market to visit a girl."

Ranne made a face at her. "Fine words from a duke's daughter in the same market."

"But not to wed," Bethia corrected with a smile and a wagging finger.

"We're not marrying." Ranne's cheeks were brightening. "We aren't even walking out together where we can be seen. His father can't know about us."

Bethia took another piece of dough and sat back. "We'll see."

"How does he find an excuse to come so often?" Ariana asked.

Ranne grinned. "He buys a lot of books," she said, "which need binding. A lot of books. He's a favorite customer in the market."

Bethia was the first to leave. Ariana stretched and said she should go, too, as she had to claim her office and workroom the next morning.

Ranne caught her arm. "Don't worry about Bethia," she said. "She's happy for you. She's your friend."

Ariana smiled. "I know."

"And she won't miss the Circle much, not like you'd miss it. She barely works as a grey mage now. You'd die without your magic."

"Well, it's not as if she'll need to be a grey mage," Ariana said. "Not if she's going to marry the prince-heir."

"See? Everything is working out," Ranne said. "Now go home, get some sleep, and go to the Wheel tomorrow as if you're claiming spoils. Because you are."

Ariana laughed. "Thanks. For everything."

CHAPTER 15

Torg took a deliberate, steadying breath. The reply to his letter had been cordial enough: *Come and look over the position, and then you may accept or return to your current post.* It was as if Shianan Becknam knew Torg's fears and meant to allay them.

The door was not quite closed. Torg entered the office.

No one sat at the paper-littered desk inside. He looked about the room—small, no more luxurious than his own, lined with cubbyholes of rolled maps, a few treatises on the Ryuven, a box of dispatches. There was no Shianan Becknam.

Torg shifted uneasily. What was this?

Then the side door opened, and Shianan entered, looking uncomfortable. "Captain Torg."

"Commander Becknam—your lordship." He had not changed much in the intervening years. He looked only a little older, more of a man, one who had seen battles both with sharpened weapons and barbed words.

Shianan exhaled in a sharp little puff of breath. "I'm sorry to make you wait, sir. I was—a moment." He did not sit but looked past Torg to the map pinned to the wall. "What can I do for you?" He paused. "You had some questions regarding the post here."

Torg was not accustomed to seeing his commanding officers stand in their own offices. He was not accustomed to seeing a boy he'd raised stand as his commanding officer. "I'm honored you thought of me, sir. I know there are many qualified men."

"And you want to know why I chose you?"

"Yes, sir." Torg gambled. "And why you gave me a choice."

Shianan moved across the room. "I thought of you because you are, generally speaking, a fine officer. You think clearly and decisively, and in trying situations you never give your men a moment to question." He turned and started back toward Torg. "You also make the effort to know each man in your command, at least something of him." He glanced at Torg briefly and then turned back, pacing again toward the far wall. "And I give you leave to choose because—because you were forced into association with a troublesome person once before, and I believe you suffered for it. Thirty years is a long time to

115

spend in the hinterlands." He faced Torg. "I would not force that upon you again."

Was it possible he held no grudge? Torg swallowed. "Sir, I—if you believe that—"

"Captain Torg, I was given into your keeping at the age of four. Since that time you have received no promotion, no increase in pay, no transfer to a less remote post. Keeping me ended your career, reduced you to a figure to be swept aside and hidden in dishonor." Shianan hesitated, perhaps a little startled by his frank speech. "I do not pretend to offer you this post as payment; there is no promotion in rank and the difference in wages is hardly worth mention. I only thought your skills could be of use here." He looked fixedly at the maps. "But if you prefer to be prudent, the choice is yours to make. There are, as you say, other qualified men."

Sweet Holy One, it was Shianan asking for *his* grace, thinking he had done *Torg* wrong. Torg tried to gather himself. "May I speak candidly, sir?"

Shianan nodded once.

"To tell the truth, sir, I had thought—I thought perhaps it was you who might have—felt cautious regarding me. That is, I mean— four is young to be placed in an outpost, and I know it was hard...." He faltered, unable to speak without saying something dangerous.

Shianan looked at him. "You thought I resented you?" He shook his head. "Captain Torg, sir, I won't deny there were moments when I hated you. But there were other moments.... In the end, it is you who could be said to have raised me. I am sorry for the trouble I caused you, however unintentional on my part."

Torg's blood thinned to water. "Sir...."

Shianan straightened. "Captain Torg, will you serve here or at your present post?"

To be in Alham again, in civilization—to break the unending cycle of his outpost and its promise of eternal obscurity, of endless punishment for following his orders—to serve within the gaze of his superiors, who might advance him yet again before his retirement— and now assured that Shianan did not despise him for his role—it was a gamble, a potentially dangerous gamble, but it would be worth the escape. "Sir, it would be an honor to serve beneath you."

Shianan's jaw twitched. "I can promise you nothing. I am not popular in Alham."

"I do not fear opinion." If Shianan were in immediate danger, he would not have risen to commander and been made a count. It was safe to serve him for a time.

"Thank you, Captain Torg." Shianan went to his desk and opened a drawer. "Here are the orders necessary for your transfer. Please make arrangements as soon as possible, and your new office and quarters will be waiting."

"Thank you, sir," said Torg, taking the orders smartly and saluting with his arm across his chest. He turned and left the office, closing the door behind him.

That had not been what he had imagined all these years. The boy had not grown to hate him, after all. It was unexpected. But if there were a chance he could rise under the bastard, he should take it. He would have no other chances.

Of course, some might be suspicious of anyone seen as loyal to the bastard. He would have to speak carefully, let a few deliberate statements be overheard. But he was glad of Shianan; he had liked the boy, after all, and liked the man he'd become.

Shianan dropped into his chair, rubbing a hand over his face and through his hair. It was done, and it had been no more difficult than expected.

Torg had been wary, of course. Shianan had been responsible for the destruction of any hopes for advancement. But he had agreed to come to Alham anyway.

Shianan straightened and pushed a hand through his hair. He should finish here, as he was to meet Ariana at the Wheel for a walk to her house and then supper. It would be welcome respite after the strain of anticipating Torg's arrival. Ariana's simplistic outlook was—

No, that wasn't right. She wasn't simple, of course; she was actually quite clever. It was only that she was so... different. Shianan was a soldier working among soldiers, and he saw things as they were. Ariana Hazelrig, younger in both years and experience, saw things as they should be. If the White Mage had concealed a Ryuven in the very heart of Alham but meant no harm, it wasn't treason, and so Shianan shouldn't be harmed by his knowledge of it. It was pure fancy, of course, but gritty reality was hard for her to grasp.

She was disturbed anew by the Gehrn, for example. Flamen Ande had brought the dark-haired slave when he arrived yesterday to inspect the townhouse and perform the Shard ritual, and while Ariana had said nothing, Shianan had seen her eyes dark with disapproval.

At least they would be finished soon. While the Gehrn had title to the townhouse, Flamen Ande himself would return to the citadel in Davan and send minor members of the order to their newest hold. Then Ande would be gone, and Shianan wouldn't have to recall Ariana's horrified, accusing eyes as the slave choked and coughed.

Enough; he was going to the Hazelrigs' tonight, and he should be thinking of more than Flamen Ande. He rose and tugged his clothing straight as he started for the door.

Chapter 16

Ariana set aside the pen and rolled her notes tightly, tying them into place. She stood, stretched, and started for her father's office.

The white door stood partly ajar. "Father? Oh, hello, Flamen Ande." She schooled her expression into politeness.

Ewan and Ande were sitting near his desk, with Tam and Luca standing behind Ande. "Hello, darling," said her father.

"Good evening, young Mage Hazelrig," the priest said. "I was just about to begin the ceremony."

"Everything is to your satisfaction?" The Circle had ordered a wooden frame built over the Shard, matching exactly the sketch Ariana had carried back from the citadel: two beams eight feet tall, connected at the top at a width of five feet. On either upright, six feet above the ground, were iron rings; when Ariana had skimmed the outline of the annual ritual, she had learned incense burners would hang from these rings as the high priest chanted and swayed over the Shard.

"Everything was prepared," Ande answered.

"Do you need anything else? Any assistance?" her father asked.

"No, thank you. I have all I need." He rose. "You must excuse me now, as I have to begin as the moon rises. Bring the bag, Luca." He nodded to Ariana and left, Luca hurrying behind him.

Ariana sat on the edge of the desk. "I'll be glad when he's finished and gone."

"Don't be rude, Ariana," Ewan said, "even if I agree with you."

"He shouldn't have Luca," Tam said. "The Gehrn don't usually keep slaves. They are supposed to live an austere life. I looked it up."

A knock sounded at the open door. "May I come in?" Shianan asked.

"Yes, do," said Ewan. "We have just sent the flamen to discharge his duty. What can I do for you?"

"My lady mage had invited me to supper."

"And you are welcome." Ariana rose from the desk. "I want to look in on the priest first. The ceremony looked supremely dull when I read over it, but I confess to a tiny bit of curiosity."

Shianan grinned. "Will you peer down the stairwell like a mischievous child, spying where you shouldn't?"

Guilt lanced her. "Something like that, anyway."

"I'll go, too," Tam said.

"I've read the chants," Ewan said. "That's enough tedium, and I want to go through the market before the last booksellers are gone for the day. I'll see you at home."

He locked the office behind them and went the other way. The building was quiet; nearly everyone had already gone. Ariana sniffed and made a face. "I can smell the incense already. That must be thick in the cellar."

Shianan was frowning at the empty corridor. "Is no one watching?"

Ariana shook her head. "The flamen didn't want the Circle present—something about outsiders and sacred rituals and purification. That's partly why Father didn't blink when I said I wanted to peek." She grinned.

"He thinks something might happen to the Shard?"

"Oh, no. The Circle picked over every aspect of this annual rite, and there's no real magic in it." She laughed. "It took weeks of preparation and more than a dozen mages to work the shield. A cranky priest and a bunch of incense, no matter how potent, won't hurt it."

The stair into the cellar was narrow, and they crept down it. Ariana felt a little thrill of excitement, as if doing something slightly dangerous. The incense was very intense here, and she put a hand over her face.

There was an odd sound, a sort of hissing thud, muffled by the smoke and coming at irregular intervals. As they neared the base of the stairs, something else, like a muted howl, overlapped the end of the first sound. "What is that?" Ariana whispered.

Shianan paused mid-step, head tipped. "I don't—it sounds like...."

Tam darted forward into the cellar. Ariana dashed after him, heedless of caution. "Tam!" But as she descended into the cellar itself she stumbled to a stop.

The incense burners were not hanging but on the floor, flanking the wooden frame. The rings held instead the black-haired slave, straddling the Shard with his arms outstretched, and the flamen was whipping his bare and bloodied back, making him twist against the wrist cuffs.

Shianan swore as he plunged past her.

Tam was nearly at the Shard, and as the priest swung again he leapt for the frame. The whip cut into him and he cried, stumbling with the force of it.

Ande paused, staring in furious disbelief at Tam. He whirled as Shianan reached him. "What are you doing?"

"I could ask you the same thing." Shianan jabbed a finger toward the slave. "What is this? I thought you were going to perform a simple ritual!"

"That follows next!" Ande snapped. "This is the purification for a new site. It requires the blood of a prisoner of war and—"

"No!" Ariana gestured sharply. "This is not what we expected. It might go wrong."

Tam came toward the priest, his face set. "You—"

Ande struck him hard with the butt of the whip, knocking Tam to the floor. Ariana rushed to him as Shianan wrested the whip from Ande's hands. "We will discuss this with the Circle."

Tam sat up, blinking hard. The skin across his temple was abraded, and Ariana brushed at it with her left hand, keeping her right free and nearer Ande. "Are you all right?"

"I gave you our ceremonial orders," Ande protested. "You must let me finish!"

"Wait!" Ariana held up a hand. "Be quiet. Can you feel it?"

"Feel what?" Shianan looked at her.

But Tam could sense the magic as well as she. "There's something wrong with the shield."

The Shard was glowing deep in its center with the indigo light she'd seen before, but its pulsing was different somehow, unsteady. And there had been no light once the shield was in place. "Get away from the Shard. Hurry!"

Shianan threw the whip to the floor and shoved Ande toward the stair. He reached for the slave's bound wrists as Ariana crouched to look at the Shard between his knees. "Something's altered it," she said. Tam crawled beside her. "Something has altered the magic." She reached her right hand to the dark liquid spattered on its surface, warm beneath her touch. Her finger came away red. "Blood. It's the blood—it's changing the properties of the shield."

The air around them was sparkling purple through the heavy incense. Shianan jerked the sagging slave free. "Can you hold it?"

"I don't know. I need some time to look at it. Move away." She pressed her hand again to the Shard, and it throbbed though her skin. "I need my father." She placed her left hand on it, trying to balance the sensation. "I think it's—"

Power shattered beneath her hands, burning her. The walls of the cellar flashed purple and an iridescent band appeared, marking the cellar-sized hemisphere that was all that was left of the shield. Shianan dashed for the stair with the stumbling slave, throwing him down as he turned back. "My lady mage!"

She closed her eyes, visualizing the failing spell, and saw a heavy plate made suddenly fragile, buckling under pressure. She reached for Tam and stood. "Come on!"

The iridescent line was creeping closer to them, the shield shrinking until it would collapse entirely upon the Shard. Ariana clutched Tam's arm and ran for the stairs, gritting her teeth against the deafening throb, knowing she would have to pull Tam through the boundary, that it would hurt him.

She struck the gleaming border as if it were stone, falling backward with a sharp, disorienting pain. Shianan shouted to her. "Ariana!"

She stared at the border, watching it advance, and it reached her foot. It pressed against her solidly and then began to push her leg across the floor. She scrambled up and backward, unable to breathe.

Shianan rushed to the iridescent rim. "Ariana!" He struck at the barrier and his fist glanced off as if beating a wall. He drew his dagger and stabbed at it without effect.

Tam caught Ariana's arm and pulled her away from the advancing wall. *It will crush us*, she thought wildly. She spun and saw the hemisphere shrinking upon them, advancing more quickly now and flickering ominously. *It will crush us, we're going to die—*

Tam faced her and seized her forearms. "Release me!"

She stared at the glistening shell contracting over them. Shianan shouted, his voice lost in the roar. She saw her father rushing down the stairs, shoving the flamen roughly aside. The rim was near enough to touch now.

Tam's fingers dug hard into her. "Release me!"

Realization came to her and she seized him. She squeezed her eyes tightly shut and saw the cables, the threads, the chains, the one all-binding lock. "*Tamaryl!*"

Power blossomed under her hands, expanding and spreading through him, spilling into her, and she felt him change as he clutched her. But it was too late, the walls were pressing against them and even Tam would be crushed.

Something very cold crashed over her and there was only black.

CHAPTER 17

Shianan stared at the Shard, at the space where Ariana and Tam had been. Where they weren't. They had disappeared in a spray of violet fluorescence, leaving nothing but the Shard itself, dull and dark. He had heard Tam screaming at Ariana, seen them grasp one another in final desperation, and then they were gone.

He thought, through the smoke and iridescent gleam, he had seen a flash of membranous wings.

Guards clattered down the stairs, weapons drawn, and looked uncertainly at the little group. "Mage Hazelrig," one ventured.

Ewan Hazelrig stared immobile at the Shard, at the space where his daughter had vanished. Shianan hadn't seen him arrive.

"Mage Hazelrig, you called us. You said something was happening to the shield."

"They're gone," the White Mage said hollowly.

"Who? Who attacked the shield?"

"The shield failed," Shianan said, finding his voice now he had someone to command. "This is the man who triggered its failure. Hold him for questioning."

"I had leave to perform our rituals!" Ande protested, himself shocked, frightened, and a bit angry. "I did—"

He was silenced abruptly as the guards took him. Shianan looked at the mage, anxious to ask questions which could not be voiced before others. "Mage Hazelrig," he said, hearing his voice quaver. "May we use your office?"

Ewan Hazelrig shook his head, his jaw hanging slackly. "No. I need a moment—here."

Shianan's stomach spasmed. The mage went to the Shard and examined it without touching, peering at the slave's blood spilled across it. He crouched and traced in the air the outline of a smudge where Ariana had placed her hand. The soldiers herded Ande and the injured slave up the stairs. "Did he attack the shield?" Shianan asked.

"I don't think so. I don't think he worked any magic." Ewan placed his fingertips lightly upon the Shard and concentrated. "There isn't any lingering trace of another effort. I think—I think it was the blood."

125

"My lord mage?"

"The blood on the Shard made it unstable. That must have been what I felt. It was weakening but still substantially the same, and it passed through us all without incident."

"But it was a barrier to them." Shianan's voice caught.

"Ariana touched it here." Mage Hazelrig swallowed, struggling to keep his own voice. "While she meant well, the shield was already failing irrevocably, and interfering only unbalanced it more. More—someone must have struck Tam."

"Yes."

Mage Hazelrig nodded. "This is Tam's blood, here. Ryuven blood was used in the formation of the shield, and then the human blood here. Tam's provided the catalyst that made it a shield to humans instead."

"That's possible?"

"It probably would have collapsed before becoming impenetrable, without Tam's blood." He straightened, his face strained.

Shianan's own limbs were beginning to quiver with shock. He had seen brutal death, but soldiers in battle—not Ariana and Tam, crushed within the shield intended to save them.

Ewan Hazelrig sank to the ground. "My daughter. Sweet Holy One, my daughter."

Shianan stared numbly. "I—my lord mage, I—I am so sorry."

Ewan shook his head and covered his face. "She is not dead."

Something rushed through Shianan. "But—she could escape the shield?"

"No. No one, not even a mage, could escape that. She would have been crushed as it collapsed into the Shard." He swallowed audibly and took away his hands, revealing reddened eyes and damp cheeks. "Did you see?"

Shianan needed only a moment to grasp his meaning. "She released him."

Ewan nodded. "She released Tam to his Ryuven form and powers. The altered shield no longer barred him as a Ryuven."

"So he could go to his own world." Ariana had allowed Tam to flee at the end, escaping the horrific death closing on them. "Better a slim chance with his own kind than certain death here." He clenched his fists. "But even if she helped him—she would have—how—you said she was not dead!"

"She is not dead," Mage Hazelrig repeated heavily. "He took her with him."

Shianan stared and then swayed, grasping at the scaffold for support. "Sweet Holy One," he whispered. "She's *there*."

CHAPTER 18

Ariana was rising, rushing up from a very deep pool of cold and black. Someone wanted her, someone somehow *willed* that she rise, that she wake.

She opened her eyes and saw a thousand colors, saw every particle of the air dancing and whirling before her in a dizzying array. A thousand sounds assaulted her ears, deafening her. She squeezed her eyes shut and slapped her hands over her ears, but still she heard them, heard the rush of the wind and the flutter of a bird's wing and the roar of the storm and the laugh of a man and the friction of grass blades in the breeze and the metallic clink of coins and hundreds of other things, all magnified beyond what her hands could blunt. The air itself bit at her flesh, the movement of the breeze whipped across her skin, the prickle of the grass stabbed a maddening attack on her body.

She screamed.

Tamaryl watched Ariana struggle to consciousness, holding his breath as she choked for air.

He had to return her. If Oniwe chose to execute Tamaryl, Ariana would suffer the same fate, or if they discovered her identity she might be used as leverage. Certainly the Black Mage, daughter to the White Mage, would be quite a prize. But he could not risk carrying her back until he knew how the first trip had injured her, lest the second kill her.

Ariana opened her eyes and gulped for air. But immediately she flinched, and Tamaryl's gut contracted—was it the sight of his Ryuven form bending over her? But she clamped her hands over her ears and hunched her shoulders, trying to hide herself, and she screamed as he had never heard her.

"Lady Ariana!" He gripped her shoulders. "My lady! What is it?"

She writhed in his grasp and began to rake at her own flesh, gouging stripes in her arms and torso. Tamaryl seized her hands to stop her, but she shrieked and jerked from him.

His senses prickled as they had done only once in recent years, and he turned his head as three winged forms strode toward them. Walking—they did not see him as a threat.

They were che, though he did not know them well. The first at least he knew by name: Umbreth, who had led the attack against him in the mountains.

He took a steadying breath, and energy burned through him. Immediately he drew another breath, and another. Magic poured through him, rushing to fill all the myriad empty spaces. Like water to the dangerously thirsty, it would need time to fully quench him, but for the first time in years, he had a cool spring to quell his parched essence.

Ariana was still screaming, struggling beneath whatever invisible attack she suffered. Tamaryl turned back, torn between attending to her and meeting the che. As he watched, her clawed fingers loosened and she passed into unconsciousness, momentarily freed from whatever plagued her. He brushed her face worriedly— yes, she was only sleeping—and with a guilty gratitude, he straightened to face Umbreth'che and the others.

They had stopped a short distance away, watching him warily. They could sense, of course, he had power now. Umbreth did not succeed in concealing his surprise and resentment. Finally he managed to speak, breaking the silence Ariana had left. "You have come home, Tamaryl'sho."

He had to press his advantage. "You seem surprised to see me, Umbreth'che."

"We left you with Oniwe'aru. I thought—but obviously you spoke privately after he sent us away."

Tamaryl did not wish to address that. "Where is Oniwe'aru now?"

"In the Palace of Red Sands," came the answer. "Who is the human?"

"I will take her to Oniwe'aru," Tamaryl answered obliquely. He stooped and gathered Ariana into his arms, taking care her arms did not dangle. She was heavy, and he needed magic to hold her. He began walking, not looking at Umbreth as he passed.

"One moment, Tamaryl'sho," Umbreth sallied. "Oniwe'aru did not say to expect your return. Nor has your sentence been lifted."

Tamaryl turned to glance at Umbreth over his shoulder, gathering his long-suppressed ability with an invigorating sense of energy and, despite the situation, a certain joy. He let a trickle of power ebb from him. "The three of you are not enough to stop me," he said bluntly. "I will go to see Oniwe'aru. We shall see what transpires after that."

He kept his head straight and high as he walked, but his mind was roiling. Could he reach Oniwe'aru through the female guard? Even if he could speak, would he die anyway? Could he risk taking Ariana back through the between-worlds? How long would the shield remain down?

The Palace of Red Sands was very near, as Tamaryl had arrived in one of its expansive gardens. That was some unconscious impulse, it seemed....

Umbreth was not the only one to note his appearance, but the others were more cautious in their response; he saw forms watching from shadowed lanes or doorways as he approached the building of gleaming white stone. The two guards, each armed with a mace, had no such recourse. They straightened and tensed as he approached, raising their wings slightly. "Tamaryl'sho," one said tightly.

"Does Oniwe'aru expect you?" the other asked, an effort to stop Tamaryl without open challenge.

"He will see me." They were males, assigned to the palace but not Oniwe's personal guard. Tamaryl did not pause but carried Ariana directly between them, and they turned, hesitated, and then watched him pass.

"Tamaryl'sho!" one called at last. "Please wait while we speak to Oniwe'aru!"

He did not slow. He guessed where Oniwe would be. He went straight down the corridor, turning at the second corner, holding Ariana tightly as he entered the cool patio. Ryuven scattered as he entered to the edges of the shaded pavilion. In the center Oniwe turned to face him, his expression solemn. "Tamaryl'sho."

Tamaryl sank directly to one knee without breaking stride. "I beg to speak with you, Oniwe'aru."

There was a long moment while Oniwe weighed the decision, and then the ruler made a slight gesture which sent the others from the pavilion. Tamaryl did not move.

Oniwe indicated the gardens around the patio, cooled with bubbling fountains. "This is not a suitable place for private conversation. Come this way."

Tamaryl rose, still holding Ariana, and followed the ruler through a door and into a small, lavish audience room. Oniwe crossed the room and sat upright in the ornate chair, settling his wings behind him. Tamaryl paused inside the door and settled Ariana's unconscious body on the cool floor. He straightened, took two steps forward, and knelt. It was not the courtier's position he had taken on the patio, but a supplicant's, on two bent knees with his hands on the floor before him, fingers spread with the tips of his forefingers touching. Oniwe would understand he meant no challenge. "Oniwe'aru."

Oniwe did not tell him to rise. "Explain why you are here."

Tamaryl chose to answer differently. "I regret our division, Oniwe'aru. It has always been my interest to serve you."

"The division was your doing."

"I meant only to serve well. I felt our path would harm us all in the end."

"So you said." Oniwe shifted a wing. "So you've come to make restitution?"

Tamaryl's throat began to close and he swallowed hard. "I beg you, Oniwe'aru, let me return."

Ariana was two steps behind him. If it seemed Oniwe would kill him, he would throw himself over her and leap between worlds with his dying effort, returning her even injured or dead to her own world.

But Oniwe merely frowned. "You have been in exile in the human world," he said. "Hidden from us."

"Yes, Oniwe'aru. I was hidden within a binding."

"A binding," Oniwe repeated. "Like a Subduing?"

"Something like that."

"You sacrificed your power so we could not find you." Oniwe scratched at his chin. "Who was it who bound you?"

"The White Mage."

Oniwe's mouth curved into a slow, grim smile. "You must have been quite a prize for them, Tamaryl."

"He did not publicize me."

"No? What, exactly, did he do with you?"

"He made me a slave."

Oniwe laughed. He laughed a long time, it seemed to Tamaryl, his wings moving with the effort. "You were a slave—a slave, without power, in the human world." He gave one final, small chuckle. "No wonder you have returned to beg for forgiveness."

"It is not forgiveness I seek," Tamaryl said carefully. "I still believe what I said then, and I still desire to serve you."

Oniwe frowned again. "How did you come here, if you were

bound?"

"My mistress released me," Tamaryl answered.

"And you have brought her as an appeasing gift to me?"

"No," Tamaryl said levelly. "No, I must return her."

"You come with many conditions to your begging."

"Only those two stipulations," Tamaryl said. "All else is yours to dictate." He rotated his hands so that the tips of the middle fingers touched and lowered his forehead to them, spreading his wings flat across the floor. "Punish me if you must. Mark me physically. Take my titles and rank from me. But let me return, please, Oniwe'aru."

Oniwe stood, shifting his wings behind him. He walked slowly forward, and Tamaryl's pulse pounded. Oniwe paused, his sandaled feet only inches from Tamaryl's skull. "You were so proud," he said quietly. "I never thought to see you take this position in my palace."

Tamaryl could not speak once he had made himself so low before Oniwe'aru. He tried to swallow the fear throbbing inside him.

Oniwe's weight shifted and he lifted his right foot to place it, as Tamaryl's posture demanded, across the back of Tamaryl's bent neck. Tamaryl's forehead ground against his numbing fingers. The pressure increased slowly, and his torso was flattened against his thighs, his shoulders pressed to the hard floor. He dragged his face to the side and Oniwe pressed hard so that his throat ached against the tile.

He couldn't breathe. He rolled one eye upward, trying to see Oniwe, but the angle was too steep. He closed his eyes and waited, burning for air.

He would not be able to reach Ariana. She would die here as well.

"I ordered your death, Tamaryl. You had betrayed me. You defied my orders."

Blood pounded in Tamaryl's ears, nearly drowning out Oniwe's words.

"You still hold those opinions which inflamed me then. You still defy what I ordered then."

The room was fading around Tamaryl. So it would be....

"I have seen what it was you feared, though. Some of the sho—the wars have not made them better leaders. Their lands have suffered, which we could ill afford. Our trade has suffered."

Tamaryl's wings shuddered. Then the pressure eased slightly, and his pulse burst through him.

"I do not deny that your contumacy infuriated me. But I think now you did believe you were serving our interests." Oniwe removed his foot and Tamaryl jerked his head from the floor, gasping for air.

"Tamaryl'sho," Oniwe said sternly, and Tamaryl pressed himself again to the floor, trying to slow his breathing. "You did defy my orders. But I see now why you did. Your method still deserves punishment, but I think so many years in exile as a Subdued slave to humans is sufficient. In fact, I consider it crueler than most of what I sentence." He paused. "Tamaryl'sho, raise yourself as befits one of your rank."

Tamaryl shifted to one knee, his hands to the ground on either side of him.

"Tamaryl'sho, I commute your sentence of death to a term of exile, which you have served. You may return to your place here, but I assign you the onerous task of repairing the damage you foresaw. I restore your rank and privilege so you may have authority to serve as I dictate. Now rise."

Tamaryl stood, knees trembling. "I—thank you, Oniwe'aru."

"You had robbed me of an excellent prince, Tamaryl'sho."

Tamaryl swallowed hard against his constricting throat. "It was not my will, Oniwe'aru."

"I know." Oniwe sighed. "To tell the truth, I wish I had listened then. But I wish you had not drawn such a sharp line. You made it difficult to hear you."

"I am sorry."

Oniwe turned, his wings shifting. "When we learned you were alive—I acted precipitously. I am not proud I was ruled by my previous thoughts so blindly." His fingers flexed slowly. "Returning, I realized I regretted my action."

Tamaryl hardly dared to breathe.

"And so, since you have survived, I view this as something of a second chance for both of us. I might regain my prince doniphan, you might regain your place. But there is little room for error, Tamaryl'sho; I cannot overturn my edict lightly."

Tamaryl swallowed. "I will give no cause to regret this action, Oniwe'aru."

"Good."

Oniwe gestured toward Ariana. "Now tell me about her."

"My mistress," Tamaryl said. "I brought her here to save her life from an accident in her world."

"To save her?" Oniwe frowned. "Quite the loyal slave, were

you? Oh, yes, she released you. I suppose you felt some gratitude. She is injured?"

"Not from that. I think it was the journey between-worlds."

"That should not render her unconscious. It is painful for humans, but not debilitating."

Tamaryl shook his head. "No, it was after we arrived. She was—she was screaming, covering her ears, scratching at her skin."

Oniwe's expression turned to grim amusement. "You were enslaved to a mage."

"Yes! Is that the cause?"

"We have brought only a very few mages as prisoners," Oniwe said. "It is never worth the trouble; they die almost immediately. From what we can surmise, the magic in their world is so diluted that they are susceptible to it here, where there is so much more." He frowned. "Even asleep, she should have died by this time. There must be something different about her."

She is the White Mage's daughter. She is stronger than any they've captured before.

"Maybe she has only a small skill?" Oniwe suggested. "So perhaps she can sense the magic but is not overwhelmed by it." He shrugged. "You have refused her to me, so she is your responsibility."

"Is it safe to carry her back like this?"

"We have never tried to take anyone back. But I wouldn't recommend it. Even if she is still alive, she probably cannot withstand the between-worlds again." He walked a few paces away. "Ask Nori'bel. She's treated the mages we brought back."

"Thank you, I will."

"And I see the humans' barrier is down. Was that your doing?"

Tamaryl's breath caught. "No. I only took advantage of it."

"Regardless, it is good to know." Oniwe regarded him. "What are you thinking, Tamaryl? I know there is more in your mind."

Tamaryl hesitated, trying to find words, and then he knelt again on one knee. "Thank you for your magnanimity, Oniwe'aru. Thank you for allowing me to return."

Oniwe nodded. "Do not disappoint me, Tamaryl'sho."

"No, Oniwe'aru."

"What more? And rise."

Tamaryl straightened. "There is someone I must find."

"Daranai'rika." Oniwe smiled. "She has not taken a mate."

"Thank you, Oniwe'aru."

Oniwe looked at him a moment. "No, that is not whom you sought. Who else?"

"I was—Maru." There was a promise, pledged years ago.

"Ah. Maru." Oniwe's expression did not change. "He disappeared for a time after you were found in the human world. After I left you there." He looked at Tamaryl. "When he returned, he refused to say where he had been."

Tamaryl's heart froze.

"I had my suspicions," Oniwe said.

Tamaryl could barely form the words. "What—what...."

"Don't look at me so! He was only shirking at worst accusation. No one had seen him with you, and even I would not kill one for burying his lord and friend."

Relief seeped through Tamaryl.

"Go and find him. He serves in this palace. But do not neglect Daranai'rika. She was very much affected when you left. Having one's betrothed suddenly declared a traitor with a price will do that."

"Yes, Oniwe'aru."

"And take this girl with you; I don't want her left in my audience rooms."

"Yes, Oniwe'aru."

"And I will have you return to tell me of the human world and this shield they've tried."

Tamaryl nodded. "Yes, Oniwe'aru."

CHAPTER 19

Shianan left the soldiers and mages arguing around the Shard. There was nothing he could do here. General Septime would speak for the military.

He left Ewan Hazelrig rigid within the shouting group, staring at the Shard. Shianan did not know how the White Mage could function at this time, how he could stand while knowing his daughter was with the Ryuven.

Tam won't be able to protect her. He had to hide here for years. They're both dead.

But Hazelrig clung to something, some shred of desperate fantastic hope allowing him to say Ariana was not dead. Perhaps the Ryuven would try to ransom her.

Shianan threw back a heavy wooden door, cracking it sharply against the stone wall. Three men started up from their table of dice. "Commander."

Shianan forced his voice to steady. "You have the Gehrn priest here."

"Yes, sir. He's been kept for questioning as you said."

No one had bothered with him yet. The more immediate concern was the shield. "And the slave with him?"

"We've got him, too, sir. Separate cells, sir."

Shianan nodded. "I want to see him."

The guard reached for a ring of keys. "He's been yelling and cursing and—"

"Not him," Shianan said. "The slave."

The guard unlocked a door beyond the guards' room and went down a short hallway before turning into a row of locked cells. Insistent cries came from some doors, while other cells were occupied but silent. The guard paused before a door and checked at the grilled window before unlocking it. "Here he is, sir."

Shianan pushed back the door and stepped into the narrow cell, less than the span of his arms. Wet straw squished beneath his boots. The black-haired slave sat in the muck with his shoulder to the wall, trying to support himself without touching his raw bare back. His head moved slightly to take in Shianan and the guard, and then he dropped his eyes.

"I'm taking him," Shianan said.

The guard looked at him. "Not the priest? I mean, sir, it's...."

"I know the usual process when there's an extra slave imprisoned," Shianan said. "There's no record of the second prisoner, he goes to the auction block, and the money is split amongst you. But you'll have to make do without this one."

The man straightened. "Yes, sir." He crossed the narrow cell. "Up with you, then." He reached for the slave.

"Leave that!" Shianan had not seen whether the guard had meant to seize the hair or collar, but he would tolerate neither. Not this night. The guard took a step back, surprised, and Shianan focused on the slave. "Get up."

The slave put a hand on the damp wall to steady himself as he unfolded stiffly, flexing his torn back.

"Follow me." Shianan went without looking at the guards, without glancing back for the slave. He could hear the uneven step behind him in the corridors, and he slowed his pace.

He had no need of the slave at all. What he had just done was illegal—no more illegal than the guards quietly selling surplus prisoners for profit, but they were mere guards and he was a commander, a count, and the bastard.

But so much was wrong, and there was only one aspect he could seize and control. The Circle, the council, and the army would want Ande. Shianan would take the slave.

They reached his quarters in more time than the walk generally took. Shianan could hear the slave faltering behind him. He went through his office and dragged a chair to the foot of the bed, its back to the footboard. "Sit there—the other way. Straddle it and face the bed." He went to a chest and began withdrawing the medical supplies he kept for his own minor training injuries.

The slave obeyed, slumping over the back of the chair. Shianan took an iron-cuffed wrist and set his hand on the footboard. "Hold there and don't move. What's your name?"

"Luca." It was hardly a voice, more an airy rasp of an answer.

Shianan stared down at the flogged back. Ande had done his work well; the cuts were deep and swollen messily. There didn't seem to be any long scars outside the stripes from what he could see, so this was the first time the slave had been scourged. He dipped a cloth into the washbasin he'd brought.

The slave flinched as Shianan began to wash away the crusted blood and fluids to expose the cuts themselves, but he remained mostly still against the chair. Shianan worked efficiently, switching from the washbasin to a little jug of watered wine—"hold tight"—to clean them of infection. Luca jerked as the alcohol entered his torn flesh and Shianan slapped a hand on the unmarked shoulder. "Hold still, and it will be done quickly." He rubbed the alcohol into the wounds as Luca sucked his breath and twitched.

Finally he tossed away the wine-soaked cloth. "That's done. Only a little more." He took out a heavy jar of numbing ointment. "You won't enjoy this either, but it shouldn't be as bad."

Luca held grimly to the footboard as Shianan rubbed the ointment into the damaged back. It didn't take long, and Shianan wiped his hands clean. "Good. Bandage to keep it clean and we'll be finished."

He lay two clean sheets over the back, sticking in the ointment, and then wrapped a few lines of bandage lightly to hold them in place. He set the top loop about the shoulder to keep it high and began to tie off the bandage, pushing the heavy black hair aside from the knot. The slave winced.

Shianan frowned and lifted the hair more carefully. Across the neck was a thick ring of abrasion and deep bruising, a mass of fresh contusion. Shianan's lip curled. "I see you must have resisted after all."

The slave nodded minutely.

A new thought came coldly to Shianan. He'd heard only one word from the slave, and that hoarse. "Can you speak?"

"Y-yes." It sounded as if he were speaking through nails. "Yes, my lord. It—it will come."

Shianan scooped his fingers into the ointment again. He rubbed the ointment into it, trying to be gentle over the battered throat, working around the chain collar.

This is what they had done at Furmelle. He had agreed to this.

He stepped back, wiping his hands again. The slave would be dehydrated as well. "Luca, was it? You're finished. There's water in the corner."

Luca rose gingerly and went for a drink. Shianan noted how carefully he swallowed. The numbing did not penetrate. "Now," he said, "I have to go back to the Wheel." He pulled an old shirt from a chest and tossed it onto the empty chair. "Stay here for now."

Luca nodded. "Yes, my lord," he whispered.

Shianan left, closing the door hard behind him. The world expanded around him again, whirling with worries of Ariana, of the White Mage, of Tam's enemies in the hostile world of the Ryuven if they had even survived. And the shield was down, there could be a wave of Ryuven preparing even now, and the king would be angry, very angry.

Little had changed in the Wheel's cellar. Shianan saw Ewan Hazelrig at the edge of the group, his face resting heavily on one hand.

General Septime found Shianan. "You were missing."

"I'm sorry, sir. What are my orders?"

Septime frowned. "Nothing, for the moment. We will increase patrols for the time being, in case of Ryuven attack. The Shard will be placed under full guard until we are certain this was only accident."

"What about the shield?"

Septime looked shook his head curtly. "It cannot be remade quickly. Something about the properties and the blood and the magic—I don't understand it."

Then they can return! Shianan quenched the thought before it could show on his face. Even without the shield, it was unlikely Tam could—or would—bring Ariana back; if so, he would have done so immediately.

"Probably the White Mage is part of the reason," Septime continued, lowering his voice. "His daughter, poor man. But you were here."

"Yes," Shianan said. "His daughter and their slave were trapped in it."

"Ghastly death, crushed like that. They're probably pressed into the Shard somehow—maybe that's the problem with the new shield." Septime sighed. "Anyway, we've got to order out those patrols."

CHAPTER 20

Tamaryl set Ariana on one of the reclining couches placed about the room. She had not stirred yet. He turned to the nim standing awkwardly near the door. Generally this room was used for entertaining guests, not for treating the ill. "I want Maru here. And the healer Nori'bel, as soon as possible."

The servant nodded and disappeared down the corridor. He had been gone only a moment when Tamaryl heard running footsteps. Maru spun around the corner. "Ryl'sho."

"Maru!"

They moved together and embraced as brothers. "Is it true? You've really returned, Ryl? You're here to stay?"

"Oniwe'aru has allowed me to return."

"I am so glad!" Maru's grin stretched wide. "I am so glad." He looked toward the couch, noticing Ariana. "The rika?"

"Ariana," Tamaryl said. "My mistress in the human world."

"Your mistress?"

"I will explain," Tamaryl said. "But first she needs care. I've sent for a healer."

At that moment a woman came to the open doorway. "Tamaryl'sho?"

He turned. "You must be Nori'bel."

She was slightly past middle age and had an air of competence. He liked her at once. She nodded. "Welcome home, Tamaryl'sho." Her voice was deep and steady.

"Thank you." Tamaryl turned toward the couch where Ariana lay unmoving. "Can you treat her? She did not come well through the between-worlds."

"Most mages die almost immediately. I managed to keep one for an hour, but he was one of the Circle. Indigo." She crossed to the couch.

"She has already been here nearly that long." Tamaryl's stomach tightened. "She was in great distress, before she fainted."

"Screaming, thrashing?" Nori bent and laid her hands across Ariana's forehead and cheek. "That is typical." She frowned. "Nearly an hour is a long faint indeed, but she is doing admirably well beneath

141

it." Nori straightened and considered her next words. "Tamaryl'sho, I am a healer. I will do my best to save this woman. You are a prince doniphan of the Ai, and I will not question. But may I ask who she is?"

Tamaryl hesitated, struggling for an answer, and then recalled in this world he was master. "Why do you ask?"

"Powerless humans are affected by the journey here, but they are only weakened. Their mages die, most within minutes. This woman seems to be enduring. She is not well, but she is not near death." Nori looked down at Ariana. "She must be a mage of great ability."

Tamaryl exhaled slowly. "What can you do for her?"

"I am not entirely certain. I am not sure what she is doing for herself. I will try to ease her suffering, but other than that, she is already beyond what I can offer."

"Thank you." Tamaryl nodded. "Do what you can, please."

A polite clap sounded from the open doorway. "Tamaryl'sho?" A boy stood wide-eyed in the entrance. "I have this for you...." His voice trailed off as he stared.

Tamaryl frowned. "Yes?"

The boy came to himself and extended a folded page. "Here, Tamaryl'sho." He blinked in solemn awe as Tamaryl took it.

The missive bore Oniwe's stamp in bright ink. *He wasted little time.* Tamaryl unfolded the textured paper, scanning.

"What is that, Ryl'sho?" Maru asked.

"I am leaving," Tamaryl answered. "I must go to Aktonn and Holbruc." Oniwe'aru had specified two estates which suffered under poor overlords.

Maru started to speak and then caught himself, glancing toward Nori'bel crouching over Ariana. "When?"

"Immediately."

This time Maru did not censor himself. "I will go with you."

Tamaryl did not answer him directly. "Nori'bel, will you watch over her for a time?"

"Of course, you have only just returned," she said. "I will take care of her."

"Thank you." Tamaryl caught Maru's eye. "Walk with me."

As soon as they were safely out of earshot, Maru pressed, "Why Aktonn and Holbruc? Why is he sending you away?"

"I am to repair the damage I once warned of," Tamaryl answered flatly. "I suppose this is both my test and my punishment."

He refolded the missive. "I leave tomorrow."

"I'll come with you."

Tamaryl shook his head. "I am going to be very unpopular in Aktonn. And there is something else—the more important reason, if I am honest." He nodded back toward the room they'd left. "I cannot take her with me, but I do not want to leave her unprotected. I want you to stay with her."

"Stay with the rika?"

Tamaryl smiled. "See, you call her the rika. To everyone else, she is the human, the mage, the prisoner."

"Perhaps it's that I have seen her awake. She is a mage, and plainly powerful."

Tamaryl nodded. "I do not want any harm to come to her. When I return, if she is well enough, I will return her to her world."

Maru looked at him seriously. "You said she was your mistress."

Tamaryl grinned. "I was her slave."

"Ryl!"

"I will tell you everything, I promise."

"You'd better. Tonight. I will have bottles of *philios* ready."

Maru's fingers were loose about the *philios* bottle. "You took a human shape? For years?"

Tamaryl had to laugh at the shock and disgust on his friend's face. "Yes— even more, a human child. A slave child. It was a nearly-perfect disguise; a slave is virtually invisible, and a slave child even more so."

"A slave!" Maru's horror outweighed his disgust. "Ryl, no!"

Tamaryl shook his head soothingly. "No, no—my nominal master knew my true self, and he was a good man. Opposed to slavery, even. Yes, I played the role of a slave, for appearances and my safety, but I did not experience the slavery typical of that place." He shrugged, anxious to dispel his friend's worry. "And behind closed doors, I was able to study human magic, which is somewhat different than ours, and their traditions, and much else of their people. Yes, it was exile, but—parts of it were even fun."

Maru made a face, imagining. "But as a human. All disfigured and a *monster*, Ryl." He hesitated. "But—could you...."

Tamaryl laughed. "Oh, yes." He pointed to a carved wooden

desk, ornate with slim winged figures captured mid-dance. "As the boy Tam, I might have lifted half that desk myself. With muscle, not magic."

Maru glanced to the desk and back. "But—a boy!"

"Yes, even as a child. In the mountains, before I was revealed, I carried a pack which would have crippled you." Tamaryl took a drink of *philios*. "It was a long while before I became accustomed to their casual strength and how they used it. And I confess I took some pleasure in my new power."

Maru shook his head in faint awe. "It would have been something, to have that kind of strength...." His eyes widened. "Could a female human lift the whole desk?"

"No, no." Tamaryl shook his head. "Their women are not so strong. In fact, they're called the weaker sex."

A quiet clap from the corridor interrupted them. Maru made a sound of annoyance. "I told them you did not wish to be disturbed."

"It can't be helped. There's fifteen years of details to be caught up, and Fasi'bel hasn't arrived yet." Tamaryl rose and stretched. "Let me answer these burningly urgent matters, and then we'll hide ourselves and talk the rest of the evening. There are fifteen years of stories to be caught up, too."

CHAPTER 21

Shianan pulled his collar close and ducked against the harsh wind as he returned to his quarters. He had not understood most of the mages' discussion, which lasted long into the night, punctuated with anger at the Gehrn, worry over the shield, horror at the loss of the Black Mage.

Ewan Hazelrig had somehow maintained composure, though he spoke little. Shianan wasn't sure either of them really believed Ariana was alive. Even if she were not crushed by the failing shield, they could not hope she would survive in the Ryuven world. Tam had feared for his life; his enemies would kill the girl he brought as well. Shianan only hoped they did not learn who she was, and that her death would be swift.

The thought broke through his mental guards and bore down hard. *Ariana, dead.*

He shoved the inner door open, cold fingers fumbling at the latch. His hands moved mechanically, unbuckling his sword belt and tossing the weapon at a table before stripping off his outer tunic. He wanted to fall into bed and disappear into oblivion, if possible. He dropped onto the sturdy mattress, pulling at his boot.

The figure across the room caught him by surprise. He had nearly forgotten the slave. Luca, his name was. "What are you doing over there?"

"Sleeping, my lord. I didn't...." His voice had improved a little.

Shianan waved dismissively. "Why are you on the floor?"

Luca glanced around him, barely lit by the low brazier. "Where else?"

Shianan dropped his boot to the floor and left it there, too weary to care. "You can't sleep there, idiot. With that back? You need a mattress and blankets."

"But there—"

"You'll share for tonight." Shianan stood and drew another blanket from the chest. "Here." Without waiting for a response, he shed his outer clothes and flung himself onto the mattress, facing the wall and squeezing his eyes tightly shut. The shield, the shield had fallen, and the Ryuven would certainly take advantage, their pride pricked by the attempt to withstand them....

The bed shifted as weight eased onto it. Something brushed Shianan's foot and he felt Luca settle at the foot of the bed. He opened his eyes and tried to peer through the dark. "It will be warmer—"

"No, my lord."

Shianan closed his eyes. It did not matter.

He slept poorly, his dreams full of menacing Ryuven with flashing wings and wicked weapons, of the king's voice cracking like a whip through the cellar, of Ariana falling, falling from the mountain as he watched helplessly. He turned restlessly, grasping at pillow and blankets, and once he woke when he kicked something. Memory came, and he drew away from the slave. He turned again, seeking a place on the pillow not damp with sweat, and dropped back into nightmare.

He woke at the first hint of dawn, not at all rested. He slid out of the bed, careful not to kick the slave again, and ran his hands through his hair, digging the heels of his palms into his eyes. His muscles dragged in protest as he drew on his clothes.

At the foot of the bed, the slave moved inside the cocooning blanket. Shianan sighed. "You awake?"

"Yes, master."

Shianan pulled a fresh shirt over his head. "Get up. We need to see to your back again."

Luca straddled the chair again, clenching it as Shianan unwound the encrusted bandages. Shianan stared at the ropy wounds, seeing nothing but torn, swollen flesh. He opened the jar of ointment and dipped his fingers. This would be painful. "Talk to me," he said to the braced, stiff form. "What did you do for the high priest?"

"I served him at meals and—" Luca caught his breath as Shianan first touched his back. He gulped and continued. "And I kept his quarters, and his articles for the rituals, and—" His fingers flexed on the chair back. "I had been with him for eight months."

"I did not think the Gehrn kept slaves." Shianan smeared ointment down a long stripe.

"My previous master died while visiting the citadel," Luca answered tightly. "So I passed to the high priest."

"By rights, you should have gone to your master's family. Did they make no effort to contact his kin?"

"It was better, he said, that I stay at the citadel where I would be useful."

Shianan began re-bandaging the wounds. "Who was your

former master?"

"A man called Renner, a sort of tinker and singer and dancer all in one. I pulled the cart, set the fire, did the wash, cooked, all the sorts of things a man keeps a slave to do. I am a good worker, my lord." It was almost a plea.

Shianan nodded. Most who could afford a slave kept one to help with the drudgery or field work. "This Renner, how did he die? He was ill?"

"He tried to hide it, but yes, for a long while. We stopped in Davan, and he was asked by the priests to repair some tools and articles for them. He died there."

Shianan smoothed the final wrap and tied it. "You're finished. You'll want to move if you can, to ease the swelling." He turned away.

"My lord," Luca said with the faintest of hesitations, "whom do I now serve?"

Shianan blew out his breath. "Flamen Ande is imprisoned and awaiting questioning. There'll be no record of your arrest. I have stolen you, no doubt an abuse of my rank. But I suppose that means you're now in my service."

"But, my lord—I do not know my master's name."

Shianan began to laugh with bitter humor. "You may be the only one in this city. I am Shianan Becknam, Count of Bailaha and Commander in the King's Army. But most of the time, people call me the bastard."

Luca plainly could not think of a safe response.

Shianan shook his head, chuckling grimly. "I'm afraid you'll find—"

A banging at the door interrupted him. Shianan pulled the door open. "Yes?"

"Your lordship, His Majesty requires your presence immediately."

Shianan's joints melted to water. "I shall be there directly," he heard himself say, and somehow the door closed. He stared at the solid unyielding grain.

He swallowed. Delay would accomplish nothing. He breathed deeply and turned back to the room. "And that," he said, wishing his voice had more strength, "is the lot of the bastard. I will likely be away for some time."

Luca nodded silently. Shianan shaved, hardly noticing when he nicked himself, and then scrubbed his teeth. He reached for his cloak

147

and started for the door, not allowing himself to pause before plunging through it.

CHAPTER 22

Luca should have wanted food, but the pain in his back dulled any hunger. That was just as well, since there was nothing in the commander's quarters.

Commander.... Count.... He did not know the proper terms for his new master's position, and there was no one to overhear. At least his new master had not seemed too exacting thus far. He swallowed carefully against his swollen throat. Had he found himself in a better place?

As long as you breathe, Luca, there is hope. Don't forget that.

Luca closed his eyes against the memory. *Liar.*

Still, at least he was no longer with Flamen Ande. But he had come to a soldier. He brushed the collar and the bruising beneath it. His new master had been at the revolt in Furmelle, too.

Luca lowered his head against the back of the chair. He was thirsty, but he did not want to move. With miserable dread, he realized the torture was not only the horrific moment when the whip flayed him, but the hours and days of swollen, aching pain which would plague his smallest movements.

He did not know how long he sat before the knock sounded at the door. He jumped, wincing at the movement, and sighed. Stripes or no, he must serve. "One moment," he called, his throat straining.

In his filthy leggings and bandaged torso, he was an embarrassment of a servant. He unfastened the lock and cracked the door. "My master is not at home."

The White Mage stared flatly at him. "You."

Luca hesitated. Had he been wrong to answer?

But the mage's face softened a fraction. "He took you?"

Luca nodded uncertainly. "He is not here, my lord. He was called by the king."

The mage looked over him, taking in the bandages and bruising. "Has someone treated you?"

"He cleaned my—wounds, yes."

But the White Mage was already coming through the door. "Sit," he ordered. Luca backed toward the chair at the foot of the bed. "So help me, if I cannot undo all he has done, I will undo this. Turn

149

away and let's have these bandages off."

Luca did not understand as he slid across the chair.

But the mage did not touch him once the clinging bandages were peeled away. Luca shivered in the cool air, not daring to turn. Better to sit quietly and take what came. It ended more quickly that way.

The White Mage's sleeves rustled. Luca shivered again and winced with it. Then a warm, dry sensation began at the center of his back. Luca tensed, but the warmth spread steadily, calming the ache. Luca shifted, wanting to turn his head but knowing better.

"This is mage healing you're feeling."

Luca twitched before he could stop himself.

"You've probably heard it's a rare and difficult thing. And it is. But what is less commonly known is that while it's intended to treat magical injury, it can often speed the start of natural healing as well." Luca caught a hint of motion in his peripheral vision and the warmth shifted to his shoulder. "It can't replace your own healing, I'm sorry. But it will help."

The sensation grew stronger until it covered most of his back, uncomfortably warm. Luca shifted on the chair. "If—"

"It will be unpleasant for a moment. Be patient."

Luca had little choice, anyway. The heat increased steadily, prickling and stinging. Luca clenched his fingers on the chair.

"Nearly finished. Hold fast and be patient."

Endure, Luca.

"There." The heat vanished. "Stand and tell me how you feel."

Luca obediently rose from the chair, cautious, but the anticipated agony did not come. As he straightened a dull ache pressed him, but nothing like what it had been. "It's better. Much better. My lord."

"Good." The mage held out a stone dangling from a light chain. "Take this. It's mostly spent, but it will do some good yet. It is already activated, all you need do is hold it over the pain." He folded his arms with an understated flourish of white robe. "You'll still have healing to do, of course, but that should have made up the first few days. Now, where is the commander?"

"He was called to the king, my lord." Luca shifted his shoulders experimentally.

The mage nodded. "I am Ewan Hazelrig, the White Mage, as you can see. Tell him I'll come again this afternoon."

"Yes, my lord." Luca stood straighter, pleased he could. "Thank you, my lord."

Mage Hazelrig's face tightened. "You'll need rest, with that." Before Luca could respond, he went directly to the door and closed it behind him.

Luca stared after him. It was his daughter, Luca thought, who had disappeared beneath the magical shield. He seemed genuinely grieved.

He moved, testing his back. He hurt, but he could function without the disabling swelling and pain of before. He had heard of mage healing, and it was unthinkable a mage would bless a mere slave with it. But he had.

Luca needed to wash his filthy clothing of blood and prison muck and to bathe himself as best he could, but there was nothing like a tub in the commander's quarters. Clearly his master used other facilities. He must wait.

It was strange and worrisome to sit quietly. He had not been allowed idleness since the cuffs had first been fitted on his wrists.

Do your best, Luca. It will be all right. While you yet breathe, Luca, there is hope. Don't forget that.

"Liar," Luca whispered.

The door opened, and Luca pushed himself upright. His master closed the door and then sagged against the frame. He moved his hand to his side, supporting his ribs in a manner Luca recognized immediately. But who would dare to hurt such a man?

The commander leaned against the wall with his eyes closed, wrapping his other arm about the first. Then he opened his eyes and looked at Luca, startled. "You. I'd forgotten about you."

Luca did not know how to respond. "Would you like something, master?"

He closed his eyes again. "Not from you." His voice was quiet, almost sad. Not dangerous. "You're doing well."

It could not be wise to speak of the mage healing. "Yes, master." He cleared his throat. "The White Mage came. He said he would return this afternoon."

"Hm."

He was not thinking of the White Mage. "Please sit, my lord," Luca tried. The longer he stood with whatever hurt he had, the more he would lash out later.

To his surprise, the commander nodded and eased himself

away from the wall. He sank into the chair with a little intake of breath.

He had not asked for drink or medicine. "Are—are you injured, master? What would you have me bring?"

He was short of breath; it hurt him to breathe. "I don't think I can ignore this one." Becknam unlaced his tunic, sliding the woven shirt to the side and exposing the skin. Deep purpling had already formed. The commander swore in a whisper. "I can't hide this."

"How should it be treated?"

He shook his head. "Broken ribs, or near enough. Nothing to do but let them heal."

Something warm might ease the hurt. There was a small towel beside the drinking water, and Luca soaked it before hanging it over the edge of the brazier. *I don't think I can ignore this one.* This was not the first time.

Becknam was quiet. When the wet towel began to steam, Luca folded it with quick, stinging fingers. Then he glanced at the commander and reached into his waistband, bringing out the little stone amulet.

It would be purest folly to reveal the mage healing. No one would condone a slave receiving such a thing.

But this man, whatever he may be, had taken Luca from the prison and treated him rather than leaving him to recover on his own. In Chrenada, the lowest slaves were not much more expensive than medicine.

And it was dangerous to serve a man in pain. Renner had not been cruel by nature; it was the pain and the drink he took for it that had made him harsh. It was better to have a hale master.

Luca folded the amulet into the hot damp cloth, hiding it completely. It would do its work without revealing the healing.

He offered the hot compress with two hands. "Here, master."

The commander looked flatly at him. "Don't call me that." He laid the towel gingerly across his battered ribs. "I don't like the way you say it."

"I'm sorry, master—my lord." Luca retreated a step, judging the commander's reach was shortened by his injury. "How would you prefer I address you?"

"I don't care. Wait." He shifted the towel, wincing. "There are enough who call me lordship or sir. They call me other things behind my back. I want you to call me something else."

"Master," Luca offered, anxious to show compliance.

The commander shook his head. "The way you say it reeks of the high priest." He flexed his fingers on his leg. "There is no one anymore to call me by name. Call me Shianan."

Luca blinked. "But—!"

The commander took no offense at his blurted protest. "Master Shianan, then, if you must hold rank." He looked at Luca. "Go on, try it."

It was a trap, a trap, it had to be a trap.... Luca swallowed and knelt, ducking his head. "Master Shianan."

"Get up!"

Luca jumped, pain snapping at his back. His master scowled as he got to his feet. "Don't do that again. 'Soats, one would think I'd been the one to pare out your backbone. I hate that Ande, do you understand? I don't want to be reminded of him, and I don't want to be treated as him." He made a small, savage gesture, cut short to spare his ribs. "Now say it."

Luca's mouth was dry. "Master Shianan."

"Again."

"Master Shianan."

"See? Now, 'I hate the high priest.' Say it."

Luca opened his mouth, but no sound came out.

"Do you want to go back in the cell with him? Say it!"

"I hate the high priest."

"Louder."

"I hate the high priest."

Shianan scowled. "I hardly believe you." He adjusted the towel on his ribs. "You might have more conviction— "

The towel wrinkled, and a thin chain fell into view. Curious, Shianan lifted the towel, and the amulet slipped free. Luca reached to catch it, but Shianan was faster, snatching it from the air as it fell. Luca's heart sank as Shianan studied it. "Is this what I think it is?"

Luca's knees trembled.

Shianan closed his fingers around the amulet. "Are you a thief?"

Luca sank to the floor, bowing his head. "No, master, no, the White Mage brought it—I did not steal it...."

The commander would strike him. Luca squeezed his eyes closed, his back quivering.

"Get up." His master's voice was thick with disgust. "It would be madness to steal a healing amulet. I don't believe you'd attempt it. And you couldn't activate it. Quit groveling."

Luca looked up.

"Get up, I said."

"Yes, master."

"Yes, Master Shianan," Shianan corrected. "Now the other one—I hate the high priest."

Luca obeyed. "I hate the high priest."

His master smiled grimly. "I'm not trying to entrap you. To the contrary—let me show you how it is done." His expression deepened into fury, and Luca's stomach clenched. But Shianan sat still in the chair, only his eyes flaring as he spoke. "*I hate the high priest.*"

Luca edged back.

"I will even tell you why: he deceived us. The annual ritual should have been harmless, and he never mentioned more. He lied by omission and unmade the shield." He swallowed fiercely. "And Ariana—Lady Ariana is gone. He killed her. However indirectly, he killed her." He squeezed his eyes shut for a moment, and Luca dared not move.

Finally he opened them and spoke again. "And that," he said, "is why I hate Flamen Ande. I know it does no good to hate him from here, but still I do." He exhaled. "And so you see, Luca, there is no trap when I tell you to say what you must surely feel."

"Master—Master Shianan—"

"Go on, say it. Didn't you ever want to strike back?"

Luca had thought often of knocking back Renner and running away, but he had been always chained to the cart, and even had he escaped, anyone in wrist cuffs and the Furmelle collar would have been apprehended immediately. When Ande took him, he had resisted a few times—paying dearly—and dreamed faintly of vengeance, but.... Daily humiliation had overwhelmed him, and he could hardly remember the ideas he'd harbored. "I did," he finally answered, "at first."

Shianan sighed. "I did, too." He looked at Luca. "We're of an age, you and I, or close enough, and it's too old to be crawling or crying for others. I cannot change what I must do, but I don't require it of you. Don't kneel and scrape all the time, do you understand? I can't stand it. Just keep a healthy respect and that will be enough."

"Yes, Master Shianan." He took a breath. "What are my duties?"

"'Soats, I don't know." Shianan looked about the quarters. "My laundry is done in the military washhouse. My meals, such as they are, are in the barracks kitchen. I sweep out this place once a week or so." He shrugged. "Stay out of the way, I suppose. But do nothing, not even that, until you've had a chance to heal that back."

Luca registered the chores listed. "Thank you, Master Shianan."

"And sit down already. You make me nervous, hovering." Shianan shifted the towel on his ribs. "This is cold."

"I'll reheat it." Luca took the towel and turned to the brazier.

A knock at the door interrupted him. Luca started toward it just as Shianan called, "Come!"

The White Mage pushed back the door. "Your lordship?"

Shianan rose and smoothed his shirt to hide the bruising. "Please come in. Luca, there's another chair in the office. Bring it, if you would."

Hazelrig eyed Luca critically. "Should he be moving so freely yet?"

"I can, my lord. I will bring the chair."

It was not a fine chair and weighed little, but his back twinged as he carried it. Still, he could hardly complain, given what should have been. He placed the chair for the two men and retreated a few steps as Shianan sank gratefully into his seat.

"I have been testing the between-worlds for traces of travel." Hazelrig looked at Luca. "Your lordship, perhaps we should go to discuss this privately."

A shadow crossed Shianan's face at the thought of moving. "My lords," Luca blurted, "you need not leave when I can go. I will wait in the office, if I may?"

He had startled Shianan. "That will be fine. If anyone enters, say I am in conference with the White Mage."

"Yes, master." Luca went out.

He leaned against the scarred desk with a flicker of satisfaction. He had spared his master discomfort and embarrassment, and surely, surely Master Shianan would think well of him. He touched the collar at his throat, careful of the swollen bruising beneath it. His new master had been at Furmelle, but he had not yet accused Luca of its associated traits. Perhaps he thought Luca wrongly seized, or maybe reformed by his punishment.

Papers littered the desk. Luca browsed some to pass the time, but there was nothing interesting, only notes regarding the replenishment of a supply house, additional training needed in the fourth squad, and a few reports to approve.

It was not long before the mage came, exhausted and unhappy. Luca let him out and returned to his master's quarters. Shianan slumped in the chair, his eyes gazing vaguely at the point where the wall met the floor. Luca went to the brazier for the towel, warm and steaming again, and offered it wordlessly.

Shianan lowered his face to press knuckles hard into his forehead, setting his jaw, and Luca realized his master was fighting tears. It was too late to return and pretend to fuel the brazier.

Shianan winced as his ribs shifted and he brushed his arm over his face. "Thanks," he muttered, taking the warm towel. "It does help." He frowned suddenly, almost forcefully, grasping anything to take his attention. "How is your back, then? I suppose I should see this mage healing. For he did give it to you, right?"

"Yes, master—Shianan."

"Well, find me the ointment. There's no point to both of us being impaired."

Shianan wiped his eyes again. Luca pretended not to see.

"Sit," Shianan snapped gruffly. "Low, and let me see you."

Luca knelt with his back to Shianan's chair. He could almost feel his scrutiny of the half-closed weals and taut scabbing.

"This is much better." Shianan dipped into the ointment and began to work along the shoulder, his brisk, impersonal reach hampered by his cracked ribs. "Much better. I wish we had another amulet." He paused. "I wish there were an amulet to heal the world itself. It might correct all that has gone wrong. Maybe to close the between-worlds...." His voice trailed into silence.

"Master...." Luca swallowed. "When the shield—when it—at that moment, inside the light, I thought.... I thought I saw a Ryuven."

Shianan's fingers convulsed and then closed firmly on his shoulder, making Luca wince. When his voice came, a long moment later, it was hoarse and terrifying. "Don't ever say that again."

Icy fear hissed through Luca, but he knew better than to struggle against the hand on his shoulder. "Yes, master."

"What made you mention that?"

He had just been forbidden to speak of it, and Luca did not know how to answer correctly. "I only—I thought you should know if I saw a Ryuven. That is all!"

The fingers relaxed. "I didn't mean—yes, we are all to report any Ryuven we sight. But there could not have been a Ryuven within the shield, could there? They would only consider your report mere raving by a pain-maddened slave whose blood destroyed the shield, and whose blood might be useful in remaking it."

Luca stopped breathing.

"No, I don't intend to suggest it. But you shouldn't draw attention to yourself."

"Yes, my lord."

Luca had expected—had hoped—Shianan would say there of course had been no Ryuven in the cellar, the idea was ridiculous. But Shianan had told him quite differently.

"There," Shianan said, dropping the little jar of ointment. "You're finished. I hope that amulet does half as well for me. I have to lead training next."

CHAPTER 23

Daranai's house was not so fine as the Palace of Red Sands, but it was grand enough to dominate the tree-lined boulevard on which it sat. Tamaryl pulled the bell cord.

A handsome dark-skinned Ryuven opened the door. He looked at Tamaryl without recognition. "I will tell Daranai'rika she has guests," he said. "Please come inside...?"

"This is Tamaryl'sho," said Maru a little sharply.

The servant's eyes widened. "Please wait in the patio. I will inform Daranai'rika immediately." He gestured toward the shaded area and fairly fled.

Tamaryl walked to the fountain, watching the water splash into the worked stone basin. "Oniwe'aru said she has not joined," he said softly.

Maru nodded. "She has courted and been courted, from what little I've heard, but nothing more."

"Tamaryl'sho!" Her voice cut through the cool air of the patio, amplified by the tiled floor. "Tamaryl'sho, are you really here?"

He turned as she swept toward him. "Daranai'rika."

"Tamaryl'sho, I am so glad!" She stopped short a few feet from him, perhaps a little startled. "You must have only just returned." There was a subtle aura of glamour about her, as always. She liked to highlight her natural beauty. And she was beautiful.

"Only a short while ago."

"And you came first to see me. I am so pleased." Her eyes traveled past Tamaryl to where Maru stood at the edge of the patio, pretending to be interested in some colored fish. "What did Oniwe'aru say? Is—is all well?"

"I am restored," he answered obliquely.

"That's wonderful!" She threw her arms around him, her wide wings stretching behind her. She was taller than Tamaryl, of course, and he was glad to lean into her smooth skin. "Then it will be as it was?"

Her sunset-gold hair draped and clung to him. "I am leaving in the morning. I have been given a task in Aktonn and then in Holbruc."

"So soon? When will you be back?"

159

He smiled up at her. "As soon as I can be."

Once he had been the chosen champion, a high prince doniphan, and half-brother to Oniwe'aru. He was far too valuable a political piece to let lie, and so a match had been arranged. Tamaryl had no objections; Daranai was of a wealthy and powerful family, and she was beautiful, and vivacious, and ambitious. Any worries he might have had regarding a dull conjoining of political convenience had been laid aside. A match with Daranai could never be dull.

And then he had gone to protest the unceasing battles, and all had changed.

"Daranai'rika," he said, "I have something to ask of you."

"Yes?"

"I brought a human woman with me, a mage."

She grimaced. "Oh?"

"She is ill with the between-worlds and our atmosphere. My house is—not yet open, and I do not want to leave her in the Palace of Red Sands. Could you keep her here?"

Daranai looked discomfited, the first time he could remember seeing her so. "A human?"

"I will leave Maru to tend to her, so you will not need to see to anything. But your home will be a better place for her than Aktonn or the Red Sands."

Daranai exhaled and nodded. "If you wish, Tamaryl'sho."

He clasped her hands. "Thank you, Daranai'rika. I will bring her this evening. And we shall dine together?"

"Won't you be with Oniwe'aru? Perhaps we could dine with him."

Tamaryl shook his head. "Not tonight. I am free to dine with you." It wasn't surprising that Oniwe had put off his official welcome. Tamaryl's return was potentially embarrassing for the ruler who had offered a price for his death, though Oniwe would surely have a solution soon.

Daranai seemed to catch his thought. "It is still Tamaryl'sho, yes?"

"I am returned to my rank and titles, yes, provided I complete this task to satisfaction."

"Then you must not fail it!" Daranai took his hand and pulled them close. "How long will you be gone?"

He shook his head. "I do not know."

She stood near him, pressing his hand, so that he could smell her, feel the warmth of her body in the cool evening air. Fifteen years....

Daranai was a head taller than Tamaryl, with high, curving wings, and when she stood near him he had a delicious sensation of potential envelopment. He looked at her neck, tantalizingly close before his eyes, and felt years of loneliness for his own kind suddenly pressing upon him.

Too soon, she drew away a little distance, smiling playfully. "But it has been so long—I don't even recall what you like. Perhaps a different glamour? What do you think?" She turned, tossing red-gold hair for effect and looking with a smile for his response.

Beautiful women had never so much as glanced at the slave boy Tam. They certainly had never flirted with him, seeking compliments as they sought to charm. Tamaryl swallowed and yet heard his voice husky as he responded, "You look splendid, Daranai'rika. As always."

"As you remembered me?" She drew close again.

Tamaryl's pulse quickened. "Yes."

He was a guest in her home; she led the evening. She could take him into the dining room, or she might lead him into a garden or private alcove....

She bent her face toward his. "I missed you, Tamaryl'sho." She reached for his face, letting her fingertips trail along his jaw. "For years, I have missed you."

Tamaryl caught his breath. "Daranai'rika...." He felt wooden with resisting the urge to take her in his arms. Her eyes gripped his, and he could almost feel her silky skin against his own.

A few droplets from the fountain spray reached them. She regarded him with artfully widening eyes. "But do you even want me, Tamaryl'sho? You have not so much as embraced me since—"

Slaves stood immobile until instructed otherwise—a prince doniphan did as he pleased. Tamaryl swept his arms around her, seeking her mouth which met his enthusiastically. Her hands wrapped around his back, teasing the sensitive roots of his wings. For a long moment they kissed, waking Tamaryl's memories of feminine delights.

Finally she pushed him away, laughing. "Did they have no females in the human world, Tamaryl'sho? You are a thirsty traveler in the desert!" Her fingers ran lightly over his bare upper arms.

Tamaryl's muscles twitched beneath her play. "I was not in a position to know many human women. And none were like you, Daranai'rika."

She smiled, pleased. "And yet you brought a human woman here with you."

"That is different," Tamaryl said, mesmerized by the way she ran her nails down the underside of his arm to take his hand. "That was to save her life."

She tugged him toward one of the alabaster archways. "If it pleases you. Now come—I would have had a lovely supper if I'd known you were coming, but we'll have to make do on my usual fare."

After her flirtatious teasing, Tamaryl was not hungry for supper, but he was embarrassed at his susceptibility and said nothing. Daranai was right: he had come through fifteen years of famine to be suddenly offered a feast. He was too eager.

They sat across from one another, and he let his folded wings settle over his chair's low back. Wine had already been poured into crystal bowls. Tamaryl took a drink and rolled it on his tongue, savoring it. Daranai offered a splendid wine.... Briefly Tamaryl wondered how his Ryuven body would handle the drink.

Daranai rang a small bell and a nim entered, this one a young male with fine features and hair so pale it shone silver, bearing a tray of steaming dishes. The food was excellent and plentiful, and Tamaryl ate with relish. Mage Hazelrig had never shorted him, of course, but Mother Harriet's meals for the household servant were not equal to Daranai's exalted house, and he had missed Ryuven delicacies.

"Thank you," he said, "for allowing Ariana and Maru to stay while I am away."

Daranai waved her hand. "It is no trouble. And if we are joined, Maru will need to understand my household." She smiled. "Do what you must. Things will be fine here."

CHAPTER 24

Luca woke at the sound of the latch. Shianan pushed back the door, grey and exhausted, and Luca got to his feet. "Master?"

"That amulet works pretty well. I hardly feel these blasted ribs. That, or I'm too tired to notice."

He had not corrected Luca's address. "Shall I bring you something?"

"No, I want nothing." He looked longingly at his bed. "Only sleep."

Luca resisted the urge to kick his blanket behind him. "Should I tell any who come you are—"

"No, no. No, don't do that." Shianan closed the door. "'Soats, if anyone hears I'm sleeping through this crisis—no." He cast another long glance at the bed. "Still...."

The man needed rest, that was plain enough, and time to heal. Suggesting a slave knew best was dangerous ground. But some part of Luca saw his master was too exhausted for anger, and some deeper part recognized something else in Shianan. He spoke before he could lose confidence. "Some say matters are clearer after sleep. There may be better news after you have rested."

Shianan looked at him a long moment, and Luca felt the ground cracking beneath him. But then Shianan gave a small, sick chuckle. "You're right. Tell anyone who comes I am—invent something. King's oats, I'm tired." He went to the bed and lay down, careful of his bruised side.

He stirred in his sleep, like his troubled dreams of the night before, occasionally catching his breath as his injured ribs shifted. Luca settled himself against the wall, intact shoulder taking his weight, and drowsed.

Two hours later, the commander woke. He sat up carefully, rubbing at his head, and looked at the high windows admitting light while guarding the room's privacy. He groaned. "So late?"

Luca stood from his place against the wall.

Shianan shifted, holding his breath as he moved. "Bring me some water."

"The pitcher is empty, master."

"Then you have your first duty."

Luca glanced at the door. "I...."

"Go." Shianan's voice was hoarse and irritable. "Bring water. And food. That's not beyond your injuries. And your own, too; you're scrawny and you'll need food to heal."

Luca went out.

He stood awkwardly in the courtyard, aware of how little he knew his new surroundings. Across the wide yard he could see the entrance to the palace itself, busy with couriers and guarded by armed men. To his left was a fountain, where someone was filling a pitcher, and a series of long, low buildings. Men in uniform were moving among them, talking, laughing, jostling one another. That would be the military grounds.

The last time he had seen so many soldiers.... He swallowed, as if the chain collar pressed his throat. They had been penned within a hastily-built solid panel fence, bunched together like so many sheep awaiting shearing. Archers waited outside with nocked arrows, ordered to aim for any flesh which appeared above the boards. They had been shoved close together, without room to sit, with barely room to breathe the suffocating hot air full of sweat and urine and blood as they shuffled forward, and as the hours passed and the sun climbed overhead some of the captured rebels had fallen senseless. What became of them Luca never knew, because he was pressed with the others into a narrow chute which squeezed them to one or two abreast, and at the end of the chute was a roaring hot smithy where a dozen soldiers waited to seize the prisoners as they stumbled out, twisting their arms and forcing them to their knees as chain collars were forged onto their necks and wrist cuffs fitted on those who did not have them.

A few enterprising merchants waited outside the forge, pointing at some they felt might be a worthwhile investment, but most would waste neither time nor money on those taken at Furmelle. Luca had been chained together with nineteen others and left in a stall for auction, sold two weeks later to replenish the army's funds after the campaign. They had brought poor prices among hundreds of rebellious slaves dumped on the market at once, but the army had been more concerned with being rid of them.

Luca pushed the image from his mind. Now he must think on serving his current master, if he meant to avoid the auctions again. Twice on the block was enough.

The dining hall stood open, showing long tables and benches. At the far end he saw the kitchen itself, separated by a wide stone arch. There was a knot of men laughing among themselves. Luca circled them, but of course they saw him anyway. "Who are you?" one called, still chuckling at his friend's last joke.

"I serve Shianan Becknam, the—"

"You're the bastard's boy? I didn't know the commander kept a slave."

"He might as well," another commented dryly. "Being he's a count and all, now."

"What's this?" Someone reached to pluck at the chain collar. "Furmelle?"

Luca shrank from the grasp. "I wasn't...."

All humor left the group. "How many of our men did you kill, boy?"

Panic rose. "I killed no one. I was taken by mistake."

"Heh! You and every other pignut we took." A soldier stepped forward to fill Luca's vision. "But you thought you could take us, didn't you?"

"No!" Luca was sweating. "I need to bring the meals."

"We feed soldiers," the cook said roughly, "and we don't give their food to dogs of Furmelle. Come back when the serving's done and you can have yours like the other slaves." He shouted over his shoulder. "Andrew! Something for the commander!"

A kitchen slave beckoned Luca to one side, and a moment later he offered a tray with vegetable soup, half a fowl, and a large chunk of bread. "I know the commander has a healthy appetite," he said, eying Luca as he produced an additional tin cup of soup, "so here's a little extra."

Luca gave him a tight smile. "Thanks."

"Watch your step. A lot of these men fought at Furmelle. Some of their fellows didn't come back."

Luca nodded soberly. He did not know how he could be anything other than what he was, but the warning was well-received.

"If you're with the commander," Andrew said, "is it true, what they're saying, that something happened to the shield?"

Luca blinked, unable to believe he might not know. The ritual, the scorching whip, the purple iridescence, the collapsing hemisphere—they were so vivid, how could anyone have missed them? "Yes," he answered. Then he hesitated. Shianan had warned him not to mention the Ryuven, but the shield itself?

Andrew's eyes were on him. "Are the Ryuven coming?"

Luca hadn't yet considered the inevitable result of the shield's destruction. "I don't know."

"Andrew!" barked one of the other cooks.

"Thanks for the food," Luca said quickly. "I'll bring the dishes later."

He paused just outside the door and hastily drained the second cup of soup before starting back. He was nearly to the office when he saw three uniformed soldiers coming toward him. He dropped his eyes, telling himself they weren't coming for him. They were only walking past him, they did not want him....

But one of the soldiers sidestepped and struck Luca's shoulder with his own. Little shoots of pain jolted through Luca's back and soup leapt from the cup. The soldier spun. "Watch where you're going!"

Luca took a step back. "I—"

"About what you'd expect from a Furmelle," observed another of the soldiers.

"Where do you think you're going?" demanded the first, stepping closer. "You think you can step into a free soldier and then just walk on?"

The three were fanning around him. "I'm sorry," Luca tried. "I didn't mean to—"

"Shut up!" The soldier struck at him, but Luca ducked with long habit and felt only a glancing blow. The second struck the side of Luca's head, making him stumble back. The roast fowl tumbled to the ground.

"Soldiers!" snapped a voice. Luca, reeling, sensed the three drawing themselves upright and he retreated a few steps.

Shianan Becknam tugged at his tunic as he strode toward them. There was no hesitation in his step; if his ribs pained him, he hid it well. "What's going on here?"

The soldiers shifted. "We were just—telling this slave— keeping him out of the public way," one offered awkwardly.

"Out of the way?" repeated Shianan. "It looked to me that you were interfering with his work."

The soldiers glanced at one another. "No, no. He can still do his work, sir. We just wanted him to watch where he was going, you see, and stay out of soldiers' way."

"Is that so?" Shianan faced the man. "Because I saw you

pushing him the other direction, making me wait for him."

Something registered in the soldier's mind. "Making—you wait, sir?"

"Would any of you," Shianan asked pointedly, "consider disobeying my orders ordinarily?"

"No, sir!"

"Then I'd expect you would not interfere with the orders I give others. And that includes my slave." Shianan's expression was flinty. "Am I understood?"

"Perfectly, sir!"

"Luca!"

Luca straightened. "Yes, master?"

"Do as you were told."

"Yes, master." Luca retrieved the fallen meat and hurried toward the office. If Shianan said anything more to the soldiers, Luca did not hear it, but when he glanced back, they were slinking away.

Inside, Shianan looked over the cup of soup as Luca tore the dirtied skin from the roast bird. "They saw the collar, I suppose? Well, we were already going to the slavers, so it's no matter. How's your back?"

Luca, stunned, could hardly answer. "Uh—it's—well enough, my lord."

"Let's go then." Shianan tossed down the rest of the soup and took the chicken to eat as he started out the door.

CHAPTER 25

Luca stared after him for a shocked moment before following. The slave market? But why? How had he displeased his master already—or had he been saved merely for profit?

He considered running, but only briefly. He would not be able to escape, not in a crowded street where Shianan needed only to shout, not with wrist cuffs and a Furmelle collar to mark him wherever he went.

Endure, Luca.

Luca clenched his fists. *Liar. Liar.*

His footsteps slowed, putting off the stables and auction block that awaited. Shianan paused at a carved sign displaying a chained wrist and spoke to the man standing beneath it. The man leaned on a heavy staff and nodded.

Shianan turned and seemed surprised to find Luca so far behind him. He gestured, and Luca went obediently to them.

"And the collar," Shianan continued.

The trader with the staff nodded. "But these cuffs aren't unusual, your lordship," he said, taking Luca's wrist and turning it. "They're very typical for field labor, actually. You want something smaller?"

"He's not field labor," Shianan said, "and I don't like the look. A friend of mine fitted his slave with smaller cuffs, and I think I'd prefer that."

The trader nodded. "Customer knows what he wants. Come on back."

Luca glanced at Shianan. Was he not being sold, after all?

They followed the trader through the chained slaves waiting for sale to the small stone forge that accompanied every slaver's stables. The trader rapped on the stone with the staff to draw the smith's attention. "Customer wants smaller cuffs."

The smith glanced at Luca's wrists and shook his head. "Nope. Don't have any smaller than that, not 'til tomorrow or the day after."

"You could come back then, your lordship."

Shianan shook his head. "Go ahead and take these off. We'll be back for the others later."

169

The smith snorted. "Even if you wanted to, it's against the law."

"I am the law," Shianan answered with a faint smile. "Aside from my current position, I was a commander at Furmelle. I don't think anyone will complain against my slave."

The smith frowned dubiously. "If you say so, sir." He motioned Luca into the building with a jerk of his shaggy head. "Wrists on the table, and don't move."

Luca closed his eyes, not wanting to see the instruments over his arms. The cuffs were not designed to be opened easily or often. But the smith removed them without undue effort or discomfort, and Luca lifted his too-light arms with a sense of disbelief.

"The collar, too," Shianan prompted.

The smith grunted and pushed Luca forward against the table, drawing his hair out of the way. "You bring this one back from Furmelle with you?"

"Not myself."

The smith rolled the chain in his hand. "I can cut this easy enough," he said. "But it looks like you've been using it. You sure you want it off? He'll be bare, then, no cuffs and no collar, and from the looks of things—" he gave the collar a little tug—"he's been some trouble."

"I think that's behind us," Shianan said easily. "He won't be any trouble."

The smith's hand rested on Luca's shoulder and, with a grunt of discovery, he prodded at the swollen welts. "You sure, lordship?"

"As I said, no one will complain against my slave."

The smith turned. "This really your slave? You're not...." He looked at the trader. "This couldn't come back on us?"

Shianan shrugged. "I didn't bring a bill of sale, but my word should be good."

"Huh." The smith pulled at the collar again. "Sorry, lordship. I just never seen anyone who wanted to strip equipment off a slave they'd had to knock back into line."

"Again, I don't believe he'll give any trouble," Shianan replied, circling the table. "Will you, Luca?"

Luca did not understand, but he was anxious to have the collar off. "Oh, no, master," he said, a nervous edge to his voice. "No trouble. I will be obedient and willing and reliable, master."

Shianan made a small gesture, suggesting this was all the proof they needed, and the smith grunted. Then he picked up a chisel and hammer and pulled the chain tight against Luca's neck.

Luca squeezed his eyes shut, but he felt nothing as the chain parted with a metallic sound. He opened his eyes and sat up, seeing the hated chains abandoned on the table.

"We'll be back for the smaller cuffs," Shianan said. "What do I owe for tonight's work?"

The smith shook his head. "Pay for the cuffs. And if you don't come for them, I had no part of any illegal freeing."

"Don't worry on that," Shianan told him. "Thank you." Then he turned and started away. Luca followed, his arms swinging loosely at his side. Emotion swelled within him and he had to hold himself to a measured pace behind Shianan.

But he did not wait long. When they had left the slavers behind, Luca sprang forward to face his master. "Thank you!" he breathed, foolish in his enthusiasm but unable to contain himself. He seized Shianan's hand, desperate for some gesture to express his gratitude. "Oh, master, thank you!"

Shianan jerked back. "Stop," he said, his voice rough. "I never liked that collar anyway. It was no great thing to have it off."

Luca bobbed his head. "But—it is—thank you!"

Shianan pulled his hand free and continued walking briskly. Luca leapt to follow. "And the cuffs. You ordered the cuffs changed."

"Tam's were better." Shianan did not look at Luca.

Luca hesitated. Tam was the slave boy he'd envied, with his small cuffs and unmarked skin and easy attitude, who had died when the shield crushed him and his mistress. Or when the Ryuven had appeared within the shield.

But Luca had benefited nonetheless. "Thank you," he repeated, and then because his master obviously did not care to hear more, he fell silent and followed Shianan down the street, staring at his pale and empty wrists.

Shianan wound through the market, between the vendors packing wagons for the trip home and a few late shoppers like themselves, and stopped at a booth of woven mats and stuffed mattresses. "Wait a moment," he called to the seller rolling a straw mat.

The seller gestured for his slave to continue packing and came to Shianan, appraising his clothing and judging his rank. "Yes, lordship?"

"I need a floor mattress," Shianan said. "What do you have left today?"

They reached quick agreement. The seller whistled and pointed, and a slave rolled and tied the mattress as Shianan counted out coins from a tooled leather pouch. "Here, my lord," the slave muttered as he passed the heavy roll from his shoulder to Luca's.

Luca blinked. He was clearly subservient to his master—and yet without the wrist bands, he was not so clearly a slave.

He eased the rolled mattress onto the shoulder without half-healed cuts and turned to follow Shianan. Shadows cast by the taller buildings fell across the plaza, throwing the marketplace into half-darkness. Around them men hoisted packs on their backs or pushed carts and wagons into the steady stream of exiting traffic, shouting at those in their way.

Shianan stopped at a wide, low building with a sign in the shape of a tankard. "I want a drink."

To the right of the door stood several wagons with slaves lounging against their vehicles. To the left, a man cupped his hands to drink at the trough of a rude fountain, an over-sized pack resting beside him. Luca understood; slaves were not permitted. He stopped beside the door and leaned the mattress against the wall.

"Luca." In the doorway, Shianan jerked his head to indicate inside. "Coming?"

Luca stared at him. Inside? But—

Shianan gestured again. Luca picked up the mattress and followed him inside.

They took a table in the corner, where Luca could lean his bundle out of the way. Shianan nodded for Luca to sit and Luca did, wary and uncomfortable.

A woman in a low bodice worked her way through the groups of laughing and arguing customers, dispensing a smile here and an admonition there, until she reached them. "Good evening to both of you," she began, displaying yellow teeth in a wide grin. Luca caught a glimpse of iron cuff as she gave their table an obligatory brush with a rag. "What's your pleasure tonight?"

"Wine for you?" Shianan asked Luca.

Luca stared stupidly. "Y-yes," he managed.

Shianan nodded. "And stronger for me," he told the woman. "The cruelest you have."

She gave him a knowing look. "There's some in the back of the cellar that we don't bring out just every night. But seeing as you have someone to steer you home...." She winked and grinned and left.

Luca stared at the table between his bare wrists. His master had removed his collar, removed his cuffs illegally, taken him inside a tavern which did not permit slaves. Why?

Master Shianan, are you giving me my freedom? But he dared not form the words.

Shianan was subtly testing his ribs with his hand. "That amulet works miracles," he muttered, "but it's not enough."

Luca nodded briefly, uncertain if a reply were required or appropriate. His back had benefited from most of the healing power. More generosity had been shed on him this day than since he had first been enslaved—since, perhaps, before.

The slave woman returned with the drinks, setting wine before Luca and a cup and dusty bottle before Shianan. "Enjoy it," she said, "and wave or shout if you want for something."

Shianan poured out a portion and drank it straightaway. "Good," he said, making a face. "This will do."

"Do?" Luca repeated.

Shianan took another drink and grimaced again. "I mean not to dream tonight." He flicked a finger toward Luca's cup. "Go ahead, drink."

Luca had not tasted wine in years. He sipped slowly.

Shianan did not speak but drank, keeping his eyes on the bottle. Luca made his wine last, not wanting the serving woman to bring another without Shianan's order. The tavern began to empty gradually as the tradesmen finished their drinks.

Shianan's movements slowed and then, as he reached for the bottle again, his fingers slipped on the neck. "I think," he said, "it is time to go home." He raised his hand to summon the woman. "Bring another bottle of this. I'll carry it with me." He looked at Luca and blinked. "Go on. I'll pay and meet you outside."

"Yes, my lord." There was no reason for Shianan to send him ahead, but Luca had given up trying to understand his master tonight. He took a gulp to finish the wine and heaved the mattress over his protesting shoulder.

The waiting slaves were gone, departed with their masters and wagons and packs. Luca walked into the street and something slammed into his skull.

Light sparked through his vision and the street fell hard against him. Hands groped over his body as the ground and sky whirled. "Nothing," a voice rasped. "Must be on the other one!"

Then there was no one, and Luca lay still for a moment, trying to bring his vision into focus again. His head was ringing, and a paving stone pressed cold against his cheek. His right arm lay across the rolled mattress.

Distantly he heard sounds of a disturbance, or maybe some sort of struggle. He should escape, crawl away from the vicious men before they could hurt him again. He pulled himself to his hands and knees.

There were three men fighting behind him. Shianan stumbled as one of the thieves struck him but he swung back, reaching with his other hand for something at his waist. The second thief hit Shianan from behind and he staggered. The thief seized his arm and shoulders and shoved him headfirst into the slaves' trough, twisting his arm to hold him under the water.

Shianan struggled but could not break the hold. The first thief began to rip items from his belt. Luca stared dumbly as Shianan's thrashing slowed. The thief holding him leaned hard, keeping him underwater.

Luca scrambled to his feet, snatching up the rolled mattress. They were intent on drowning and robbing Shianan and did not see him coming. He swung the rolled mat hard against the thief holding Shianan and felt the jolting impact as the man stumbled backward, raking Shianan roughly over the trough's edge.

Luca turned to face the other thief, who danced backward. Shianan gasped raggedly for air behind him. Luca heaved the mat again, but the thief ducked nimbly out of range and the heavy mat sailed wide, leaving Luca unguarded as the thief moved forward. Luca flinched away from the swinging cudgel and pain flared through his temple.

The thief grunted as dull steel flashed across his side. Shianan wheeled, but the other was already fleeing. He turned back, but the attacker stumbled backward, hands to his bleeding flank, and ran down the street.

Shianan dropped to his knees and then to his hands, panting hoarsely. Luca looked after the thieves, racing in opposite directions to discourage pursuit, and blinked blood from his eye. He knelt beside Shianan. "Master!"

Shianan's head drooped toward the paving stones, and he was shaking with exertion or injury. He tried to speak, but the sound was lost in his gasps for air.

Luca could not see for the wet hair hiding his face and his folded posture. Had he been stabbed as well? Had he been too long underwater? "Master?"

"You great stupid fool." Water ran from Shianan's hair and torso, puddling beneath him. "That was your chance. Why didn't you run?" He pushed himself slowly upright. "You could have been a free man."

Luca stared at him. He had no collar, no telltale wrist cuffs. If he could hide the pale streaks on his arms for a few days—

"They would have killed you," he said numbly.

Shianan shrugged. "And what of it?" He clenched his fists. "My last thought would have been that at least you would go free." He shook his head, staring at his fists in his lap. "But no, I could not even do that."

A chill ran through Luca. He gulped and said, "You're bleeding, master. Let me help you."

Shianan made a disdainful sound. "This?" He put a hand gingerly to the cut over his swelling eye. "It's nothing. At least it gives me an excuse for the dent in my ribs."

Luca's back was beginning to scream, though he'd not even thought of it during the attack. "And your money—they robbed you."

Shianan shook his head. "I never carry more than I'll spend." He sighed and wiped bloody water from his face. "Where's my drink?"

Luca found the bottle beneath the trough. He picked up his mattress and started after Shianan, limping uphill toward the military grounds.

Wielding a mattress had been too much for his back, even half-healed, and his head pounded. Luca gritted his teeth and shuffled the last distance, hardly noting how Shianan clutched his side as he reached for the door. They went through the office and barely into the living quarters before Shianan fell into a chair and Luca dropped the mattress to the floor, careless of reprimand. He lit a couple of lights, creating a narrow circle of illumination.

"You should've run," Shianan said gruffly without prologue. "That was your best chance."

Luca could think of no safe response. He gripped the back of the other chair and leaned on it.

"But you ignored your chance and came to me. So you're still a slave, and I am still alive." He frowned at Luca. "You're terrible in a fight. Go put something on that."

175

Luca turned and went to the little chest of medical supplies. They had nearly exhausted the rags and bandages, but he took two of the few remaining and handed one to Shianan, pressing the other against his own head.

Shianan pushed the wadded rag against his split eyebrow. "Sit." He opened the second bottle and took a drink. "I should sit with a slave. I cannot even die properly."

Again cold raced through Luca. "No, master," he heard himself say. "You wouldn't—"

Shianan took another drink and looked fiercely at him. "Why not?" He drank again, huge swallows that made his throat strain. He coughed, eyes watering with the alcohol, flushed even in the candlelight. "There are enough people who would be gratified by my death; I could oblige them."

No. Luca looked down, horrified. *No, master. Live—live, so I may stay. Don't send me to the block again.* But of course he could not say that. He swallowed.

Shianan took another drink, his eyes on the wall. "I gave the Gehrn their house and their ritual. The failure of the shield is my fault. Ariana—she's—Mage Hazelrig has to know she's gone because of me. The king.... He's furious. The entire kingdom is at risk because I agreed a Gehrn priest could come to the Shard." He made a sharp gesture toward Luca. "Even you. If not for me, you wouldn't have been strapped to that scaffold and skinned." He took a deep drink from the bottle.

The room swayed a little around Luca as he shifted the clotting rag. "No, master."

Shianan looked at him with reddened eyes. "Didn't I tell you to sit?" He stared pointedly at the chair until Luca lowered himself into it. "I can't even look after my own men. Do you know how many have died in my command?" He swallowed. "I killed Ariana, too. And Tam. And if the Ryuven come—if they come while the shield is down, how many more will I have killed?" He snorted. "Partial triumphs, he said. But they were all just slow deaths."

Luca gripped the edge of the table. "Master," he said urgently. "I was told once, while you yet breathe, there is hope. You don't know what may come." The words tasted foul.

Shianan took another drink and looked across the table at Luca, blinking hard. "What may come? The Ryuven may come. The Ryuven may come and kill every one of us. And it will be my doing."

His words were blurring.

"Not yours," Luca said automatically. "That was master—the high priest." He squeezed his fingers on the table. "He broke the shield."

He could not tell whether Shianan heard or understood. Luca lowered his bloodied cloth and looked at Shianan, drinking again. His face was purpling. He should have had cold meat on it.

"While you breathe, eh?" Shianan said after a moment, his words even less clear. "That's pretty." He fixed reddened eyes on Luca. "Do you believe that?"

Luca dropped his eyes to the table. *While you yet breathe, Luca, there is hope.*

He clenched his fists. *Liar.*

A frenzied banging at the outer door made Luca jump in the chair. "Commander!" shouted a voice outside. "Commander! Ryuven!"

Luca shoved himself away from the table, fear pricking him so that his fingers fumbled on the latch. The door was flung back and Luca stumbled as the soldier burst inside.

"Commander! The mages have sounded the alert. There's a Ryuven here, sir, here in the hold!"

"Ryuven, eh? Already?" Shianan nodded and reached for the bottle. "Well, invite him in for a drink."

The soldier's eyes widened and he backed a step. "I'll go to General Septime, sir," he said, and he fled.

CHAPTER 26

Luca pushed his hands through his hair and ran, ignoring the ache stabbing through his shoulders. Beside him Shianan scraped at his dusty tunic with one hand and shielded his eyes from the morning sun with another.

"What are you doing?" Shianan demanded, squinting.

"Accompanying you," Luca answered. He was almost afraid to have his master out of sight, after Shianan's drunken talk the night before. And with angry soldiers and even Ryuven outside, he felt safest near him.

Shianan scowled and jerked at a lace. "I don't need you in the king's offices."

"Then I will wait outside," Luca answered quietly, surprised at his boldness.

They passed between liveried guards, leaving the sunny courtyard behind. The door banged behind them, making Shianan wince. "Keep well out of the way," he conceded, lacking the energy to order Luca home. "And 'soats, hide your wrists; I don't even want to think what will come if someone sees you without cuffs."

Luca tugged his sleeves over his hands. They went up stairs and through corridors and came to an anteroom. The secretary looked at Shianan with pursed lips. "You'd better go right in, your lordship."

Shianan's rigid shoulders rose another quarter-inch. "Thank you." He turned and strode forward, pushing back the doors determinedly. Luca caught a door before it rebounded and followed.

Shianan took a few steps into the room and dropped to one knee, bowing his head. Luca blinked, seeing richly dressed men standing around the suddenly silent room, and threw himself to the floor. If his master knelt, Luca could not do less.

"My lords," said a broad man in the center, "what have we here? Look, General Septime. Do you recognize this man?"

The general shifted. "Majesty...."

"Ah! Wait, it could be Bailaha. Is it? We did not at first see past the bloodshot eyes and bleary countenance. Stand, Bailaha, and join our conference."

Shianan straightened, keeping his arm close to his injured side.

179

"Your Majesty."

Luca knew better than to rise, but he risked shifting his head to look at the room. A few slaves stood against the wall, but he didn't think he should move to join them. He saw the nobles and military men look away from his master, distancing themselves.

"We were talking, Bailaha, of the appearance of a Ryuven in our midst last night. You might have heard something to that effect?"

Shianan's head was bowed. "Yes, sire."

"Oh, that's good. At least you won't claim a dimly remembered dream or some other feeble drunkard's tale." The king tapped a finger on the table. "It was late when our Amber Mage, who had not yet retired, sensed the arrival of a Ryuven." He nodded toward a woman in appropriately colored robes, who bobbed respectfully in return.

"Why only one mage?" asked Septime. "Why didn't others sense this?"

"It was, as the king says, late," offered the White Mage gently from a corner. Luca had not noticed him before. "Most of us were sleeping, and a single Ryuven of lesser power would not generate enough of a disturbance to wake us."

"I suggest a night watch," General Septime put in. "We've never expected a single Ryuven to enter Alham alone, and so we've relied upon advance warning. But this shows otherwise."

"An excellent idea," the king said. "Our mages and soldiers will work together to watch for Ryuven and deploy appropriate counters. But we will take care to keep Bailaha from the night watches. We would not want to disturb his libations."

Shianan flushed scarlet. "Your Majesty—"

"You were drunk, were you not?" demanded the king. "When the Ryuven appeared—when we might have been under attack—you were drunk?" He took a step forward. "Answer, Bailaha!"

Shianan flinched. "Yes, Your Majesty. I was drunk."

"And when this threat was announced, did you seize a weapon and rush to command your men, as is your duty?"

Shianan had to try twice to speak. "I—no, I did not."

"And why not?"

Shianan swallowed. "I will offer my single excuse, Your Majesty. It was night, and I had no duties. As the time was my own—"

"Your time is not your own!" thundered King Jerome. "Your time belongs to this kingdom. Your first duty, from which you are never released, is to come to this kingdom's aid. In neglecting that

180

duty, Bailaha, you failed us all."

Shianan's head sank lower. His mouth opened, but he did not speak.

"But the Ryuven fled immediately," the White Mage said from the side. "Why? We know he was in the Wheel, and nothing is missing. What he did want that he was here for mere moments?"

"We don't know," the king snapped. "Perhaps he was verifying the shield is indeed destroyed—but we cannot be certain, since he was not captured." He looked darkly at Shianan. "He went practically unchallenged in our very stronghold!"

The men shifted uncomfortably and looked away.

The king stepped nearer to Shianan. "Lift your head," he said curtly. Shianan obeyed, showing his blackened eye and jagged cut, and Luca saw tight lines etched around his mouth. "What is this?" King Jerome circled Shianan, who stared fixedly ahead. "Did you fall against the door in a drunken stupor?"

Shianan swallowed. "I was attacked, Your Majesty, and defended myself."

"Attacked? Not by our Ryuven; you never made it so far. Where was this attack?"

Shianan gamely answered the tapestried wall. "At the Brining Tankard."

The king's eyebrows lifted. "Oh? So a tavern brawl first—a fine occupation for a count of our nobility. Then you went home to drink yourself further into oblivion."

One of the other men coughed. "Your Majesty, if we could—"

"No, no, Your Grace." King Jerome waved in protest. "We know what you wish to say, and it is well-intentioned but incorrect. This is certainly the business of the court, because it is the business of the kingdom. Here is a noble, an officer entrusted with the safety of the crown and the people, and he is found drunk at the very moment when he is needed. My lords!" He stepped back and pointed at Shianan, who stared blinking ahead. "You who serve well, you who perform your duties conscientiously—look at this man and mark him. We want that none of our servants bear such shame." He faced Shianan. "You may take your leave, Bailaha. As we have not yet found evidence that alcohol is a potent weapon against the Ryuven, we do not require your assistance at this time."

Shianan bowed stiffly without speaking and backed to the door. The king turned his back before Shianan reached the

181

antechamber. Luca scuttled backward and closed the chamber doors firmly, then turned to find Shianan already disappearing down the corridor. Luca ignored the staring secretary and ran after him.

Shianan was traveling fast, his stride lengthening nearly to a run as he shot down the corridors. He burst from the Naziar into the courtyard, ignoring the guards on either side. A group of slaves carrying packs and baskets of vegetables crowded the yard, and Shianan shoved his way through. Luca wove more slowly behind him.

Shianan jerked open the outer door and went through his office without hesitating. His hand fumbled with the latch of the inner door, but before Luca could reach him Shianan shoved back the door and went into his quarters. He staggered a few steps and fell on his knees, folding his arms across his chest and groaning.

Luca hurried to him. "Master! Are you—"

"Get away!" roared Shianan, flinging his arm backward at Luca. His teeth flashed like an animal's as he snarled. "Out! Let me be!"

Luca stumbled backward, dragging the door shut behind him. Slowly he sank to the floor. From the other room he heard a low keening, as from someone mourning or in pain.

The bastard—Luca had not understood at first. The physical resemblance was not blatant, but it was there, and King Jerome could not ordinarily afford to treat his nobility so contemptuously.

Luca felt himself trembling and squeezed his fists, driving his nails into his palms in an attempt to quell the savage emotion which roiled suddenly within him. He had thought he'd forgotten—but the rage had not gone. It had only lain dormant.

Endure, Luca.

Liar! Traitor!

The keening faded. Luca took a long, shuddering breath and swallowed. He understood now what Shianan had meant. *I cannot change what I must do, but I don't require it of you. Don't kneel and scrape all the time, do you understand?* Shianan was no more to his royal father than Luca was to any master—than Luca had been to his own father. Shianan knelt for abuse just as Luca had before Ande.

Luca pushed himself to his feet and faced the door. He should not enter, he should not intrude on his master's grief and shame, but it was somehow as wrong to leave him alone.

He set his forehead against the door, hearing nothing. Wounded animals were most dangerous. Had his master not just shouted and struck at him?

Luca gritted his teeth. He owed Shianan Becknam this much.

He opened the door quietly. Shianan sat against the footboard, his knees to his chest, a boy hiding from some terror. Luca closed the door behind him and crept forward a few steps before crouching silently.

Shianan lifted his head from his knees. "What are you doing?" he rasped. "Get out!"

Luca twitched but remained where he was. "You were right, master, when you spoke of retaliation."

Shianan blinked. "What you say is treason."

"You said there could be no retaliation for you. I understand now."

Shianan uncoiled, his expression darkening. "I cannot believe you would intrude only to say you comprehend my shame."

Luca closed his eyes, expecting to be struck. "No, master." He sensed his next words were his most dangerous. "It was my father who sold me."

Shianan rubbed roughly at his face. "What makes you think the history of a slave matters to me?"

Luca stared at his clenched hands. "He sold me to be summoned and ordered and beaten and humiliated. I hate him more than I hate the high priest."

Shianan's eyes narrowed. "You see too much. I should have— but you knew yesterday, didn't you?" He tightened a fist in helpless fury. "I could not hide it yesterday."

Luca swallowed and said nothing.

"So you think we're alike, do you? You think our positions are the same—me, a count and a commander, and you a slave?"

Luca had made a mistake, a terrible mistake. He should never have come, should never have spoken, should never have opened the door....

Shianan swore. "Tam said as much."

Luca could not help the question that burst from him. "What?"

"Tam said I took orders as a slave did. That I am a slave to—the king." He twitched. "I was angry then, but it's true, isn't it?"

Luca bit his lip. This was not as he'd wanted it. He would do nothing but provoke his master into demonstrating his power.

"So were you a bastard too, sired on some slave girl and disposed of when you became inconvenient?" Shianan's voice was harsh. "It might have been nice to have been a forgettable mistake."

183

"No, master. I was an own son, born a freeman."

"Freemen don't sell their sons."

"They do, when they are indebted and the price of negotiation is the sale of a child."

Shianan's mouth hardened. "Your father sold you for credit?"

Hot tears threatened Luca's eyes, making him turn away. "He put the shackles on my wrists himself." Old anger and grief surged within him. "Himself, do you understand? He bound me for the trader himself!" He gulped. "And my brothers—he kept them. He sold me into slavery and my brother just watched me dragged away."

Shianan's face turned a deeper red. "Your family."

Luca could not answer him.

A long moment passed. Shianan ground a balled fist into the floor. "A nice trick. I am too angry at your father to think of—the king." He rubbed savagely at his face. "All of them—I hate them all." He gave Luca a hard look. "Why did you come here?"

Luca was unprepared for the question. "What?"

"You disobeyed me, came when I told you to go and stayed when I told you to leave. You saw my humiliation and claimed we were equals. Is your slavery so heavy that you wished for death? What possessed you to be so stupid?"

Luca's throat constricted. "I—I thought...."

"Did you already miss the feel of the whip?"

Luca shrank. "I'm sorry, master."

"We're both sorry." Shianan gestured abstractly. "Look at us, cringing and sniveling and practically moldering in our own tears. There's not another more sorry pair within the Alham walls." He sighed.

Luca bowed his head.

"I couldn't speak of this in front of anyone but a slave." Shianan rubbed his sleeve across his mouth. "Even so, Luca, my slave, I will make you an oath—if I find that you've used this in any way, I will make Ande's tortures seem mild, do you understand?"

"I will never mention it."

"In any way," Shianan repeated. He dropped his head. "You wouldn't, though, would you? And not even for fear of punishment." He looked at Luca with unguarded, miserable eyes. "No other man in the king's chamber today would have had the heart or the stones to come in here."

"The White Mage is a good man," Luca said quickly,

uncomfortable with Shianan's bitter praise.

"Yes." Shianan gave a long sigh. "I cannot afford to wallow in my sorrows. I cannot be caught unprepared again, no matter the cost." He gestured toward the stand across the room. "Is there water?"

"Yes, master."

Shianan held up a finger. "Yes, Master Shianan. 'Soats, you can't argue we are the same and then address me as if I were that mongrel of a Gehrn." He got to his feet and went to the washstand. "Find me something to eat, would you?"

"Yes, Master Shianan."

Luca went out through the office and into the street, busy with morning activity. He paused at the fountain and took a long, careful breath. Finally he cupped cold water in his hands and splashed his face, shocking away the clinging agitation.

A hand settled on Luca's shoulder. "How is the commander? Did they chew him out much?"

Luca steeled himself to meet the strange soldier's eyes. "My master is very well, thank you. He will be in his office after his breakfast."

He eased forward, letting the hand slide from his shoulder, and started for the kitchen. No one called him back or held him, and he lengthened his stride with a small measure of relief.

He brought breakfast from the kitchen, musing that the trip was too far for cold weather. He would have to use warmed stones. Shianan was in the office when he returned, looking over papers. Only the darkened eye and cut marred his face; his expression was unruffled and attentive. He nodded as Luca set down the breakfast and continued reading.

Someone rapped at the door behind Luca. "Commander?"

Shianan gestured, his mouth full of bread, and Luca opened the door. A man stepped inside, holding a letter. "The White Mage sends you this, sir."

Shianan took the letter, folded but unsealed. "He did not write this?"

"No, sir, it was open when he entrusted it to me. He said he found it near his offices but believes you should see it. He is still with the king at this time."

There was no name on the outside of the letter. Shianan opened the letter with one hand, using the other to take another bite of his meal. The soldier, dismissed, departed.

185

My dear master, the letter began.

Shianan's stomach tightened. Mage Hazelrig had unconventional ideas regarding slavery and had kept only Tam, so far as Shianan knew.

My dear master, you will be gratified to know our journey has gone well, though we have been delayed. My mistress is ill with traveling but comfortable, and the consulting physicians say she should rest for a time before trying to proceed home. I will of course continue to serve her to the best of my ability as I know you would instruct me. Do not worry on her behalf, master, as I will do my best to bring her safely to you when she is recovered.

Shianan stared at the letter, hardly daring to breathe. There was a short signature at the end: *Your devoted servant, T.*

The letter was unassuming and unidentified, should anyone else see it, but to Mage Hazelrig it could only be from Tam—

"She's alive!" Shianan breathed, the letter trembling in his hand. "Sweet Holy One, she's really alive."

CHAPTER 27

Energy shifted subtly, and Tamaryl sagged in relief. A few minutes later Maru appeared in the center of the room, breathless with the effort of leaping the void. "Left beneath his door."

"And no one saw you?"

"Some mage must have sensed my arrival, and I was pursued." He grinned. "But I was quicker, as you can see."

Tamaryl shook his head. "I did not want you so near to danger."

"I'm fine, Ryl'sho. How is the rika?"

Tamaryl turned toward Ariana, motionless on the bed. "She should have awakened by now."

"Nori'bel said perhaps she would protect herself until she reconciled her body to the magic here."

Tamaryl sighed. "I hope that is it." He faced Maru. "I am going now. I will go to Aktonn first. It seems Rarn'sho and Do'che have especial need of my guidance."

Maru gave him a guarded look, but even after so many years Tamaryl could read his thoughts. Maru knew Oniwe had given him a difficult task, one that would benefit all if he succeeded and leave Oniwe blameless if he failed. "I will watch over the rika as best I can," he said.

Tamaryl nodded. "Thank you."

"But...." Maru looked uncomfortable. "If she should wake—if she is alarmed...."

"Yes?"

"She is a mage, isn't she? And the most powerful ever to come here, or she would not be alive."

"She will remember you," Tamaryl said, hoping it were true. "My name in her world was Tam—use that if necessary. But she will remember you. She has not met so many Ryuven. And she is not so foolhardy as to open battle here alone."

Maru nodded. "If you say so." He put on a smile. "Travel safely."

Fifteen years had passed since Tamaryl had really used his wings, except for diving after Ariana and struggling with their combined weights and his neglected skill. Still, his Ryuven body was at ease in the winds, and the night was clear, and it was an easy flight to

187

regain his confidence and find his way to Aktonn.

Tamaryl soared higher, squinting against the burn of the wind. He could feel himself grinning.

Fifteen years was a long time to miss his home.... And now he had his former place, something he had never dared to dream. He folded his wings and rolled forward into a somersault, air screaming past his ears. Then he spread his wings to catch himself and laughed aloud.

Daranai would be waiting for his return. The thought excited him. Conjoining meant affirmation of his regained position, a companion who would never be separated from him, precious after his exile. And Daranai was eager for him, too; he could see it in her hungry glances, feel it in the way she teased with word and casual action.

He dove into another roll, giddy with the rush of wind and adrenaline. This time he turned over twice before snapping his wings to their impressive span. It was a child's game, one young Ryuven played to amuse themselves while incidentally building confidence and skill. One had to open his wings just at the precise instant, or they would not catch the air properly. Of course, the game inevitably degraded to challenging one another to see who could fall the furthest before opening his or her wings, where it taught the pitfalls of folly and recklessness as well—whatever they could not heal themselves, they took to the healers, who scolded them fiercely as they treated them. Tales of those who had died kept most from trying it at higher altitudes.

Tamaryl did another short roll. Daranai admired him, and that was a warming thought. That too was gratifying, after so many years of being overlooked or disdained.

Tamaryl checked himself—Hazelrig had never disdained him. In fact, they had developed a strange friendship, a hidden respect between the human White Mage and the princely warrior Ryuven. Tamaryl could not complain of his stay in the mage's house; he had played the demeaning role of a slave only in the public eye. He dove again through the rising wind. But, though she had always been more than kind, he had always quietly resented that Ariana had seen him only as a young slave.

His wings cracked open audibly, but there was no abrupt pressure as they caught the air. Tamaryl felt a sickening lurch as he realized he had opened too early. He wrenched, trying to catch the wind with the forward crest, but the trailing edge had already caught and he dropped like a human soldier.

Panic seized him and he thrashed in the air, clawing for something to break his fall, but there was of course nothing. With iron control he forced himself to be still, to curl into a ball of arms and legs, to fold his wings tightly against his back with only the tips trailing in the violent wind of his plunge. Then he flung himself forward, kicking out with his legs to right himself, and with arms and legs splayed wide he opened his wings again.

The snap of resistance jerked at his torso and snatched his breath, but he gasped with more relief than pain. Then the ground rushed toward him and he barely had time to drop his legs before he landed with crushing impact, flattening his feet and jarring his teeth.

He sank with the force of the fall, dropping to one knee as if greeting Oniwe'aru, and grunted with dull pain. For the first time he noticed the warm rain falling over him. He flexed his wings to check for damage and, finding none, he rocked backward to sit on the ground. His feet and ankles tingled with healing.

That had been foolish, he thought ruefully. He rubbed at his neck, already stiff. He knew better than to allow himself distraction while playing at acrobatics. And he had no call to be thinking of his human mistress at all, not alongside thoughts of his bride.

That was not true, either; it was only right that he should be concerned for Ariana's welfare. She lay in a state which was hardly living, and he was duty-bound to return her to her own home world. This sense of obligation might understandably encroach on other thoughts.

He sighed and stood gingerly, testing his prickling feet. His wings and torso ached with labor, and with chagrin he noted he was out of condition. He arched a wing to shield himself from the rain. He could rest a bit and still reach Aktonn well in time for a suitably impressive entrance.

Rarn'sho had not been warned of Tamaryl's coming. Any harbinger could have preceded him by no more than a few hours, and Tamaryl hoped his unexpected return would impress Rarn'sho.

He frowned to himself. It had been merely Rarn'che when Tamaryl had gone out to that last battle, from which he had not returned. Some act of crazed bravado on the field had won him higher rank and the rule of Aktonn, and as Tamaryl had once warned, the new lords were more interested in personal promotion than in careful governing of their awarded lands. What exactly did Oniwe'aru expect

Tamaryl to do in Aktonn? What could he accomplish in a single visit that would enrich Aktonn and make Rarn a more conscientious and knowledgeable lord?

Maru was awakened by a small sound in the darkness. He lay still, listening, and it came again—a kind of gasping moan.

He rolled from his bed and sparked a light for the candle he'd left nearby. As the wick flared to life a sharp cry came from the opposite bed. He eased forward. "Rika?"

Ariana thrashed in the bed, throwing her arms before her face. "No! Get it away! Away!"

He hesitated, lifting the light higher to see her. "Rika...."

"Ow! It burns, it's hot! Take it away, oh please!" She twisted in the bed. "So bright, so bright...."

Maru, startled, pushed the light behind him. "Is that better? Rika?"

She quieted a little. "Oh, don't shout, please." She clawed at her arms. "It bites me."

Maru set the candle on a low table and crept forward. "Can you hear me, rika?"

"Shh! Please don't shout." She squinted at him. "It's so bright...."

Maru was unsettled. "There's only the one candle, rika."

She twisted on the bed, raking her fingers over her clothing. "It bites, it itches, make it stop!"

She felt things more keenly—too keenly. "I will give you some medicine to make you sleep." Maru turned in the dark, seeking the packet of herbs Nori'bel had left. There was water on the table, and he emptied the packet into it and sloshed the water to mix it.

"Quiet," she protested from the bed, her hands to her head. "Make them be quiet."

"I'm sorry, rika," Maru whispered. "Here is your tea." He tiptoed to the bed and held it out carefully.

Ariana twisted toward him and unshaded her eyes, apparently seeing him for the first time. She screamed and recoiled, thrusting her hands before her.

Maru leapt backward, recognizing the angle of her hands. He would never dodge in time—

But nothing happened. There was no crack of power, no

sudden pain in his chest.

Her jaw worked in shock, and then she looked at Maru. "Get away!"

Maru held up a hand, the sloshing infusion between them like a shield. "Rika, listen," he said, as if speaking to a child. "I am Maru. We met before, remember? Tamaryl'sho asked me to stay with you. You must remember Tamaryl'sho—Tam, he said you called him. You remember Tam?"

She blinked at him, wide eyes shining in the dark. "Tam?"

"That's right. Tam asked me to look after you. You've been ill." He held up the cup. "Will you take some medicine?"

She looked around the room, shielding her face from the candle. "Where am I?"

He slid forward and held out the cup at arm's length, almost afraid she might touch him as she reached for it. Welts were rising where she'd clawed herself. "We are in the house of Daranai'rika."

She took the water. "The Ryuven world."

"Yes."

The cup of water shook in her hand. "Why does it hurt so much? The light hurts my eyes. And these clothes—they bite me. They have fleas, they itch, they hurt me." She sipped at the tea, rubbing at her shoulder.

"The medicine will help."

She made a face. "It scrapes my throat." She looked around the room, her eyes wide. "The Ryuven world."

"Yes. It's all right. I'm here to watch over you. You don't need to worry."

But she was breathing faster. "I couldn't—why couldn't—I know there's magic here. There has to be magic here. I can't—I can't be...."

"Drink your medicine," Maru repeated helplessly. "It will help you."

She looked distrustful, but she drank. "Where is Tam?"

"Tamaryl'sho was called elsewhere. He asked me to stay with you until you recovered." He started to reach for the candle and then remembered her earlier complaint. "Does the candle bother you?"

"Candle? It feels like a bonfire."

Why was everything magnified so dramatically to her? "Tomorrow," he said, "I will ask Nori'bel to look at you again."

191

Ariana muttered something into her tea and sipped a little more. After a moment she sagged, and then she drooped against her pillow. The cup fell from her hands and spilled across the bed and floor.

CHAPTER 28

The wind came howling down the passage, kicking dead leaves into the doorway where Luca pressed his arms more tightly across his chest and tucked his hands into his armpits. Shianan hadn't asked him to wait outside the general's door—had not, in fact, asked him to accompany him at all. Luca had followed him, explaining others would be less likely to interfere with him if they saw whose he was.

Luca did not care if his master thought he feared the soldiers. What did that matter? He needed to know his new master. He could not afford to lose this man.

The door opened and Shianan emerged, carrying a stack of ledgers. Luca got to his feet, and Shianan frowned. "You're still here?"

"I thought I might be needed, my lord." Luca gathered the stack of books from Shianan's arms. "You see?"

"Hm." Shianan looked unimpressed. "Your insistence on standing in the cold will cost me money."

"Master Shianan?"

"Because you must have a cloak." Shianan gave Luca a small smile and started down the angled passage to the courtyard. "We have to go to market anyway, for the cuffs. It's good no one's noticed." He glanced at Luca's wrists, nearly hidden beneath the stack of books. "Today."

But when they reached Shianan's quarters, he sat at his desk with the ledgers. "My just punishment, I suppose," he said unhappily.

Luca, lacking instruction, began to clean the office. The shelved maps were full of dust and grit that would shower onto the floor when removed, so he began wiping those. Shianan spread the ledgers over the wide surface of the desk, opening some to compare with others, and scowled over the neat columns of numbers. "This writing! How does anyone read these ant prints without going blind?"

Luca grimaced as a particularly large cloud of dust billowed. "Master Shianan, would you rather I finish this when you are away?"

Shianan grunted, bent over the desk.

Luca was uncertain of his meaning. "Master Shianan?"

"Go ahead," he said wearily. "A little dust is appropriate to this." He sighed and set a stack of surplus books on the edge of the wide desk, fanning a sheaf of letters on the top. Then he moved his chair to the far end, giving himself more work space as he squinted from one book to another.

Luca moved to the next map and his stomach tightened. *The Wakari Coast.* He glanced at the familiar shape of the coastline—there had been many maps in their office—and gingerly brushed the dust from it.

Behind him, Shianan began drumming his fingers on the desktop. Luca replaced the final map and began to sweep the floor made filthy with dust.

"This makes no sense," Shianan muttered. "Why did we need another five hundred spears so soon? Hadn't they just two weeks before—? Where's that other book...." He drew another ledger to him and flipped to the end.

Luca gathered the first pile of dust. When some trickled to the swept floor he almost expected Ande's sharp reprimand, but Shianan only stared at the ledgers.

"Bah." Shianan rapped his knuckles on the table in frustration. "This is like trying to trail a rat through a warehouse. Everything is entered in three different places, and they don't always agree. Hand me Morn's letter of requisition, will you?" He gestured to the fanned letters at the far end of the desk, where Luca stood. "Oh, let me think, it will be, um, the third one—"

But Luca had already selected the correct letter. He held it toward Shianan, but the commander looked over it at him without taking it. Luca froze.

His master appraised him. "You can read, can't you? And fluently?"

"I can...."

Shianan took the letter, still looking at Luca. Luca hardly breathed. There was no reason for guilt, he had done nothing wrong, but few slaves were educated. Ande had laughed once to find Luca cutting his scraps in the proper fashion and had confiscated his utensils, making him eat from a bowl on the floor that night to remind him of his position.

"You were a freeman's son, you said," Shianan mused. "An educated one, it seems."

"Yes, master. Ours was a merchant house. We were all taught to manage the shipping affairs."

Something sparked in Shianan's eyes. "You managed the

office."

"Yes, master."

"Bookkeeping?"

"Yes."

Shianan fairly leapt from the chair. "Then sit, please, and take this! I am making no headway at all." He gestured to the chair. "Sit."

Luca hesitated and then moved behind the desk. "Master?"

"This is the standard yearly approval, only this year it's fallen to me, no accident. I should just sign the thing, as I'm sure the generals do each year, but...." Shianan took the broom from Luca's hand. "Just check over it, make sure nothing is glaringly wrong, and then I'll sign it as completed."

Luca nodded mutely, surprised, and surveyed the ledgers before him. There was one for each month, another master ledger, and an unwieldy collection of requisition letters, merchant invoices, shipping logs, and other miscellany.

"Go ahead." Shianan moved to the far end of the desk and began sweeping.

Luca leapt to his feet. "Master! I will finish—"

Shianan glanced from Luca to the broom and back. "Oh, this? King's oats, man, who do you think cleaned this place before you came? I'd rather sweep than slog through that mess, anyway. Now sit down and do it."

"But...."

"That is an order," Shianan said firmly. "What's the point of having a slave if I can't have him do the things I don't want to do? Get to work."

Luca fell silent and sat at the desk again. He tried to ignore the soft sounds of Shianan's sweeping as he scanned down the first column.

Shianan had been right, it was a difficult system to track. Luca wasn't sure why the accustomed notation was so complex, but he supposed it had always been so and would not be easily changed in so unwieldy an entity as the military. It wasn't long before he found the habit of correlating letters, logs, invoices, and receipts, and he began making a running list of transactions on a spare sheet for simpler reference.

Shianan finished sweeping the floor and moved into the next room, stripping the bed and the smaller mattress on the floor. Luca blew the ink dry and started a new column of transactions.

195

The light had shifted considerably through the window when Shianan returned and stood beside the desk. "You didn't have to put that much effort into it."

Luca stood and rotated his notes. "I thought a master list would be simpler to review. The primary ledger, with all the year's transactions, is not itemized."

"So I noticed," Shianan answered dryly. "Why do you think you're doing it?" He looked down at the sheet. "Still, this is considerable work for something no one will ever examine."

"I don't mind. I'm happy to do it."

Shianan snorted. "I thought I'd told you not to grovel."

Luca shook his head but remained silent. In truth, he had found a kind of solace in transcribing the numbers. He had not even held a pen for so long, much less exercised his previous training.

Shianan picked up the sheet. "What does this mean, here, this SW mark?"

"Swords," Luca supplied. "And these are spears, and these are wagon wheels, and axles, and harness for the draft slaves, and raw metals for repair, and smithing equipment, and—"

"You do enjoy this, don't you?" Shianan looked surprised.

Luca half-grinned, embarrassed. "This was my special province. My father and brothers met with clients and captains, wrote the contracts, arranged the payments. I was the primary bookkeeper, though of course we all did parts of all of it."

Shianan stared at him and then looked away. "Clear this away for now. We need to go to the market for your cuffs."

Luca nodded, hiding the twinge—though he had known better, some part of him had hoped he might remain unfettered. But even a commander and count could not risk defiance of the law. He tucked his notes inside the master ledger and stacked the books.

They descended to the market, navigating hilly streets less crowded with the chilling weather. When they reached the slavers, Luca exhaled against the hard lump in his throat and followed Shianan inside.

The merchant needed reminding, but the smith took a single glance at them and nodded. "I have them right here, lordship. Slimmer than he had, but still plenty functional."

Shianan nodded approval, and Luca reluctantly approached the fastening table. The smith, impatient with his slow approach, reached for Luca and pulled him forward. "Hurry up. Won't change anything, so don't even think about it." He slapped Luca's wrist onto the table. "Hold still."

Luca turned his head and closed his eyes. The process shouldn't be painful, but he had seen it already.

The cool metal cuff slid around his wrist and the smith rotated it, checking the fit. Then he riveted the cuff into place, making it a permanent part of Luca's arm. Luca flinched at each bang of the hammer. Then the smith pulled at the cuff, testing whether it could be greased to slide over Luca's hand. Luca braced himself against the table with the other hand, remembering his first fitting, but this smith was more easily satisfied, and there were no abrasions on the arm he dropped. "Next."

Shianan began counting out coins, and Luca retreated from the table. The cuffs were already familiar against his skin.

"He gives you trouble," the smith said, "bring him back. There's a man here who can—"

"Thank you," Shianan said, handing the last coin to the trader. "Have a good day."

Shianan went down the windy street without looking back, for which Luca was grateful. He felt weak as they left the slavers, passing under the carved sign. It was far too easy to slip into that place, waiting again for the bidder with the deepest purse to take charge of Luca's destiny.

"Keep up."

Luca quickened his pace. "Yes, master."

"Master Shianan," the commander corrected. "Don't let that smith worry you. I've never seen the point in paying good coin to have someone else loosen up the hide of a slave one could intimidate oneself."

Luca heard the tentative reassurance behind the ostensible threat. "Of course, Master Shianan."

"So get back to those ledgers." He made a face. "Better you than me."

They turned through the market, passing a gaming booth. The gamer was having a hard time soliciting customers in the chill. Then he saw Shianan. "Good sir!" he called. "Where is your lady friend today? Care to win her a flower?"

"Not today," Shianan answered sharply, and he started up the hill at a brisk pace. Luca hurried behind him, observing by Shianan's tense posture he should not ask about the incident.

Buying a used cloak was a matter of minutes and they returned to the office, where a soldier awaited shame-faced. "I'm Harl, sir. I was sent to you."

Shianan looked at him. "For discipline, I take it?"

The soldier sagged. "Yes, sir."

"We'll hear it in a moment. Luca, clear those books to the next room, please?"

Beyond the office door, Luca settled himself on his mattress with books and papers in a wide arc around him. There was something interesting in the books, he sensed. It was difficult to discern, but occasionally the master ledger and the monthly ledgers did not seem to match exactly, or they differed from the associated requisition letter, or invoice, or receipt. It could be simple errors in entry—certainly possible in such an imprecise and complex system—but he had been trained in accuracy to the minute detail, and a puzzle to unravel was welcome distraction from reality.

The outer office door opened and closed, and then opened and closed again. Luca kept working, gnawing occasionally at his lip.

Then the inner door opened, and Shianan entered with a tray. "Here," he said. "You didn't have lunch."

Luca jumped to his feet. "I'm sorry. I should have gone."

"Quiet. I went myself. I used to do that every meal, you know." He indicated the tray. "This is yours. I've already eaten. Return it when you've finished. I'm off to supervise training and make arrangements for Harl."

Luca asked before he could stop himself. "What's happening to him?"

Shianan sighed. "He was drinking, and when confronted he became belligerent and tried to hit Captain Torg." He shook his head. "Captain Torg isn't one to be taken by a drunk man, but the assault was there, and it's my place to deal with it."

Luca knew the penalties for a slave striking a master, but not for a soldier who struck his officer. "And... you did?"

"He'll be in the pillory tomorrow," Shianan said flatly. "I should have had him strapped a little, but since he didn't actually land a blow, I let that go." He sighed. "I'll return after training."

"Goodbye, Master Shianan." Luca took a piece of bread from the tray nearby and turned his attention again to the ledgers.

CHAPTER 29

Twilight came early with the advancing season. Shianan stretched his arm overhead, and his ribs twinged. He probably should not be training again so soon, but he had no excuse to offer for his absence. It was easier to work in short sessions than to devise a reason he shouldn't.

Resentment flashed hot through his mind. It had not been his fault the shield failed, not really. But the king had found it easiest to blame him.

But then the resentment faded, leaving despair in its wake. Whether he bore the blame alone or not, Shianan had failed, and now the shield was gone and Ariana was trapped in the Ryuven world. Battered ribs were a small penalty for risking the kingdom and sacrificing Ariana.

He passed the fountain and then the platform and pillory, brought out for Harl's punishment in the morning. There was little light visible in his quarters' high-set windows. He let himself into the office and then into the next room.

The room was dark, with the exception of a single candle near Luca's low mattress. By its light Shianan could see the slave studying a ledger, one leg folded beneath him and supporting the book, the other propped comfortably upright. It was the most at ease he could recall seeing him.

He closed the door quietly behind him, noting the slave had not yet leapt to his feet as he was inclined to do whenever seeing his master. "Luca?"

Luca jerked, dropping the book in his haste to rise. "Master Shianan! I—"

"You didn't hear me. What are you doing in the dark?"

But instead of apologizing and offering to bring lights, Luca seized the book from the floor. "I've found it. I've found the system. It's sloppy, which is why it was easy to find. They're cheating you."

Shianan looked from the nearly untouched tray of food to Luca's excited face. "What?"

"Whoever is supplying your foodstuffs and your weapons, and they are different houses, but they're cheating you. Handsomely, too!

199

And your steward, or quartermaster, he is a part of it."

Shianan looked at him more closely. "You're sure of this?"

"Absolutely. As I said, they have not covered it well."

"They knew none of us ever really checked the books," Shianan said. "Why would we? We're fighting men. Only the quartermaster sees this, and some runny-nosed noble son with a bought commission, and we sign it. You said they are cheating us handsomely?"

Luca nodded. "I have not had time to review the year in full, but judging from what I've seen, I would guess they are reaping perhaps a fifth."

"A *fifth*?" Shianan repeated in shock. "You can't be right."

But Luca merely nodded insistently. "A fifth, easily. Every year you pay a fifth more than you should."

"But for the army, in a year, that would be—" Shianan paused to calculate. "By all that—that's a fortune." He looked narrowly at Luca. "Are you certain of this? I can't go to General Septime and accuse our suppliers and our quartermasters of theft and treason, not without proof."

"Give me until morning," Luca said eagerly, "and I'll have your proof. It won't be complete, but it will be enough for you to present to him, and any clerks he brings to pursue it will be able to find the rest easily enough."

Shianan stared at him. "What is there for you in this?"

Luca looked confused. "My lord?"

"How do you profit if I report this? And how if I report it falsely? You won't be freed if I'm caught in a false accusation."

Luca's eyes widened. "No! No, Master Shianan, no! I only—you told me to look over the books, and I did. I have not fabricated anything!"

Shianan sighed. "I'm sorry, Luca. That was—I had no reason to suspect you. It's only that a fifth is an enormous amount. Unbelievable."

"Then see for yourself." Luca opened the book and laid his notes alongside. "They have overcharged here—most entries show fifty axles ordered, but here they ordered forty and yet paid the price of fifty. This same purchase of pork, delivered every two weeks, was entered once in this month's ledger and once in last month's, only a day apart. One shipment, paid twice. And there is more, that is not so quick to the eye—"

"I believe you," Shianan said hastily. "I'm sorry I doubted you."

He looked at him. "You can really have a report by morning?"

"I can." Luca actually smiled at him.

"Then get to work," Shianan said, a little surprised by the smile. "And eat something."

"Yes, Master Shianan."

Luca returned to the office, where Shianan had a supply of paper, and began outlining clearer notes. Shianan began to clean his teeth, wondering at what Luca had revealed. A fifth—that was a phenomenal amount. How long had they been cheated?

Luca lit a fresh candle in the office, and Shianan closed the door against the light before going to bed.

When Shianan opened the office door in the morning, Luca was still scratching notes, though his writing was no longer as neat and orderly. He turned reddened eyes to Shianan and stood. "I kept finding more," he said hoarsely, "but I think it's coherent enough." He blotted a page. "Your general should be able to follow it."

"I thought you would come with me to explain it."

"Me? No, Master Shianan. You will have everything here."

"But you did all this."

Luca shook his head. "The general does not know I exist, much less that I'm reviewing his army's accounts." His voice dropped. "Please, Master Shianan, I don't want to go."

Shianan frowned. Was this the first time Luca had asked for something? He couldn't remember.

Luca held out the folded sheets. "This is your work, Master Shianan. The master always is credited for the work of his slave. The smith is paid for the metals his slaves worked. The architect builds a bridge, though it is never his hands on tools or stone. And when the army conquers, isn't it said King Jerome won a battle?" Luca halted with a catch of breath, eyes wide.

"What you say," Shianan said flatly, "has too much truth for me to dispute your calling me a slave." He tucked the papers safely inside his tunic. "Thank you for your work this night. Now get some rest."

Shianan went out into the courtyard laden with ledgers, wishing he had a hand free to pull his cloak against the wind gusting around the corner. It was not yet the cold of winter, and yet it was a shock from the comfortable temperatures of the weeks before.

A small crowd had gathered to watch as Harl was inserted into the pillory. Two officers were present, one locking Harl into position and the other announcing his crime and punishment. Neither was Captain Torg. Shianan wanted to avoid the appearance of retaliation rather than discipline.

A few jeers came from the onlookers as Harl's neck and wrists were locked into the stocks. That was to be expected, and Harl studiously ignored them. The officers stepped away, leaving him to his humiliation and discomfort. There was no guard, as the prominent location helped reduce the risk of the more dangerous pranks.

Shianan went to General Septime's office, where the general's servant relieved him of the books and stacked them neatly on the desk before asking him to wait. Shianan stood beside it and waited.

"Good morning, commander," Septime offered as he entered.

"Good morning, sir. I've brought the accounts, but it's more than just returning them."

Septime gestured. "Have a seat." The servant reappeared, bearing a tray. "May I offer you tea?"

"Thank you, sir."

The slave poured out two measures of steaming tea, already brewed. Shianan must have caught the general at his meal. Septime took the lid from a small jar and dipped a drizzle of honey into his tea. "Go ahead," he said, indicating the honey. "I know they ration it dearly in the hall."

Shianan smiled. "Thank you, sir."

The tea was excellent. Shianan savored it, wondering how to begin his revelation. He heard the quiet rattle of stoneware and then the slave returned with plates of eggs, sausage, fruit, and porridge. There was also toasted bread with generous slabs of butter. "Sir," Shianan said, "I would have breakfasted with you every morning if I had known."

Septime laughed. "Yes, having my own kitchen is an advantage. But you are not entirely without comforts, my boy. I see you now have a slave to keep your quarters." He gave Shianan a significant look. "Did you get him at a good price?"

Shianan's heart sank. "I don't follow you, sir."

"I think you do." Septime cut apart a sausage. "But don't worry. Where do you think I found Petar?" He nodded toward the slave. "He should have been sold along with other confiscated property. But it's not such a bad lot here. He keeps my quarters, runs errands and messages, and cooks his breakfast alongside my own, except when I have an unexpected guest. Benefits to all." Septime took another bite and gestured a dismissal to Petar. "Now, you said you had more business than merely returning the accounts, which I assume you have examined, more or less."

"More than less," Shianan answered, "which is what I wanted to show you." He withdrew the notes Luca had made. "We—the king's army—we're being cheated."

"Cheated? How so?"

Shianan moved his plate aside and spread the notes, taking a ledger from the stack at the edge of the desk. "Look here, sir. There's a delivery of pork for the commissary every two weeks. And yet here are two payments, recorded on the last day of the month and the first day of the next. Both were paid in full to the merchant. Both were recorded, but in separate books, so the duplication might be overlooked though the accounts balanced."

Septime put down his tea and leaned forward. "Go on."

CHAPTER 30

Shianan returned to his office with an unfamiliar sensation burning warmly in his chest. Septime had been at first keenly interested, and then shocked, and finally outraged at the financial treachery—no doubt fueled by the knowledge they had likely missed the blatant robbery for years, with little interest and less training in examining the complex accounts. He had praised Shianan warmly for the discovery, and if he had noticed that Shianan's notes were not in the same hand as his military reports, he had said nothing.

Shianan whistled a little as he opened his door, pleased at seeing his superior impressed rather than recalling his bone-melting humiliation before the king and others. He crossed his office, ignoring the papers on his desk, and went into his living quarters.

Luca was sleeping with his back to the window, snoring softly. Shianan stopped whistling. If he had not noted Luca's ability to read, he mused, the deception might have continued for years more.

He reached for his sword, and the belt dragged across the chest at the foot of the bed. Luca jerked upright.

"I didn't mean to wake you."

Luca shook his head, blinking, and got to his feet. "No, I've slept. I'll see to the laundry."

Shianan began buckling the sword in place, mentally recounting points he wanted to review in the afternoon's training group. Luca followed him out with a basket of clothes.

They were halfway to the fountain when a chorus of rough laughter drew Shianan's attention. Some of the soldiers had armed themselves with old fruit and were lobbing pieces at Harl. Something dark and juicy struck his temple, spattering over his face.

"Soldiers," Shianan called, his tone colored only slightly, "if you've the time to spare, I have more duties to assign."

Most of the men heard him and recalled business which took them across the courtyard. A few were too involved in their fun to notice and launched another volley, making Harl flinch as half-rotten scraps struck his face.

"Enough!" snapped Shianan. "Unless you'd like to be beside him, get to your own work."

They looked over their shoulders in surprise and scattered. Shianan watched them go as Harl tried unsuccessfully to stretch his fingers to dislodge a piece of sticky fruit from his face.

When he turned back, Luca was staring at the pilloried soldier, the basket tipped unevenly in his loose grasp. His eyes were blank, seeing something more than just Harl. Shianan reached to tap him on the shoulder. "Hey."

Luca started, nearly dropping the basket. "I—I'm sorry."

"What were you thinking?"

Luca shook his head. "Nothing, master."

Shianan noted the change in address. Beyond them Harl twisted, trying to scrape pulp from his eye, but he could not quite reach. Luca swallowed and glanced at Shianan before looking back at Harl, his expression shielded once more.

Shianan exhaled sharply. "We'll see." He gestured toward his quarters. "Put away the clothes."

"Master Shianan?"

"Go."

Luca did, perplexed but obedient. Shianan calculated; morning training had ended only a short while ago, and if he ate lunch over his reports, he could spare an hour or so now. When Luca reappeared, he motioned for the slave to follow.

The soldiers performed their drills and some sparring in a large square. Around it were several smaller areas for group training, and set among them were a few rings, twenty paces or so in width, for individual practice or instruction. Shianan chose one of these, turning to face Luca once they were inside. "Do you know what this is?"

Luca swallowed. "It looks like the holding pens at Furmelle."

"No, no." Shianan went to the wall, made of heavy lumber to withstand impact—they occasionally fought more than each other here—and withdrew two staves from the mounted rack. "You won't have many choices of weapon, but there's usually something to hand that can be used as a staff. We'll start with it."

Luca's eyes widened. "Master Shianan? I—I haven't...."

"Take this one." Shianan tossed the staff toward him.

Luca raised an arm to shield himself, and the staff bounced off his forearm to the sand. "I can't!"

Shianan looked at him. "Take it."

"No! I cannot. I am a merchant's son, a bookkeeper—"

"Are you?" Shianan demanded. "I thought you were a slave. My slave, bound to obey my orders." He pointed to the staff. "Pick it up."

Luca did, moving slowly.

"Hold it in both hands, like so." Shianan demonstrated. "Now, when I come at you—"

"Master, please," Luca protested, his voice shaking. "I cannot do this."

Shianan shrugged. "As you like. I am going to swing at you; you may block or not as it pleases you." He made an exaggerated attack from the side, aiming clearly at Luca's head.

Luca flinched, involuntarily jerking his arms. Shianan altered the path of his staff so that it rapped Luca's smartly between his hands and bounced away. "That will do for a start."

Luca raised his head, opening his eyes wide. "But I...."

"You blocked my attack, as I wanted." Shianan was beginning to sense how very tenuous Luca's hold was, riding the edge of panic. "Again." He made another deliberate and obvious swing, and Luca almost against his will ducked beneath the staff. Shianan again missed the easy target and let his staff bounce off Luca's. "You see?"

Luca stared at him. "You want that I should learn...?"

"I'm teaching you to fight," Shianan answered. "Not as a soldier; you won't be able to hold off a Ryuven. But I'm not asking you to do that. I want you to be able to hold off a similarly armed man."

Luca stared at the staff in his hands. "Why? I'm...."

"Because the Ryuven are not our only enemies," Shianan replied flatly, "and having a helpless slave at my back is no protection. I do this only for my own safety, of course. No one can argue with that." He gestured with his staff. "Be ready; I'm coming again."

The next dozen movements he made were designed not to test nor even to instruct, but simply to induce Luca to manipulate the staff. Emboldened by his accidental successes, Luca began to move a little more freely, actually shifting the staff to meet the coming blow rather than merely flinching behind it.

"Good," Shianan said. "Now, consider that you have several primary angles of defense." He demonstrated each, talking Luca through the corresponding movements. "Let's try each of them."

A few minutes later, Luca was sweating but moving readily to interrupt each of Shianan's blows. "Very good," Shianan said, and he saw Luca's expression shift almost into a smile. "Any questions?"

"No, Master Shianan."

"Good. Then let's reverse it. Come and attack me."

Luca froze.

"Come, you're wasting time."

Luca withdrew a step.

Shianan lowered his staff. "I see. You think this is a trap—that as soon as you touch me, I'll claim you struck me. Do you think that little of me?" He sighed. "Hit me as hard as you can, Luca."

Luca hesitated.

"Strike me. This is my command as your master. Do you disobey me?"

Luca gulped.

"Do it!" Shianan shouted.

Luca swung wildly, squeezing his eyes shut. Shianan moved his staff a few inches and deflected the blow into empty air. "You see? There's no danger at all of hitting me." He spun the staff and grinned. "Feel better?"

"I—no."

Shianan laughed. "Then I suppose you'll have to try again. Go ahead."

Luca raised the staff and then hesitated. "Master—I cannot strike you."

"It's Master Shianan, I told you." Shianan sighed. "Luca.... Within this ring, what passes is not between a master and slave, but instructor and student. You will not be held by the laws governing slavery here, but by the accepted rituals of training. There will be moments when I pass through your defense, but that is no punishment except for flaws in your technique. There will be moments, I hope, when you pass through my defense, and as an instructor I will be glad of that. Do you understand me?"

Luca nodded slowly. "If that is what you want."

"Right now, I want you to come at me from each angle, just as we discussed a moment ago."

"Yes, Master Shianan." He targeted a reluctant swing toward Shianan.

The unskilled attacks had little power, but Shianan did not criticize. As earlier, his first task was simply for Luca to discover there was no threat to these exercises. He remembered demanding whether Luca had ever longed to fight back. It seemed Ande had seen to that.

Finally he signaled a halt. "That's enough for a start. Now we each have other work." Luca nodded, lowering the staff. "Bring your meal and mine to the office." Shianan held out his hand, expecting

Luca to toss the staff to him.

But Luca merely took a few steps to cover the distance between them and offered it to him with a small bob of respect, a slave serving his master. As he handed off the staff, he said quietly, "Thank you, Master Shianan."

CHAPTER 31

"Daranai'rika wishes to see you." The servant eyed Maru disapprovingly. "She's in her garden."

Maru knew no reason for his faint hostility and merely thanked him. There was no profit in being anything but amiable to those with whom he would be living and working later, when he was a part of the household Tamaryl and Daranai would share.

The private garden was shielded well from external eyes. Stone walls had been built to resemble mossy ruins, and climbing flowers covered the net which guarded the sky. A fountain played on one side, its splashing offering a steady and pleasant undercurrent of sound. Maru stopped in the wall's gap and clapped softly for admission.

On the far side of a flowering hedge, Daranai reclined on a narrow couch as the silver-haired servant massaged oil into her feet. "Ah, Maru." She sat upright, withdrawing her feet from the servant, and reached for a piece of fruit from the basket near her.

"You wished to see me?"

She made a dismissive gesture as she peeled the fruit. "It is not urgent. How is the human?" She motioned over her shoulder, and a second servant Maru had not noticed stepped forward to take the rind. "Will you be staying with her?"

Maru had thought she understood this already from Tamaryl. "She is stable but unwell, Daranai'rika. We must stay until Tamaryl'sho opens his own home again."

"And then you will go to his home?" She raised an elegant eyebrow.

"I thank you again for your hospitality to the human rika. I know it must be an inconvenience to you."

Daranai smiled. "Hardly an inconvenience. An affront, perhaps, but no inconvenience."

Maru did not know how to respond to this. "I am sure Tamaryl'sho appreciates it."

She nodded. "Hm." She remained looking at Maru for a moment, saying nothing, and he wondered if he had left something unsaid. Protocol bound him to stay until she dismissed him.

Daranai'rika raised a long finger to brush hair from her face.

"Maru, you have served in Oniwe'aru's house, is that correct?"

"Yes, I have. Oniwe'aru was the nearest lord of obligation. My service fell to him when Ryl'sho disappeared."

"Ryl'sho," she repeated softly with an amused smile.

"I am sorry. Of course he is Tamaryl'sho."

She nodded. "I was only curious. You may go."

"Thank you, Daranai'rika." Maru left the garden.

Daranai sat still a moment. The silver-haired nim near her feet made a small movement. "Shall I continue?"

"No," she answered slowly. "No, I don't think so." She motioned to him. "Stand and let me see you."

The nim who had taken the rind stepped forward. "Daranai'rika, would you like me to—"

"Quiet a moment." She looked back and forth between them. "I am thinking of sending one of you away."

The silver-haired servant glanced down. "I will—"

"Do not interrupt me," she said lightly. She looked at the black-haired Ryuven waiting, his eyes fixed on her. "Jeros has served me before and I know what to expect of him."

Jeros nodded tightly, looking as if he wanted to speak. She raised a hand and casually trailed her fingers over his chest, noting the slight change in his breath and how he shifted his weight forward. He would be eager today.

"But while I rely upon excellent service," she continued, "I cannot bear monotony." Jeros's expression tightened, and she knew he feared disappointment. "Taro, you are a handsome young thing, even incapable of glamour. That is what first prompted me to purchase your debt from Heka'che. Your attentiveness since has also caught my attention."

Taro swallowed. "It is a nim's duty and pleasure to serve," he replied, his eyes on Daranai's feet.

"Duty and pleasure," she repeated. "I've always thought that a wonderful phrase." She looked back at Jeros, who remained obedient if no longer hopeful beside her. "Oh, Jeros, don't look so sad." She reached to caress his cheek and ran a hand down the line of his throat, over where his nipple lay under the thin fabric, and down his torso, drawing her hand away with a little downward flick of the fingers just where his hip curved. "I'm sure I'll find another use for you soon."

"Yes, Daranai'rika," he said hoarsely, and she knew he had been anticipating since she first summoned him to fan away the insects and the heat.

"You may go," she told him, "and be sure to drape the vines behind you. I do not want to be disturbed again."

He flattened his wings and retreated. She turned her gaze on Taro, still at the foot of her reclining couch. "And you, come closer."

He swallowed again. "Daranai'rika, is it—"

"Don't speak yet." She gestured, and this time he obeyed, coming slowly to stand where Jeros had been. "You have done well this first week here."

"Thank you, Daranai'rika."

"I like to reward those who serve me well." She faced him, still seated so that her eyes were even with his chest, and reached to him. His skin twitched as she touched him, sliding the tips of her fingers along his arm. "As you noted yourself, a good nim delights in the opportunity to further serve."

He gulped and stared fixedly at the fountain behind her. "Daranai'rika—"

"Hush."

"Daranai'rika, this is—"

"Quiet." She placed a hand on his hip and turned him so that he faced away from her, his wings folded tightly against his back. "If I choose to take a lover from a lower caste, that is my choice." She reached to the sensitive skin at the roots of the wings.

Taro caught his breath as she stroked him. "The—the...."

"Hush," she soothed. She stroked the tender skin for a long moment, enjoying how he slowly began to breathe against her steady motion. She took the edges of his garment where it split to accommodate his wings and pulled them a little further apart, making him shift slightly. His fingers flexed at his side.

She continued, letting her fingers trail to the base of the wings and wrap around the roots, and his wings began to tremble. She smiled to herself. "Why don't you relax a little?"

His knees weakened, and with a few strokes down the length of his arms she enticed him to sink to the ground beside her couch. Now she reached one hand over his shoulder as she teased his wings, and when her fingers brushed his nipple through the slick garment he tensed.

"I think you are beginning to enjoy yourself," she whispered.

213

"Let me help you." And she slipped her hand beneath his clothing.

It was a simple matter from there to tease and arouse him, licking and kissing his neck or ear as she felt inclined and tantalizing him with fingering. He was still reluctant at first, but no male could remain firm with one hand on his bare flesh and the other on his responsive wing, and when at last she invited him to turn and face her, he was anxious to release the energy she'd built within him. He knelt beside the couch and leaned forward, as greedy for her touch as Jeros had been.

Usually she only teased them at first, building their desire into something she could use, but the handsome silver-haired nim soon broke completely, shivering and leaning into her as she drew her fingertips from abdomen to shoulder. She did not mind frustrating him if it meant he would be more eager the next time, but she was enjoying herself and did not want to be denied. Still, he was a pretty prize and not to be wasted with haste, and so after a few minutes, as he reached for her neck with his lips, she caught his shoulders and held him back. "There," she whispered, smiling, "that is enough for now."

He looked surprised. "But—I—"

"That is enough for now," she repeated. "You have been here only a week, Taro. Be a good and attentive boy, and there will be more later." She found the handful she wanted and gave it an invigorating stroke.

Taro struggled for speech. "I—yes, Daranai'rika. Of course." He licked his lips.

She gave him a little push. "Go back to your quarters." *Go, and reflect that there is no meet substitute for finishing with me.* But she was aroused herself and anxious for her own pleasure. "Send Jeros to me as you go." It did no harm to cultivate a little jealousy among them.

Taro's eyes widened a fraction, but he did not speak. He pulled the garment over his shoulders again and retreated uncomfortably from the garden.

It had been a good start with Taro. His initial reluctance had been broken down and he would be wondering when next she might favor him. It would not be long before he would be desperate to give her pleasure in the hopes that she might reward him.

Jeros arrived quickly; he had not gone far after his dismissal. "Daranai'rika?" he asked, trying to hide the anticipation he hardly dared hold.

She smiled at his excitement. "I am in desire of a devoted

servant."

His face broke into a relieved, eager grin. "I will do my best for you, Daranai'rika."

CHAPTER 32

Luca was checking the drying laundry when a knock came at the door. He went to answer it, as Shianan glanced up from his writing.

The man outside wore royal livery. "The Count of Bailaha is summoned to His Majesty's presence."

Luca's throat tightened. "I will tell him."

His master had heard the message. He sat very still at the desk, staring at the squat ink bottle before him. "Well, then, there's nothing for it," he said finally. "Luca, is there a dry tunic with a better appearance than this one?"

"I'll find one, Master Shianan," Luca told him.

Shianan's fingers were slow on the laces of his fresh tunic. Luca exchanged his own well-worn shirt for another Shianan had given him. Shianan hesitated, his face ashen, and breathed deeply several times, as if fighting a sneeze. Then he crossed quickly to the night relief pot in the corner and vomited into it.

Luca stared in surprise and then hurried to the wash stand. When Shianan straightened, Luca mutely held out a damp towel and a cup of water.

Shianan exhaled a shuddering breath. "How they'd laugh to see that."

Luca said nothing.

Shianan took the water and rinsed his mouth, spitting into the pot again. "Blech. Thank you." He swallowed and wiped his pale face. "I didn't know I'd reached such a low point." He looked at Luca. "Why are you changed?"

"I am accompanying you, Master Shianan. In case you need something during the audience."

Shianan's stone face cracked into bitter laughter. "You little fool. You double-dyed little fool." He sighed. "You cannot help me here, Luca. What would you do, argue with the king himself? You'd save me nothing and earn yourself a week of whipping."

Luca swallowed. "But I may accompany you as far as the audience room?"

Shianan blinked, surprise overcoming the cynicism. "You— you can. You may. I don't know why you would want to, but of course you may." He hesitated. "Thank you."

"I'll get your cloak."

They did not speak as they went to the palace and then wound their way through the corridors. Shianan asked and was told the king was meeting with military officers and advisors in one of the newer chambers.

Shianan exhaled slowly. "That is good news and bad," he confided softly to Luca as they walked. "He meets me alone in the upper chambers, and he is sometimes more—demonstrative—there. I doubt he would be so open before the others. But he is not afraid to shame me before them, as you saw. And there is no reason for me to be telling you this."

Luca merely nodded, unsure how to respond. Something had opened between them, exchanged their secrets, and it was a treacherous road for a slave to walk. Easier and safer by far to simply perform the duties required and avoid notice—but he could not be that any longer with this master who was as much a slave as he was.

They reached the chambers and the man outside recognized Shianan. "Go on, Bailaha. They are expecting you."

Shianan took a deep breath and entered, sinking almost immediately into a kneeling position. Luca dropped to the floor behind him. He meant to retreat and wait in the antechamber, but then he saw two other men in wrist cuffs standing against the wall. "Rise, Bailaha," said the king, and as Shianan straightened Luca moved beside the other slaves.

The room was less full this time, and those present were obviously military. Luca kept his eyes down but wished he dared watch. "Bailaha," the king began, "General Septime has brought something to our attention."

Something flared through Luca, a resentment that Septime should receive credit instead of Shianan. Before he could marvel that he retained a sense of injustice, the king continued.

"The army is a critical limb of this nation, protecting our people from other lands, from the southern warlords, from the Ryuven, all active threats to our safety. It is vital to our survival. But while we value the army, we cannot afford to spend unwisely in its maintenance, wasting the people's taxes."

Luca swallowed and clenched his fists. Why didn't he get to the point? It was agony to hear him, dreading what was to come. He could not imagine how his master suffered, standing before them all.

"Your Majesty," Shianan began, his voice uneven, "I know we cannot afford to waste our resources. If we had been able to learn sooner—"

"But we did not," King Jerome interrupted. "No one did, not until now. I am told the books were complicated and deceptive. That is why we are so pleased you uncovered this treachery."

Luca caught his breath. Pleased?

"If Bailaha had not found this, we should have been robbed further and further. A fifth of our spending! That is a princely amount. We have already spoken on dismissing and trying our present officers and suppliers—though I confess to some surprise you were not here for those discussions."

Shianan struggled for words, clearly off-balance. "I thought only to report the findings to General Septime, Your Majesty. I believe him capable of addressing them."

"You did not seek recognition for this work?"

Shianan bowed his head. "The recognition is given always to the master. If Your Majesty has charged certain subjects with fulfilling certain duties, it is credit to you that they perform those duties."

"Well spoken!" The king laughed. "Did you hear that, gentlemen? A philosopher as well as a soldier. Let's drink in honor of that thought and of the recognition he has earned from his master."

The king continued to speak, but Luca, nearly wavering with relief, hardly heard. The king had not attacked Shianan, had not humiliated him and cut him. Luca's work had not endangered his master but benefited him.

Royal servants carried around beverages as the talk shifted to the problem of profit-minded purchasers and conspiring merchants, and Generals Kannan and Septime promised to pursue the wrongdoers. Luca's feet began to ache, but he had long practice in waiting motionless before Ande and with less optimistic prospects. Finally the king dismissed them and Shianan bowed and backed from the room with the others, Luca scrambling on numb legs to follow.

Shianan nodded to the other officers, made a few friendly comments and good-byes, and strode down the corridor. Luca hurried to match his pace, his legs tingling with pooled blood. They left the palace and went into the cold air, now dark with advancing twilight. Why did his master hurry so? Was he upset?

But then Shianan reached a corner and turned abruptly. Luca followed and found him leaning against the wall, his head thrown back in ecstatic relief. "He was pleased," he whispered, beaming at the stars. "Did you hear him? He was *proud* of me!"

Luca's shoulders slackened. "Yes, Master Shianan."

Shianan looked at him seriously. "I haven't forgotten this was your doing. I know a slave's work belongs to his master, but you sought that out on your own."

"I am happy to have been of service, Master Shianan."

Shianan laughed. "Do you know, I think this might be the first time I actually believe a slave saying that." He reached out impulsively and seized Luca's forearm, clasping over the cuff as he would clasp another man's wrist. "Thank you, Luca."

Luca stared down at their hands. "Master Shianan," he managed.

"Luca, Luca, I have ruined you already." Shianan sounded a little giddy. "I teach you to fight, I let you demand to accompany me. What is a handshake?"

Luca looked at their overlapping hands and then seized Shianan's wrist. "Thank you, Master Shianan." He held the wrist tightly, clinging to the first sympathetic touch he'd had since Furmelle—since before Furmelle. "There is no one I would rather serve."

"Then you are a bigger fool than I thought, because even in my current rapture I still know that mere hours from now I will be the bastard again, but so be it. I will not argue with you." He sighed and released Luca, rubbing a hand across his eyes. "I drank too much, I think. I couldn't believe my fortune, and I had two or three glasses of that stuff. Four. I think. It's headier than our common tap, anyway."

"I'll build up the brazier when we return and bring some water to cut the drink."

Shianan shook his head, leaning backward against the wall. "No, no. Don't cut anything. I want to savor this." He grinned at the dark sky.

Chapter 33

Ariana woke, not screaming this time but befuddled with her drug-induced sleep. Maru left the candle—a mixed blessing in the windowless room—on the far side of the room and went to her, careful to avoid touching or jostling her. "Rika? How do you feel?"

"Make it stop," she mumbled.

"I'm sorry, rika, there is nothing more—"

"You made it stop." She flexed her fingers slightly. "Doesn't hurt so bad."

Nori'bel's herbs were working. "Good. Good, rika. How do you feel?"

"My name," she said with a tone managing to be haughty even slurred, "is Ariana."

He smiled. "Ariana'rika, then."

"M'lady mage."

He chuckled. "You must be feeling better."

She moved her hand slowly across the bed. "Mage."

"Yes, I know. Tamaryl'sho told me you were a mage." *And you tried to strike me magically only last night.*

"No. Not a mage. That mage."

"What mage?"

"Black Mage!" she snapped into the pillow.

"You are the Black Mage, yes," he repeated. "A member of the Circle."

Tamaryl had told no one else Ariana was the daughter of the White Mage. Every mage was a prize, and one of the Circle even more, but possessing the only child of the Circle's highest mage might be a significant advantage. Tamaryl could never keep her.

"Hungry," Ariana muttered.

Maru glanced at the closed door, the luxury which kept Ariana from the rest of the household. "It's the middle of the night," he apologized. "I'll bring something in the morning."

She mumbled something unintelligible in which he could distinguish only the word "Tam."

"Tamaryl'sho is away," he said. "He's been given a task from Oniwe'aru." He seated himself on the side of the bed, adjusting his

221

wings over the edge. "Ryl is in a difficult position, I think. That is why he left you to my care."

She made an effort to speak. "You call him Ryl."

"Yes, I do. Tamaryl is his given name, but I have called him Ryl since we were children." He smiled. "I shouldn't, though, at least not in front of others. It's not fitting to make easy with sho names."

She opened her eyes unnaturally wide. "I'm not sleepy," she told him urgently, her words slurred. "Not real me. My mind is awake."

He nodded patiently. "Of course."

"No," she mumbled into the pillow. "I think. Body won't move."

The soporific drug would weight her limbs. "It's all right."

She closed her eyes again. "I want Tam." A small circle of damp appeared on the pillow beneath her eyes. "I want home."

Maru felt a sudden sympathy. This young human female had been seized from her own world in a rush of betraying magic and dropped in an enemy atmosphere that was deadly to her. She could survive, but the cost was agonizing. Even as a human, she was owed his pity and his sympathy. "Hush," he whispered, wondering if he dared touch her, whether it would soothe or hurt her. "Sleep again. Tamaryl will return, and he has promised to take you home again when he can."

He wished Tamaryl good fortune and speed on his journey.

Tamaryl struck down the first Ryuven with ease, directing the powerful magic with a gesture that sent him flying to the side. The second he spun away and the third he used as a weapon to strike the fourth. The last hesitated, alarmed by the fate of his companions, and Tamaryl pinned him beneath a barrier, immobilizing him. Power coursed through him, invigorating him with the joy of magic which had been almost entirely denied him for so long.

The Ryuven regarded him with wide, frightened eyes. "Tamaryl'sho!"

Tamaryl scowled. "You did not think so a moment before." He turned to face Rarn'sho. "Are we finished with this?"

Rarn's throat worked visibly. "Forgive me. I thought—it has been so long—and there was no word of your return...."

"Only a fool would falsely claim a traitor's name," Tamaryl growled, releasing the remaining Ryuven with a magical shove that sent him sprawling. Around them the others were regaining their feet and regarding him cautiously. "That should lend some credence to my claim. Oniwe'aru has sent me to deal with you."

"Deal with me? Why? I have done him no wrong."

"Apparently that is not true," Tamaryl returned. "Aktonn's taxes and tribute have dwindled from what he once received."

Rarn'sho grew defensive. "How can I help that? The land is not as rich as it was. Is that my doing? Perhaps it was failing before he awarded it to me—does that make it my fault? Or did he intend for me to be a scapegoat?"

Indignation ran hot through Tamaryl, and his wings flexed. "If you would not dare to say that to Oniwe'aru himself, do not say it to me." He turned on the watching che, seeing them flinch. "Do you have here any of those who served the former sho? An overseer, a steward?"

They glanced among themselves. "Unum'che is left," someone offered. "He is not here, but he lives near."

"Bring him," Tamaryl ordered. "Perhaps he can make some sense of what you have done."

Rarn'sho frowned at this usurping of authority in his own hall, but he did not challenge Tamaryl's order. Perhaps he sensed that Tamaryl was bathing in power, reveling in the magic inherent in the very air. The human world was sparse in magic, even in a mage's home, and bound in the form of human boy without any mageskill, Tamaryl had starved for magic like one might starve for food.

He had almost unconsciously limited himself while in and near the Palace of Red Sands, not wanting to appear flagrant before Oniwe'aru. Now, really dipping into power for the first time since his return—since his departure—the temptation to simply play with it and thrill in its kinetic vibrancy called intoxicatingly to him. But Tamaryl could not afford to show childlike wonder to Rarn'sho, and so he resisted firmly.

He turned back to Rarn'sho. "It seems we will have some time to wait while this Unum'che is summoned," he said evenly. "May I prevail upon your hospitality?"

"My hospitality?" Rarn'sho seemed to come to himself, realizing only now how fully he had trespassed. He looked uncomfortably at his remaining che and then lowered himself to both knees, placing his hands flat on the floor before him. He spread his fingers so that the tips of the forefingers touched, wincing a little with the humiliation of the gesture. "I offer you my apology," he said uncomfortably. "Your welcome was—not at all proper. Please accept

223

my hospitality for your stay."

Tamaryl nodded graciously toward Rarn'sho. "I am pleased to accept both your apology and your hospitality. Thank you."

Rarn'sho rose and quickly called for a meal and drinks. Tamaryl took an offered seat and sampled a fruit he had not tasted in years and years.

He was no longer the human slave boy.

CHAPTER 34

Shianan slept late, and Luca was already taking down the dry clothing when he woke. "Good morning, Master Shianan."

"Hm." Shianan sat up groggily and pushed a hand through his hair. "I did not think I had drunk so much last night, but…. No, I'm not quite ill with it. Ow." He looked around the room. "Bring some water?"

Luca went to the stand. "There's only a little here."

"Bring what's there—my throat is scratchy. Why isn't there fresh? It's not as if there's too much for you to do."

Luca stopped moving.

Shianan shook his head. "I didn't mean anything by that," he said, rubbing his eyes. "I don't feel quite centered. That drink was certainly different from the ale in the serving hall or even the potent brew at the Brining Tankard. Don't hold to anything I say."

It wasn't the drink. By evening, Shianan was irrefutably ill. He complained of cold, shivering even after Luca roused the brazier to open flame and brought him a blanket as he worked—an act which irritated him. "I'm no old man to be bundled and carried," he grumped, rubbing his arms. "Leave me alone."

Luca said something about fever and brought a small pot of broth from the kitchen, keeping it warm in the brazier. "I've brought something warm to drink. And it's growing late. Shall I lock the door?"

"One more," Shianan said hoarsely. "I have to see the White Mage yet, about the shield."

"Are the mages raising it?" Luca's voice was taut. Shianan felt guilt for his suggestion that the blood which had destroyed the shield might be thought useful in remaking it.

But the thought of the shield frightened him too. "They cannot," he answered. "Not yet." He clutched his mug of broth close and shook his head. "Bring me a heavier tunic. It's chill out there."

He swayed as he pulled the tunic over his head and reached for the wall's support, cursing the fever. He had no time for illness. Weakness frustrated him. He tugged his cloak over his shoulders. "I doubt anyone will come this late, but if so, say I'll see them tomorrow."

Shianan stepped out into the dark, and the cold seeped through his cloak. It did not take long to reach the White Mage's office in the

Wheel.

Hazelrig looked unhealthy, leaning on his desk as Shianan let himself in. He got to his feet hastily. "Your lordship!"

"Please, my lord mage, let's sit," Shianan said, looking at the chair longingly. "Two men with such a secret cannot afford to stand on ceremony."

"As you say." Hazelrig returned to his chair and looked at Shianan, clearly trying for a more normal conversation at least to start. "How is the slave?"

"Luca?" Shianan shrugged. "He's recovering. But, king's sweet oats, he's—I don't know."

Ewan raised his eyebrows. "Yes?"

Shianan sighed. "Have you ever offered a scrap to a street dog? And even while you're tossing the meat, it's cringing away from you, certain you're going to kick it? And it's so—frustrating, you're half-tempted to throttle the thing anyway?"

One corner of Ewan's mouth shifted. "That might hamper earning its trust, perhaps."

Shianan made an irritated sound. "I know. But sweet all, it's annoying."

Ewan leaned back in his chair, his voice light. "So why feed the street dog at all?"

"I don't know," muttered Shianan, regretting saying anything. "I just thought, you know, it might be a good dog." He rubbed his eyes. *And stray dogs pack together.* "Have you heard more from them?"

"No," answered Hazelrig unhappily, leaning again on his desk.

"So we have to stall." Shianan gestured. "You can't let them do it!"

"I know that, but how? There are debates on how Ande caused its failure, but there's no question whether we can recreate the shield itself."

"Can't you say it might just collapse and harm someone again?"

"These are mages, your lordship. Of the Circle. They understand magic. They know human blood catalyzed the shield against human flesh. They know human blood alone should not have affected the shield without something from the original spell to unmake it. You understand? They suspect Ande of sabotaging the shield."

Shianan stared. "To what purpose?"

"Right now, the supposition is that he planned to seal off the city of Alham and seize power for the Gehrn. Some are presenting evidence that—"

Shianan groaned and dropped his face into his hands. "That will be the final knot to secure the millstone about my neck."

"I beg your pardon?"

Shianan waved weakly. "I'm sorry. Go on."

The mage looked at him a moment before continuing. "I cannot see any way to stall the recreation of the shield without drawing suspicion. And yet of course we cannot allow that."

Ariana would be trapped forever among the Ryuven. "Then we must do something else."

"You could steal the Shard."

Shianan blinked. "I'm sorry—what did you say?"

Hazelrig looked at the desk, disassociating himself from the words. "If the Shard is missing, we cannot remake the shield."

"You want me to steal the Shard of Elan? How? Where would I hide it? And—why me?"

Hazelrig sighed. "There must be someplace a military commander could hide an object. A rarely-visited outpost, or a warehouse crate marked 'bedclothes.' And it should be you, because you can travel with less suspicion."

And because the bastard has less to lose, Shianan thought. *The king has already half-accused me of conspiring with the Gehrn. His hand moved to his sore ribs. If the Shard disappears, it will be my fault anyway. Why not at least earn the blame?*

"I'm sorry. I know it's an enormous risk—"

"It is no risk," Shianan interrupted. "It is certain arrest."

"What?"

"The king has already chastised me for bringing the Gehrn within our walls, even before the shield fell. If he hears now the Gehrn planned the failure of the shield...." Shianan shook his head. "Someone will accuse me of accepting a Gehrn bribe along with the Shard itself, and the only witness to what happened in Davan is not here to speak."

"Then...."

"Then I will be arrested and made to confess."

Hazelrig stared. "He would not turn on you so quickly. There would have to be evidence."

"Would anyone need evidence?" Shianan could hear stark bitterness in his voice. "But I won't confess to knowing about Tam. I'll only admit I was paid by Ande to allow access to the Shard. That should allow you time enough to hear from Tam again, I hope."

"You can't mean you'd allow yourself—"

"I won't have much choice in the matter, will I?"

"But, your lordship, you could plead ignorance."

Shianan gave him a frank look. "That will not be enough. If the king can be angry that I did not prevent the shield's collapse, he will be far more so that I allowed the Shard to be stolen."

Hazelrig shook his head. "If you believe that's so, then forget it. We will find another way."

Shianan took a breath. "No, I will do it."

"Your lordship! You've just said—"

"I will do it. I want—we have to give them every chance. Tam—Tamaryl will return her if he can, right? We have to give them as much time as we can." He placed his hands flat on the desk to still their fidgeting. "Will you take care of Luca? He deserves better than the block after I'm taken."

"Your lordship, I don't want to see you arrested. There must be another way to help her." Hazelrig leaned over the desk. "This is for her, isn't it?"

The words hit solidly in his stomach. "You—what do you mean?"

"Your lordship... Do not throw yourself away for her. None of us want that."

Shianan dropped his head, his fevered eyes burning. "I have nothing else to offer."

"You don't know what may come. We'll find another way."

Shianan exhaled. "You must think me an enormous fool."

"To the contrary," Hazelrig answered carefully, "I think you somewhat impulsive, but not a fool. I suppose I should be flattered you find my daughter worth the risk of torture."

Shianan smiled bitterly. "I confess, I am not eager to prove that. But there are very few friends among whom I may count the lady. I would not want to lose her."

"I see." Hazelrig shifted. "Your lordship—Becknam—neither she nor I would be pleased to have her home again at the cost of yourself. Please don't make her carry that guilt."

Shianan flinched. "You argue unfairly, my lord mage. But I understand." He inhaled. "Do you have other instructions for me?"

"If I think of a way to stall the remaking of the shield, I will tell you. In the meantime, if you think you are under suspicion already...."

Hazelrig looked solemnly at Shianan. "Be careful, Becknam—may I call you by that name?"

"As I said, men who share secrets cannot stand on formality."

"And if you—I cannot say I would have chosen you," Hazelrig said frankly, "but I am not distressed to hear of your interest, either. Let me—"

Shianan shook his head quickly. "I have not professed anything, my lord mage. I am not fool enough—I say only that I would help a friend in any way I can."

"Of course." Hazelrig sat back. "I apologize for speaking out of turn."

"Thank you, my lord mage." There was a sudden brittle formality between them, both anxious to deny the unexpected exchange. "And now I'm afraid I must ask to leave you. I am not quite well, as you can see. Is there anything else?"

"No, your lordship. I will let you know if I think of anything."

Shianan excused himself and went out into the cold wind, his cheeks burning with emotion and fever. The wind whipped at his face and tore at his hair. He pushed aside the mage's conversation and thought anxiously of warm soup, a heated bed, undreaming slumber. He wanted to bury himself in blankets and escape in sleep.

CHAPTER 35

Oniwe nodded with an approving smile. "Restoring an old steward—very good. I wonder that Rarn'sho did not think of that himself."

"It was not difficult," Tamaryl said modestly, before Oniwe heard it from another. "The che knew where to find him. But Rarn'sho was anxious to make the rule entirely his, and no one dared recall a relic from the previous lord."

Oniwe sniffed. "The previous lord turned his back in battle. Do not let your tone mock Rarn'sho too much." He gestured for Tamaryl to rise. "So you think yourself finished there?"

"I spoke at length with Unum'che," he answered, "and I reminded Rarn'sho that depriving you of taxes and tributes was poor gratitude for such an honor. I think you should see a marked change within months, though it will need a year or two to recover, of course."

"And what will you do now?"

Tamaryl gestured. "I have yet to visit Holbruc. But I thought first to report to you."

"In case I, in a fit of benevolence, restore you as well?" Oniwe smiled. "Not yet, Tamaryl'sho. Not yet. But I am impressed by your confidence after Aktonn. They listened so eagerly to you?"

"I did not receive a warm welcome—as I expect you anticipated, Oniwe'aru."

The ruler chuckled. "It has been a long time."

"And you foresaw I would need to fight for recognition."

"And how better to know if you had degraded during your time in the human world? By the Essence, what if you had been tainted and could no longer comport yourself as sho?"

"Our blood, Oniwe'aru, does not dilute so easily."

Oniwe raised his eyebrows and nodded in acknowledgment, smiling. "A worthy point, half-brother. You contend, then, you are the warrior you were? Even after your Subduing?"

Tamaryl sobered. "It was a binding, Oniwe'aru, by a mage of exquisite power. I assisted in it. It was not a Subduing."

"I see." Oniwe's mouth curved. "What a sight it must have been, turning your own power against yourself."

Tamaryl ignored the sting of the words. Oniwe meant little by them, or he would have saved the insult for an audience.

"So." Oniwe turned to the low table beside him and poured a drink. "When will you bring this girl to me?"

Tamaryl blinked. "Oniwe'aru?"

"Your mistress. I would like to see her. I want to know what kind of human could command a Pairvyn. When will you bring her?"

Tamaryl hesitated. "I have not seen her yet, but she was not well when I left. I do not know how she fares."

Oniwe made a vague gesture. "If she has not died yet, she will probably live. Bring her tomorrow, before you go on to Holbruc."

Tamaryl bowed, his heart racing. Had Oniwe'aru guessed her identity? Or was he merely curious?

Oniwe extended an arm, offering a cup to Tamaryl. "We shall see what kind of human can compel my finest warrior."

Ariana squeezed her eyes against the light, but the heat beat upon her face no matter how she writhed. "Sun...."

The arms cradling her did not shift. "What's that? Hush, it's all right. Don't squirm so. What is it?"

"Sun...!"

"Oh!" Tamaryl paused, her weight steady in his arms. "Maru, please?"

Hands reached to adjust the wrap around her body and head, shading her face. She relaxed marginally.

Tamaryl had returned the night before—she thought it was night, because she'd heard him say "supper" to someone, but it was difficult to distinguish night and day. Her room had no windows, for which she was vaguely grateful, and she could not track the passage of time in her drugged state. But Tamaryl had returned, and she had been glad to hear his voice and to sense him near her, looking over her, speaking to her. Maru had given her the stupefying drug again, which she craved and hated, but she had tried to tell Tamaryl she was glad to see him and that she wanted to go home. He had not understood, and she'd heard Maru explain that she was insensible but for brief periods, when she needed the drug again.

That was not true. She did need the mixture, even begged for it at times. But the drug did not make her senseless, it only dulled her senses and deadened her movements and speech. She could still hear, could still see when she could make her affected eyelids obey her will. She could still think, when not pressed into unrestful sleep. She was incoherent, but not incognizant.

But it was nearly impossible to tell them so when her words came out slurred and slow. She could not even manage to shade her own eyes; how was she to make them understand she was still herself?

But she wasn't. She had not been able to summon magic to her defense when startled by Maru. It was this place, the Ryuven world— it was foreign to her. Here magic was everywhere, as plentiful as air, and it did not heed her arcane training. It bombarded her, plagued her, made her feel the touch of every fiber in her clothing, the scrape of every hair across her skin. It magnified the sound of every footstep, the creak of every board, the whir of insect wings, the rush of breath as Maru slept across the room, the cutting breeze, the glare of a candle, the scorch of a light, until she thrashed and scratched and begged for the drink that made it all subside into a dull blur.

Tamaryl was carrying her to Oniwe'aru, he'd said. Some part of Ariana not completely muted by the drug recoiled and shouted desperately that Oniwe'aru was the lord of the Ai, the most powerful clan of the Ryuven, and he could not have kind thoughts for a mage of the Great Circle. But she had not been able to articulate her fears, and no one had heard. And then Tamaryl had lifted her into his arms, and a comforting familiarity settled over her. Tam wouldn't let anything happen to her. Tam was faithful, trustworthy. As long as she was with Tam, she would be all right.

She knew she did not wholly believe that. Tam had lied to her. He had hidden his true self for years. But she was lost and helpless, she needed to trust someone or she would go mad, and so she trusted Tam.

They entered a building, cool with shade and carefully-directed breezes. Tamaryl spoke with a female guard and then handed Ariana to Maru. Maru was a little shorter than Tamaryl and the difference bothered her, though she wasn't sure how she could even sense the height with her eyes tightly closed.

"Oniwe'aru," Tamaryl said in Tam's voice, aged years.

"Enter, Tamaryl'sho," came a resonant answer.

This was Oniwe'aru. This was the Ryuven who had nearly killed Tamaryl, who had killed thousands of human soldiers in invasions to her world. Ariana blinked her eyes open, trying to see, and then Maru fell.

It seemed a dizzying plunge and she gasped as the air rushed past her. She thrashed for purchase, and Maru's arms tightened as he caught his breath. "Ariana'rika!" he whispered, the sound loud in her ears. "Hush! Hush. I have you."

He was only kneeling, like Tamaryl. Like anyone might do before a monarch. It was only her sensitivity which made it so frightening. Ariana turned her head, feeling foolish.

"Quiet," he whispered, his lips barely moving. "I nearly dropped you. Be still. Nothing will happen."

Why did he feel the need to reassure her?

"Rise, Tamaryl'sho," the rich voice said. "And Maru, bring her forward. I want to see her."

Ariana worked her fingers into position to cast a defense, but only empty air hung between her fingertips. She grasped at the wrap, absurdly wanting to shield herself.

"She is still unwell," Tamaryl was explaining. "Nori'bel has kept her alive and with us, but our atmosphere afflicts her and she must be kept drugged."

"Drugged?" Oniwe'aru stood enormous over her, staring down. She felt his eyes, heavy and burning, and even with her own eyes tightly shut she felt him, felt his hot breath touching her skin, felt the weight of his gaze—

"It burns!" The heat of his breath, the warmth of Maru's skin, it was too much, it reached through the wrap and her soft clothes and burned her. She twisted, sweating, and tried to shield herself with her hands. "Go—let go—let me go...!"

"Ryl'sho," Maru said, and her head vibrated with the sound. Tamaryl took her and the weight of her body pressed the weave of her clothing against her like a thousand needles into her flesh. She moaned and pushed at him, and in the dark of her mind's eye she saw a bright glowing reservoir of power hanging above her. But it was unreachable and she turned away, seeking relief, and then Maru slid a hand beneath her hair, cradling her head, and offered her the drink.

It was bitter as always, as if it would peel her tongue, but she drank it eagerly, and only a moment later the torment began to ease. She sighed and felt her muscles loosen.

"Well." Oniwe'aru sounded surprised. "This is the female who kept you for so many years?"

"It was another who first bound me," Tamaryl answered. "But she was my human mistress."

Oniwe'aru chuckled. "I wish I could have seen you kneeling

before her, begging forgiveness for some negligence. All is forgiven, Tamaryl'sho. I could not demand a harsher penalty than what you inflicted upon yourself." His voice grew formal. "Return to your former place and take again your champion rank."

"Oniwe'aru...!"

"Do not be so amazed. Have you not wondered why no one had taken the title? There were some who tried, of course. But none of them were your equal. In truth, I felt I could not award it to anyone inferior, and I waited to see who should rise in your stead." He chuckled. "I never imagined it would be you again."

"Thank you, Oniwe'aru." Tamaryl handed Ariana to Maru again, where she lay dreamily, only half-hearing, and knelt. "My pleasure is always to serve you."

"Rise, Tamaryl'sho." Oniwe moved a few paces. "I return to you your position, your rank, your title, and your friend—Maru was of course bound to the nearest lord of obligation, but I return him now to your service."

"Thank you, Oniwe'aru."

"And this human." Oniwe's voice grew amused. "I see she is not likely to be of much use. She does not look very much in control even of her own speech."

Tamaryl cleared his throat. "Actually, Oniwe'aru, she may speak—Maru has talked with her."

"Yes?" Oniwe looked at Maru and Ariana.

Maru nodded tightly. "When the drug is wearing away, I speak to her, and she answers. She tries to tell me things."

"What kind of things?"

She could feel Maru's breath shorten. "She says she can feel the cold. She says she wants to go home."

"That is all?"

"If I speak to her, she will usually respond. Rika, can you hear me?"

Oniwe laughed. "Rika?"

Maru stiffened. Tamaryl shifted forward. "She is a mage, which is a position of some standing in her own world. Maru acknowledges her personal rank."

"Of course. I'd forgotten mages are accorded rank for their rarity. Maru, do you think she could offer any useful information?"

Maru hesitated. "I cannot pretend to know what would be useful knowledge. But she is not well, Oniwe'aru, and she cannot sustain rational speech."

Oniwe'aru sighed. "Well, then. What do you intend to do with her, Tamaryl'sho?"

He stepped closer to her. "She saved my life by releasing the binding when we were about to be killed, and I saved hers by bringing her here. I mean to carry her again to her own world."

"You would return a mage to them? To fight us in the future?"

"As she returned your Pairvyn to you."

Oniwe'aru laughed. "Well spoken, Tamaryl'sho. Though, I do not think she looks capable of withstanding the between-worlds in this condition. If she improves, I would like to see her again, but she is yours to do with as you will."

"Thank you, Oniwe'aru."

A word pricked at Ariana, a vague urgency, but she was drifting in a soft place where there was no itching clothing, no blaring noise, no burning heat.... She dimly recognized the movement of Maru's kneeling once more, and then she was asleep.

CHAPTER 36

The first merchant caught Shianan and Luca off their guard. "Just a drink together," he suggested with a smile, and as Luca poured the wine he'd brought, he made small talk about the advancing season, and the state of trade, and then he began detailing his reliable and cost-effective supply of spearheads.

Luca worked it out before Shianan, of course. Though Commander Becknam wasn't procuring supplies for the army, as the officer credited with exposing the fraud, his approval and endorsement were logical assets in the fight for the newly available military market. The second merchant brought a smoked ham one evening and explained how his house had come to be a respected provider in Alham and elsewhere.

The food and drink surprised Shianan. "I can't be seen receiving gifts," he protested, and Luca knew he was thinking not of his position as commander, but as bastard. "Thank you, but I must—"

"Oh, it is nothing more than a gift," interrupted the latest merchant smoothly. He drew a bottle of wine from a bag. "Honest men such as you cannot be influenced by material goods. But it is important you trust our supplies, and so you must have a sample. Here is an excellent vintage, suitable for officers like yourself—so you may know our product, of course." He smiled broadly.

"Of course," Shianan repeated, his smile less broad. "Thank you for your consideration."

The next had the decency to appoint a time for dinner in Shianan's office. As Luca admitted him he noted the bright red sash crossing his chest. From Vandoga, obviously, and probably anxious to sell leather goods.

"Good evening," Shianan offered. "Please have a seat. Luca, the drinks?"

The conversation began on pleasant, neutral topics—the changing weather, the happy reprieve from fighting the warlords, the new southern market. And then, as Luca served, the Vandogan skillfully turned the topic to the provision of military goods. Luca had been right, he had leather harness to sell as well as hardened leather armor.

As they spoke, Luca waited a few paces away, ready to supply more wine as the cups ran low. Vandoga's vast grazing ranges lay between their mercantile and industrial cities and the profitable markets of Alham and others. They relied on sea trade to deliver their goods. Luca's father had been negotiating a profitable deal shipping Vandogan cargo when the loss of the *Alamar* had lessened confidence in their house....

Luca respectfully retreated a few steps and then turned toward the other room. They would be ready for bread and honey soon. He checked over the tray and brought it to the table.

"Your prices do appear reasonable," Shianan acknowledged. "And your proposed delivery does seem efficient."

"I know you have several others seeking this same arrangement," the merchant said modestly. "May I pour you a drink?"

Luca felt a prick of guilty apprehension that he had not been quick enough to refill his master's wine. But the Vandogan added only an inch to Shianan's half-filled cup. Shianan reached for it automatically, and as the Vandogan raised his own wine a tingle of recognition ran through Luca.

"Master!" he burst. "I—a message has just arrived for you, my lord. An urgent message, by the other door."

Shianan paused, his wine halfway to his lips. Luca kept still, counting that the merchant did not know there was no second entrance to Shianan's rooms and that Shianan trusted him enough to accept the interruption.

At last Shianan spoke. "Urgent, you say?" He set down the wine. "I hope the patrols haven't been seeing imaginary Ryuven again. Will you excuse me?" He nodded to the merchant and rose, and Luca followed him into the other room.

Luca closed the door behind him as Shianan turned to face him. "I suppose you have something important to justify this."

Luca nodded eagerly. "That merchant is Vandogan."

"I know that."

"By Vandogan custom, the acceptance of a drink, poured and taken together, is a binding contract."

Shianan frowned. "Oh. Oh, I see." He considered. "So I was a sip away from committing to accept his bid."

"Yes, Master Shianan."

One side of Shianan's mouth quirked into a half-smile. "And I suppose our friend outside counted on my ignorance of this? We could hardly renege on a contract, and I could not argue without embarrassing myself and the army." He exhaled. "Luca, you are the saving of the king's army, I'm afraid."

Luca flushed and added hurriedly, "He's already poured the wine. You cannot drink it even now."

"Then I'll have to be careful to avoid drinking," Shianan replied. "Now, let me return to my guest."

Luca held the door for him, and Shianan resumed his seat with a casual air.

"Nothing terrible, I hope?" asked the Vandogan.

Shianan shook his head with a smile. "Not at all. I am free to remain with you."

"Excellent." The merchant lifted his cup in an easy manner.

Shianan's hand moved toward his wine and then he arrested it with a frown, reaching instead for a piece of bread. The merchant's eyes followed his movement.

"Would you like some samples of our product?" he asked after a moment, taking bread and honey.

"Thank you," Shianan replied, "but I have no venue to test them myself. I have only Luca, as you see, who needs no harness for his duties here. I might give one or two to the caravan masters and ask their opinion."

"Certainly!" The merchant nodded. "I'll have several delivered tomorrow."

"Thank you." Shianan's hand moved unconsciously toward the cup again. He paused, regarding his treacherous hand, and then reached clumsily for the wine, upsetting the cup. "Oh! What a mess. Luca?"

Luca successfully contained the spill and then, righting the empty cup, poured fresh wine. He kept his eyes carefully on the soiled table, not risking a conspiratorial glance with Shianan or a peek toward the merchant.

"Thank you, Luca." Shianan lifted his cup and drank, and then he looked toward the merchant, his expression friendly. "If I can be forgiven for my clumsiness.... I think your offer is very fair, and I will be pleased to discuss it with my superiors."

The merchant smiled, the pleased smile of a man who knows he's been bested but enjoyed the game. "Thank you, my lord." He gestured toward Luca. "Your servant is quite efficient. I'm sure you must receive many compliments on him. Is he perchance for sale?"

Luca tensed. But Shianan chuckled. "Thank you, but no. I find him indispensable."

"I thought as much," the Vandogan answered with a smile, "but it was worth the asking, anyway. Have you any more questions for me, your lordship?"

"I don't believe so." Shianan rose and gave a small bow. "Thank you for your time this evening."

"The pleasure was mine," the merchant responded. "And in appreciation, let me offer you this. Any man of responsibility appreciates a chance to relax. This is a token for the Kalen baths."

Shianan looked surprised. "Thank you. Thank you very much."

"Enjoy your visit, with my compliments." The merchant offered a deeper bow. "Good night, my lord!"

After Luca had locked the door, Shianan faced him. "You looked a little alarmed at the end. Did I err somehow?"

"No, not at all. He knew what you did, but you did not err. I—I only worried for a moment, when...."

Shianan turned to look across the room and reached a hand to Luca's shoulder. "He could not afford your price," he said simply. "Come, clear away this mess. I have notes to record and other work before sleep."

CHAPTER 37

Luca reversed the staff in his hand and felt a satisfying impact, and Shianan nodded as he stepped back. "Exactly," he said. "Better than swinging a mattress, yes? Now remember to keep your heel on the ground."

"Yes, Master Shianan," Luca answered, a little short of breath. "Again?"

Shianan grinned. "You're not starting to like this after all, are you?"

Luca felt himself smile. "Yes, a little. I mean, yes. May I try again?"

Someone laughed from outside the practice ring. "That skinny thing? You're wasting your time, commander!" More voices joined in laughter.

Luca froze. Shianan's grin vanished and he stepped back. "Giusto," he called, "come here."

There was a pause in the laughter and then new guffaws broke loose. "Ha! The commander will tan you now!" someone jibed.

Shianan shook his head as a wary soldier entered the ring. "Not at all." He tossed his staff toward the soldier, who caught it with awkward surprise. "Luca, go ahead and try it again—on Giusto." He smiled.

Giusto and Luca both stared at him. "Are you—sir, this is ridiculous!" Giusto protested. "I'll kill him!"

Luca silently agreed.

Shianan raised an eyebrow. "So confident? You think I have no faith in my student? Maybe your friends should do a little wagering."

Giusto looked indignant. "I'm your student, too."

"Then perhaps I think Luca is a better student." Shianan gestured casually. "Stop protesting and prove yourself."

Giusto looked across his shoulder at Luca, disdainful and resentful. Luca quailed before the look and fought the urge to drop his eyes in a slave's posture. Why had his master set him to this impossible match? What would—

Giusto took a step toward Luca, twisting his body as he prepared to deliver a smashing blow. It would shatter Luca's arm, it would send him reeling across the ring. Luca saw it and felt his arms move as his weight shifted.

The sweeping staff cracked against Luca's and slid as it rebounded. Luca remained frozen a precious second before realizing he had deflected the onrush. Giusto wavered, off-balance with his own momentum, and growled with rage as he renewed his attack.

This time Luca moved more smoothly, almost expecting to succeed, and Giusto's staff sailed wide over his head. Luca shifted his left hand's grip to a position below his right hand, whipped the tip of the staff low over the ground beside his right leg and skimmed it directly into Giusto's groin.

Giusto grunted, shocked from his charge to a standstill. Luca froze, terrified of what he'd done. He hadn't meant—! Behind the fence there was a moment of stunned silence and then the spectators began whooping and howling.

Shianan put a hand to his mouth, trying unsuccessfully to conceal his pitying laughter. Luca stumbled backward, dragging his staff, his breath catching in his throat. Giusto's face contorted as he bent over the injury, and then he raised the staff as he lurched forward unevenly.

Shianan stepped into the path of the angry soldier, twisting the staff easily from his grip. "That's enough, Giusto. Walk it off."

Giusto turned hot eyes on his commander. "He—I'll take him into—"

"That's enough," Shianan repeated, his tone firmer. "Walk it off."

Something penetrated the haze of Giusto's pain and humiliation, and he gave Shianan a curt nod before limping away. Behind Luca the spectators laughed and jeered; one voice demanded payment for a bet. Luca watched Giusto's departure, taut with worry, until Shianan called his name. "Luca! Didn't you hear me? Put away the staves; we're done for today." He tossed the second staff.

Luca fumbled the weapon as he caught it. He had struck a freeman—a soldier, even. He replaced the staves in the racks, his hands moving woodenly. He could not think further than that. He had struck a soldier, and—significantly.

Shianan scooped his cloak from the bench and swung it around his shoulders, not bothering to fasten it in place. He grinned at Luca. "That was better than I'd hoped, even," he confided. "Giusto is full of himself. There's nothing wrong that a little practice couldn't fix, but of course he's far too talented for that. You showed him up quite nicely."

"I didn't mean—"

Shianan looked at him sharply. "Don't you dare to finish that. Remember, within the training ring there are only instructors and students who train to meet or surpass them. You did exactly as you should have done, if with a more particular aim than I'd anticipated, and you should be proud of your work."

Luca hesitated. "But—I hit him...."

"And what in the name of all the sky's stars were you supposed to do?" Exasperated, Shianan stopped and pointed backward. "Within that ring, you are not a slave. Do you understand me?"

Luca followed his master's finger and saw the soldiers laughing among themselves. "Yes, Master Shianan," he answered unhappily. "I understand."

Shianan sighed. "You don't sound very convincing." He started walking again. "Go and bring something to eat, if you would; I have reports waiting for me."

Ariana was sleeping. Tamaryl stood beside her bed, but she did not seem aware of him. Maru had said she was often like this.

There was a whisper of sound from the open door, and he turned to see Daranai. "We've taken good care of her, as you can see," she said.

"And I am grateful," Tamaryl answered. "I'm sorry to impose both Maru and Ariana on you. Oniwe'aru has promised to have my house open for my return."

"Oh, but then you will have no cause to visit me." Daranai sulked beautifully.

Tamaryl smiled. "I am certain you might convince me somehow."

She kissed him deeply, inviting him to pursue the hungers she stirred.

He knew on some level that he was infatuated. He was not so young and foolish as to believe he loved a political match chosen for him long ago. He was giddy with joy and power and lust as much with Daranai'rika herself. But there was much to be said for joy and power and lust, and Daranai was a formidable rika and a worthy consort.

He would return quickly.

Shianan glanced up from his desk, his hair disarrayed from unconscious fingering. "Good, you're back."

"Did you have something for me to do?" Luca asked.

"I have something for you." Shianan held up a wooden badge. "I have here a token for the Kalen baths. You have done quite well of late—the accounts, of course, and last night you caught the Vandogan's game, and then that round with Giusto."

"I don't understand you, Master Shianan."

Shianan grinned. "I'm sending you to enjoy the Kalen."

Luca's stomach lurched. "I can't!"

"Of course you can. You'll have this token, and if anyone notices you, they'll think you're serving one of the guests. But once you have your room—the Kalen baths are all private rooms, did you know?—you'll be the guest yourself."

Luca tried to swallow. "Master Shianan...."

"Go on." He extended the wooden badge. "You'll enjoy it, and once inside no one will think to question you. If you get into any trouble, tell them I sent you ahead for me."

"You would give this to me?"

"Take it. I've never been to the Kalen baths, myself; they're beyond the means of a mere commander, and I've not been a count long enough to have the inclination. Consider this reconnaissance, and tell me if I should bother."

Luca's fingers closed numbly on the polished wood. "Thank you, master."

"You'd better hurry. You'll want the entire evening, I suspect."

CHAPTER 38

Luca hesitated outside the wide, gilded doors. What if he were caught? But Shianan had seemed unworried. He had sent Luca out the door with a cheery wave, telling him to enjoy his reward.

Reward. Luca had not expected that. Renner, who might have been a fair man before illness took him, had often given Luca his leavings when he intended to drink the rest of his supper. Ande had never even jested of generosity, occasionally making Luca beg even for necessities. Shianan had already bought a serviceable cloak and removed the abominable collar—why further reward his slave with the merchant's expensive gift? The accounting had not been so much, had it?

His master would not have sent him here for sport. The token was too expensive for that. Shianan must have expected he could indeed take a guest room. Luca swallowed and pushed open the gilded doors.

The lobby itself was an ostentatious display of luxury. A fountain splashed quietly in one corner, and flowers perfumed the room so that it seemed nearer a garden. Luca thought briefly of the courtyard of his home, filled with flowers and moonlight, and he shoved the wrenching image away.

A man sat at a narrow counter, scratching at some papers. Luca held his breath as he pushed the token over the counter, trying to let only his fingers show above the polished surface.

The man looked up sharply—the fountain had masked Luca's quiet entrance—and blinked once at Luca's rumpled and sweaty appearance. Luca stood absolutely still, his hands at his sides, knowing the man could see relatively little of him over the tall counter.

He took the token. "Good evening. Welcome to the Kalen." He turned over the polished wooden piece and eyed a marking on the back, then compared it to a small ledger beside him. "Ah, welcome, your lordship. You've been training, I see?" He turned over his shoulder and called to a curtained doorway behind him. "Seven for Bailaha!" Then, smiling, he turned back to Luca. "Room number seven, if you would, my lord. Thank you."

Luca blinked and managed to nod before walking on to the

doorway. That had been simple.

The hallway beyond the door was comfortably warm, and Luca pushed back his cloak. Two slaves passed him, one carrying a stack of fluffy towels and the other a tray of jars and bottles, and Luca pulled his cloak forward again to hide his telltale wrists.

Room number seven sat at the junction of two corridors. Luca pushed the door open tentatively.

The room was small but rich, all jewel-toned fabrics and dark woods. Along the right wall was a high couch padded with silky emerald and cobalt sheets, folded back invitingly. A tiny brazier warmed the air near the door, and directly opposite was a wood and stone basin, already filled with water.

Luca closed the door firmly behind him and went toward the bath itself. The water was actually flowing, a current between openings at either end of the basin. Somewhere below or behind the walls, slaves would be turning giant screws and fueling fires to supply this heated, flowing water, but here in the private room, it looked suddenly irresistible.

Luca stripped off his clothing and eased into the basin, twitching a little as the hot water stung, and sank to his chin. Relief poured over him as his water-borne limbs relaxed.

It was wonderful.

For a long, long moment he simply lay there, feeling the hot water move over and around him. There was a faintly bitter odor to the water—perhaps the heat came from natural hot springs and not only furnaces—but the perfumes in the room more than compensated. Luca turned in the bath, letting the water roll over him from a different angle, and rested his head on the stone and wooden edge.

He must have drowsed, for he wasn't sure if he'd actually heard a knocking sound or if it had been only the water lapping around his ears. He held his breath, his heart pounding. Had he been discovered?

"Hello?" he called quietly, hoping desperately there would be no answer. There was not. Luca lowered himself into the light current once more, feeling little twinges as his muscles fought between recalled tension and warm relaxation.

At home, long ago, this would have been followed by a massage to work out stiffness from bending over desks and ledgers.

He sighed and looked at the low table set beside the bath. There were several bowls and bottles, powders, oils, and lotions. The bowl nearest him was filled with scented salt crystals, dampened and colored to match the wall hangings. Luca scooped out a handful and smeared it over his arm. Then, pleased, he rose from the water and crushed salt over his body, scraping away the sweat and dead skin and filth.

The skin over his back was still too new to be scrubbed with the big crystals. The mild abrasion felt pleasant elsewhere, however, and when he'd scoured himself he sank into the moving water again, gently rubbing it away.

There was another bowl with a milky soap, which made a delicious smooth lather. A colored glass dish held a peppermint-scented soap which he used to scrub his scalp clean. He began to wish he'd brought another set of clothes.

He stretched, his muscles lengthening like a cat's. He had not felt this good in a long, long time. The exertion followed by the hot water and then the scrub had worked well together. He could forgo the massage of nostalgia.

There was a mirror of real glass and silver opposite the couch, and as Luca climbed out of the warm water, he paused at it.

He had not often seen himself since leaving home. He looked very different from the young man who had greeted his father's clients and employees. He was thinner—scrawny, Shianan had called him, though he thought he'd gained some weight since—and his hair was ragged instead of carefully trimmed. Most shocking was his own face. The face in the mirror at home had usually been comfortable, content, the face of one who knew he could not outshine his elder brothers but would be satisfied with what they left. Even after his decadence here, however, his expression was wary, a little haunted. Afraid.

Luca squeezed out his dripping hair and pushed it aside, turning. Ugly pale and puckered weals crossed his back, making him flinch to see it. He turned away.

He lifted his shirt distastefully, unwilling to put the dried sweat and grime on himself again. Maybe he could wait a little longer.... He looked at the hot bath and smiled to himself. It would probably be the first time anyone had done laundry at the Kalen, but that milky lathery soap would do admirably.

He washed out the shirt, braies, and leggings—the tunic would take longer to dry, and it did not rest directly on his skin, anyway— and hung them as best he could over the low table, near the squat little brazier that warmed the room. Then he slid between the sheets on the couch, marveling at their delicious texture, and let himself drift toward sleep again.

The bed was so smooth and warm. It was easy to dream....

"...I have come again and again, and there was no tag on the door," a voice said distantly.

Luca nodded against the silken sheet. The servants should have known not to wake him....

"And so I thought perhaps you meant to bathe yourself, but I—"

Luca woke with a stomach-wrenching start and twisted on the couch, wrapping himself in the emerald and cobalt sheets. A woman stood inside the door, startled as he whirled. "I'm sorry, my lord! I did not realize—I did not mean to wake you!"

Luca kicked his legs free and stumbled over the opposite side of the couch, clutching the sheets from inside the twisted bundle. "What? I'm sorry—I—"

"I'm sorry, my lord. I thought I maybe missed the bell. I—I can go if you're not yet ready."

Luca leaned against the wall hangings, his knees trembling within the concealing sheets. She was pleasant-looking and wearing light wrist cuffs. He forced himself to breathe more slowly; they would not send a single female slave to seize him. "I'm sorry," he said, trying to control his voice. "What bell?"

She looked mildly surprised. "The bell, the one here." She pointed to a tasseled rope hanging in the corner. "For summoning your attendant."

"Attendant?"

"For scrubbing your back, applying the salts and soaps, for...." Her voice faltered as she looked at the low table, its bowls and bottles and jars mostly emptied and pushed aside now to accommodate the shirt and leggings.

"I took care of that myself, thanks." Shianan Becknam's name would be mocked for months to come.

"I see." She bobbed her head in a slave's acceptance of a master's quirks. "Of course. Would you like your massage now?" She indicated the couch with an unsteady gesture.

Fresh terror pulsed through Luca. If she saw.... "No. I don't want a massage. No, thank you." He gulped, the soft wall close behind him.

But the woman did not leave. Instead, she looked at the floor and bit at her lip. "Then, maybe, my lord would prefer—would he like—" She hesitated uncomfortably.

Luca wanted nothing more than for her to go, to let him dress and flee. He shifted along the length of the couch.

The woman started toward him, her eyes fixed somewhere in the area of his stomach, her breathing shallow and uncertain. "I will be happy to provide whatever service my lord wishes."

Luca recoiled from her. "No!"

She reached one hand almost pleadingly toward him, across the couch, and he slapped it away as he stumbled backward.

She stopped, staring at his cuffed arm, and Luca realized his mistake as he backed against the basin. She blinked at him. "You are a slave?"

Perhaps he could beg her not to betray him. "Please, I—"

"No," she whispered, horrified. "No, I can't do this."

"You don't have to do anything. You can go and pretend you never saw me, just say I never called—"

"No!" She stepped back, staring at her hands. "I would have—no, no!"

Luca tightened the slipping sheets across his torso. "Why did—oh!" He stared at her, suddenly comprehending. "You were sent to—to lie with me?"

She shook her head desperately. "I can't—not when you're—no!" She was beginning to cry. "I'm sorry, I'm so sorry!" She was fumbling with a large pouch on her belt, trying to retrieve something. "Look," she sobbed, "look. I'm sorry—"

"Go!" Luca snapped, turning away. "Get out. You shouldn't have come; they had no call to send you. They have no—it's not right to send you for this!"

She sobbed harder and fled toward the door.

"Go!" Luca heard the door close and he clenched his fists, crushing the sheets. Empathetic fury burned through him. They had sent a slave, just another luxury to be enjoyed with the oils and the steam. Only chance separated her from Luca. Only Luca separated her from Sara. *You would not have me sell your sister, would you?*

Luca yanked at his damp clothing, anxious to leave the luxurious room, now a gilded cell. The attendant in the lobby spoke as he passed, but Luca rushed by him as if he did not exist.

The wind cut coldly through his damp leggings where the cloak shifted with his stride, but Luca did not care. All his anxiety and the sick familiar terror of coercion fueled his growing rage as he stalked toward their quarters. Thrown to a guest's pleasure like a bone to a hound—!

He flung open the door, expecting no one in the office at the late hour, but Shianan was still at his desk. He looked up with a startled expression. "Luca?"

The angry words stuck in Luca's mouth. Fury throbbed in his chest and he could not speak it, not toward his master.

Shianan grew concerned. "Luca, what is it?"

His master was waiting. His master, who had sent him to that place and that unhappy slave, waited for his answer. Luca hung a moment without breathing, wavering between righteous outrage and acquiescent subservience.

His master grew impatient. "Luca!"

Luca bowed his head. "Master—come to the practice ring with me?"

Shianan regarded him skeptically. "The practice ring? Now?"

"Please, master!"

Shianan dropped his pen. "Why not?"

Luca's throat closed and he could not reply. His pulse beat through him. He remained still until Shianan had donned his cloak and reached the door behind him, and then he followed his master outside.

Shianan walked briskly in the cold dark, glancing occasionally at Luca but waiting to see what lay at the practice ring before asking further. Luca swallowed hard against his pounding heart, trying to form his wild thoughts into coherence.

Shianan walked into the ring without hesitation and went directly to the center, where he turned and faced Luca. "Now, what is it?"

Luca's hands moved without his thought or consent, taking two staves from the rack and tossing one toward his master even as a part of his mind recognized he was killing himself. "Take that, please."

Shianan caught the staff mid-air and spun it into readiness, his eyebrows rising. "Yes?"

Luca moved forward into the ready posture he had been taught. "How—how dare you?" He swung the staff in a wide, angry arc.

Shianan deflected and stepped back. "What?"

Luca saw in his mind's eye the frightened woman backing away from him and he swung again at Shianan. "How could you think that would please me—that I would want such a thing? A show of how little we are to you?"

Stop! Stop! he screamed silently. *Don't do this! You can't do this!*

"When it can as easily be me—another plaything for whatever twisted pleasures a rich man can fathom?" He jabbed the end of the staff at Shianan, who parried without returning.

You're killing yourself!

Shianan slid out of range of the next fierce sweep, his staff quiet in his hands. "What are you talking about?"

"I could never be pleased to see another slave prostituted!"

Shianan's staff spun and smashed down upon Luca's, jarring it from his stinging hands and leaving Luca unarmed and half-stooped with the force of the blow, staring breathlessly at his master.

Run! Flee! Beg!

Shianan's eyes bored into Luca's. "You say a slave was sent to bed you at the baths?"

Luca's fury vanished, leaving him utterly alone to face the fruits of his insanity. His breath caught in his throat and made his voice stumble. "Y-yes."

Shianan straightened, letting his staff come to rest against the ground. "The Kalen baths do not offer prostitutes."

Heat rose in Luca again. "She was there! She—"

"The Kalen baths do not offer prostitutes," Shianan repeated firmly. "I am certain of that. Though it's certainly common enough elsewhere, there was some question of taxation two years ago and it's been an occasional point of discussion since. Wait, though—I do believe you when you say a woman came to you." He frowned.

Luca's knees began to tremble in the hollow aftermath of his rage, and he did not know whether to straighten to face his master or to drop to his knees and beg for his life.

Shianan looked at Luca again and his puzzled frown faded. "Luca," he said slowly, and his expression softened. "Stand upright. That was well played."

"Master?"

Shianan smiled faintly and gestured to the ring about them. "If you are no slave here, you can of course speak freely, even in anger. I give you full credit for using your advantage, though now I'll remember to avoid this place if I feel you're giving me trouble."

Luca breathed.

Shianan spun his staff absently. "Perhaps the Vandogan merchant arranged for an extra service," he mused. "Did he think that would seal the bargain he missed?"

He did not seem upset. He did not seem even to be thinking of Luca. Luca straightened, his eyes on Shianan's whirling staff.

He had been angry, he had been angry at his master and at his slavery and at—everything. It had been a long time since he had dared to feel fury.

Shianan shook his head sharply. "Oh, that would be grand—to say the bastard might trade military funds for a pretty piece of flesh." He spun the staff abruptly into the ground, making Luca jump. "No, that won't do. Put these away. We're going to see the Vandogan. I can't let it be thought that I—" He paused and looked at Luca. "You did refuse her, didn't you?"

"I never touched her!"

"Right. I didn't think so." Shianan started for the ring gate. "Now, Luca! I want to catch him before he sleeps, before he has a chance to tell anyone of the visit."

Luca hurried to match his pace. "They—they thought I was you." He gulped, realizing how that might sound. "That is, there was a mark on the token—"

"So I was there tonight, yes? Did I do anything in particular?"

Luca shivered, cold in his damp clothing and emptied wrath. "You—I—you went directly to your room, number seven, and you bathed. You never put a tag on the door for the attendant—I didn't know, but I couldn't have—with these—you know—I bathed, I mean you bathed, and then I washed out my clothes because they were so dirty from the—"

Shianan laughed aloud. "You did your laundry? I'm sorry, go on." He chuckled. "What else?"

"I went to sleep on the couch while I was waiting for them to dry, and she came in, while I was sleeping, and she—she wanted to massage me but I said no, and—she offered—and I was afraid she'd realize and I tried to send her away, but—she saw my wrist cuff and she stopped." Luca's face was burning hotly. "Then she was very upset, and I told her to tell no one that she'd seen me, and she left."

Shianan nodded, taking long strides which made Luca hurry. Then he smiled suddenly. "Luca," he asked, "if your clothes were drying, then when she came in...."

Luca had not thought it possible for his face to grow hotter, but he had been wrong. "I—I was—I was in the couch, in the sheets...."

"So when she was offering her services, you were naked?"

Luca ducked his head. "I sent her away!"

"I know, I know. I believe you. I was just... picturing it." Shianan grinned.

The heat of his flush ran down Luca's neck and back, and he swallowed hard.

"No, Luca, don't be upset. I was only teasing you." Shianan smiled to relieve the sting. "Is there anything else I did which I should know about? And is the girl the only one to know you were a slave?"

Luca started to shake his head and then nodded, confusing himself. "I left immediately after she did. And no one else saw my cuffs, I think. I told her to say she hadn't seen me, but...."

"We'll see."

The military guesthouse had few lights in the windows. Shianan frowned and then selected a door at the end of the building, rapping sharply on it. Luca stood to one side and slightly behind him, shivering with the cold and a little afraid of the coming conversation. Would it come out that he had been the one at the baths? The Vandogan merchant could not be anything but offended to find Shianan had passed his gift to a slave. Would the baths' proprietors demand punishment for the brazen slave?

A light-haired man opened the door, tired but courteous. "Yes?"

"I'm Commander Becknam, and I've been discussing a supply contract with your master. May I speak with him?"

The slave looked appropriately contrite. "I'm sorry, my lord, but he's just had someone else come in. If you'll wait, I will tell him that you are here, or—"

"Thank you," Shianan interrupted, "but I will come again later."

Shianan led Luca around the corner of the guesthouse. "Someone else just arrived, eh? At this hour? Do you think that might be someone from the Kalen?" He eyed the high windows and then pointed to a half-emptied crate. "Help me move this, but quietly. I want to see if you know this visitor."

Luca thought of the man behind the counter, the slaves he'd passed in the corridor. He didn't know if he could recognize them again. But he took one end of the crate and set it below a lit window.

Shianan mounted the crate and gestured for Luca to follow.

"Stay a little back from the glass. Quietly!" He turned to the window. "Well—is this what I think it is, Luca?"

Luca stepped onto the crate and looked in the window. The unhappy slave woman stood before the Vandogan merchant, her posture plaintive before his angry demeanor. Luca's blood chilled—what was she telling him?

Shianan tipped his head closer to the window, his jaw hanging slightly as he strained to hear. Luca held his breath and imitated him.

"I tried, master, but he sent me away—"

"One task! I set you one task! Is your freedom so little a prize?"

She drooped, looking even smaller from their high angle. "Master, I did try, I swear—I offered him whatever he wanted, but he wanted none of me...."

"Perhaps he would prefer a pretty boy?" The merchant scowled. "And could you not get within even an arm's reach of him?"

The woman flushed and bowed her head. "I'm sorry, master. I'm sorry."

"Then you'll be successful the next time?"

She bit her lip. "I—I cannot do it, master. I cannot!" She rubbed at her face with the back of her hand and reached into the pouch at her waist. "No matter what you offer." She withdrew a knife and extended it on flat palms. "Take it back, please, master! Even for my freedom, I cannot kill!"

Luca's heart stopped.

The merchant seemed to swell in anger. "You defy me?"

She cringed. "It is not defiance to fail—I only.... Why? Why must he die? Master, don't do this! I cannot let you, I won't let you kill him—"

The merchant seized the knife with one hand and her hair with the other. She recoiled, eyes wide, and instinctively raised her hands. But the blow swept the hands aside as it carved through her throat. She staggered as the merchant released her, grasping at her gaping, spurting throat with half-severed fingers, and then Luca was on the pavement vomiting and choking, his mind reeling with horror.

"Get up, Luca." Shianan's voice was low and curt. "Get up!" He seized Luca's collar and hauled him to his feet. "Move!" He kicked debris over the puddle of vomit and pushed Luca forward. "Go!"

Luca stumbled across the yard, unable to think, unable to do anything except hurry alongside Shianan. His master kept a hand on his shoulder until they reached Shianan's own office and quarters, where he turned to latch and lock the door. Luca's knees failed and he fell beside the desk, trembling and feeling as if he would be sick again.

Shianan stared at the door. "Why?"

She had offered to massage him—she had reached for him, was ordered to bed him for her freedom—but she was to kill him, to kill him with a knife, and now she was murdered—

"Luca!" Shianan crouched, forcing Luca to see him rather than the scene in his mind. "Are you all right? Are you with me?"

Luca gulped and nodded. "I—yes."

"Good. I want you to think back to the baths. Did she say anything more than what you've told me?"

Luca stared, unable to recall anything of the baths, unable to think of anything at all.

Shianan took a slow breath. "Luca, stay with me. Think. Someone would have killed you in my place had you not been so scrupulous. He will probably try again, and I need to know everything you might have heard. What did she say when she came to you?"

Luca blinked at him. "She would have killed me, instead."

"Your particular morality spared you. Now tell me, what did she say?"

Luca closed his eyes and tried to remember her with her throat still closed. "She—she came while I was asleep and—she could have killed me then." Gooseflesh spread over his arms. "But she said she didn't realize I was asleep."

"Maybe she didn't," Shianan said. "Go on."

Luca shook his head. "I told you everything, before. That's all of it."

Shianan blew out his breath in frustration. "We know the Vandogan is involved—what is his name? Karlm. Who else is part of this, and why? Why me?" He straightened and turned away to pace. "In his room, did you see anything that—"

Luca vomited again, his body spasming to reject the bloody image scorched into his memory of the room. He coughed and spat, his eyes tearing, and realized Shianan was beside him, one hand on his back. "I'm sorry," Luca managed.

"Most new soldiers react in some way," Shianan said, "and they're expecting to see it, on a battlefield. Not in a guesthouse." He stood and went into the next room. A moment later he returned with a handful of dried rushes for lighting the fire and candles and dropped them over the viscous puddle. "Most new soldiers, though, have the courtesy to be outside." He smiled grimly and held out a cup toward Luca.

Luca took it, weak and miserable, and sipped automatically at the water.

"Karlm's slave will say I came to see him, but is he likely to guess that I spied through his window?" Shianan stared across the room, looking empty and faintly stunned. "Why me? What advantage to a merchant could there be in killing me?"

CHAPTER 39

Luca was scrubbing at the dried residue on the office floor when the outer door opened. "Is your master in?"

"Captain Torg," called Shianan from the next room. "One moment, please. I'll be right there."

Shianan looked haggard when he came, as if he had not slept well—which he had not. "Good morning, captain."

"Good morning, commander. I have a question about the fourth squad—"

"Leave that for a moment." Shianan gestured to a chair as he sat behind his desk. "Captain Torg, I called you from the hinterland, and only recently. You did not know I would invite you."

The captain looked faintly startled. "No, sir."

"And I can't imagine you were making alliances from that distant post in the expectation of finding yourself suddenly in Alham, which, thanks to my childhood, was very unlikely."

Torg regarded him. "What are you asking me, sir?"

"Someone tried to kill me last night, Torg. And you're nearly the only man I can trust to ask about it."

"Tried to kill you?" The captain was appropriately disturbed.

"Yes." Shianan ran a hand through his hair. "You don't know of anyone who might try such a thing, do you?"

Torg blinked, hesitated, and shook his head. "Of course not, sir." He shook his head again. "How?"

"He sent a slave to whore in the baths," Shianan said testily, "and she was supposed to put a knife into me. Fortunately, I don't have a taste for coerced women, and she never got a chance."

Torg nodded. "How did you know that was her purpose?"

"I had a look in her master's window. Apparently she had a change in heart, because she told her master she couldn't kill after all. More, she said she wouldn't let him do it, and I suppose he felt she had enough knowledge to be a threat, because he killed her."

Torg whistled under his breath. "So you have evidence. Why not arrest the girl's master?"

"I have no evidence at all," Shianan corrected. "I overheard a slave say she would not kill at his order. A slave's word is only barely admissible as evidence, with conditions, and that particular slave will never testify. I saw him kill a slave, which is uneconomical but not a crime."

"And no one else saw this?"

"Luca was with me." Shianan nodded toward him. "But again, a slave's word carries almost no weight, His witness, even under torture, wouldn't be enough to overturn the man's denial while I have no other proof."

Luca scrubbed vigorously with the brush, working bits from between the floorboards. His word's lack of worth had spared him from Ande's hearings thus far. He might be needed for the final trial, he had been warned, but not for the preliminaries. He hoped vehemently he would not be needed at all.

His knees ached. He had been working at this for some time. He wondered if Karlm's light-haired slave were simultaneously scrubbing at a large dark stain.

"He's a merchant, come to negotiate a supply contract. I'd never met him until a few days ago. What reason could he have to kill me? He must be working with someone, and I have to find who that may be."

Torg steepled his fingers. "Could it—no, no."

"You have an idea?"

Torg glanced toward Luca. "May I speak freely?"

"Luca has already seen as much of this as I have."

"A slave can be bribed or threatened."

"No." Shianan shook his head. "In many cases I might agree, but this is different."

Torg looked between Shianan and Luca. "No taste for coerced women, but coerced men have a different seasoning?"

"Captain!" Shianan's steely tone made Luca jump. "I can relieve your mind on that score."

Luca, red over his face and neck, dumped the brush into the dirty water and retreated into the sleeping room.

Torg cleared his throat. "I'm sorry, sir," he offered, with a quiet emphasis on the final word. "I should not have suggested...."

Shianan exhaled, a little of the tension going out of his shoulders, and glanced at the door Luca had closed. "I've had Luca only a few weeks, true, but in that time he has saved my life. He stays because I trust him—and if I did not, no other reason could keep him here." He sighed. "I'm sorry, captain."

"No, sir, I am the one to apologize. I forgot my place."

Shianan smiled bitterly. It was more than a little awkward, having their roles reversed. "Now we've settled that question, what other suggestions do you have?"

"Of course, there's the Gehrn. Their high priest is imprisoned here, and you're the reason he came."

Shianan swore. "That's an excellent point."

"What little I know of the Gehrn, though, they wouldn't favor subtlety. They'd be more likely to march on the city, I think. Kill you in the street."

"Still, it's worth considering. If you hear anything, on any front, will you let me know?"

"Of course. Who sent the slave he later killed?"

"His name is Karlm. I cannot imagine he conceived a grudge for me in Vandoga and came all the way here just to act upon it, so he must be in alliance with someone else."

"I'll keep my ears open, sir."

Torg closed the door to his quarters and leaned against it, trying to calm his rapid pulse. He thought he had hidden his agitation well, but that would not be enough if his fears were realized.

Years ago, he had blunted the king's intent to dispose of his bastard son. Now someone again meant to kill Shianan.

Torg closed his eyes and thought. The king had changed his mind about Shianan, hadn't he? He had brought him to the capital, ennobled him. Surely he wouldn't turn again to kill him—and if he did, he wouldn't need a foreigner's slave to work it.

Shianan didn't know of the king's early order, or Torg's part in it. There was nothing to suggest he'd guessed he was meant to die that night.

Torg liked Shianan a great deal. He could not stand between Shianan and the king, but he did not want to see him killed by another malefactor. He would listen, for what good it would do.

CHAPTER 40

After Torg had gone, Shianan drummed his fingers, staring at nothing.

He had faced harm early and often as a soldier. On the roads there was danger, too, from robbers eager for coins, weapons, armor. But those were impersonal threats, a mere transaction of unsavory business. A soldier or a bandit did not choose Shianan particularly.

But this attempt had been for Shianan himself—direct, specific, personal. That somehow felt very different, and his mind wanted to shy from the thought. There was no reprieve in denial, however.

Who would benefit by his death? Almost no one, directly. He stared at his notes. His guesses were wild and baseless, conceived almost wholly on the basis of his parentage.

The queen. Queen Azalie had resided outside Alham since Shianan was first called to the city, having told her royal husband she would not enter the Naziar while Shianan was attached there. She had the sense and decency to publicly pretend her habits were not rooted in her resentment of the bastard, but Shianan knew better. If she had tired of arranging her calendar about his existence, or if she had tired of waiting for him to die in battle, she might have arranged to hurry his death.

The idea was extremely far-fetched, however.

Soren. The prince-heir had no likely reason to want Shianan dead, but he could conceivably be guarding his position. Half-royals had claimed the throne before. Again, it seemed unlikely.

Alasdair. The younger prince might be likewise jealous of a half-royal, and possibly more so since Shianan had the advantage of age. He might also, at twelve, lack temperance.

Another officer? Shianan had racked his memory for any officer who might have desired Shianan's position or been jealous of his relatively quick rise. There had been a few raised eyebrows, of course, but had anyone resented him enough to kill? He could think of no one, but perhaps he had missed something.

The Ryuven. Shianan did not flatter himself that the Ryuven feared him personally, but it was possible they were seeking to weaken

261

their enemy by assassinating military personnel. But General Septime and others were a more logical choice than Shianan, and he could not help but think the magic-rich Ryuven would have chosen a more direct method than convincing a human merchant to send a slave to seduce and stab him.

Luca. Shianan had written this only out of a need for completion. Slaves did kill their masters; Furmelle was evidence enough of that. And Luca had been free once, and might seek to be free again.

But he had given up his chance in the beginning, when he had come to Shianan's aid rather than taking the opportunity to flee. And he did not behave as a slave who loathed his master—the opposite, in fact, perceiving Shianan's condition and emotions with uncomfortable accuracy.

And while he could have invented the story of the slave's proposition, he had not been the one to kill her. Shianan could not imagine a plot so complex as to include Luca.

He glanced up with relief when the door opened for Ewan Hazelrig. "Good afternoon, your lordship. Do you have a moment?"

"As many as you require, my lord mage." Shianan indicated the chair which Torg had used.

"Thank you." The White Mage seated himself and glanced about the office. "May we speak freely?"

Luca was working in the next room, but the door was closed between them. "Go ahead."

"The Circle has determined to remake the shield tomorrow night. I cannot stall any longer. The tests on the Shard have been completed, and it has been determined there is no lasting damage. The evidence against Ande will include the presence of Ryuven blood to disrupt the shield and unmake its properties, and while I have not found a way to reconcile that with my conscience, I have not found a plausible alternative, either." Hazelrig sighed. "At any rate, if we want to allow for Ariana's return, we must do something to prevent the remaking of the shield."

Shianan swore softly. "Forgive me, my lord mage, but I had not expected this. I... have been distracted by other developments." He gnawed at his thumbnail.

"Distracted?" Hazelrig's voice was cool. "Is there something more pressing than regaining my daughter? Your friend?"

Shianan bit into the quick of his nail. "Someone tried to kill me last night, and I have no idea who it might be." He looked suddenly at the mage. "I don't suppose there are any magical aids that could help with that? A potion which might, when deposited in a cup of ale, force a man to reveal his plans and accomplices?"

Hazelrig, initially stunned by the announcement, shook his head and smiled faintly at Shianan's speculation. "I'm afraid not. But can you tell me what has happened?"

Briefly Shianan wondered if Hazelrig had any possible motive, but if the mage wanted his help with the Shard, he could not want him dead. "In short, one of our visiting merchants made an attempt—unsuccessful, obviously—and he executed the slave who failed to kill me. I have no evidence on which to arrest him, and I cannot fathom why he would have done this."

"You have no guesses?"

Shianan shook his head. "Nothing worthwhile."

Hazelrig glanced toward the door. "Then, if I may offer a suggestion, you might send away the slave for a time. It's possible that someone—"

"Why does everyone think of Luca?" Shianan sighed. "Luca—is not a typical slave. I trust him. Besides, I have put too much time into training him thus far. Why, he actually attacked me with a staff last night."

Hazelrig stared at him, and Shianan shook his head apologetically. "I'm sorry, it has not been an easy night or day. If you hear anything that might help me, please let me know. Now, to the Shard—so we must steal it, then?"

"That is the best action I had thought of, yes."

"Right." Shianan sighed. "I think I can hide it."

Hazelrig looked at him. "You thought before you would be under suspicion if it disappeared."

"So I did. So I would." Shianan winced as his thumbnail tore further. "She can't return on her own?"

"Only Ryuven can leap the between-worlds. She must be carried, and Tamaryl can't travel through the shield."

"And he can't just, I don't know, push her across?" Shianan ran fingers through his hair. "I'm sorry, I know it's beyond me. I can't think of any other way. You would have thought of anything magical."

"There are several magical blocks," Hazelrig said, "but none that could not be immediately detected and quickly overturned. That would betray us without serving our purpose. And of course, it would be futile to explain we believe her alive. At best, I would sound like a deluded man insane with grief. At worst...."

"We are both executed as traitors, and she dies there." Shianan exhaled. "Then I suppose we have no choice."

Hazelrig's expression was full of conflict. "I want my daughter, Bailaha. I want her returned more than anything else. But I don't want to sacrifice you to that end."

"I don't want to sacrifice myself, either. I will be careful."

"How will it be done?"

"I will come to visit you in your office," Shianan said. "I'll take it from the cellar then, but we'll have an alibi in each other. Then I'll have the Shard well away and hidden before the Circle convenes."

"Where will you hide it?"

Shianan shook his head. "No, this is my crime, my lord mage. You cannot lie if you do not know the truth."

And I will solemnly try my best to say that only I was involved, though they ask me with hot irons. Shianan gnawed at his thumb, tasting blood.

CHAPTER 41

Maru was calculating remaining doses of the herbs when the door opened. He turned, surprised. "Daranai'rika. Good afternoon."

She glanced about the room, past Ariana's sleeping form. "It's stuffy here, without a window."

"Yes, but that is beneficial for her. The fewer sensations, the better."

"Hm." Daranai paced a few steps. "Tamaryl'sho is not returning so quickly this time."

Maru nodded. "I think Ryl is—"

She laughed, interrupting him. Her laughter was not unpleasant, only amused.

Maru regretted his error. "I'm sorry, rika. Tamaryl'sho."

She sat on the empty bed, Maru's bed, and smiled at him. "I understand long force of habit." She bent one elegantly curved finger to catch red-gold hair fallen over her eye. Maru could sense the aura of glamour around her but was not sure how much of her appearance was altered. "Tamaryl'sho has always been kind to you."

"I consider him the best of friends, rika."

"And I am glad you've had that pleasure," she said. "Once Tamaryl'sho and I are formally conjoined, of course, you will not be able to visit so freely. As a prince doniphan, Tamaryl must pay stricter tribute to social custom, and fraternizing with nim...."

The words cut through Maru. She spoke everything he feared. Even through the years when he and Ryl had been close, Maru had always quietly worried that responsibilities would eventually demand his friend. And it was already true: Tamaryl, once returned, had been repeatedly forced elsewhere by Oniwe'aru's orders. Maru did not resent it—Tamaryl could not do otherwise—but to hear his fears confirmed aloud was cruel.

Daranai looked impersonally over Maru and smiled, catlike. "There might be a place for you in our household, though."

For a moment Maru's breath caught—he had never considered that there might not be a place for him, that Tamaryl might release him to the next lord of obligation—but then he pushed away the thought. Of course he would stay. His friend might have more responsibilities, but even Oniwe'aru had respected their friendship and restored Maru's service to Tamaryl's estate. It could not be otherwise.

Daranai let her eyes move to Ariana, huddled and shivering on the bed. "I don't mind that Tamaryl'sho has played with other toys before now," she said. She looked back at Maru, her expression hungry. "I can understand the attraction of something wriggling and helpless."

Maru's stomach clenched with abrupt realization. His throat twitched as he swallowed.

Daranai laughed. "Don't play so ignorant, nim. There's nothing more helpless and wriggling than a handsome young male pinned by the balls."

Maru did not meet her eyes. "You are my lord's bride. I cannot, rika."

"I am your lord's bride," she repeated, "your mistress, and you will do my will."

"Rika—"

She stood and walked toward him, her stride never changing as he backed away until he found himself against a wall. She stretched her fingers to his chin and tipped his face up. "Ah, Maru," she said, apparently pleased. "I don't mind a little reluctance. It makes the play more fun." Her eyes narrowed. "But don't overdo it."

Maru's pulse pounded as he squeezed to the side. "Daranai'rika, I will be your obedient servant in all matters, but I cannot do this. If you will not accept my will, then please accept that I cannot betray my lord of obligation." He appealed to Tamaryl's authority—she surely could not argue against that.

She smiled, unaffected by his rebuttal. "I have a meeting in a few minutes. I will return in an hour. You have until then to think it over." The smile chilled. "I urge you to see this my way, Maru. I have had a very trying morning with taxation and agricultural records and I am not in a mood to be patient. I will be gratified one way or another." She turned for the door, leaving Maru frozen where he stood.

Ariana rose through the misty greyed darkness and found herself in her usual room. Her mind was matted with tangled sensations, but they did not hurt her; she was still safely under the sway of the drug. It was fading, though, and she would need another dose soon.

Maru was pacing the length of the room. She could just see him from where she lay. She tried to move her head, to call him, but the drug was not exhausted enough for that, so she lay in her dreamy, hazy repose and watched him pace.

Then the latch on the door moved, and Maru whirled, his wings shifting fretfully. A female Ryuven entered, closing the door again behind her. "Well?"

Maru sank to two knees. "Daranai'rika, please understand, I cannot in good conscience do this."

"You choose that conscience, then. I see disobedience to your mistress's orders."

Ariana strained to hear more.

"Stand," Daranai ordered.

Maru rose slowly, reluctance evident in each small movement. Daranai cupped his face with one long-nailed hand. She leaned down, holding him steady by the jaw, and kissed him. Maru remained stiff and unyielding, and as Daranai released him he regarded her with wide eyes.

"That isn't what I'm looking for," she said darkly. "We will try again. Do not disappoint me."

"Ri—" Maru's protest was lost as she covered his mouth with hers. He leaned backward, his hands twitching as if he wanted to push her away but did not dare.

Abruptly she ceased, giving his face a little shove. "Little nim fool," she snapped, her eyes flashing. "If you won't give me what I want, I will take it."

"Daranai'rika—" Maru shook his head. "You can't do this."

Her hand cracked across his face and he reeled. "Do not presume to tell me what I cannot do!"

Ariana was transfixed and horrified. She could not move.

When Maru straightened, there was a streak of seeping blood marring his cheek. It did not heal as he faced her again, his eyes wide.

Daranai mollified her tone. "I see you do know better than to defy me."

Maru dropped his gaze to the floor. "I cannot do this, Daranai'rika."

She laughed. "A fine, healthy male like you? I think you can. I'll help you." She placed her hands on his shoulders and slid them inward. "You'll like it, I promise. I'm not usually cruel in my pleasures."

This was wrong. Ariana did not know who this female was, but this was clearly wrong. But she could not speak, could not move.

Maru blocked her hands with his wrists. "Daranai'rika, please—there must be others who would be glad of your attention...."

"And why shouldn't you be?"

"You are not my bride. If Tamaryl'sho were here—"

There was a concussion of power and Maru cried out as he tumbled along the floor. Ariana winced as the burst battered her through the deadening potion.

"Tamaryl'sho isn't here, is he?" Daranai leapt to where Maru had fallen. "He has not been here for so long. And you are his servant, are you not?" She knelt on his wing and placed the other knee squarely in his chest. "So you should do his work, shouldn't you?"

"No—"

"I told you before," Daranai warned, "I'd rather not force you. But I will if I must."

Maru pleaded, "Rika, please...."

"Unless agreeing to serve me, you should be quiet before your mistress." She began to tease him through the thin fabric.

Maru twisted unsuccessfully. "Stop!"

"No, no, not yet." She forced one arm down with enhanced strength and blocked the other with a wing. "Now, let's have a better view of what we're doing." Cloth ripped and slid.

Maru flinched away from her fingers. "Rika!"

She laughed, her expression predatory, and Maru recoiled against the floor. "No! Get away! Stop it—"

Stop it! Don't hurt him—stop it! Twinges crawled over Ariana's body with the drug's fading, but she was helpless to intervene.

Daranai laughed over Maru. "You didn't think you'd enjoy this, did you? In fact, I think you're ashamed right now, ashamed you are excited by it." She teased her nails over his ribs, making him tremble. "You could have had this—" she caressed his chest—"without all this fuss. But, I'm afraid you chose the more difficult path."

Stop it! Ariana wanted to weep, but her body would not respond.

Maru rolled and succeeded in throwing Daranai off. Daranai twisted and rose, dragging Maru upward and heaving him with a flash of power into the wall.

Ariana's cheek was damp. She was crying. *Maru....* She had to help him. He wasn't healing. She had to do something. She slid her arm forward against the fading drug and grasped at the edge of the bed.

Maru slid along the wall, raising one wing as if to shield himself. Ariana flinched under the tremors Daranai's magic left in the air as she stalked Maru like cornered prey.

CHAPTER 42

Shianan burst into the office, moving directly to the desk. "Luca, my friend, I have a task for you." Luca blinked at him, not trusting his ears. But Shianan rushed on, a frantic edge to his voice. "Where is that roll of accounts which arrived last week? From Fhure?"

"In the bottom drawer there, my lord."

"I want you to take it to my steward. Say I am not sure he has the accounting right, and I would like him to check and return it. You understand?"

Luca nodded, confused. "But, Master Shianan—"

"Quiet. Those are my orders to you." He twisted and slid something from beneath his cloak. "You'll travel with this pack, which you'll find partly filled. Do not unwrap the bundle inside. Somewhere between Alham and Fhure, find a lonely bit of road and a readily identifiable marker, and bury it deep. Make sure no one sees you. Then forget about it and go on to the estate, where you'll do as I have already said."

Luca nodded again, more slowly. "Yes, Master Shianan."

"Good." Shianan pointed across the desk. "In that top drawer, on the right, you'll find a sealed document. Carry that with you. If there is any trouble when you return, if for any reason, you cannot find me or if anyone is—worrying you, then open and use that letter. Do you understand?"

Luca hesitated. "Master Shianan—is there anything.... Can I help?"

"You can do as you're told," Shianan answered curtly. "Do not uncover that bundle, and I'll swear on the rack you knew nothing of it. Hurry. You'll leave now. I'm giving you money enough so you needn't wait to pack provisions."

Luca's mind whirled. He took a few spare pieces of clothing and pressed them into the bag above the wrapped bundle, tucked the sealed letter and his master's coins into a travel pocket, and shouldered the heavy pack. He looked at his master, uncertain and uncomfortable. "I will return as soon as the steward has given me a new accounting."

Shianan seemed distracted. "Good enough. Now go. Hurry."

"I'll hurry, my lord."

Shianan swallowed visibly. "Good-bye, Luca."

Daranai held Maru's jaw and gestured toward Ariana. "Are you worried about her watching? Don't be. It's like a little pet in the room." She laughed.

Maru pressed himself against the wall. "I cannot."

"You will not, you mean." She sighed, her voice deceptively regretful. "This is not how I'd prefer it, nim."

Cold terror bit through Ariana, bleeding into hot rage. *Let him alone!* She wriggled, sharp pains shooting through her. The drug was wearing dangerously thin, and she would soon lose her shield against the painful atmosphere. She reached toward Daranai. *Don't!*

Daranai shoved a forearm across Maru's collarbone, pinning him. Her other hand drew a small, hard object from her belt and angled it carefully toward him. Magical reverberations filled the room, ripping across Ariana.

"Stupid nim. Is there even enough magic in you for this to work?"

Maru made a pained sound. Ariana thought of all the attacks she had learned, of the defensive spells which might protect Maru, if she could but act. She tried to hold the magic about her, but it was everywhere, *everywhere*, and it threatened to overwhelm her if she touched it—

Maru cried aloud.

Don't hurt him! Ariana closed her eyes and saw the brightly glowing power that was Daranai. Where Maru writhed against the wall was a flickering, weak light, burning orange where the small object brushed it.

"Stop," Ariana whispered aloud. "Don't."

Daranai paused in her arcane attack, rotating the object's face away. "This is your choice, Maru. Am I really so revolting that you prefer this to me?"

Maru only panted for answer.

"Stop." Ariana's weak voice frustrated her. Her fury mounted, making her limbs twitch. How dare she—how *dare* she...!

Daranai reapplied the torture, moving the object so the magic flamed a hungry red. "You think you're so favored!" She leaned hard into her forearm as it slid from his chest to his throat.

Maru cried and choked.

Force begets force. It is always more efficient to channel power than to counter it.

"Let him *be!*" Ariana flung out her hands and seized the swirling power that filled the room, blinding her. The protective levies of her frail resistance crumbled and the magic crashed over her, crushing her, suffocating her, but she was desperate for it and did not fight it, she dove into the torrent, and it scorched excruciatingly through her and filled her, overflowing her organs and mind and bursting through her fingertips and crackling through her hair and—

Daranai swore.

Ariana opened her eyes and saw the room in gaudy color, glowing with unreal energy. She was looking *down* upon the two Ryuven who stared open-mouthed at her, half-standing on the bed and half-suspended on the tide of power rushing through her. "Let him be!" she snarled, and her voice reverberated in the small room.

Daranai stumbled backward, her eyes wide. "What—how...."

Ariana's hair crackled. "Let him go!" she ordered, and Daranai stepped away from Maru without looking at him. Maru gaped with naked fear.

The power did not hurt her. She was numb with rage and fear and exultation. "Get out."

"But—"

"*Get out!*" Invisible lightning sparked around her, hissing her wrath.

Daranai ducked beneath her wings and ran for the door, pulling it closed behind her.

Ariana's fury ebbed, and the agony of the too-full power pushed itself on her again. She fought the instinctive urge to resist. She could not fight it, she must control it. With every grain of concentration she visualized the power, saw it pouring through her in a rainbow of brilliance, possessing the blood vessels and nerve paths and bubbling through the very pores with its pressure, and she carefully slowed the flow, damping its rushing entry, until it merely burned in her. Her ankles took her weight. She blinked, seeing nothing of the room, only the multi-hued energy, and watched the power fade under her concentrated command. The burn faded, and her hair drifted to her shoulders, and only a tingling in her fingertips remained to testify to the mighty crash.

Her vision returned to normal. She took no time to marvel at her accomplishment but stumbled forward on awkward tingling feet to Maru, collapsed against the wall. He shifted weakly as she approached, his eyes wide and staring, shaking with pain.

"Maru!"

He recoiled. It was not pain that made him shiver, but fear. He was terrified of her.

"Maru, it's all right. I'm all right, I feel better. I—I won't hurt you. Maru!"

He stared at her as if she were a demon of flame. "A—Ariana'rika...."

She impulsively reached for him and caught his wrist, making him jerk backward. "Maru, wait. We're friends, aren't we?" Holding him, she moved forward. "Let me help you."

He held very still. He was hurt and frightened, and his natural power was weakened, burned away in the red-orange glow. She could not restore it to him, and she had no chocolate to offer as they had given to Tam. "Maru," she said softly, "please don't be afraid."

He blinked at her, conflicted.

"Please, Maru. Let me help you as you helped me."

His lips worked tentatively. "Tamaryl'sho—he said you called him Tam. He said you would not open battle here." He looked at the fingers still on his wrist. "Tamaryl'sho said you would remember us. That you would not hurt us."

He was afraid of her. "Maru.... You're hurt. What can I do to help?"

"I don't know." He looked at her, wide-eyed, and hesitated. "I just—thank you." He swallowed.

"Rest," Ariana said quietly. "It's all right."

Maru, pale and staring, looked at her and nodded.

CHAPTER 43

Tamaryl soared toward the Palace of Red Sands, overlooking the city spread beneath him in happy bustle. A few other Ryuven were in the air, waving politely or intent on their own business. Tamaryl cupped his wings to slow his speed, banking toward the gardens of the palace.

An explosion of power rocked the air around him. Tamaryl's wings stuttered and he looked around as he stabilized, but he saw only two other fliers looking stunned as well. He turned and searched in the direction from which the jarring sensation had come.

That was Daranai's roof.

Tamaryl raked his wings through the air and dove. The burst of power had ebbed, but something was still very active in the house beneath him. Tamaryl reached for it, but he could not identify the Ryuven who had called forth such a marked blast.

What if someone had come for Ariana? Some would resent the human mage's presence—some rika might have decided to take matters into her own hands, or perhaps a group had come for her.

He rocked his legs forward and landed running, folding his wings behind him. Maru would have been helpless against that kind of power. Daranai was capable of deflecting most of it, but it would have cost her.

He nearly knocked her to the ground as he tore around a corner, one wing extended for balance. He slid to a halt and turned back. "Daranai'rika! What's happened? Is she all right?"

Daranai stared at him. "You—she—you!" Her face twisted in fury. "You brought her here!"

They had come for Ariana, endangering the entire house. "I'm sorry, I have to go to her."

Daranai screamed something after him as he swept down the corridor. He flung back the private door.

Ariana knelt on the floor, obviously well, with Maru's head cushioned against her shoulder. She looked up as he entered, her fingers on Maru's neck. "Tam!"

He stared. She was not injured—Maru was not moving—she was not even ill—the power....

"Tam, can you help him?"

Sweet essence, Maru. "What happened?"

"She hurt him."

"Don't trust her," Daranai said from the door. "Come with me, Tamaryl'sho, and I will explain—"

"Get back!" ordered Ariana in a tone Tam had rarely heard. She rose on her knees, her eyes hard, and a small eddy of power whipped up about her, tugging at her loose robe and hair.

"Human toad," snarled Daranai. "I would not need to be near you to kill you." But she retreated a step.

Tamaryl stared between them as the eddy spun away and was gone. "That—that was you?"

The magic and Ariana's movement had roused Maru. "Ryl!"

His clothing was torn, and his innate energy was unnaturally thin. "Maru, my friend, what happened to you?"

"She did," Ariana muttered viciously.

"I'm sorry, Ryl—I'm so sorry."

Something enormous had happened, something no one wanted to say directly. "Tell me! What happened here?"

Ariana turned icy eyes on Daranai. Maru looked sick. "I—she wanted to bed me. I refused."

"Don't be ridiculous," Daranai snapped, tearing Tamaryl with denial and accusation.

Ariana leapt to her feet, swaying. "You lie!" Her hands rose to form an attack.

Tamaryl shaped an inversion well and absorbed the stinging power Ariana had gathered. "Stop! I—"

"She came for him! And when he refused again and again she hurt him!"

There was nothing but anger in her expression. Tamaryl turned and looked at Daranai, who elongated her slim neck and raised her chin indignantly. "This is a nim and a human—a sick, weak human who has not even been able to speak or move until this hour. You take their word against me, a rika and your betrothed?"

Things broke inside Tamaryl. There could be no good end to this. "Daranai'rika—what happened?"

"Your servant came to me—"

"He didn't!" Ariana shouted, her hands clenched into fists. "I saw everything!"

"You lie!" Daranai snarled. "You were a senseless, oblivious heap!"

"Never senseless," Ariana countered with a weird grin. "Never senseless. No, my affliction was sensing too keenly. I heard everything and saw much."

Maru grasped at Tamaryl's wrist. "Ryl," he whispered, "it is true. I'm sorry—I'm so sorry."

Tamaryl's heart seemed to stop beating. He rose and turned to face Daranai.

She knew his decision. Her expression changed, her eyes narrowing from wide indignation to a feline sneer. "Oh, don't play at the high ground, Tamaryl'sho."

"What?"

"Come now, do you mean to say this human you brought and kept—in my own house, mind you—is nothing to you?"

Tamaryl's jaw slacked. "Lady Ariana is...."

"No?" She smirked. "Then why do you guard her so carefully? Set your precious Maru to watch her?"

"She is my friend."

"A human friend," Daranai'rika repeated scornfully, as if the words betrayed themselves. "And as you value your friends so well, of course, you held her in a world which might have killed her?"

"I didn't know how the journey would harm her!"

"Of course," Daranai agreed smoothly. "Staying was deadly torture to her, but she couldn't risk a brief leap across the between-worlds."

"That's ridiculous." How had he taken the defensive?

"It's clear she is either too dear to release, or her use to you is greater than your concern for her." Daranai shrugged. "So, is she your plaything, or something more serious? And I know how those lines can blur, but don't worry, I don't really mind. And Maru—no, I don't mind him either, so much. Bring your nim, bring your human, bring whatever you like. I'll make no jealous demands on you. But don't pretend to be shocked. We are more sophisticated than that."

"Daranai...."

Her lip curled in disgust. "Please, you're not hurt. You never cared for me. Even back then, you didn't care enough to warn me you would sacrifice our match with your betrayal, much less that you would flee to the human world. You left me the traitor's tainted betrothed, questioned endlessly and locked in uncertain status, not quite under suspicion and yet not exonerated, fit for no one." Daranai gave a triumphant, brittle smile. "Only a moment ago you knocked me to the ground and in the same breath asked if the human were safe. And when you returned, didn't you search out Maru before me? You came here at last only because you needed me to shelter him and your wretched pet human." She scowled. "Your wretched pet human, which attacked me.'"

"You were killing him!" Ariana shot.

Daranai laughed. "Stupid human. *Fup* will not kill nim. They're too weak."

"You used *fup* because he would not lie down for you?" demanded Tamaryl.

"Enough." The voice came from the door, calm and undeniable. They turned together toward the tall female with emerald-dark hair.

"Edeiya!" Daranai started toward her, relieved. "I'm so glad you—"

Edeiya lifted a hand which stopped Daranai as effectively as if it were a shield. "Say Edeiya'rika, please. I am here as Tsuraiya."

Essence and flame, she was Tsuraiya ni'Ai now. Irrelevantly, Tamaryl could not recall whether his rank owed her a nod of acknowledgment or greater obeisance.

Daranai saw her gesture as fresh betrayal. "There is no danger here, Tsuraiya. I thought you might have come as my own blood."

Edeiya raised an eyebrow. "No danger, when a human mage has worked magic strong enough to shake my own house down the way?"

Daranai grasped after the missed opportunity. "She attacked me, in my own home where I sheltered her—"

"I attacked no one," Ariana snapped. "I only underscored my request that she leave off forcing Maru."

Maru turned away, shamed and humiliated. Tamaryl reached down to him. "Can you stand?"

"Yes, of course." But he was unsteady as he rose.

Daranai wheeled on them, determined to lose no more face before Edeiya'rika. "Get your nim and your human out of my house. And you get out as well. I am done with you." She flung herself past the Tsuraiya and into the corridor.

Edeiya'rika glanced after her and then at Tamaryl. "You have this?"

"I think so." He hesitated. "Er—many compliments. We could not have a better Tsuraiya."

Edeiya's lips curved. "Thank you, Tamaryl'sho." She turned and left, pressing no questions.

Tamaryl turned back. "Maru?"

"I will be fine, Ryl." He smiled wearily. "I would not turn down something sweet, though."

"Let's go." Tamaryl settled Maru's arm over his shoulders and looked at Ariana.

"Don't worry for me. I'm well enough for now. Take care of Maru."

He nodded and started for the door. There would be time to question Ariana on her recovery when they were away.

They were nearly to a door when a voice called tentatively behind them. "Tamaryl'sho?"

A nim stood in the entry behind them, shifting his weight and shuffling his wings nervously. Tamaryl recognized his silvery pale hair, the one who had served at supper. "Yes?"

"You're taking him away?"

He must mean Maru. "I am."

The nim took a deep breath. "I was obligated to Heka'che. Daranai'rika purchased my debt and remaining service, and I came here. May I—if you please, I have two years left on my debt and I... I will be an excellent servant, Tamaryl'sho, if you should need one."

Tamaryl turned slowly so that Maru did not stumble. "You too?"

The nim nodded jerkily, his expression tight.

Tamaryl stifled an oath. "What is your name?"

"Oh, thank you!" The nim dropped to two knees, the gesture from nim to sho. "I'm Taro. Thank you!"

Tamaryl nodded. "On your feet and to your duties, Taro. The rika is not pleased with me at the moment, but I will see if I can purchase your debt." He turned back to the door Ariana had dragged open and helped Maru through.

CHAPTER 44

Shianan had sorted most of his paperwork, leaving his desk neat for whoever would use it next. He had canceled the evening training. He did not want the men to see him taken for questioning.

He heard raised voices outside, and his heart quickened even as he schooled himself to sigh in resignation. The time had come. A moment later, there was a sharp knock at the door and it opened without his call to enter. "Sir!" a soldier said breathlessly. "The Shard has been taken!"

Shianan reflected that it was perhaps too early for orders regarding him to have been issued. Of course the alarm would be sounded first.

"The mages say it was stolen, sir. And Prince Alasdair is missing."

A winter storm was blowing in, and as the wind picked up the cold rain fell more steadily. Shianan wrapped his cloak around himself and looked up the dark road. He wasn't worried about searchers happening across Luca to the north-east, as someone had seen Alasdair's hunting group start to the west. Still he felt uneasy.

Somewhere to the south, Prince Soren was searching with another group of soldiers. With both the Shard and the younger prince missing, the stakes were too great for the prince-heir to be seen doing anything else. Only Shianan knew Alasdair's disappearance had nothing to do with the Shard.

Prince Alasdair should have returned from his hunt well before dusk, but neither he nor the two slaves accompanying him had reappeared from the barren hills. The rain was coming down harder, now, and it was more impossible than before to see through the dark night.

Shianan hated the rain. He trudged on, cold water coursing over the edge of his hood, and dutifully called, "Highness? Your Highness?" He did not expect an answer.

The footing was becoming treacherous, the rain turning the steep hillsides to mud. Shianan reflected bitterly they were likely to lose more men than they sought in this dark weather.

"Commander!" called a voice through the rain. "Sir?"

"Over here! What is it?"

A soldier slogged toward him, slipping in the mud. "Sir, they say we're finished here, there's nothing this way. We're moving west."

West was further yet from Luca's road. "So noted, soldier. Go on, I'll follow."

"Yes, sir."

Shianan looked out a moment longer, unable to see the rocky wall he knew he faced. For anyone other than a prince, the search would have been delayed until morning. He hated the chill rain. He sighed and turned back.

He had gone about a quarter mile, sliding in the mud and feeling his way against the rock wall, when his questing fingers found a gap in the rock. He reached forward, feeling into space, and smelled woodsmoke. Light flickered around the corner.

A natural cave, and occupied! This might be a contingent of soldiers evading their search duty, or it might be Alasdair himself sheltering from the storm, or it might be a coterie of bandits in hiding. Shianan lay a hand on his weapon and felt his way into the dog-legged opening. There was a small fire burning inside, and Shianan remained on the far side of the wall until his eyes grew accustomed to the light. Then he moved around the corner, looking across the fire.

Prince Soren looked back at him, firelight reflecting in his startled eyes as he reached for the sword at his hip. He hesitated, recognizing Shianan, and they stared at each other for an eternal heartbeat.

"Your Highness." Shianan found his voice first. "Are you all right?"

"Bailaha." The prince-heir nodded slowly. "I was taking a few moments to warm a drink." He gestured to indicate the flask sitting near the small fire. "Thank you for asking, I'm fine."

Shianan nodded curtly, already uncomfortable. "I see."

"Would you care for a drink? It's cold out there."

"No, thank you, my lord." Water dripped into Shianan's eyes. He shifted his weight awkwardly. "If Your Highness will excuse me...." He shifted toward the rocky doorway.

He had nearly escaped when he heard the prince's sharp exhalation. "Heh. As expected."

Shianan stopped. "Highness?"

The prince made a frustrated gesture. "You prefer the rain to sharing a warming drink with me. So be it." He shook his head, looking away.

Shianan straightened and faced him, anger stirring. "I intended only to relieve my lord of my presence," he answered more sharply than was wise. "I did not mean to offend."

"Oh, well said," the prince replied, his tone biting. "It's hard to find fault with you. Except I believe I invited you to stay." He faced Shianan sternly. "It is my desire, commander, that you share a drink with me."

Shianan clenched his jaw and drew himself to his full height. "I await your pleasure, Highness." He bowed formally.

"'Soats," muttered Soren. "What have I ever done?" He picked up the flask. "I should order you to explain exactly how I've earned your hatred." He took a short gulp and wiped his beard.

"My hatred? My lord, I have never—"

"You are an abominable liar, commander."

Shianan glared at him. Could he truly not see why Shianan would resent him?

Shianan expected arrest at any moment, with interrogation to follow. In this final wild night, what had he to lose? "I regret, Highness, I did not understand you. Is that indeed your order?"

The prince eyed him over the flask. "Why not?" He took another drink, almost savagely. "It's only you and me out here, with no gaping courtiers. We'll never have another opportunity like this so long as we live. Let's be honest. Why do you disdain me so, when we've barely spoken?"

Shianan swallowed against swelling outrage. "It is my prince's desire that I am honest?"

"Perfectly." Soren glared back across the fire.

"Then I shall be honest." Shianan bowed in sardonic courtesy. "I do resent my prince."

Soren snorted. "You wish you'd been born on the right side of the bed."

"No! No, if I had any choice in the matter, I would be the son of an ugly pigherd and his uglier wife."

"And I should believe that?" Soren took another drink. "Come, really. If you were the son of a pigherd, you would not be a commander. You would not have a string of victories behind you and a dozen commendations and a—" He stopped himself abruptly, looking at the flask.

Shianan could not restrain a bitter laugh. "Commendations?" He crossed his arms, made daring with the certainty of impending arrest. "In obedience to your wishes, my lord, I will be perfectly honest—I could bring the head of Pairvyn ni'Ai to our king, and it would not garner half the praise of your wearing the latest fashion in cunning hats."

The prince jerked, his eyes flashing, and then he crossed his arms gruffly. "Honest," he growled. He looked narrowly at Shianan. "And I suppose all those military promotions mean nothing? Years of freedom, away from the pressure and the demands and the scrutiny and the what, was it only once a week or so that I had to listen to your latest accomplishment?" He tipped the flask again and looked past the fire. "'Soats, how I envied you."

"Envied?" Shianan repeated. "You, who were at court? Who had real tutors and classes? Who grew up with hunting parties and dances and respect? Did anyone whisper it was unlucky you were developing your father's jaw and too bad you hadn't enough stubble yet to disguise it?"

Soren stared at him. "You—you're serious?" He leaned forward, suddenly intent. "Listen—I truly envied you. I couldn't help but believe your outpost must be more adventurous and carefree than the stifling, staring court. And you hadn't the weight of all the kingdom waiting for your shoulders." He shook his head. "And I resented you, too—but why mince words? I still resent you, commander. I hate you for every big and small victory he hangs over my head to show just how far short I fall." He took another gulp, swallowing hard.

Shianan blinked. "That's impossible."

Soren shot him a defensive glare. "Not so much."

Shianan shook his head angrily. "No—no, because it is you he holds up as a perfect subject, an accomplished and talented courtier, a—a— " *A son.*

"Me?" Soren faced Shianan. "Your lordship," he said slowly, "I think we have stumbled upon something."

Shianan looked at him, unsettled as his world shifted. "My lord?"

"The king has used us against one another." He stared at the fire's base. "We have been manipulated." He exhaled slowly. "Sweet Holy One, I see it now. He has each of us dancing to the tune he claims the other is playing."

Shianan stared. "But—but why?"

Soren shook his head. "I doubt he even knows he does it," he said quietly. "He says so many things.... He cannot hear himself anymore." He glanced at Shianan and held out the flask. "Drink?"

Shianan accepted it numbly. "So—my lord—you would tell me you do not despise me?"

"Despise you?" Soren laughed bitterly. "Never. I hated you, of course, for being all I wasn't and having all I didn't, but I could not despise you. One has to be better than another before he can despise him." He smiled bitterly. "What a waste of effort that was."

Shianan tipped the flask and was shocked as the liquid hit his lips. "This is tea!"

Soren smiled, a small but friendly smile. "I'm sorry. I prefer tea in the cold."

Shianan drank. "I cannot believe I have been struggling to follow you...." He looked hard at Soren. "You would not deceive me on this, for sport? You really mean he has sometimes praised me to you?"

"We are in a tiny cleft of rock in a pouring rainstorm, met only by accident, and I have no audience to appreciate my wit. What kind of sport would I seek here?" Soren held out his hand for the flask. "I should ask if you are serious about his praise of me."

Shianan chewed at his lip. That the king might praise him behind his back was mind-boggling. That he might do so to Soren was staggering.

"'Soats, what a mess." Soren's mouth twisted sardonically. "King's oats—that's a fitting enough phrase, I suppose, since we're the living harvest of his sowing." He regarded Shianan frankly. "I've sometimes wondered why they didn't simply drown you at birth."

Shianan's throat worked. "I am sure my lord is not the only one to think so," he managed gruffly.

"Wait!" Soren shook his head and held up a hand. "No, I said that all wrong. I meant, after the trouble they went through with me...."

Shianan swallowed. "The arrival of an heir is hardly trouble, my lord," he said with a brittle coldness to disguise the sting.

Soren looked at him. "Sweet Holy One, you don't know. Oh, but who would have told you? Of course you don't know." He exhaled. "Sit down, please, commander. Bailaha. You of all people deserve to understand this."

Shianan obeyed slowly, wary.

Soren took a drink and considered. "You know our father was not the prince-heir."

Shianan knew better than to answer that question directly. "Before King Jerome took the throne, his brother—"

"Oh, enough of that," Soren snapped. "Do you think I don't know who sired you? Do you think anyone will think better of you if you refrain from bragging?"

"Bragging?" Shianan shot him an angry glare. "The first time I repeated what I had overheard, that I was the son of the king's mistress—I'm not sure I even knew yet what that meant—I was thrashed very soundly. So no, Your Highness, I do not seek any particular favor, only the preservation of my own back."

Soren looked startled in the firelight. "I did not realize—but I suppose it might have been so. There was a time when it seemed everyone pretended you didn't exist." He paused. "But by that logic, no one should ever be permitted to say my name."

Shianan did not understand. "My lord?"

"Soren was the first heir to our grandfather's throne—yes, *our* grandfather. I will say it plainly." It seemed to Shianan he took unhappy pleasure in referring to their mutual blood. "But the younger prince took an affair with his brother's betrothed bride, and Prince Soren, who apparently truly loved her, killed himself."

"But—"

"It was publicly alleged to be a hunting accident, I know. But I listened when I was a boy—people say things in front of children, thinking they're too young to understand—and I've done some research of my own. Prince Soren's fall from a precipice—not far from here, actually—was no accident. His servant saw him leap." Soren drank from the flask. "Prince Jerome, left the only heir, took the bride and eventually the throne, though there was quiet talk he was unprepared. He had not been trained so carefully as Soren, after all. But he managed, and the kingdom did well enough.

"But it seems King Jerome and his Queen Azalie suffered some guilt regarding his brother's death. I don't know whether my mother loved Soren or not, but she hated her part in killing him, and she resented my father for it. And she named her first son Soren."

"She named you..."

"She named me for my dead uncle, whom she should have married. Whose throne was taken by her husband." He smiled bitterly.

"I am a walking reproach."

Shianan had no response.

"And then he went and got you."

"And the queen hates me."

"She hates what you represent, I'd say; I'm not sure if she's even seen you, no?" Soren shrugged. "But that is enough, I'll grant."

Shianan stared into the fire, knowing he was ruining his night vision but for the moment beyond caring. "It's enough."

"I'm sorry, Bailaha. For my error in judgment. I never thought but that you must feel as superior as you were portrayed."

"Superior?" Shianan repeated in dull disbelief. "And my lord! A prince need not apologize to his subject."

"To the contrary," Soren returned, "the prince must be the first to apologize. He is held to a higher standard." He gave a weak chuckle. "Though it seems you are no stranger to the higher standard, either."

"I'm not sure that's the right phrase for it."

"Regardless." Soren extended the flask to him. "Here, finish it. I'm sorry I've nothing else to offer, but tea is actually more warming than liquor."

"Thank you." Shianan drained the liquid.

"And now, with our excuse for lingering finished, I suppose we must go out and find the little turd."

Shianan blinked. "My lord?"

"Oh, come now. If you resented me at all, you must certainly know whom I mean by the little turd."

"I only—I have never heard him called so, my lord."

Soren laughed. "I'm glad to hear that. If the court called him such, Holy One knows what they'd call me." He rose, making Shianan scramble to reach his own feet first. "He is my brother, and a prince, but he is also something of a turd. However, I would not want the general populace calling him that."

"My lord." Shianan would not repeat the term—of course not.

Soren faced him. "I—I am glad you happened across this place. I'm glad we spoke. May we be friends?"

Shianan tensed, distrustful. "I...."

Soren's face twisted. "Or perhaps you still hate me?"

"No—I...."

Soren regarded him critically. "You distrust my invitation, yes? Perhaps you even think this is some elaborate plot to entrap you. Perhaps I would be happy to see the bastard arrested for some trifling offense into which I'd manipulated him through overtures of friendship. Perhaps he could be locked away and forgotten, or even executed, and I would be free of his wretched competency."

"I had no such thoughts, Your Highness. I only...."

"You only what? Did you think I did not mean what I said?" Soren demanded.

"Yes," Shianan answered without thinking. "That is—yes, I distrusted it. I am—"

"You thought I would offer my hand in the dark of this cave, but before the court I would make sport of you for my friends." Soren sighed. "Commander, it is the will of your prince that you come to my office tomorrow afternoon, unless this search is continuing. Do you understand?"

"Yes, my lord." Shianan bowed. "I am sorry to have distrusted my prince's word."

Soren shook his head and sighed again. "I might have been suspicious if you had come to me with sudden amiability."

Shianan was unsure how to respond, but Soren did not seem to mind that he said nothing.

They wrapped their cloaks tightly before kicking out the fire and leaving the shelter of the little cleft. The slicing rain made it easy to stay hunched within the hoods rather than trying to speak, and they slipped up the road in silence.

Still, Shianan was uncomfortable walking alongside Soren. Their conversation had shaken him and he wanted to escape, to think alone for a time. How strange it was, he mused, that at his prince's order he would march into fighting and death, but he did not trust that same prince's word that they might be friends.

Soren spoke first. "We'll cover more ground if we separate. That only makes sense."

"Yes, my lord," Shianan answered too quickly. "I will go to the northeast."

"Watch your footing." He sighed. "May we find him soon, and not at the base of a cliff."

Shianan nodded. If Prince Alasdair were found dead at the same time the Shard went missing....

He left the prince with a bow, backing a few steps until Soren had moved a suitable distance away, and then he pulled his cloak tighter as he ducked against the rain.

He slipped in the mud, catching himself with an outstretched hand which landed hard against a boulder. To his right was a short fall into a ravine. If he had slid over that, he might have broken a leg and been lost himself.

Shianan blew out his breath in sharp irritation. This was useless and dangerous. They should have waited until morning, when at least there was light to counter the rain's danger. The steep foothills were too dangerous in these conditions.

He was trying to kick heavy mud from his boot when he thought he heard a human voice.

CHAPTER 45

Shianan froze, lifting his head, but there was only the rain. He dropped his hood and rotated, straining to hear. Rain ran coldly down his neck.

There! Was that a voice? He couldn't be sure. "Hello?" he called.

He wasn't sure if he heard a response. The steady drumming of the rain muted most other sounds. "Hello?" Shianan rubbed water from his eyes and edged toward the ravine's lip, bracing himself against a scrubby tree. He didn't need to fall while chasing a phantom. "Hello! Can you hear me?" He leaned over the edge, eyes aching with the effort to see.

Perhaps a dozen feet below there was sudden movement. "Hey!" Two figures scrambled up from the ground beside a swelling stream. "Hello! I'm here! Can you reach us?"

"Your Highness?"

"Yes! Who are you? Can you reach us?"

For a single heartbeat Shianan wanted to answer that he was a Ryuven captain, but of course he did not. "It's Bailaha." He unfastened his dripping cloak, peeling it back so cold rain pounded into him. "I think I can bring you out."

Alasdair's face was pale in the darkness and for a short moment he did not speak. Plainly he did not relish being rescued by the bastard. "Where have you been?" he sallied angrily. "I've been trapped here for hours, and no one came to our calls."

"I think the walls shaped the sound away, my lord," Shianan answered, rolling his cloak at an angle to form a twisted rope. "I could only barely hear when I was just above you." He wrapped the cloak about the lowest branch of the tree and shook it down. "Can you reach that?"

"The walls crumble away when we try to climb, and the water's rising."

"Use the cloak to take your weight and walk up the wall. I'll pull as well. Ready?" Shianan gripped the sodden cloth, planting his feet as firmly as he could manage. Alasdair placed a foot in his slave's cupped hands and leapt for the cloak, and it stretched in Shianan's hands as it

291

took weight.

Shianan slipped dangerously as he dragged the cloak backwards, and for one terrible instant he thought he would tumble in on top of the prince and the slave, but he found a ridge of stone to brace himself and Alasdair scrambled over the edge, undignified as he scrabbled for a handhold. He got to his feet, slathered in mud and barely recognizable, and looked at Shianan uncertainly.

He was trying to decide whether or not to thank him, Shianan realized. Alasdair owed gratitude to his rescuer, but the prince owed nothing at all to the bastard. Shianan turned back to the ravine, shaking out the cloak a second time. *It would not harm you to say the words*, he thought bitterly. He glanced over his shoulder at the prince, slimed in mud, and suppressed a vicious grin. *The little turd, indeed.*

He tossed the cloak's end toward the slave. "Catch it!" But the cloak passed over the slave's reach and slapped against the wall. "You're going to have to jump higher," Shianan told him unnecessarily.

The slave nodded, shivering. "Yes, lord."

Shianan swung the cloak again, and the slave leapt, but his reach fell short again. Shianan would have demanded better effort from men he trained to survive battle, but there was no battle here, and the slave was cold and exhausted. "One moment, I'll come down." He turned to Alasdair. "Your Highness, you'll have to pull us up."

Alasdair blinked. "You want me to what?"

Shianan indicated the cloak. "I can climb this, but I don't want it slipping, and any help you can give would be appreciated. Your Highness?" He waited. Somehow the dark and the hills made him feel more a commander and less the scorned bastard. This was no royal audience—there was a man who needed retrieving, even if only a slave, and the task made him stronger.

Alasdair looked as if he would protest and then reconsidered. "I will do it." He took the cloak, setting his feet in the trenches Shianan had dug.

Shianan smiled to himself. It might have been unthinkable for the young prince to admit he doubted his ability. "Thank you, Your Highness."

The steady rain made the sides of the ravine treacherously slick, but the cloak's rough weave provided a firm grip. Shianan slid to the end and braced his boots against the muddy wall. "Here," he said to the slave, "do you think you can jump to me?"

"I'll try, my lord."

Shianan twisted the cloak about his wrists. "Go ahead, then."

The slave caught an arm about his waist and swung, tearing at Shianan's hold. Shianan grunted and squeezed hard at the cloak, feeling his grip slide as the fabric tightened about his wrists. "Hold tight," he muttered, and he worked one hand carefully free. Then he began to climb hand over hand, walking up the muddy side of the ravine.

He had nearly forgotten the prince, concentrating on simply dragging their weight up the wall, and he was almost startled to see Alasdair's white eyes leaning over him. The boy was indeed pulling on the makeshift rope—he hadn't a chance of actually taking their weight, despite Shianan's hopes, but he was trying.

Shianan grabbed for a branch and his arm trembled. "Take him," he grunted.

Alasdair stared at him and then at the slave, who stared back in equal astonishment.

"Take him!" Shianan repeated, his words clipped by lack of breath. "Hurry!"

Alasdair reached for the slave's arm and pulled him awkwardly onto the ledge. Shianan welcomed the relief to his shoulders. "Now me." He didn't trust the footing at the edge of the ravine, where water ran steadily into the gorge, or his quivering muscles.

The slave and Alasdair together pulled him to firmer ground, and the three of them stood tiredly facing one another. Alasdair straightened to his relatively short height. "We will go back now."

"Yes, Your Highness." Shianan untied his cloak with fumbling fingers. It shook out of its tight twist reluctantly. He swung it over his shoulders and it slapped against him with frigid impact. "We should let the others know you've been found."

Alasdair nodded. "Clemb twisted an ankle in the afternoon and couldn't keep up."

There had been two slaves. "And where is he now, Your Highness?"

"We went ahead, but we didn't know the way, after all. Then the storm came up, and...."

Shianan felt a hot stab of anger. "You left him to crawl home?"

Alasdair's eyes widened. Perhaps no one spoke to him in such a tone. Certainly Shianan never had. "He—he wasn't crawling. He was just slow. And Jaid here already had the weapons and the deer...."

293

Shianan shivered. "And here you are without the weapons, the deer, or your servant who actually knew the way home."

He'd pushed too far. Alasdair was angry. "It was just a little deer, anyway. And the weapons fell in the ravine. And who are you to criticize me, anyway? You—you're just a dog!"

"This dog, Your Highness, would like to get out of the rain. This way."

Alasdair swelled with outrage as Shianan turned. "How dare you?" A royal never saw a courtier's back.

Shianan pretended not to hear. He was tired, and frustrated, and angry, and cold, and he hated the rain that chilled him both without and deep within, and he almost wished for arrest already so that he no longer had the agonizing suspense of wondering when it would come.

The rain continued, cold and incessant. Shianan clutched at his cloak, shivering harder. He hated the rain, hated it. He could hear Alasdair and the slave slipping behind him, struggling in the heavy mud. Shianan's fingers and toes were numb.

"Hello?" someone called from the road ahead. "Who's there?" It was the soldier Harl.

"It's your commander." Shianan's voice was rusty. "I've found him."

There was a split second of hesitation, and then Harl raised the cry. "The prince has been found!" The sound was echoed along the lines of searchers, and within minutes they were surrounded by soldiers.

"Let me through," ordered an authoritative voice, and Soren pushed his way to the center. "Alasdair! Are you hurt?" He seized him by the shoulders.

Alasdair shook his head. "I'm fine."

"We found Clemb," Soren said. "We were afraid you'd had an accident. Come this way. We have a fire and warm drinks." He looked over the young prince and saw Shianan. "You found him, Bailaha?"

"I did, my lord." Shianan clenched his teeth to minimize their chattering. "My lord, may I—"

"First, come to the fire," Soren said firmly. "And you'll have something warm to drink."

That had been more or less the request Shianan wanted to make. He followed the princes to an oiled tarp stretched between two dripping trees and a smoky fire beneath it. Shianan rubbed at his eyes.

Beside him, Soren was speaking to Alasdair. "What were you thinking? You have a guide for a reason," he said, his voice quiet but forceful. "And where is the Shard?"

Shianan's heart seized mid-beat. Alasdair shrugged at Soren. "What do you mean?"

"The Shard of Elan. It's missing. We thought you were both taken."

Alasdair shook his head. "I don't know anything about it."

"You're certain?"

"I went hunting. Why would I take the Shard?"

Soren exhaled. "Someone has stolen it. And we've lost time searching for you."

"It's not my fault!" Alasdair protested petulantly. He gestured. "It's not like you could have found anyone tonight, anyway."

"We found you." Soren turned to face Shianan. "Bailaha, we owe you thanks."

Shianan saw Alasdair shift uncomfortably. "It was my duty, my lord."

"It was the duty of every man here, but you were the one to find him." Soren looked at Alasdair. "Did you thank his lordship?"

Alasdair's jaw set. "I...."

Soren could match the stubborn set of Alasdair's jaw. "It will be his task to find the Shard, and he has lost this night in hunting you instead. More, you owe him your safety."

Alasdair turned to his elder brother in dismay. "But—but he is...."

Soren's eyes narrowed. "He is a count and a commander in the king's army." His voice was steely. "Now, thank him for his efforts."

Alasdair hesitated, but he could not argue with Soren's logic. "Thank you for your help, Bailaha."

Shianan bowed. "I hope to be of further service in the future."

Alasdair retreated, sipping at his soup as he looked deliberately toward the fire. Shianan accepted a mug of soup from another slave and wrapped his icy fingers about it despite the burning discomfort. Someone began unfastening the tarp's ties.

Shianan gulped the hot soup. If they were starting home, he wanted to be at the front of the line. The sooner he could escape this rain, the better.

Cursed idiot fool of a princeling.

CHAPTER 46

Luca spread his cloak over the damp ground and settled comfortably. As he bit into an apple purchased at a crossroads stand, he withdrew the rolled accounts with his free hand. He could check for obvious discrepancies or improbabilities. Shianan didn't seem as if he should be familiar with the accounts of a typical estate and might be easy prey for a greedy majordomo.

He knew, of course, the accounts were not the primary reason Shianan had sent him. Luca's first priority was to find a safe place to hide the heavy wrapped bundle, whatever that might be. But he did not assume the accounting excuse was wholly fabricated. After unraveling the military accounts, it would be logical for Shianan to want to review his own.

The tramp of feet drew his attention from the neat rows of numbers. He glanced up and saw a contingent of soldiers jogging toward him, weapons and packs slung across their backs. Luca's pulse quickened and a bit of apple stuck in his throat.

No, he was on his master's errand. They were only using the same road out from Alham. They would have no interest in a slave, they would pass him by.

But a sergeant at their head called an order, and the company came to a halt. Luca's stomach clenched.

"You," called the sergeant, as the men panted. "What's your business?"

"I'm carrying my master's accounts, my lord."

"Who's your master?"

"Commander Shianan Becknam, Count of Bailaha. I carry accounts of his estate Fhure."

The sergeant grunted. "On your feet when I'm talking to you. You coming or going?"

Luca stood, the apple in one hand and the sheaf of papers in the other. "Coming, my lord." Was that the right answer? He did not quite understand the question, but nerves kept him from saying more.

"Good thing, that. It'll be slower going if you're leaving the city. Have you met anyone suspicious going out from Alham? I don't know if he would have gotten this far yet."

297

"What do you mean by suspicious, my lord? I've seen only vendors and merchants."

The sergeant grunted again. "I don't know, myself. But someone's stolen the Shard of Elan, and we're looking for him—or them. Only an idiot would be carrying it, but it's my orders to ask." He grinned, showing brown and broken teeth. "Seen anything?"

Luca's head shook almost without his volition. "No, my lord."

"Eh." The sergeant looked around at his men, some of whom had sprawled at the side of the road. "Guess we'll keep on our way, then. Good thing you're on toward the city, as we're setting up road checks ahead. You won't have the delays going into Alham, though, and maybe you'll be quick enough to save your back, even if you stop to laze along the way." He turned toward the soldiers. "Breather's over. Form up! Ready, move! Hurry!" He plucked Luca's apple from his hand and jogged off to join the company.

Luca's throat was too tight to eat, anyway. They were looking for the Shard, which lay in the pack at his feet.

Why had Shianan stolen it? It was plain he had to get it out of Alham before it was discovered. And he had sent Luca, sacrificing a slave—

No, not exactly. *I'll swear on the rack that you knew nothing of it.* His master had urged secrecy for both their sakes. *Luca, my friend, I have a task for you.* Luca had not dared to think on that—but it implied Shianan had not willingly sacrificed him. Didn't it?

Luca wiped apple juice onto his leg and rolled the sheaf of accounts into the bag. He hefted the damning weight of the Shard to his shoulders and glanced after the military company. As they disappeared over the next hill, he turned and moved away from the road.

There were two large oaks before him, ideal markers for a hiding place. He could bury it in the ample space between them. But they were spaced several dozen paces apart, and the Shard might be left long enough for all signs of digging to fade. Luca rotated, scanning the landscape around him. There! Two white birches fifty paces away, perfect for his purpose. He placed himself exactly between the two oaks and then crept sideways until one birch disappeared behind the other, appearing to be a single tree. He dropped the pack and went in search of a sturdy stick.

It was hours before he finished, but he was confident his work would go unnoticed. He had carefully peeled back the sod first, loosening it and scraping it free below the roots, buried the Shard, and then replaced the sod over the refilled hole; the grass would recover within a few days, given the damp earth, and within a week or so it would look undisturbed. The excess earth he'd carried by hand and scattered over a wide area, so there was no obvious detritus to attract attention. And the place was an arrow's shot from the road, where few would see it.

He brushed the larger chunks of mud from his hands, took the remaining apple from the considerably-lighter pack, and settled the straps on his shoulders. Now he had to deliver the accounts, as his master had sent him.

Shianan tried to swallow, but his mouth was too dry, and he felt he might gag instead. He scraped his palms across his tunic and tried to breathe normally.

The door opened easily under his hand, and he entered the audience room and knelt. The king's voice commanded, "Rise, Bailaha."

Shianan did so but kept his eyes low, not trusting himself to keep a steady expression. Courtiers and advisors filled the room around them, and he could feel their eyes boring through him.

"The Shard is our most precious resource at the moment," King Jerome opened curtly.

"I know, sire. We are working to find it." Shianan licked his lips.

"Can you explain how this could have happened?"

"I can't, Your Majesty...."

"Sire," interrupted another voice. "The commander spent most of the night in the search for Prince Alasdair, like myself. I suspect he, like myself, has had little time to examine what evidence we have or to formulate any plans of action beyond what was immediately done."

King Jerome and Shianan both looked in surprise at Soren. Shianan caught himself first, swallowed and nodded, amazed his voice responded. "We have sent companies to all major crossroads within a day's march, Your Majesty. Even had they found the Shard already, news could not have reached us yet."

The king nodded thoughtfully. "True, true. And we hear you were the one who found our prince Alasdair. That was well done." He smiled. "We are very grateful for that."

Shianan flushed with heat. "Thank you, sire. I am happy to have

299

been of service." He swallowed. "I think perhaps we should have had a stricter guard on the Shard itself, Your Majesty. It was in the lowest level of the Wheel, which has a guard at each entry, but it was not watched specifically."

The king nodded. "That will be remedied after its recovery. Bailaha, we charge you and General Septime with the safe recovery of this vital safeguard. The Circle is ready to recreate the shield; the thief must be a traitor who seeks to keep us vulnerable to the Ryuven. Find this treasonous cancer so that we may cut it out."

Shianan gulped and bowed. "As you command, Your Majesty." As he straightened, Ewan Hazelrig's eyes caught his. Shianan tore his gaze from the mage and faced the king. "If Your Majesty has no further questions of me, I will return to organizing a more comprehensive search."

This frank request startled the king, but he nodded. "Go to your work, then. We will expect regular reports."

Shianan bowed and backed to the door, waiting until it closed firmly before fleeing the antechamber. His mind spun; he had to invent something to give the appearance of industrious search without endangering Luca and actually capturing the Shard.

Almost he wished for arrest and the relief of the suspense, the solid knowledge of what he would face. Almost.

Perhaps a miracle would save them—Hazelrig might find a way to reach across the between-worlds, or Tam might return her this very day. Then Shianan could discover the Shard's hiding place and be the kingdom's hero.

He blew out his breath bitterly. Such dreams would only disappoint him more keenly; better to focus on what he could do to delay his arrest and interrogation.

CHAPTER 47

Shianan tugged nervously at his tunic and entered the massive door to the elder prince's antechamber. The secretary gave him a dubious look, and Shianan said, "His Highness asked me to come this afternoon."

The secretary nodded authoritatively and rubbed at his nose. "Wait here, please, your lordship. I'll speak to His Highness."

Shianan paced for the duration of the secretary's absence. But when the inner door opened, it was Soren who emerged. Shianan dropped into a bow.

"Bailaha, I am sorry, but I cannot stay. I appreciate your coming as asked, but—well, I'm sure you have as many demands as I do today. With any luck, the Shard has already been recovered and is on its way home, but until it arrives...." Soren exhaled. "Perhaps we can find time later." He nodded. "I'm sorry, Bailaha."

Shianan bowed again. "Your Highness." When he stood, the prince was gone and the secretary was already seated, making a few notes and ignoring him. Shianan left.

Nothing had changed. He hadn't thought it would, not really. It was not disappointment he felt, but the cold certainty of confirmation. Nothing had changed.

He returned to his quarters long enough to exchange court-worthy clothing for training gear and went to the practice yard. The men not dispatched in search of the Shard deserved a day of lighter drills, after last night's difficult search, but Shianan would see their routine was not too simple. Nothing in the military changed.

The oversized oaken doors of Fhure's main house were locked by the time Luca arrived, shortly before midnight. He beat at the door and called until a watchman came. "Who are you, coming at this hour?"

"I carry papers from our master, Shianan Becknam."

The watchman grunted. "Come in, then."

Luca looked around the modest but elegant entry, heavily shadowed by the lantern. "Where is the majordomo?"

301

"In bed, like sensible people," grumbled the watchman. "Didn't you think of the bandits?"

Luca shook his head. "I didn't know you had bandits nearby." He withdrew the accounts, secure in their oilcloth wrapping. "I want to deliver this and be on my way as quickly as possible."

"What is it?" A thin man in nightclothes with a cloak drawn over his shoulders entered and looked at Luca expectantly. "I'm Kraden, the majordomo. Who are you?"

Luca gave a small bow, for the majordomo's position far outranked his own. "I bring a message from our master." He extended the wrapped packet. The watchman hung close behind, anxious to hear the news.

"He ignores us for nigh a year and then sends midnight messages? What's it, then?"

A sturdy woman who had followed Kraden moved to the fire, prodding it to greater flame and pulling at the blanket around her shoulders. "You walked through the dark, lad?"

"What?" Kraden stared from the accounts, spread in one hand, to the letter in the other. "He doesn't trust the accounting and wants it redone."

"What's that?" The woman heaved herself about and snatched the letter. "Those numbers are good, I'll vouch for that," she said indignantly. "I checked them twice." She grinned at Luca. "Yes, it's mine. Kraden's a dear, managing things, but I can render accounts in a third of the time and leave him to manage the place."

Luca nodded. "That's good. Er, please don't be offended. If you've heard about the military funds—"

"Right, right." Kraden nodded. "Didn't we say every lord in the land would be checking his accounts more closely? He's just giving us the chance to be sure of things." He took the accounts back. "You are sure of these, Marta?"

"Sure as sunrise," Marta answered confidently. "I never send without checking twice." She turned back to Luca. "But why rush this, lad? You could have slept safe and brought it in the morning."

"I hadn't the time," Luca answered. "I need to leave again by dawn."

Marta gave him a skeptical glance. "He can't expect you to do that trip again in a day!"

It wasn't Shianan's orders that drove Luca, but he could hardly explain that. "I should hurry."

"Blasted unreasonable bastard," Kraden muttered, "and he can stay in Alham for all my pleasure. Marta, get the man something warm to drink, will you?"

CHAPTER 48

Tamaryl drew one knee to his chest and rested his chin upon it. He had retained some boyish habits, it seemed, after fifteen years posing as a child.

He glanced at the package resting beside him. It felt far too small. Maru had suffered for Tamaryl's poor judgment, and no offering could make things right. And there had been a promise....

Tamaryl had been only a child—a real child—when the attack had come. The Lian had threatened the Ai for some time, but this was the first time fighting had reached so far. It had caught them by surprise, and Tamaryl had not time even to escape inside. In the garden he huddled within sheltering flowers, curled tightly into himself.

Only steps away, his mother fought. Even through his terror he was in awe of her as she flung bolt after bolt into their foes, snatched down Lian warriors with savage magic, whirled to destroy another opponent. She was deadly, graceful, powerful, unstoppable.

But Caliel'silth was only one. Their garden was not netted, and there were too many Lian dropping from the sky. Even in her fury she fell behind, now deflecting as many bolts as she threw. A hot blast of magic scorched the earth beside Tamaryl, withering and crisping the flowering vine, and when he looked again his mother was facing three Lian males.

But another form rushed from the side with angry magic. She had to fight at closer quarters and her attacks did not utterly disable her targets; she was nim. But she disrupted their concerted assault upon Caliel'silth, and together the two females killed two of the Lian while the third fled, badly injured. They did not pursue him but faced the continuing Lian onslaught, fighting together in terrible harmony, Caliel'silth destroying those above while the nim Rizalet dispatched those who penetrated Caliel's barrier and wider attacks.

When the Lian had at last been repelled, the two females stood panting in the bloodied garden, eying the array of dead warriors. They had hardly assured themselves of the enemy's flight before they turned to opposite sides of the garden and called anxiously.

"Tamaryl!"

"Maru!"

Their sons came hesitantly, fearing the dead Lian and the open sky. Tamaryl flung himself into his mother's arms and clutched her tightly. Beside him, the strange boy wailed. "Mama, you're bleeding!"

"I'm all right, Maru," his mother soothed. "Take my hand. We must go."

"Nonsense," Caliel'silth said, speaking to the stranger for the first time. "You are wounded."

Rizalet shook her head, breathing shallowly. "No, Caliel'silth, thank you. I only saw you were fighting alone and I hid my son in your garden. I did not mean to stay." She rose to her feet. "We—we are going to...." Her eyes rolled and she fell forward onto her son, who shrieked.

Caliel'silth set aside Tamaryl and gathered the injured nim into her arms, carrying her into the Palace of Clouds and calling for the scattered servants. Special care was given to the nim who had aided the silth in her own garden, and Rizalet stayed in the palace itself while healers attended her. Their sons eyed one another warily before settling to play at knocking imaginary humans in the head with garden sticks. In the end, Rizalet confessed she had lost her small holding in the Lian attacks, and Caliel'silth promised that she and Maru would always have a place in her household.

Maru was the only other child in the Palace of Clouds, and he became Tamaryl's fast friend. When Rizalet fell ill, years later, young Tamaryl had gone secretly to her and promised anew that Maru would always have a place in the household, that he would be safe even after she was gone.

And then Tamaryl had abandoned him. Twice.

At last he sighed and picked up the package as he rose. He passed the servants industriously restoring the mansion and went directly to the open room where Maru lay on a sleeping couch. It took time to recover from *fup*. "Are you awake? How do you feel?"

Maru gave him a tired smile as he sat up. "I'm all right, Ryl."

"You're better, certainly, but I don't know that you're entirely all right." Tamaryl seated himself on a stool and held out the packet. "Here; eat it all."

"Chocolate!" Maru's face broke into a more honest smile. "Better than honey!"

Tamaryl smiled. "I'll get more this afternoon, so be sure to finish that." He sobered. "Maru—I did not know what you would face in Daranai's house. I never would have asked you to stay...."

"Ryl," Maru interrupted, "you do not need to apologize. You hold no blame."

Tamaryl swallowed hard against the lump in his throat. He had hurt Daranai, if unconsciously, and left his unprepared friend to suffer her revenge. "But still, you suffered for my lack of insight."

"Well, I would not have it repeated," Maru said grimly. "But none of it was your doing." He took a bite of chocolate. "How is—the rika?"

Tamaryl noted the hesitation. "She is doing well. She is practicing, trying to become familiar with our own magic." He shrugged. "If you're feeling well enough, you should come with us this afternoon."

Maru thought only a moment before smiling. "I am merely tired. I will go to the market with you."

"Good." Tamaryl rose. "I have some things to see to. I'll come for you when we're ready."

He left Maru and found his steward, reclaimed from a wing of the Palace of Red Sands. Fasi'bel had returned willingly to Tamaryl's service, happy to have the responsibility of a full estate again after years of working beneath another steward.

"Tamaryl'sho," she greeted. "I have spread word that we need a few more servants to complete your household. We should have a full contingent within a few days."

"There is no hurry, Fasi'bel," Tamaryl told her, "but thank you for your efforts. Actually, that is another task I have for you."

She produced a slate for notes.

"In the house of Daranai'rika, there is a nim called Taro. I want you to purchase his debt so his obligation is to this house." He hesitated. "You will probably find Daranai'rika is... not receptive to any offers originating from me. If you can trust another to do it, you may find it an easier task."

"Yes, Tamaryl'sho."

"I don't know the exact amount of the debt, but he owes something like two years of service. I am willing to pay a little more to have him, if necessary. Use your own judgment. It has always been excellent."

"Thank you, Tamaryl'sho." Fasi smiled beneath the praise.

Tamaryl went next to the room given to Ariana. He rapped the wall beside the archway—a courtesy concession to human preference in the open Ryuven house—and called, "Mistress Ariana?"

"Come in. The door's open, anyway." She laughed. "I'm practicing. I thought I could manage a light," she explained with mild disappointment, gesturing to the unlit candle beside her, "but apparently that's more control than I can muster yet. How's Maru?"

"Recovering. How is your practice coming?"

Ariana shrugged. "Your magic is everywhere! So easy to draw! It's harder to control, though; I'm not used to such abundance flowing quite so freely. Hence my difficulty with the candle. And to be honest, delicate work has never been my forte. But I cannot use much power, yet. It hurts."

"It hurts?"

"I want instinctively to suppress it, to limit it. But that's.... It's difficult. And painful. I think it is better to simply channel it and trust it will do as I ask, but that's—frightening. I am used to more control. And, it's exhausting."

"Your kind is not accustomed to our magic, nor trained to handle it, nor perhaps even capable of withstanding it." He looked at her seriously. "It has killed every mage brought here—you are the first to survive. Only a mage of very great talent and skill could manage what you have done thus far."

She sobered at this daunting statement, but she answered as if he only complimented her. "Thank you, Tam—Tamaryl—but I don't mean to stop just yet. It's right there, just out of reach, and I had it once. I can do it again. After another nap." She smiled. "You said we would go out this afternoon?"

He nodded. He wanted to test her defenses before he carried her again into the between-worlds. He had to know if she were strong enough... and he secretly, privately, hoped she was not. Once he carried her home, the shield would be restored and their worlds separated forever, and now—so soon after Daranai's offense, still uncertain in his return to the Ryuven court—now he did not want to lose her. Not yet.

Chapter 49

The Ryuven city was... different. Of course. They walked through a market, familiar in its spreading variety, but many of the goods were strange to Ariana. The streets were wide and open to the sky, full of light where she was accustomed to stacked buildings and close roofs.

Ariana felt eyes always as they walked. Barter and conversations slowed as she passed. She tried to ignore this. She was, after all, an oddity and even an enemy here. How would people react if a Ryuven walked openly down the street in Alham? What if Tamaryl walked beside her father in his true form? There would be panic and resentment. They would certainly stare.

That was all, she told herself. She was a human, and they were staring. She glanced at a small Ryuven, wings shifting as she gaped, and saw her mother pull her away as they passed.

They're just curious, maybe worried. I'd feel the same way.

"Is that the human mage?" someone asked in a hushed, urgent voice.

"She didn't die?!"

"She's a human who uses our magic!"

Conspiratorial voices rippled around her. "Is she here to treat with Oniwe'aru?"

"She must be very powerful."

A Ryuven boy dashed across the clearing they made as they walked and snatched at her clothing with the air of completing a daunting dare. He raced away again, glancing wide-eyed over his shoulder.

"What is she doing here?"

"What does she want?"

Tamaryl glanced at her. "Ignore them, my lady," he said softly.

Ariana swallowed. She was trying.

"Go back!" someone called, hidden in the throng. "Monster!"

Monster? That was an epithet for Ryuven....

"We can't have humans here!" shouted someone else, more sharply.

Ariana tensed. Were the Ryuven gathering closer now? There

309

were so many.... The angry muttering increased, marked by occasional shouts. Ariana glanced worriedly at Tamaryl and Maru beside her.

An object flew through the air. Ariana saw it and reached for the magic to form a shield. But the unfamiliar energy slipped through her fingers, eluding her, and she felt the awful sense of failure, only this time it was no mere entrance exam—

It was a vegetable which struck her, a reddish-brown tuber which slapped solidly into her shoulder as she ducked. It bounced to the ground, and more voices joined, and Ariana's heart leapt in sudden terror.

Tamaryl moved and a brief hail of vegetables rebounded off the shield he flung about them. "Enough!" he shouted in a furious baritone. "Stop, now!"

"We don't want the human here!" came a chorus of shrill replies. "It's not safe. She's dangerous, she's an enemy. We don't want her!"

"She is not here for you!" Tamaryl's wings flared as he glared around them. "This human is mine, my own, mine by right of spoil. I carried her back from the human world, and Oniwe'aru has left her in my keeping. Which of you will challenge for her?"

The Ryuven shifted and threw frustrated glances at each other, but no one opposed Tamaryl. He turned and snapped, "Let's go."

They walked down the street, eyes burning them, and around the corner. Ariana walked a little closer to Tamaryl even as she clenched her fists. "Was that really necessary?"

"What?"

"You told them I was—your possession!"

"It was the way to have them let you be. I am the—no one will challenge me for right of spoils."

"But it's what you said!" Ariana struggled for words. "You don't understand. A—a thing! A mere piece of loot. It's awful! It's like—"

"Like being a slave?" Tamaryl's mouth formed a faint smile.

Ariana's stomach clenched. "Tam, I didn't mean—I'm sorry. I'm so sorry. But you weren't treated like a slave, not like other slaves...."

"I did serve you and your father," Tamaryl corrected her mildly. "And to you, I was a slave. I was treated well, yes—I know that—but you always thought of me as a slave boy, didn't you?"

Ariana looked straight ahead. "How was I supposed to know differently?"

"You weren't," Tamaryl answered. He paused in the shadow of an awning and turned to catch her eyes. "But I often wished you would not see me as one."

Ariana was suddenly, urgently aware of his proximity and his size and his strange Ryuven build. "You—Tam—I...."

He glanced away and his intensity faded. "But I knew that was impossible. In your world, I could be nothing more." He turned back to the street, where Maru stared fixedly at a market stall a few paces away. "Coming?"

Ariana's mind was whirling, but her feet began moving. There were still Ryuven eyes on her, but she did not look back as they passed through the busy market.

CHAPTER 50

Shianan looked over the men as Torg called orders, mentally critiquing a few crooked lines and sloppy postures. He could address those when Torg was finished.

Shouts came from the nearby gate, where a caravan fought through storm muck in the dip long traffic had worn, draft slaves slipping and struggling with the wagons. Shianan glared at the soldiers whose attention drifted. Most looked hurriedly back to Torg. Shianan started forward through the ranks. On either side he sensed men tensing, straightening, holding their breath. Before he reached the first sloppy posture, it was corrected.

Shianan eyed them critically. If they meant to march before the king in a few weeks at the festival, they would have to be drilled considerably before then. But in the meantime, they had more important duties. "Captain Torg," he called. "I want a company guarding the Mages' Wheel."

Now the caravan master was snarling threats to an overseer, who took them seriously enough that he began pushing at a mired cart himself. For a moment he and the single draft slave worked together, feet slipping in the muck, and the cart rocked promisingly, but it did not break free of the mud. Then the overseer angrily shoved away from the cart. "Push!" he shouted, slashing with a switch.

The slave jumped as he yelped and strained forward.

"Move!"

The slave gasped. "Please!" he tried, slipping as the mud liquefied beneath his efforts. "I can't—"

The overseer glanced worriedly up the line. "Move it!" He began to flail the switch. The slave ducked away from the blows, crying aloud, and hid his face against the crossbar as he dug against the muck. But the switch did not pause, and the slave wailed and tried to shield himself with his arms, abandoning any attempt at freeing the wagon. His panicked cries stopped activity in the courtyard.

Shianan started for the gate. But before he could reach them, a dark-haired man seized the arm of the overseer. The overseer half-turned, frenzied, but caught himself. The man twisted the switch from his hand. "You're accomplishing nothing here."

313

The overseer was winded. "But—it's not moving. Master Orcan will flog me as well if it doesn't move!"

"Then you'd better try something more productive." The dark-haired man pushed past the overseer and looked down at the mud-covered slave. "Let me see you."

The trembling slave obeyed and lifted his head. The man looked at his face briefly and then turned away.

Shianan saw the overseer stiffen as the caravan master approached. "What is this?" he demanded. Without waiting for an answer he lashed his own switch over the slave, who reached for the crossbar, slipping in the mud.

"Orcan!" The dark-haired man faced him squarely. "This is fruitless, wasting time and ruining our labor." He gestured toward the rest of the caravan. "Bring a team to help free this."

"As you say, then." Orcan turned on the overseer, who jumped. "Go and bring the slaves from the first wagon to be parked away."

The merchant was firm. "You have other wagons to see to, Orcan."

Orcan set his jaw. "Of course." Holding his switch firmly, he stomped up the line.

The merchant exhaled a long breath and then turned toward Shianan, still watching from a few paces away. "I'm sorry—I think you were coming for the same reason?"

Shianan made a small gesture. "No one likes to see that."

"Orcan would sooner cut a drudge than a cheese." He rolled his eyes. "He says labor is the least of our costs. He may be right, at that, but I'm not sure it justifies all."

"You must be another of the merchants come to compete for the opportunity to supply our army."

"I hope the competition is not as fierce as that," he replied with a smile. "Jarrick Roald, at your service."

"Commander Shianan Becknam," Shianan replied, offering a hand. The merchant tipped his head, as if trying to remember something. "You might have heard it as the Count of Bailaha."

Roald looked startled. "Then I should take seriously your comment about the competition."

Shianan liked him already. "Don't worry just yet. Though it's not my decision, I'll be happy to hear why we should choose your house over another."

"I'd very much appreciate some of your time."

"Tomorrow evening, at my office?"

"Thank you very much." Roald offered his hand, and Shianan clasped wrists with him. "I'll bring wine, if you'll have some cheese or a good cut of meat."

Shianan nodded. "Fair enough." He turned and called to Torg. "I want five men to move this cart." He pointed. "And another company—Sergeant Alanz—that dip needs repair. You'll find shovels in the warehouse."

"That's slaves' work!" someone muttered resentfully from the ranks.

"There'll be slaves to finish the stonework," he announced loudly. "But you'll do the base. And if you'd rather not do the stonework, too, see that you turn out more smartly tomorrow. Now move."

Mage Hazelrig called a weary response to the knocking at his office door. Elysia Parma opened. "Someone to see you," she said gently, and she held the door and gestured.

It was the bookbinder girl—Ranne, he recalled. "Yes?"

"My lord mage." Her face was strained. "I've brought this...." She placed a wrapped book on his desk. "This was—Lady Ariana's. She'd left it to be repaired.... I'm so sorry, my lord mage. But I wanted to return it to you."

"Thank you." The poor girl believed Ariana dead, and he could not disabuse her, not yet. "Thank you for bringing this."

She nodded, clamping her lips together tightly, and made a quick curtsey before rushing for the door. He heard a stifled sob before the door closed.

Poor girl. But she would be glad again when Ariana returned from the Ryuven world, safe and whole. He folded his hands and clenched his fingers tightly. When Ariana returned....

The Silver Mage locked the door and swept around his desk. Without speaking she sat on the arm of his chair and wrapped her arms about him.

His notes blurred and he rested his head in his hands, despair and worry and fear rising in him. "She's...." But he couldn't tell her. Not even Elysia.

Her fingers wrapped about his, and he squeezed her hand. Ariana would return. Tamaryl had promised to bring her when she was able, and Becknam had promised to make it possible to bring her. She would return. She would return.

CHAPTER 51

Tamaryl paid the seller and handed a large packet to Maru. "Eat all of that."

Maru chuckled. "If I must."

Tamaryl handed a smaller square to Ariana. "I do not know if sweet food will be of any help, since your magic is not inherent but drawn, but I doubt it could hurt. Maru, shall we show Ariana our old lookout?" He turned to Ariana. "Do you feel up to a steep walk? I can't fly with you, I'm sorry."

"You caught me when I fell from the cliff."

"And took you straight to the ground. I only managed to slow our fall to something manageable. Human bodies, even the slightest and most lovely, are unwieldy, weighty things. All that bone!"

"But they say the Ryuven carry humans in battle."

Tamaryl sobered. "A Ryuven may indeed lift a human, when he is already at speed and simply snatches one from the ground. But he never lands with one."

Ariana had a sudden awful image of a Ryuven dropping a human over the swirling maelstrom of battle and wished she had said nothing.

"Come. If you tire I'll help you." He gave her an enticing smile and led the way out of the city.

The climb was steep as promised, but Tamaryl took her hand over the rocky areas. There was no trail, as the Ryuven could simply fly to the summit. But they did not have far to go before Tamaryl and Maru paused. "This is the first stop," Maru said. "Look." He gestured over the view below them.

The city spread before them, gleaming white and multi-colored in the sun. Winged Ryuven sailed from one rooftop to another, and Ariana noted the taller buildings had entrances on multiple levels. To one side, the Palace of Red Sands lay under a glittering net which kept its walled gardens secure and more or less invisible to eyes overhead.

"It's beautiful," Ariana marveled aloud. "Absolutely beautiful." She watched a winged figure land gently and embrace another waiting for him. "Why would...."

Tamaryl looked at her. "Yes?"

It was difficult to ask. "Why invade our world, when they have such an amazing world of their own?"

Tamaryl sighed. "Look at the fields beyond the city." Without city walls, it was easy to see distances. The fields were green and brown, mottled with grey-black. "That blight has affected crops here for a generation. Food stores are precious, and some years we have famine. It has become more common for nim to beg money and indenture themselves for the debt, providing for family and guaranteeing their own food and shelter in the house's service. We haven't steady resources, our social structure is changing, che and sho are desperate for glory and power and security."

"So you want our food. And battles."

"Some years are more urgent than others. And in truth, it's worsened since I left."

Tamaryl settled on his stomach in the hillside grass, wings folded compactly on either side. Ariana settled cross-legged beside him, more weary than she wanted to admit. The magical atmosphere was demanding, and the climb had tired her.

She closed her eyes and tried to see the Ryuven magic, as she perceived her magic at home. Here in the Ryuven world, however, magic was not something which could be seen. It was sight, sound, taste, scent, pressure, heat, cold, all at once, overwhelming her if she tried to approach it like the tame magic of the human world. It came at her in a dizzying rush, crushing her in a roaring wave, tugging her under—

She opened her eyes and pulled a deep breath, her heart racing. The world settled about her, the magic pulsing just below the fabric of reality, ready to surge again.

Tamaryl turned to where Maru still stood. "Come join us," he prompted. "We can relax for a few minutes."

Maru sat a few paces from Ariana. She hesitated and then ventured, "I don't often bite, despite my vicious human appearance."

Maru glanced down, sheepish. "No, I suppose not."

"You took care of me when I was a senseless heap. I can't be too fearsome. I'm not nearly so dangerous as your own kind." Immediately she regretted the words. She hadn't meant to refer to the attack, and the incident was not a subject for jest. "I'm sorry, I didn't mean.... She's a brute, a horrid—there aren't even words for her. She muddies lust with power and ruins both."

318

Tamaryl regarded her with a raised eyebrow. "And I had thought my lady innocent."

Ariana flushed. "I am innocent, but not ignorant. My father said those who are ignorant will not long remain innocent." It was time to change the subject. She pointed. "Which is your house?"

Tamaryl was chewing on a piece of grass, so Maru answered, "The bright one there traditionally belongs to the Pairvyn, and the Tsuraiya's is across the way. Ryl, what are you doing? Are you a grazing beast?"

Tamaryl laughed. "When human children have clean grass in their reach, they often chew it. I'm not sure why, but it does offer an interesting flavor—though I perceive now our grass is more piquant. Anyway, I took up a number of childish habits. Useful camouflage."

Maru shook his head. "That you should be—"

"Your grass is tasty!" announced Ariana around a stalk. She laughed. "Try it, Maru!"

He looked skeptical, but he gamely plucked a stem and tasted it. "Hmm."

"Isn't it, I don't know, almost savory?"

Maru's expression was not quite patronizing. "As you say, Ariana'rika."

She laughed and tipped her head. "Does rika mean mage?"

"No, no." Maru grinned. "We have no need of such a word, of course. Rika is a—a title? An honorific? A term of respect. A rika is a female where a sho is a male. And then there are bel and che, and then nim."

"Silth and aru are our rulers, you would say," contributed Tamaryl. "King and queen."

"Does Oniwe'aru have a silth wife, then?"

Maru blinked at her in confusion, and Tamaryl chuckled. "No—if Oniwe'aru takes a mate, she will be rika. My mother was silth while she ruled, and rika after."

"Your mother was a ruler?"

"Yes, for a long time. And then Susanoni'silth after her, and then Oniwe'aru. My mother was also Tsuraiya after her rule—that is, she led the Ai host."

"The Ai host... like an army?" Ariana frowned. "But we've never seen female Ryuven in raids. Don't you guard them, like Damas wives?"

Tamaryl chuckled. "My lady mage, Ariana'rika, you

319

misunderstand. We do not protect our females. Quite the opposite, in fact."

"What's a Damas wife?" asked Maru.

"Damas is the capital city of the Damas region," explained Ariana. "Confusing, I know. The women there stay always in their houses and are never seen by any man other than husbands or fathers."

"Why? Don't they love their mates and children?"

"What? No, the men don't allow them out, from what I understand."

Maru looked as if she'd explained water ran uphill.

"A moment, both of you." Tamaryl had given up trying to hide his amusement. He turned to Ariana. "Your armies are predominantly male. That was one reason we first thought you barbarians, using males in defense. Don't argue, I understand better now. For our part, we have two hosts. The males are deployed exclusively for battles of conquest."

"On the surface, that does not sound so different."

"Ah, but we have also the host of females. It is they who defend us from invasion or attack."

"I see." Ariana considered. "And why is this? Is it to keep your women only for more desperate need?"

"I suppose it might be." Tamaryl smiled. "But there are two better reasons. The first is that, as in most species, the female is a greater defender."

Ariana nodded. "A wolf should face the boar before the sow with her piglets. And the second reason?"

Tamaryl ran his thumb along his cheekbone. "As a general rule, our females are larger and stronger. This happens in your world, too, as in birds of prey? There are exceptions, of course, but we keep our fiercer force for our own defense."

"Stronger, you say?"

"Your father is no doubt a match for most Ryuven males. Only a few of the sho could challenge him seriously. But even the White Mage would be hard pressed by our rika."

Ariana bristled. "Surely you exaggerate."

Tamaryl chuckled. "Not intentionally, but I confess we learn early to respect our females. As children, we see them defend us from other clans—Maru and I watched our mothers repel a palace attack— and then as inexperienced warrior initiates, we go to battle another clan's defending host, where we are thoroughly blooded by their females. It leaves an indelible impression." He shrugged self-deprecatingly, smiling.

"That's intriguing." Ariana watched distant Ryuven in the sky. "Are they really so fierce?"

"It is why we raid your world," Tamaryl said carefully. "We would rather face your barbarian armies with their brutal muscles than another clan's defensive force."

"And the blight isn't only here in Ai lands," Maru added. "It's more profitable to raid where there's a harvest."

They sat in silence for a few moments, the words hanging in the air.

"Look." Tamaryl pointed to a group of young Ryuven diving over a field. "That's what tag looks like here."

"Oh, how fun!" Ariana yawned. "I'm sorry! I'm not bored, I promise. I'm always tired. I'm sorry."

She sat still, watching the city and the tiny Ryuven in the sky, and a warm hand crept over hers in the grass. "I'm glad you could see this," Tamaryl said quietly. "I wanted to show you my world before you go home."

The word quickened her pulse. "When?"

"In a few days, when you're stronger. Do you remember the between-worlds? You should be whole. In a few days." He squeezed her hand. "I promised your father I'd take care of you. I'll see you safely home."

CHAPTER 52

Shianan shed his cloak, grateful for the thin warmth of the office. The day was cold, and in the night he had dreamed of slaves wailing in the courtyard. He hung the cloak over its peg and leaned against the wall, tired not in body but in mind.

If only Hazelrig had a way to contact the Ryuven world. If only they knew whether Ariana could return at all....

Shianan closed his eyes. When the White Mage had pierced all his words and found the heart of his willingness to steal the Shard—a motivation Shianan had hardly admitted to himself—he had wanted to run, to deny all and flee. It was worse than stupid to want the White Mage's daughter. Such a prize could not come to the bastard.

From long ago, it was accepted practice for bastards of the Laguna line to be gelded, eunuchs to prevent further illegitimate shoots off the royal family tree. As far as Shianan had been able to learn, he was the first openly known by-blow in several generations, and while the custom had been neglected, he did not wish to tempt fate.

No, Shianan Becknam would not be permitted to marry. And Ariana Hazelrig, Black Mage of the Great Circle, would go to someone more worthy.

He went through the office to his sleeping quarters. Clothing hung where he'd left it to dry and muddy tracks marked the floor. Shianan frowned. He had not noticed how much he'd come to leave to Luca.

With a start, he noticed Luca on the low mattress. "Luca?" There were muddy boots at the foot of the mattress. "How are you here already? I did not expect you until tomorrow."

Luca missed Shianan's gesture to remain where he was. He blinked red-rimmed eyes and surreptitiously braced a hand against the wall behind him as he stood. "I hurried. I ran as much as I could, and walked when I was too winded." He sounded faintly proud of himself.

"There was no need for that."

Luca swallowed. "I met a company of soldiers who said the Shard had been stolen. I knew my master would face many demands and would stand most in need of service."

323

The answer had come too glibly through his exhaustion. It was an answer rehearsed over miles. "You unwrapped the—"

"Oh, no! Not against your order. No, I buried your package safely as you instructed. Even if you suspect your majordomo of misplacing funds, your coin will be safe there, and if you find the accounting is correct after all, it can easily be retrieved."

Shianan stared. This slave could hang him in a moment's work, but he would not. "Right," he said. "Well done, Luca. Thank you." He swallowed. "Later you can explain exactly where it is. Meanwhile, take a few hours and sleep. I'll want you this evening for another merchant."

"Thank you, Master Shianan." Luca slid to the mattress again.

"New, then?"

The recruit made a face. "I'd rather be counting profit in the granary than wearing down my heels in drills. But they said one of us had to go in the army, and I pulled the short straw."

The soldiers laughed. "Well, put some of that straw in your boots, rookie."

"Boots?" said another. "I'd say rather to pad your limbs. It's weapons where you'll feel it first, with the commander."

"The commander?"

"Commander Becknam. Er, he's a count now, too, but here he's just the commander."

"Not just! He's a demon, he is. You ever had him demonstrate a pass on your skin?"

"'Soats, it was me and Ald together he took on at once. Knocked us both down and wasn't even winded."

"Like I said, he's the demon commander."

"You're all full of it. He's the bastard, sure, but he leaks to the front and dumps to the rear, same as anyone."

"And were you leaking and dumping yourself in Stir Valley?" demanded a gruff voice. "That was a hide of hell, to be sure, and what of us made it out never want to go in again. But if ever I have to face such again, I'd want to be right behind Commander Becknam."

"On your feet," called a sergeant's booming voice. "Form up with wasters."

They arranged themselves, clutching wooden swords, and the commander appeared. He motioned a soldier out of the line. "We'll start with what ended yesterday. Here's the parry, half-time. Come over my left shoulder." He nodded for the soldier's attack and negated it neatly. "Now show me what you remember."

He moved among them, making a few corrections, and then called a halt. "Now we'll add another counter." Shianan gestured to another soldier. "Slowly—as I step forward...." He brought his sword toward the soldier, who parried correctly and responded. Shianan countered and laid his sword against the man's padded chest. "You see? Try that."

Shianan walked through the drilling partners, observing and occasionally commenting. At last he called for them to put away their equipment and end the session.

Returning from training, Shianan opened the door into Luca, who yelped and skipped back with the broom. Shianan looked around at the swept floor, clean of mud, and the made bed. His dried clothing had vanished. "Luca, I don't deserve you. Weren't you sleeping?"

"I thought it should be done."

"We have as much as an hour before the merchant comes," he said. "I'm going to change and rest for a few minutes. You could do the same."

Luca nodded. "After I finish this floor."

Shianan found a clean shirt and tunic and then propped his feet against the wall, enjoying the delicious stretch in his calves and hamstrings. He let his head fall against the back of the chair and closed his eyes, just for a few minutes. He heard Luca go to his mattress. *Just a few minutes.*

A knock at the door woke him, and Shianan jumped in his chair as his feet dropped. The knock came again at the office door outside, and he glanced toward Luca, scrambling from his mattress. Shianan looked at the cheeses and bread, uncut and waiting to be assembled onto a serving tray. "Take care of that. I'll let him in."

"Yes, master." Shianan distantly noted the subservient address—Luca worried over his lapse—and went into the office, closing the door behind him. He unlatched the office door and pulled it open.

"Good evening, your lordship!" Jarrick Roald made a small, friendly bow. "I bring wine, as promised." He presented a dark bottle.

"Come in, please." Shianan beckoned him inside. "I'll take your cloak. My servant is preparing a tray for us. Please sit down, and I'll take this to him." He took the wine and returned to the living quarters.

Luca was making quick, efficient cuts through the cheese. "One moment, and then it will be ready. I'm sorry—"

"Leave off, Luca, it's fine." Shianan glanced toward the door. "This one isn't such a stuffed shirt. I think he has a soul somewhere inside." He grinned.

Luca relaxed and gave him a smile in return. Shianan went back to the office, letting the door swing shut behind him. "Thank you, Roald." He took a seat across from the merchant. "So, tell me why you can supply grain at a better price than anyone else."

"Not only a better price—better grain." Roald smiled, self-deprecating. He knew his seller's song was not new to his listener. "But it's true. We can bring you Tyrgian grain directly by ship, delivered to Alham as quickly as anyone else can bring harvest from nearer fields overland. Your own supply trains can distribute it from the capital. And you know of course Tyrgian wheat is considered the finest."

"By ship? Then you—"

There was a flash of motion at the door and then a terrific crash. Shianan turned to the door, hanging half-open and vacant. There was no sign of Luca. He glanced at Roald, puzzled but too polite to comment. "Excuse me," Shianan said with a quick, uneasy smile.

"Of course." Roald nodded.

Shianan rose and went to the other room. Bread and cheese were scattered across the floor. Luca sprawled against the wall, his fingers on the empty tray, puddled with wine.

Shianan's first thought was that he was ill, but Luca stared suddenly up at him with wide white eyes. He made a grasping motion toward the door, reaching and yet recoiling, and Shianan pushed it closed. "What's wrong?" he demanded.

Luca's mouth worked without sound. His face was very pale— perhaps he was ill after all. But by his position against the wall, Luca had whirled away from the door and dropped the tray. Shianan crouched to look at him levelly. "Luca, what is it?"

Luca gulped. "My—my brother."

The words registered slowly. Luca's brother....

He sold me into slavery and my brother just watched me dragged away.

Luca dropped his eyes to the fallen tray and shook his head slowly. "Please—I can't go out there—please, master, I beg you, don't—not out there...." His head moved faster and faster. "Master, please...."

326

"Quiet," Shianan said. "We can manage without you." He took a breath. "Where is the wine the other one brought? In the chest?"

Luca blinked at him, uncomprehending, and Shianan left him and opened the largest chest. The bottle of wine was indeed there. He took it and the cups that lay beside the dropped bread.

Luca was frozen against the wall, his eyes wide and unseeing. Shianan was not sure he was breathing. He crouched again to meet Luca's eyes, which blinked and focused on him in fresh panic. Shianan gestured with the cups to the splattered floor. "Clean this?"

Luca nodded dully.

"Good," Shianan answered with a tight smile. "We'll talk when this is finished." He rose, straightened his shoulders, and passed through the door.

Roald gave him a politely curious look. "Is everything well?"

Shianan saw him as if for the first time—medium height, dark hair, a familiar outline to the face. Now he could see the resemblance. It was the confident, friendly smile, so foreign to Luca, which had set them apart.

Shianan had not yet answered the question. "My servant is ill. Nothing catching—I'd sent him out of the city with a message and he ran the entire route. Nearly killed himself, the diligent fool." He set the cups firmly on the table. "I'm afraid the wine you brought was lost in the crash. Was it an especially good vintage?"

"Fair." Roald peered at the bottle Shianan brought. "Ah! But this is an improvement. Perhaps we should thank your diligent fool. Shall I pour for us?"

"If you would." Shianan took his seat again. "Tell me about your ships."

"We have exclusive contracts on half of our ships and own another third." Roald dispensed dark wine into Shianan's cup. "The remainder are open contracts. They are speedy ships, for the most part, sloops that can take the sea faster than your wagon caravans travel overland."

Shianan made himself think of ships. "And during the stormy season?"

"They need come only from Tyrg, your lordship. The storms are not so severe." Roald tasted the wine. "They have been very reliable for us."

"In your country?"

"And others. Our house contracts all around the sea."

327

"Which is why you can broker the best rates." Shianan stared at the bottom of his cup, wondering how it had emptied.

"It does help." Roald grinned. "I spent a quarter of last year in Tyrg myself and another two months in Damas. We've managed to secure prime contracts in every major port."

"How excellent for you." Shianan toyed with his empty cup, afraid to refill it just yet. The first had disappeared too quickly.

Roald glanced about the office. "A little sparse, is it?"

"Austere," corrected Shianan. "I am a military commander before a count."

"Forgive me, I meant no offense. I only meant to say it is eerily efficient. There's nothing of the man in this office; it is an office that could belong to anyone." Roald smiled. "So your private treasures are in your living quarters rather than here. A clever defense, your lordship. I cannot comment favorably on any of them. You give me little to work upon in winning your trust."

Shianan liked the smile in spite of the way it sat unfittingly on what was faintly Luca's face. He liked the easy charm with which Roald gently mocked his profession and the mission they both knew had been assigned to him. And he disliked how he liked them.

"Tell me about your family," Shianan said with deliberate lightness, pouring wine into Roald's cup. "Your father created your mercantile house, I know, and he's obviously done well. Have you any siblings?"

"I do," Roald answered with a nod to acknowledge the wine. "I have an elder brother, heir to our father's house. Thir is his name. Then I have a sister, Sara, who is engaged to wed shortly."

"A marriage." Shianan smiled and gave a little half-bow in his chair. "My compliments to your sister, then."

"I thank you on her behalf."

"No others?"

"No others." Roald looked into his cup. "This is excellent wine, your lordship."

"A high compliment from so expert a traveler." Shianan clenched his fingers beneath the table where Roald could not see. "No other family, then?" His voice sounded sharp.

Roald looked up, startled. "No...." He swallowed. "You seem to disbelieve me."

Shianan shrugged jerkily. "I only asked."

"I—I did have another brother, a younger brother. But we lost him a few years ago."

"You lost him," Shianan repeated gruffly. "How sad." He flexed his fingers on the wine. "I should ask how he died, but I was led to believe he had been misplaced rather than lost."

Roald's mouth opened soundlessly. After a moment he managed, "But you...." He blew out his breath nervously. "It's obvious your lordship has done more research into our house than we expected. Yes, I confess, I had another brother. But as your lordship must understand, if you know that story, it is not one we like to tell."

Shianan crossed his arms. "We are seeking new suppliers due to fraud. You must understand we are leery of merchants who do not tell the whole truth."

"Then I will tell you the truth," Roald said heavily, "and you may compare my story with the one your agents brought you." He rubbed his face. "It is to our shame, all of it. Some years ago our house was heavily in debt. That is another thing we are not proud of, and we do not like to say we were ever in such a position, but to understand what happened you have to know we were in danger. You see that? In desperation my father had negotiated credit with our primary rival, who had been very careful to buy up our debt, and if we defaulted we could have lost everything."

"Go on."

"The ship we desperately needed was late. We'd lost two that year and thought her lost as well. We were near defaulting, and my father went to negotiate for an extension. Remember, he had found credit only with Sandis—oh, I have said his name, and I should not have told you."

"It does not matter."

"Anyway, Sandis was glad to have his most hated competitor in his hand, and he could have crushed us then. But Sandis has a cruel streak, and it was not enough merely to destroy our trade and finances, which he was reasonably sure of doing. He allowed an extension of credit if my father would sell one of the family into slavery."

"That seems unlikely."

Roald looked at the table. "I am relating it to you as my father explained to us, your lordship. Sandis wanted a certain sum paid on the loan, and we did not have it—Sandis told my father then to sell a child...." His voice wavered. "Can you imagine it? Can you conceive of such a decision?"

Shianan swallowed and clenched his fists. "There must have been another way."

"There was not. At least, my father could not find one. He decided to give up his youngest son."

"Your brother."

"Yes, your lordship."

"Did this brother have a name?"

"His name was Luca." Roald gave Shianan a bitter look. "I'm sure your spies, or agents, or whatever you prefer to call them, didn't miss that detail."

Shianan ignored this. "And so this brother was sold, and your house's credit was extended."

"A few days later the ship arrived, and with her cargo we were able to pay enough of the loan to reduce the danger."

"And did you buy back the brother?"

"No—no, we didn't. We were still short of funds, and—he was already sold."

"Couldn't you find him? Surely there was a record of the sale."

"The trader had sent him inland...." Roald looked down, his face reddening. "Your lordship, let me try to explain something. To sell one's own son—you cannot imagine it. My father could not bear to think on it. And so Luca simply ceased to exist for us. He made no further search because he could not admit what he had done."

Shianan stared. "He sold his own son and then willfully forgot it? Pretended it had never happened?"

"We couldn't have found him, your lordship. He was sent to be auctioned in another city."

"It must have been far indeed if a trading family could not have followed him."

Roald flinched at the words. "My father felt.... It was easier to pretend it had not happened. And I think he was afraid to look—he wanted to believe Luca had found good service because of his training and education, and he was afraid of finding otherwise. And he—I think he was afraid of facing him, too." His voice wavered, unhappy. "So, your lordship, now you know the truth of it. My younger brother was sold for debt and lost to us. Now, as I said, I have only an elder brother and a sister."

"I see." Shianan glanced at his hands. "And how will this history affect our trading? A man who will sell his own son for profit might do more—might cheat an army, as our last merchant partners did."

Roald shook his head. "Oh, no, your lordship. We have learned that debt is fatal. We are now a very conservative house, and you would not be disappointed in us."

"Nicely said." Shianan squeezed his fingers on his wine. "Your father would be proud."

Roald stiffened. "I am not proud of all my father has done, but he did what he thought he must at the time—and he is still my father."

"Only because he chose to sacrifice your younger brother instead of you." Shianan shook his head. "No, I'm sorry. I do not mean to argue over a man I have never met. You came here to persuade me your house would be an ideal supplier, and that is my official concern. Your family affairs make no difference to King Jerome."

Roald's throat worked. "We would be a good supplier."

"Though a few years ago your house was nearly destitute? Saved from ruin by the price of a single slave?"

Roald flushed. The charm had vanished entirely. "Word got around of what had happened. It was bad for Sandis. Who would contract with a man who took a son as interest?" He shook his head. "Even strangers came to our house to show their sympathy and outrage. Sandis' cruelty undid him. He still trades, but he has lost nearly all of his custom to us."

"So your brother really was the saving of your house."

Roald looked down, his shoulders slumping. "Your lordship," he said quietly, "I was instructed to come here and sign a trade agreement with you. I intended to do so. But if you would rather I depart now, I could simply—"

"No, stay. Drink your wine." Shianan swallowed. "As I said, King Jerome's interest is in your mercantile promises, not in your family affairs, and you have made a very attractive offer."

Roald smiled thinly. "The king is interested in our mercantile promises, and it is only you who finds us distasteful?" He sighed. "I cannot blame you, your lordship." He reached for the bottle. "I find us distasteful as well."

Shianan looked at him.

"Oh, yes. It's true." Roald took a drink. "This is entirely the wrong conversation for this wine. We should have something cheap which we can knock back without shame."

Shianan lifted his cup and stared at it without drinking.

"I will tell you something none of my family knows." Roald leaned over the table. "I tried to find Luca."

"You did?" Shianan could hear his own surprise.

"Yes. Not right away—not soon enough—but when I went out on business, I tried to trace him. I thought it would be possible; he was well-educated, and how many clerks could there be?" He shook his head. "But I was wrong. I underestimated the man who would break us. Sandis had not only demanded my father sell a son, he had paid the trader to—to sell him as labor instead of as educated help."

Shianan shook his head. "He would have lost too much money."

"That's why Father was sure he was all right. But the trader told me Sandis had made up the difference in price, just for the satisfaction of seeing Luca sold as common labor and Father's shame if we looked for him. Holy One knows he stood to profit enough on the interest." Roald rubbed a hand over his face. "Luca was my brother. I was horrified at the idea of him grinding in a mill or working a mine or pulling a wagon or dragging a plow. I've seen—it's not easy work."

Shianan clenched his jaw. "Why didn't you find him?"

"He was taken to Furmelle for auction." Roald looked down. "This was before the rebellion. I found someone to go through the old accounts for me."

"Did you not find his purchaser?"

Roald shook his head slowly. "I thought I had. The records weren't complete; there had been a fire. But I had thirty names who had bought labor slaves that day. I thought there was a good chance I had found him." He bit at his lip. "He wasn't there. I wandered the streets, hoping to see him bearing a litter—that's popular there—or pulling a wagon or maybe selling vegetables, I don't know. But I didn't see him, and then the rebellion started."

"And that interrupted your search."

"I had to flee, like so many others. But—you can't imagine what it was like."

"I was there." Shianan looked down. "You would not have been able to find one man. Families were killed in their beds. Slaves fled or banded together to fight, it was chaos. We didn't keep records of prisoners—there were too many."

Roald nodded. "Even if I'd been able to track him before, I could not have found him after the fighting."

He was ashamed of what had been done. He had searched for Luca. He might not be the same man who had watched his brother dragged away in chains. Shianan took a long, shuddering breath. "If you could find him now, would you—"

"He is dead."

Shianan's jaw hung for a moment. "What?"

"Furmelle—it was bad. You know that, lordship. He died there."

"He died there?"

"I'm sure he did. I can feel it. There was so much fighting, and it was so—I have to believe he died there, you see. Luca was not a fighter, he was a clerk. He could not have survived."

Shianan laced his fingers together fiercely. "I was a commander at Furmelle. We sold hundreds of slaves after the fighting. Don't you think he might have been one of them?"

"I heard what kind of men were sold then, lordship. Luca could not have been one of them. No, Luca died in Furmelle. I have only an elder brother and a sister."

Shianan swallowed. No, Jarrick did not want to find Luca. He only assuaged his conscience by imagining he had searched for his lost brother. He was willing enough to accept defeat, to lay his brother's loss to impartial death instead of their own fault.

Shianan clenched his fists beneath the table. He would not have Luca. Luca deserved better.

"Finish this," he said gruffly, emptying the bottle into Roald's cup. "And you don't have to tell your father you've failed. The contract is yours."

Roald glanced up, clearly startled. "But...."

"Your house needs this contract, yes? That is why he sent you, though we're a long journey from the Wakari Coast. He could not leave this in the hands of a hired representative." Shianan looked steadily at Roald, whose dull look confirmed all. "Your mercantile house is recovering, but it is not quite as comfortably reestablished as you'd like me to believe. But it is secure enough to succeed with this contract, or you would not risk everything you've rebuilt on this." He dug his knuckles into his thigh. "If you fail now, then the sacrifice of your brother accomplished nothing. Correct?"

Roald swallowed visibly. "That is—correct."

"Then you may tell your father his sacrifice was profitable. Bring me a contract, and I will have it signed by all the relevant parties." Shianan stood abruptly. "And now, Roald, I think we have said all that matters. May I bid you good night?"

Roald stumbled out of his chair. "Your lordship." He bowed deeply. "I—thank you—the contract—I will come again.... Thank you, your lordship." He bowed once more and nearly fled the office.

Shianan locked the door behind him and turned. After a moment he crossed to the living quarters.

Luca leaned with his shoulder against the wall, huddled beside the door with his arms about his knees. His face was damp, and as he glanced up he rubbed briefly at his cheeks. Shianan looked at him with a hollow ache. He'd listened to every word. "Luca...."

For once, Luca did not scramble to his feet. He sniffed. "Thank you."

"Thank you?"

"For giving him the contract." Luca sniffed again.

Shianan's jaw clenched. "I could have him arrested. I could ruin him. I could—take you to him."

Luca shook his head slowly. "I don't want to see him," he whispered. "I don't want him to know I'm here. I just want him to go home." He dug his knuckles across his face. "I'm sorry."

"Sorry for what?" Shianan turned away. He could not imagine what Luca must feel. If his brother had watched as his father sold him away....

It might have been the other brother, he reflected. Thir, the eldest. But he guessed it had been Jarrick who watched.

If Jarrick Roald learned of Luca and was not glad to find him now—that might be worse. Shianan understood why Luca did not want to see the merchant.

He walked to Luca's back and sat against the wall beside him, staring across the room. He wanted something to say, and yet there was nothing.

A slave did not have family, did not have relations, did not have connections—just as a bastard had no family. And yet Luca wept for his brother.

CHAPTER 53

"Tamaryl'sho." Fasi'bel paused at the open doorway to the courtyard. "One would like to speak with you."

Tamaryl straightened from dangling his fingers in the fountain. A few colorful fish darted toward the surface as water dripped from his fingers, hoping for bits of food. "Of course."

It was Taro who entered at Fasi's beckoning wave. He knelt upon two knees. "Tamaryl'sho—I thank you for your kindness."

"I am not sure it deserves special thanks, Taro. If you were asked for more than you had sold, you were wronged."

"Nonetheless, I thank you, and I will repay you."

"Thank you." Tamaryl was spared from further response by a sudden and demanding knock at the far exterior door. Fasi gestured, and Maru hurried to answer.

Two females, wearing the blue sashes of Oniwe'aru's guard, pushed their way inside. "Tamaryl'sho," one began, seeing him across the courtyard. "You are summoned with the human mage prisoner to the presence of Oniwe'aru, in the Palace of Red Sands."

Maru looked worriedly at Tamaryl. "We will come immediately," Tamaryl said. "I presume you are sent to escort us safely to the palace?"

"We are." She gave Tamaryl a guarded look.

The two members of Oniwe'aru's elite were not for security, but to make obvious Tamaryl's trespass. He nodded. "Maru, go and ask Ariana'rika to join us. Be sure to knock at the wall beside her entry. Humans are very particular about that."

Tamaryl entered the audience chamber and dropped to one knee, bowing his head. Behind him Ariana curtsied deeply.

"Tamaryl'sho." Oniwe'aru stalked across his dais. "I thought you were beyond disobeying me whenever it suited you?"

Tamaryl caught his breath. "You know I honor you, Oniwe'aru."

"Then why do you parade this human, claiming her as spoils, when you were to bring her to me if her condition improved?"

Tamaryl went to his second knee and placed his palms on the floor, forefingers just touching. "I apologize, Oniwe'aru. It was not my intent to disregard your instruction. I only had not yet brought her to you."

"Hn." Oniwe'aru did not seem appeased. "Stand, human."

He had not told Tamaryl to rise. Like the guards, this was a rebuke.

Ariana did not know how to comport herself in this foreign court, and her voice wavered. "Your Majesty."

Oniwe chuckled. "That is a human honorific, you know. You may address me as Oniwe'aru, unless you would prefer to use my full title."

"What is that, my lord?"

"Altayr ni'Ai cin Celæno, Alcyon ni Pairvyn, Majja to Pleione." He smiled at her dismay. "As I said, you may address me as Oniwe'aru." He seated himself regally in his chair, adjusting his wings behind him. "This is Edeiya'rika, my Tsuraiya ni'Ai. Do you understand this?"

Ariana looked at the tall Ryuven female with emerald-dark hair. "Not entirely, I'm sorry."

"You do know the Pairvyn ni'Ai."

"Yes." Her single syllable was tight with wariness and contempt. "Your warlord who wreaked horrific destruction on us."

"I can see how you became a mage instead of a diplomat," Oniwe observed dryly. "Say rather, the Pairvyn is my male champion. The Tsuraiya is my female champion. As such, she will safeguard my person during our interview, in case of any such display as the one in the house of Daranai'rika."

Ariana's jaw worked uselessly until she found words. "I offered no threat! I only defended a friend! You have to understand—"

"I must do nothing demanded of me by a human prisoner," rumbled Oniwe. "You are the first human mage to survive. You will not be the first to strike a blow in our own court."

Edeiya'rika made a sound somewhere between a cough and a dismissive chuckle, almost too faint to catch.

The aru turned to her. "Yes?"

"I do not think there is much worry, Oniwe'aru." Edeiya passed her eyes over Ariana as if overlooking litter on the street. "She could not have presented much of a threat, or Daranai'rika would not have left her untouched."

Tamaryl stiffened. What was Edeiya'rika playing at?

Oniwe's curiosity was piqued as well. "Oh?"

Edeiya gave an elegant little shrug. "By my questioning of her household, when this human awoke, Daranai'rika simply... left the room. I ask you, is that the action of a rika who senses danger in her own home?" Her voice was cool and nearly toneless.

Oniwe's smile came slow and insuppressible. "It certainly doesn't sound like it."

Tamaryl blinked as, with a soft word, Ariana was excused and Daranai's standing was destroyed.

"But as Tsuraiya, I am interested to know if we should expect more human mages here. I am anxious to hear your questions answered."

"Indeed. And so, human mage, you will answer."

Tamaryl risked a glance and somehow met Edeiya's eyes. She gave him a significant look he did not quite understand.

"Now," said Oniwe, "what can you tell about the disposition of your troops?"

Ariana faltered. "Your—Oniwe'aru—I don't know. I'm not an officer, I am a mage."

"A Circle mage is expected to battle on behalf of the king and must march forth with the soldiers."

"But I only go where I am told, and in fact I have not yet faced battle myself."

"No?" He frowned. "What is your position?"

Tamaryl, trapped in his penitent's posture, held his breath. Ariana would say nothing of her parentage. Surely Oniwe'aru had no reason to suspect....

"I am the Black Mage in the Great Circle."

"Of the Circle, yes. But only the Black?" Oniwe was openly surprised. "I should have thought, given that you are standing here, you must have been more—or less. Perhaps your king is more desperate for mages these days?" He smiled coolly. "But isn't it odd you are the only mage to have lived more than an hour here, and you have recovered completely?"

Tamaryl peeked to see Ariana standing erect. "I cannot speak to that, Oniwe'aru, since I have not known other mages' circumstances."

Oniwe looked at her a long moment. "Are you quite sure you can tell us nothing of your defenses?"

"There are soldiers in our keep. I cannot say how many, I do not work with them. I know there are outposts throughout the countryside, each manned by at least a hundred soldiers. Some have more. But I do not have specific information."

"Not even if I ask again under less cordial conditions?"

Tamaryl's muscles clenched. He started to move, to protest, when he heard Ariana's hasty answer, "I cannot tell you what I do not know, my lord. A lesser mage is not consulted in the army's deployment." Her voice was unsteady, but she did not flinch.

Oniwe grunted. "To my regret, I find that believable." He glanced across the room. "Tamaryl'sho, have you repented yet of your negligence?"

Tamaryl lifted his head. "Oniwe'aru?"

"Rise, Tamaryl'sho. I think the point has been made. You were not one to abuse privilege in the past, and I mean you to exercise your privilege and rank now." He gestured for Tamaryl to stand.

Tamaryl's pulse leaped through him. Not now, not before Ariana, not yet.... He shifted to one knee, paused briefly in the courtier's position, and then got to his feet. "Oniwe'aru," he ventured. "As to that.... If you would, I should like speak with you." He swallowed. "Privately."

"Oh?" Oniwe raised an eyebrow. "I hope you do not mean to refuse me."

Essence and flame—Oniwe would see it as a second betrayal, a fresh rejection of his authority. That would end Tamaryl and Ariana both. Tamaryl shook his head. "Of course not."

"Good." He looked back at Ariana, stiffly facing him. "So you know nothing of the army's affairs. I accept that. But a Mage of the Circle must know something of the barrier erected between our worlds."

"Actually, my lord, I was not yet a member of the Circle when the shield was erected—"

"Do not toy with me!" Oniwe snapped.

Tamaryl glanced worriedly at Ariana. She did know most of the shield's workings but would be reluctant to betray them.

Oniwe faced her sternly. "What is this shield?"

"It—it is a barrier...."

"I know it is a barrier. I have seen its effects to that purpose, and indeed I called it a barrier myself not a moment ago. How is it done?"

"I did not help to create it—I only observed—"

"Keep in mind, please, only the mages died upon their arrival.

Others died more slowly as we found ways to question them. You might not know the military situation, but you know of this. How is it done?"

Ariana paled. "I—it is a barrier inhospitable to Ryuven—it is a magic woven by the entire Circle...."

"It is powered by condensed starry ether, Oniwe'aru," Tamaryl intervened. "The shield fueled by the ether is calculated to act upon the nervous system and the organs specifically. Any Ryuven attempting to pass through would leave his organs behind. It is a secure magic of overlaid bindings, mostly of what humans call the Tolemic type, and cannot be undone except at the source of its power, the condensed ether, what the humans call the Shard of Elan."

Oniwe'aru raised an eyebrow. "You know a great deal of this."

"It was of obvious concern to me." And he had helped to create the method of it.

"And you offer this information with interesting timing."

"I did not know you were in need. I assumed you would have already discovered the shield." He kept his eyes from Ariana.

"Discovered it, yes," Oniwe answered sourly. "By accident, as half a hundred warriors tried to cross the between-worlds. The majority of our force was spared only by fortunate timing." He crossed his arms. "You say it cannot be undone?"

"It would require the Circle's magic to be unwoven about the Shard itself. It is impossible to break from outside the barrier."

"Hm. But the shield is broken now. You are here."

Ariana was staring at Tamaryl. He ignored her. "Yes, Oniwe'aru. A careless, ignorant human altered the spell and collapsed the shield."

"And it has not been recreated. Once it was discovered, we knew what to look for, and we know that it has not been restored." His voice became commanding. "Pairvyn ni'Ai!"

Tamaryl straightened even as his stomach fell. "Yes, Oniwe'aru?"

"Take a force to the human world. The area northeast of Alham, with fewer posts of soldiers—they have storehouses freshly filled with the harvest. Go and bring food for our people, and remind the humans we are better fled than fought."

Shock and horror radiated almost palpably from the human figure beside him. He could not look at her. Instead, he nodded once. "As you command, Oniwe'aru." He left the room, knowing Ariana would follow.

She did. "Tamaryl!" She choked. "It—it isn't so. It can't be."

He stopped but did not turn.

"It's not true. Pairvyn? Tell me it's not true."

He could not.

She circled and faced him. Fire lanced her voice. "You killed thousands! We lost so—entire villages! All of Luenda, scorched after the fighting, and it was all, all you!"

He closed his eyes against her furious hurt. "It was empty glory. We advanced worthless power-hungry maniacs who cared nothing for those they killed, human or Ryuven, and we let conditions worsen here as we relied more and more on raids. I told Oniwe'aru I would no longer lead his warriors."

"And he cast you out."

Tam shook his head. "No. If he had believed me, he would have killed me then. But he thought I was only angry at some of the che." This should have been Ewan Hazelrig's task. This was not how Tamaryl would have told her. "I did not fight. I stood and waited to die. But even so I outlasted the nim around me, and Oniwe'aru heard. I was waiting for them to find me, but your father found me first."

"And everyone supposed Pairvyn ni'Ai dead."

"I was no longer Pairvyn ni'Ai." He stepped around her and began walking.

"Until now!" His long strides made her run, but they did not leave her behind nor take enough breath to stop her protests. "You can't do this!"

"I must, Ariana'rika."

"You're going to attack us?"

"I am going to retrieve food for my people."

"You're going to kill and steal!"

"I can take you home."

"I don't want to go home to a battlefield!"

"It is your chance to go home and mine to take my place here."

Ariana snatched at his arm and pulled him around, drawing herself to her full height. "Tam, I forbid it. I order you not to do this!"

"In your world, my lady, I would obey you. But here, I am Pairvyn ni'Ai." His chest ached. "Ariana'rika, I promised your father I would take care of you. I must return you home."

She stared at him with wide, pained eyes. "You were Tam, my Tam, my sweet-natured boy. I never—you killed so many people." She gulped. "I don't want you to kill more people."

Her impending tears ripped at him, clawed his stomach and made him want to hold her and weep with her. But that of course was impossible. Instead, he swallowed hard and flexed his wings tightly against his back. "I don't either, my lady."

"Then—"

"You are a Mage of the Circle," Tamaryl said sharply. "What will you do when you are ordered into battle?"

She stared at him, her mouth open but saying nothing. He turned abruptly and walked away, hating her, hating himself, hating Oniwe'aru and Daranai'rika and King Jerome and everything.

CHAPTER 54

Shianan ran his hands through his hair, dimly aware of the fidgety gesture but powerless to stop it. He was unhappy with his update on the failing search for the Shard. He wanted to speak with Ewan Hazelrig but dared not. And at any moment Jarrick Roald might walk through his door, and Shianan could not decide whether to throttle the man or drag him into the next room to shove him face to face with Luca.

The door burst open and Shianan glanced up angrily, almost glad of a chance to vent some of his frustration. "You will knock—"

"Urgent dispatch, sir!" barked the soldier, his face pale beneath the sweat of exertion. "Ryuven attack!"

Shianan rose, reaching for the extended paper. "Where?"

"Caftford, sir."

"Does General Septime know yet?"

"I'm just on my way to him now, sir."

"Then go!" Shianan gestured the man out the door and scanned the dispatch. The words struck him like physical blows. Caftford had been raided and their winter stores stolen. There had been no warning.

He read and re-read the final sentence, as if it might somehow change: *Pairvyn ni'Ai has returned to battle.*

Pairvyn ni'Ai—they had thought the fearsome Ryuven warrior dead. They had not been foolish enough to believe they had somehow killed him; it was thought he had died in some inter-Ryuven conflict, a political scuffle which cost their best asset. But if this report were correct, and Pairvyn ni'Ai had returned to fight once more....

Shianan sank slowly to his chair. They would suffer devastating losses as they had not seen since Luenda, when Shianan was a boy and terror of the Ryuven immense in his mind. Hundreds, even thousands would fall to the Ryuven, because the shield which should have protected them had been sabotaged by a desperate bastard.

Caftford's warehouse had been emptied. Ryuven raids would leave the countryside to starve, and as the army requisitioned grain to feed patrolling soldiers the villagers and farmers would grow more and more resentful of those who beggared them to save them. Riots would injure those the Ryuven left unharmed. And the Shard which could have prevented all was buried leagues away.

Shianan dropped his head to the desk, welcoming the dull pain which flashed through his skull. The search for the Shard would intensify, and even without evidence, they would demand a scapegoat. It would not be long now.

He sighed and pushed aside some papers, uncovering a contract. Roald had not had the courage to bring it to Shianan's face but had left it on his desk. Shianan's knowledge of Luca's history had been unsettling, indeed.

He forgot the contract on hearing the gathering of voices outside. He stepped onto a chair and peered through the high window, seeing a clot of soldiers arguing among themselves with frequent glances toward his office.

It's here.

"Luca!" He tore open the top right drawer, seizing a sealed document. He whirled and nearly stumbled into the slave, still holding a broom. "Keep this with you. If anyone comes for you—soldiers, I mean, or slavers or anyone—use it."

"Master Shianan—"

"Quiet! There's no time." Luca could not escape with the angry soldiers outside. "Get underneath the bed."

"What?"

"Do it! Under the bed and stay. That's an order."

Luca folded the sealed document into his shirt and obediently dropped to the floor beside the bed, slipping beneath it. Shianan wanted to speak but could not think of anything before the door opened without a knock.

"Commander Shianan Becknam," said one of the half-dozen that pushed their way inside. "We are here with a warrant for your arrest, for questioning in relation to the theft of the Shard of Elan."

Shianan faced them. "I will go with you."

They stared uneasily at him, uncomfortable with the task of arresting their commanding officer. "Sir...."

"I'm coming."

But before he could reach for his cloak, more men shoved into the office. "Is it true?"

Shianan remained very still. "I am going to answer questions about the Shard." No resistance, no excitement, do not antagonize them....

But another man stepped forward. "They say you maybe stole the Shard."

"They say you took it because you were jealous and wanted to try for the throne yourself."

The group shifted toward him. "You were the one who brought the Gehrn to destroy the shield!"

Shianan held up his hands in a calming, submissive gesture. His sword lay across a table in the far corner, and he did not want to fight. Some of these were his own men. "Wait. I'm wanted for questioning, I understand, but—"

"My people live in Caftford!" snapped a man on his left.

Shianan dropped backward and struck the man's arm as it swung, but the motion triggered the others. A fist caught him from the other side as he stepped backward, driving through someone, and they flowed around him, entrapping him. A dizzying rush of movement came from all sides and he could not defend himself from everything.

He tried to shield his head but they hammered him down. Before he reached the floor the group had closed, seizing him and dragging him through the door. He tried to regain his feet, but they were still hitting him as they shouted. "You took it! You killed those people! You let the Ryuven in! Murdering bastard!"

There were more now, he thought, but it was hard to tell. They threw him from one side to another, hitting him and shouting. He whirled and hit the ground hard as someone's boot caught him in the ribs. Someone else kicked his head. Sound and vision together swirled into a dull dark blur.

Dimly he realized no one was kicking him, the jeering had slowed. There was another voice instead, an angry, familiar voice, and as it cut across the group he recognized General Septime speaking, though he could not understand what was said. Then hands pulled him from the paving stones and jostled him forward though the hurts.

Septime's voice faded away, and the air became the clammy cold of underground. He vaguely recognized the dim corridor. Cold metal shackles were fitted on him and then he was dragged again and dumped roughly to the ground. Foul-smelling straw prickled at his face, surprising him with the sharp sensation through his hazy consciousness. A door slammed and it was dark.

The office had been empty over an hour, but Luca had not yet moved from beneath the bed.

He had seen them attack Shianan, seen them drag him outside where there were more cries of rage, and Luca had been too easily able to picture the mob, tossing Shianan from abuse to abuse, perhaps ripping him apart in the street just as in Furmelle....

He squeezed his eyes tightly closed. He did not want to go and see Shianan's body in the yard. He did not want to be seized by the angry soldiers. He did not want to think of what would come next.

Shianan would not return. He had known what he plotted, he had known what would come. But Luca could not remain in hiding.

If anyone comes for you.... Shianan's last act had been a final instruction. It was too much to hope—if he could save his slave, he would have saved himself—but perhaps it held the key to escape. Luca withdrew the paper. The seal, softened with his body heat, opened easily.

It was a bill of sale, that was all. It was dated a few days past, documenting the payment of a low average sum for a serving slave, a transfer of ownership to Mage Ewan Hazelrig.

Luca stared, his mind working slowly. Shianan could not legally free him except by his death-will, and if convicted of treason his property would be forfeit to the crown. Luca would be assigned to the army warehouses or sold at market, common labor to be prodded until exhausted and useless.

But if sold, Luca was safe from the law's seizure. And it was Mage Hazelrig who had kindly treated Luca after his scourging. Shianan had found his slave safety and comfort.

Luca was crying. He wept for Shianan, killed by the mob or soon to be killed by the king, and for himself, losing his master and—and his friend.

He slid from beneath the bed, rubbing tears from his eyes, and tucked the precious bill of sale away again. It did not take long to gather his few belongings and stuff them into a soldier's bag. He hesitated a moment and then pulled a few of Shianan's shirts from the chest. They would only be taken, and Luca could use them as well as anyone, and he would at least think kindly of the man who had worn them before.

He took a deep breath, rubbed the last of the damp from his face, and steeled himself to open the door. There was no red pulpy mass. The mob had not killed him, at least not here.

Luca pulled the bag over his shoulder and ducked his head,

hoping no one would recognize him as Shianan's servant, and hurried toward the Wheel. He arrived without incident and found his way to the White Mage's office.

The white door was open. Luca swallowed and knocked at the frame. "My lord?"

Hazelrig looked up from his writing. "Yes? Oh—you're Becknam's servant, yes?"

Luca hesitated. "They've taken him, my lord. They arrested him."

Hazelrig's expression fell. "Did they." The mage was not surprised.

Luca withdrew the saving paper. "My master gave me this." He shuffled across the office, his eyes respectfully lowered, and extended it across the desk.

Hazelrig pursed his lips over the bill of sale and then looked at Luca. "Clever." He dropped the paper to the desk. "Then you'd better come home with me."

Luca clutched his bag of clothing. "Yes, my lord. Master."

CHAPTER 55

Ariana glanced up irritably as Maru entered the open archway without knocking or speaking. Before he could speak she complained, "I know there's not an actual door, but—"

"I'm sorry, Ariana'rika," Maru interrupted, "but Ryl sent me for you. He's coming to carry you over."

Ariana's chest tightened. "Let's go, then."

Maru led her down a mostly-empty street and out of the city, to a field of tall grass recently trampled. There was no one else; whoever had stomped the grass flat had gone. Maru stopped a third of the way across the green and sat.

"What is this place?" The wind pulled at Ariana.

"This is the Leaping Plain. It's easier to cross the between-worlds from here."

Ariana was intrigued, and she quested into the magic around them, but it slipped past her, elusive as ever. Frustrated, she formed a little ball of smoke, just to prove she could.

"Ariana'rika?"

She let the smoke dissipate. "Why this place?"

Maru shrugged. "I'm only nim. I can tell you only there is something different here."

She sighed, resigned to ignorance, and glanced at the sky.

"Here." He proffered a small bag, tied tightly at the neck. "This is what remains of your medicine. In case, if you adapted to our world, perhaps yours will feel strange? Or maybe there is something in the between-worlds?" He shook his head. "I don't mean to frighten you. But it was mixed for you, and so you should take it."

"Thank you." She tucked the bag at her waist, knotting its drawstring safely about her belt. "I hope I won't need it."

Tamaryl came alone to the field, descending with a sweep of wide wings to land gracefully before them. "Hello," he greeted them both.

She didn't look at him. Had he come from a raid? She didn't want to know.

"Thank you, Maru, for bringing her. Ariana, are you ready to go?"

She hadn't thought she would have any reason to remain, but the question gave her pause. She might be the only human to have spoken with Oniwe'aru, she wasn't sure. She had experimented further with the natural Ryuven magic, though she was far from mastering it. She glanced at Maru. She had made at least one friend here, even if he were a little frightened of her.

But she did not belong here. She turned to Maru and reached for his hand, glad when he did not hesitate. "Maru, thank you for looking after me. Take care of yourself."

"You too, rika."

Ariana drew him close and embraced him. "I wish I could see you again."

"Be well, Ariana'rika."

She turned to face Tamaryl and took a breath. "You are all I was taught to fear. You were the monster beneath the bed all my childhood. But you say you want to end this war—and once, you acted on that. And you are my only chance of returning home or surviving here." She was afraid to stop speaking, lest she lose her words or her nerve. "So I choose to believe you. I choose to trust you. And I swear, I will end this, with or without you."

"Noble words." She could not read his expression. "I hope you may honor them."

Her voice was almost steady. "Did my father know?"

Tamaryl understood the question. "It should have been the stuff of legends, the White Mage and the Pairvyn ni'Ai meeting in battle. It would have been story and song for generations." He tried to smile. "But as there was no one to witness it, we chose something else."

Ariana did not answer.

Tamaryl stepped behind her, embracing her tightly. His chest pressed her back through the thin Ryuven clothing. "Are you ready?"

She nodded, careful of his face. "Yes."

He spread his wings and a massing of power pressed her ear drums. Then Maru spun away and the cold dark crashed over her.

The between-worlds was black and cold and terrifying. For an instant Ariana could not breathe, could not feel, could not sense anything, but then she felt the warm pressure of Tamaryl against her back and his arms wrapped around her. "Only a moment," he whispered in the void.

And then light burst around them and she saw blue sky, green-brown vegetation, trees in late autumn color. For a moment of pure delight she gazed down at her own world, and then panic seized her as she realized they were falling.

The ground rushed toward her and Ariana's fingers tightened on Tamaryl's arms. He murmured a reassurance and there was a crack as his wings caught the air. Their descent slowed with a jerk, and she clutched at him, but he did not let her slip. The ground came more slowly, but still too rapidly.

"Pick up your feet, please," Tamaryl instructed. "And you might want to run as we land."

Tamaryl's wings worked around them, making his arms flex with effort, and then he hoisted her upward as he jolted into the ground. He grunted and shoved her ahead. "Go!"

Their momentum carried her for a few paces and then she steadied, coming to a halt. She turned and saw Tamaryl with his hands on his knees, breathing hard. "Are you all right?"

"I'm fine." Tamaryl straightened. "Now, we must hurry. Some mage will have felt that entrance, near as we are to Alham."

"You—you're staying?"

"For a short time, at least. I want—to tell your father goodbye." He shifted the small bag which hung across his torso and withdrew the silver cuffs. "I can change myself this time, but you must still seal the binding."

A wave of cold touched Ariana. "You're sure?"

"My lady mage, there is no time for hesitation. They will be coming."

She nodded, straightening. "Then let's hurry."

CHAPTER 56

Shianan's head had cleared by the time they came for him, but the throbbing ache gave no sign of ending soon. The guards were curt and avoided eye contact, uncomfortable with an officer as prisoner. His wrists were bolted behind him between two crimped iron bars, and he could not wipe the itching clotted blood from his face or probe the numerous hurting bruises.

He ascended dozens of steps, shuffled across a room, and climbed dozens more. He did not know how they had settled upon him at last, but at least it was done. He knew exactly what to expect.

The thought brought no comfort.

The guards pushed him upward to the older wing of the castle. Shianan's fingers coiled and uncoiled around what he could reach of the unyielding shackle. He swallowed bile.

"Inside," someone ordered gruffly, and Shianan moved obediently forward and then dropped to his knee.

For one hideous long moment nothing happened, and Shianan held his breath as he knelt, head aching and wrists weighted behind his bent back and guards waiting ominously on either side. He could think of nothing at all.

"Bailaha," ground the king finally, his voice thick with disdain and anger.

"Your Majesty." The usual salutations were far out of place.

The king frowned down at him. "I see you resisted arrest?"

"It was the men, Your Majesty," the guard captain offered. "They were angry about Caftford and kind of seized on the arrest. We stopped it as soon as we could."

King Jerome grunted. "So your own soldiers dislike and distrust you."

Shianan said nothing. There was nothing to say.

"You were to recover the Shard," the king said darkly. "And now we find you yourself may be the thief."

Shianan scraped his fingers against his shackles and swallowed hard. If he confessed now, he would have only his secrets left to be wrung from him. If he held his tongue now, he could surrender the information he had already determined to offer. But it was all he could do to keep from blurting that he had taken the Shard.

"You have no response?"

Shianan tried to make his mouth form words. "Your Majesty, I ask the basis of this accusation." He had fully expected to be arrested as a scapegoat, but did they know anything? Had he been careless?

"You were seen. A man saw you leaving the east door of the Mages' Wheel three nights ago carrying a wrapped bundle."

Shianan's head twitched with surprise. He had left by the western door, with the Shard in a pack beneath his cloak.

"Bailaha!" the king demanded.

"It is not true," Shianan managed. It wasn't.

"No? You call this witness a liar?"

Shianan gambled. It was only a matter of time, anyway. "Your witness must have been mistaken, Your Majesty. I was in the Wheel that night, but I left by the western door."

Fury radiated from the king. "There was no reward—this man did not profit by reporting you. Why would he have seen you at the east door?"

Why, indeed? "I don't know, Your Majesty."

"Perhaps we were deceived."

Shianan's heart quickened.

"Despite all my generous gifts, I always wondered if you might betray us one day, and this is the realization of all my fears. You were so anxious to protest your fealty to us. But after your protestations, still you brought the Gehrn, you were at the shield's collapse and the murder of our Black Mage, and you were admittedly present when the Shard was stolen on the eve of the new shield's creation."

Sweet Holy One, did they think he had helped murder Ariana to break the shield?

"You have not found the Shard, due to guilt or to simple incompetence, but you were seen carrying something from the Wheel. It's possible you are the traitor who laid us vulnerable to attack."

It was only the falsified witness which convicted him?

"Get him up," snapped King Jerome. "I know, Bailaha, there is scant evidence yet to convict even one so suspicious. But a confession can do a great deal in the Court of the High Star. Take him out and get the truth from him."

Shianan's heart stopped, and for the first time he pulled against the guards. They gave him a reflexive jerk that brought him around by his trapped arms.

Someone rushed into the room, a blur on the edge of Shianan's hazed vision. "Stop this! Father—what is this?"

"Keep quiet, Soren. He was seen."

"Someone saw the Shard? I don't believe it, Father. He's innocent."

Shianan stared at Soren. That the prince would come to defend him—and now, of all times, now when there was nothing to defend....

"No," he heard himself say hoarsely. "No, I'm not."

The room went silent as Soren's head turned. "You stole the Shard?"

It was too early yet to confess—but he would confess eventually, and somehow he didn't want Prince Soren to believe falsely in him. Shianan gulped. "I—did."

"You—!" The prince's eyes widened. He glanced down and then back at Shianan. "You did?" Abruptly he pushed past the captain and drove his fist hard into Shianan's diaphragm, jolting him from the ground and making the startled guards stumble.

Shianan fought a long, heart-stopping moment for breath. Even if he'd been able to draw air, he could not have met the prince's eyes.

"Soren," interrupted King Jerome. "If you're satisfied, we were about to send him to be questioned."

"I'll do it myself," Soren growled. "Give him to me, please."

"To you?" King Jerome looked puzzled, then worried, then vaguely resigned. "Then you may have charge, if that's what you want. Only remember we need the Shard recovered, and there must be enough of him left to execute."

Soren made a sharp gesture toward the captain. "Take him to the eastern walks," he ordered. "We'll do it there." He turned to the king and bowed. "Sire, I apologize for my intrusion. Thank you for the chance to avenge myself of my embarrassment."

The guards pushed Shianan toward the door.

"Why did you come at all? Why did you think him innocent?"

"I thought he was not the kind to betray you. But it seems I was wrong."

The guards bowed in the king's direction, shoving Shianan's head down with them, and then backed out the door. Once in the corridor their pace increased, as if by unseen signal, and Shianan stumbled as they dragged him along.

They hauled him up narrow twisted flights of stairs without

355

room for even two abreast, Shianan tripping sideways up stone steps as they pulled and shoved. When they reached the top and emerged into evening light, the captain turned and struck him.

Pain burst through Shianan's bruised and swollen face. Arms braced him from behind as he rocked and held him steady for the next blow.

It will be worse.

The captain hit him again, and Shianan grunted with the impact. The open sky whirled about him.

"Men are out there dying, and you stole the Shard." He threw another punch into Shianan's face. "I guess since they're common honest men, it doesn't matter? Not royal bastards?" He hit him again. "Because only a royal bastard would do such a thing!" And again.

You don't understand, Shianan thought blearily, reeling. *You don't understand a thing.*

"Oh, I understand just fine," the captain snarled. Shianan hadn't realized he'd spoken aloud. "And I hope there's no soft gloves for you, whoreson." He struck Shianan again. And again.

"Captain!" came a guttural whisper from one of the guards. Shianan hung in their grip and caught his breath, tasting blood. When his eyes focused again he blinked and saw fine leather boots.

"I see you started without me," Prince Soren observed dryly. "Caftford, eh?"

"We didn't have to have Caftford," the captain muttered. "But I'm sorry, Your Highness, for going ahead. I should have waited for if you wanted something different."

Soren gestured to the crenelated wall. "Fix him to something there, maybe that torch ring. I don't want him leaving while we— talk."

Shianan wanted to look at Soren, to show he was not intimidated, he was not broken yet, but it hurt to move his head, and one eye was swelling closed.

They had to unfasten his shackles to get his hands over his head—they weren't to the point of breaking his arms and shoulders, not yet—but there was no chance of flight. They bound the iron bars to the ring and stepped back, leaving him leaning against the stonework.

"Bring a light, one of you," the prince ordered, "and then leave us for a while."

They went. Shianan dragged his eyes upward. "Well?"

356

Soren looked coldly at him. "It really disagrees with me, beating a man already battered." He drew back and hit Shianan hard in the gut. "But then I think of those lying dead at Caftford, and I wonder how many will be dead in the next raid, and suddenly I feel no qualms at all."

Shianan coughed and fought to speak. "You—you could save—time."

"Oh, no. Before any of that, I need you to tell where the Shard is now. So keep that in mind, Bailaha—you prolong everything while you keep that secret." He crossed his arms. "And aside from the king's order, I have my own question: Why did you do it?" He looked probingly at Shianan. "I ask because I believe you when you say you stole the Shard. But I also believed you when we talked over that pitiful little fire in the rain, when you said—though not aloud or in so many words—you would do anything for a scrap of praise." He exhaled. "I know that sounds harsh, but it's what I heard. It wasn't difficult to recognize it."

Shianan stared with his one eye.

"And since that conversation must have taken place only hours after you stole the Shard, I cannot reconcile it in my mind. Did you think committing the greatest of crimes would call his attention to you? Did you think conspiring with the Ryuven would somehow avenge yourself on him?"

Shianan shook his head and looked at the edge of the walk. "No. Never."

"Never?" Soren regarded him from inches away. "Then what possessed you?"

Shianan licked his bleeding lips. "I—I did it to save a life."

Soren struck him again, this time across the face. Shianan reeled and the shackles pulled him upright.

"To save a life?" Soren repeated furiously. "To save a life?" He jabbed a finger to the northeast. "Is that what happened in Caftford? Did you save them?"

Torn muscles ground as Shianan shook his head. "There had not been a raid in months, and I—I thought—a few days...."

Another blow. "Explain!"

"Stop." Shianan tried to spit blood, but it only dribbled from his mouth. "I'll tell you—you should know, you—but don't hit me. I'll tell you myself."

"The time for that has passed," Soren growled, but he crossed his arms again and waited.

Shianan's head throbbed. "The shield—when it fell...."

The door to the tower stairs opened. "Brought your light, Your Highness."

The guard set the lamp and left. Soren turned back to Shianan. "I chose this place because I want everyone in that yard to see." He pointed toward the busy courtyard below them. "Every soul there knows you're being questioned. But the wind will carry what we say over the wall." He hesitated. "That's not to say I will protect you. If you stole the Shard, you must pay for that treason. But I want to know for myself what madness took you."

Shianan swallowed painfully. "Ariana Hazelrig did not die."

"Ari.... The Black Mage? She was killed in the collapsing shield."

"She did not die. She was carried away by a Ryuven."

"She was inside the shield. That's not possible."

"I saw it, Your Highness. I saw the Ryuven, I saw him take her. The shield was unstable, Mage Hazelrig said that. The ritual had undone it—I don't know, I'm not a mage. But I saw the Ryuven appear and I saw him take her."

"She would have been killed. They've never returned a captured mage."

"She was not killed. There was a message."

"What?"

Shianan would have to go carefully here. "The night the Ryuven came here, when there was a—"

"The night you were drunk," supplied Soren disdainfully.

"They never found a reason for the intrusion. It was because he came only to leave a message, that the Black Mage was safe and would return when she had recovered from the crossing."

Soren stared. "And you told no one?"

"Her father. But we were afraid to say the Ryuven had given us a message."

"Why? Why spare her at all?"

Shianan tried to shrug but was hindered by the hurt and angle of his arms. "Perhaps they respect the White Mage."

"So you stole the Shard?"

"If the shield were remade, she wouldn't be able to come back."

Soren gave an incredulous sneer. "A brilliant ploy to keep the shield down. They dangled a story, and you gave them all of Caftford. And more."

There was a startled cry from the yard below. A runner burst through the gate, shouting faintly, "Ryuven! Ryuven, in Alham!"

Chaos boiled below as mages and soldiers hurried to respond, and Soren whirled furiously on Shianan. "I hope they find you bound here," he snarled. "There hasn't been an attack on Alham in ten years or more—and you've just let them in."

But someone cried and pointed toward the open gate, and the activity paused. A feminine form ran through the gate, followed closely by a boy in dull silver wrist cuffs. Ariana scanned the yard and ran to the mages already assembling. Most stared in amazement or shock, but the figure in white robes dashed forward and threw his arms around her.

"The Black Mage," breathed Soren. He watched as father and daughter embraced while the servant boy stood respectfully a few paces behind. "She's come back alive. And she saved the slave, too." He looked over his shoulder at Shianan. "You were telling the truth about that, at least."

Shianan could hardly breathe. *Sweet Holy One, she's safe. Thank you.* She'd returned. She had really returned....

"But to trade her for Caftford? Her life for the kingdom? What madness—" Soren stopped, observing Shianan. "Oh," he said dryly. "That madness."

Ariana stood back from her father and explained something animatedly, gesturing once or twice to Tam. The preparatory action slowed, as Ariana presumably explained a Ryuven had come only to deliver her and depart. The other mages were listening intently. Shianan knew the real story would be explained once she and her father and Tam were alone.

"And you knew you would be arrested and sentenced by the Court of the High Star?" Soren sighed. "Oh, you poor sop, you've got it bad."

Shianan tore his eyes from the scene below and looked at Soren. "I...."

Soren gave him a steely glare. "So you let Ariana Hazelrig come home, I'll grant that. And the slave boy, too, it seems. The Ryuven must really honor Ewan Hazelrig." He moved closer. "But to do it, you murdered those in Caftford and you condemned others there to starve, unless we provide them from our own stores which should have been supplemented by theirs, shorting our own men. And, commander, you gave the Ryuven an easy victory, so they will return."

With abrupt force he drove his fist into Shianan's gut, crushing him against the stone. "And you've brought Pairvyn ni'Ai into our world again. Every man who dies facing his command, you murder. And you killed them all for a pretty girl." He struck again, making Shianan gasp weakly for air.

Soren turned away, his throat working visibly, his profile to Shianan. "You did this alone?"

Shianan licked his bloody lips. "Yes." He hesitated, hardly daring to hope but needing to offer, "Since she's come back—the shield is—I can retrieve the Shard...."

"Oh, you will," Soren snarled. "You will return the Shard, that's certain. Where is it?"

"It's...not here." Shianan didn't want them to take Luca—a slave would fare even worse. But he did not know the exact location.

Soren moved, raising his gloved fist again, and Shianan flinched away. Soren hesitated. "Bailaha, this is not a typical scene of interrogation. We have not even begun, by the standards of what lies in those chambers."

"I wasn't lying. I was trying to—it is hidden, buried, outside of Alham. I cannot tell you how to find it."

"The men below could make you tell," Soren replied grimly. "After they've plucked every fingernail and used them to peel the flesh off you, you'll find a way to describe the hiding place." He sighed. "But I hope it won't come to that. At first light, as soon as you can see to dig, you'll go for the Shard." He stepped back. "In the meantime, you'll spend the night here. And if the Ryuven do come—I hope Pairvyn ni'Ai finds you here. I hope he makes you beg, Bailaha, like those in Caftford begged for their lives. But I hope he does not kill you, because you need to find the Shard in the morning."

CHAPTER 57

Shianan shivered and wished he had not; the movement jarred too many pains. The wind which had protected his conversation with Soren beat against him. He flexed his cold fingers in the shackles and leaned his head against his upper arm, trying to conserve heat.

Chained overnight on a crenelated walk.... He had not thought of that in a long time. He tried not to think of it now.

While mages had crowded eagerly around Ariana, Shianan had seen the White Mage step back. Shielded from most of the yard behind a wagon of supplies, he had embraced the slave boy, earnestly expressing his gratitude.

For hours that image echoed in his mind. Hazelrig had not offered even momentary protest to Shianan's arrest. Hazelrig had his daughter, and Shianan had a painful public execution to await.

He leaned against the stone, wishing he could shift his arms. But Ariana was safe. Sweet Holy One, she was safe and at home.

But Shianan was here, and he did not know where to find the Shard.

The lamp beside him wavered and then guttered out. There was a subtle scrape of flesh against stone, and something moved through the crenelation where the dead light rested. Shianan blinked and the form resolved into the shape of a winged man. A Ryuven.

Shianan's voice caught in his throat. If he made a sound, the Ryuven would certainly kill him—but he had to raise the alarm—but no one would hear, on the walk above an empty yard....

"My lord commander, don't be alarmed."

The voice was vaguely familiar, but he could not place it. Shianan swallowed. "What do you want?"

"I wanted to speak with you." The figure came closer.

It was Tam—or the Ryuven that was Tam, at least. Shianan felt relieved and foolish and angry. "What are you doing as a Ryuven? I thought you were Subdued."

"You don't sound well, commander." He came closer, and Shianan could just make out his features in the moonlight. He paused, near enough to see Shianan as well. "Oh."

Humiliated anger rolled over Shianan. "We don't all heal so

quickly."

The Ryuven folded his wings tightly, probably cold in his native form. "I am not Subdued, to answer your question. I was bound again, but Mage Hazelrig was good enough to open the binding just enough for me to assume this form."

"So you're a Ryuven without power?"

"For the time being."

"Why would you expose yourself to such risk? If anyone sees you, you're a dead man."

He tipped his head to regard Shianan. "And why would you expose yourself to risk like this?" He paused. "I wanted to speak with you, and the tower stair is guarded."

Shianan waited. He was trapped here, but he did not have to speak. If the Ryuven wanted to talk, he could do the talking.

"The house is very full tonight. My lady has not had a moment without questions since she arrived. But I was able to speak with the elder Mage Hazelrig, and he told me what you had done."

Shianan looked away. "What of it?"

"Thank you." The Ryuven's voice was strangely quiet. "It must mean a great deal to you that—that she be safe."

Shianan was glad his reddening skin would not be seen in the moonlight. "She is my friend." Defensively he added, "And your mistress. Did she give permission for her slave to go out tonight?"

"As I said, my master released me to come here." His voice was nearly as humble as a slave's ought to be. He faced Shianan. "I do not think she knows."

Heat raced through Shianan's cold limbs and he twitched against the shackles. "Nor will she," he snapped. "What does it matter to you? Can't I hang in my chains without your torment?"

Tamaryl turned away. "If you will be executed anyway, why return the Shard at all?"

"Because I am not a traitor," Shianan snarled. "Because I do not want to see my people murdered and starved by yours."

"I do not want to see mine starved, either."

"And so mine must die?" Frustration made Shianan quiver in his shackles. "And they say Pairvyn ni'Ai was at Caftford. If that's true, if he's alive—"

"They do?"

"Is he?" Shianan demanded. "We thought him dead. It's been since the Luenda battles—" He stopped, icy horror scorching through him. "No...." he breathed. "No, please, no."

But Tamaryl simply looked unhappily at him.

Shianan lunged, hoping to kick him, shove him off the walk, something, but the shackles tore his wrists and he fell back hard against the wall. Impotent fury filled him. "I should have killed you when I first had the chance!"

"And then where would my lady mage be?" Tamaryl answered quietly. "Do you remember I told you it was my choice to leave the fighting?"

"Apparently it's your choice no longer," Shianan raged. "You'll kill as many as ever and leave the rest to starve. And someday you'll face the Circle and you'll kill Ariana."

"No," Tamaryl cut in firmly. "No, I will not."

Shianan sagged against his bleeding wrists, his muscles screaming for relief. "Ariana should never have touched that Shard. None of this would have happened. I should have killed you in the beginning. Hazelrig never should have brought you."

"I helped to invent the shield. I was as anxious for it to work as you." He paused. "And what of the slave? Mage Hazelrig said you took him after the shield collapsed. Sparing him from the Gehrn was surely a good—"

"Luca." Shianan stared at the ground. He needed Luca if he were to recover the Shard.

"Mage Hazelrig said you sent him for safekeeping after your arrest."

Shianan seized on this. "He's at Hazelrig's house now?"

Tamaryl looked mildly surprised. "He's serving the guests come for Lady Ariana."

"Then he will be safe." Somehow he felt a little relieved knowing Luca was with the mage—though he could never say now Luca knew where to find the Shard. It would implicate Mage Hazelrig, even if the Pairvyn didn't take Luca first.

"You think Mage Hazelrig is safe?"

Shianan eyed him coldly. "Even knowing what you are, I won't betray him." He breathed slowly, gathering his strength. "It was Caftford that did this. They had no real evidence against me, but Caftford demanded a scapegoat. And the reappearance of Pairvyn ni'Ai—that's what upset them. They weren't asking questions."

"I am sorry, your lordship."

"Don't call me that! I'm no one's lord commander now—just a

traitor. But I am still loyal for all that, and I won't see my people murdered!" He stepped forward as far as he could, arcing backward against the shackles, and kicked hard at the Ryuven. Tamaryl was caught unprepared and deflected the kick as he stumbled at the edge of the walk. Shianan caught his breath as the Ryuven flailed and then the great wings snapped out, curving into a powerful thrust which pushed him onto solid footing again.

Shianan shouted, "Ryuven! Ryuven, here! Pairvyn ni'Ai is here—"

Tamaryl's hand clamped over his mouth, stifling his warnings. Shianan struggled but the Ryuven was strong for his kind, and Shianan had no leverage chained against the wall.

"I will leave you, my lord commander. I am sorry for your state, but I can do nothing. Yet again, I thank you for what you did." Tamaryl withdrew his hand and vaulted over the wall into the open air.

Shianan screamed in rage and pain and humiliation until his voice broke into sobbing cries, but the wind whipped it all away and no one heard.

Tamaryl slipped into the mage's house and found Hazelrig waiting for him. "You knew I was coming?"

Ewan Hazelrig smiled. "It is not enough power to draw attention," he said, "but if one knows to look for it, you can be sensed."

Tamaryl concentrated and began to reshape his body, molding it into that of a human boy. He held out his wrists, and Hazelrig took the cuffs in his hands. "You found him?"

The binding closed on Tamaryl again. It was not painful—Hazelrig had not undone it, so it did not need to be remade, and he was, after all, the White Mage—but it was an eerie, unsettling feeling. "I did." Tamaryl shivered involuntarily as the great lock sealed. "I spoke with him."

"How is he?"

"He said they were angry over Caftford and the Pairvyn." Guilt twisted in his stomach. "They've beaten him."

Hazelrig's jaw clenched. "Is there any hope?"

"He's confessed. He said he is to return the Shard in the morning, and then he will be executed."

Hazelrig crossed the room. "I haven't been able to think of a way to save him. Even if I confessed everything myself, he would still be held as a complicit traitor."

"Being rescued by a Ryuven wouldn't help him in the end, either." Tamaryl glanced down. "I think he's given up. He confessed, but they had not forced it from him. He's chosen."

"Fool," snapped Hazelrig. "We might have—he had no reason to kill himself." He worked his fingers in frustrated energy. "And when Ariana learns, she will blame herself." He paced. "If we had the Shard.... If we could bring it, would there be enough evidence against him? Why don't you go to him and—"

Tamaryl barked a bitter laugh. "Oh, no. He will not tell me where to find it, not even to save his life. He guessed who I am." The thought hurt, oddly.

"Oh." Hazelrig slumped into a chair. "He just might listen to me, but I cannot reach him there." He clasped his hands. "And so we wait."

CHAPTER 58

Dawn's cold light had just come when the tower door rasped open. Torg was with them.

Shianan lifted his head, shooting pain through his arms and neck. Soren stopped and appraised him, his expression closed. Torg, waiting with the guards, looked unhappily away.

"Here we are," Soren said finally, his voice pitched low and vicious. "You'll want to know, the Black Mage is whole and well. She's spent the night being welcomed home and answering questions from the Circle. And you're probably dreaming she'll throw her arms about your neck, gushing with gratitude and pledging her undying love. But no, it was all for nothing. She hasn't even asked after you."

Shianan felt kicked. *But—but it wasn't for nothing. She's safe.*

Soren raised his voice. "Unchain him. We need the Shard."

Torg looked sick as he approached Shianan, but he dutifully reached for the shackles. Every small movement made Shianan's shoulders scream, and then suddenly the iron bars released him and his arms fell. The sudden drop made him gasp and he stumbled as he tried to balance, his bruised torso aching.

"These men will accompany you to the Shard. They will make sure you do not waste time or fail. Then you will bring the Shard, and your trial will begin."

Shianan's heart would have sunk, had it not already been at its lowest reach. "Your Highness."

Soren left then, and the guards stood about Shianan. One reached for his skinned wrists. "Can't have you running on the road," he said, fastening the shackles onto him again.

Shianan did not care. He was exhausted, cold, hungry, pained. He did not care if his wrists were free.

"Move."

The stairs were difficult, his legs stiff with kicks and the night of standing and shivering. Shianan stumbled down, braced against the guard before him. Torg was somewhere behind him. He was clearly not in command, and this was a good way to demonstrate his loyalty was to the king and not his traitorous commander.

The yard's early traffic stared at Shianan with angry, accusing eyes. He tried not to look at them and when they stopped at the main fortress gate, he sagged gratefully against a post.

"Which way from here?" asked the guard captain.

He had sent Luca to Fhure. "Northeast."

"That way, then." The captain took a handful of Shianan's vest. "There won't be any delaying or putting off. Every time you name a place where the Shard isn't, we'll every man take our belts to you. Buckle ends. Understand?"

There was no choice, and he couldn't reach Luca now even if he wanted. Shianan nodded and started stiffly down the steep hill.

They had gone only half the distance to the northeastern city gate when someone ran across the street, skidding to a halt beside Shianan. The guards tensed, ready to defend their only hope for the Shard against an angry citizen, but Luca offered no threat. He stared at Shianan. "Master, I've come."

Luca—! Shianan felt simultaneous joy and guilt. Luca could save him pain, but in the end they would both die.

"Get out of the way!" snapped a guard. "Keep moving."

Luca simply started walking, trying gamely to hide his dismay at Shianan's battered face. "I'm coming with you."

"What?" A guard cut in before Shianan could respond. "Get on!"

"I can dig!" protested Luca with more vehemence than Shianan had seen from him. "Look at him—he won't be quick. I can dig for you."

Shianan shook his head desperately—Luca was betraying himself—but the guards seemed pleased to have a slave for the labor. "Move on, then. If he wants to break his back, let him."

They left Alham and started down the road, weaving through the heavy morning traffic of merchants and vendors and buyers and pickpockets entering the city. Luca stayed close to Shianan, saying nothing.

Tam slipped behind an overloaded wagon in the morning traffic and fell into step beside a hooded man, who glanced down at him. "What have you found?"

"They're outside the northeast gate. And you were right, Luca is with them."

"I thought that must be so." Hazelrig paused. "I don't know

that we can follow all the way. We don't know how far they have to go."

"We don't have to follow them to the Shard. We can separate them and let Shianan Becknam make his escape from there."

"If he has the sense to do it." Hazelrig nodded to himself. "I'll take charge of that. Go back and keep the door while Ariana gets some rest, and by all that's holy, don't tell her of this."

It would have been quite a sight to see the White Mage running down the road against the morning traffic, white robes flapping against his legs, but almost no one noticed the man in typical burgher garb, possibly looking for a wayward child or a lost friend. He alternately walked and jogged along the road, one hand on the bag slung across his chest.

Shianan stumbled frequently. His sleepless night of muscle fatigue and shivering had sapped him, and the limited use of his arms affected his balance and movement. But he kept going, though Luca stayed close and once or twice reached to steady him when he tripped.

The sun was nearing its zenith when the guard captain suggested, "Let's take a leak and eat something. That hill looks like a soft spot."

Shianan dropped gratefully to the grassy hillside, closing his eyes. He felt as if he could sleep immediately, but someone shook his arm gently. "Not yet," Luca said. "I have water for you."

Shianan opened his eyes to see Luca drawing a stoppered bag from his small pack. Beyond Luca, the guard captain was frowning at them, but he said nothing as he withdrew his own lunch. They didn't have to provide for the prisoner, but there was no reason another shouldn't, if he'd keep a better pace in the afternoon.

Luca removed the cork and pushed the bag into Shianan's fettered hands. "Drink. And I have some food, too."

The water was mixed with a salted broth of some kind. Shianan sucked at it eagerly though it stung the cuts in his mouth. Luca munched an apple, one eye on his master and his back to the road so he could see the guards.

Torg sat behind Shianan and kept his eyes on his meal, meat and cheese rolled into brown bread. The keys at his belt clinked as he shifted away from his commander. He did not join in the guards' small talk.

Shianan finished the watered broth and lay in the long dry

grass, his back to the guards. He stared at the road, empty but for a single traveler following, and then closed his eyes.

"Master, do you want something to eat?"

Shianan shook his head without opening his eyes. He wanted sleep more than anything else—preferably in a soft bed with several feather pillows and fluffy warm quilted blankets, and as long as he was dreaming fantasies, with Ariana beside him, talking happily of flowers and sunlight and deeds well done....

He slept.

Hazelrig left the road and chose a place beside prickly bushes which still held their leaves. Most of the guards were enjoying the pause, stretching their legs and drinking. They had been roused early for this duty. Luca was sitting near Shianan, glancing from the commander to the guards, who ignored him.

Hazelrig sighed. If he'd known from the beginning Luca would be with them.... But the slave had slipped out of his present master's house to follow his former master. There was a story there, Hazelrig thought, if only there were time to pursue it.

Shianan seemed to be sleeping, which made sense. He would have to take rest when he could. Hazelrig could not act now, but he could prepare for when the moment was right.

He opened the bag slung across his chest and withdrew a vial of coarse sand, another of powdery particulate, and a tiny athanor and crucible. He poured the sand into a shallow dish and arrayed his materials before him, and then he began to sketch patterns into the sand and the grass.

"That's long enough," announced the guard captain. "Time to go." He turned toward Luca. "Get him on his feet, or I will."

Shianan stirred reluctantly at Luca's urging, disoriented for a moment, and then sat up. He raised his joined hands to rub dried blood from over one eye. Luca stood and extended a hand. Shianan blinked blearily at it.

A sudden breeze wafted by them, carrying a smattering of dust. Luca automatically lifted a hand to shield his face, still holding the other out to Shianan. And then the breeze exploded into a whirlwind and smoke enveloped them.

The guards gave startled cries as they disappeared from view. Luca could just make out Shianan as he leapt from the ground and spun, blurring into the dusty wind.

"Grab the prisoner!"

Luca moved after Shianan and saw him jerk a flailing Torg backward and drive his shackled hands downward like a hammer.

"Get the keys!" Shianan snapped.

Luca leapt forward. Torg lay still as he yanked open the buckle and pulled free the ring of jangling keys. Shianan must have hit him hard. But then Luca heard a hoarse whisper, "Run!" and he knew the captain had chosen not to resist.

"Who has him?"

But Shianan was already running, slipping on the grass as he struggled up the hill. Luca followed, the smoke dissipating around them. He glanced back to see the whirlwind still obscuring the group, coughing guards stumbling to the edges. He turned forward again and seized Shianan's arm, pushing him over the crown of the hill and down into overgrown concealment.

The guard captain waved his arms through the fading smoke as if it would disperse more quickly, cursing violently. "Which way did he go? Why didn't you stop him?"

Torg was kneeling, one hand clutching his bloody mouth. "It wasn't as if I simply handed him the keys," he retorted.

The other captain regarded him suspiciously. "You have a history with the commander, Captain Torg," he said darkly. "A long history, don't you?"

"I have a longer one of fighting the Ryuven," snapped Torg, spraying blood. "I have as much reason to want the shield in place as anyone." He glared at the guard captain. "If you've got something to say, you'd better say it."

The captain scowled. "Maybe the two of you staged this to free him."

"Maybe, but I'm no mage—I couldn't have done that trick of the wind. And Shianan Becknam's no mage. And I'm reasonably sure his slave is not a mage, either. So either there's someone else here working magic on his behalf, or he had a Ryuven ally who did this, or that really was some freak gust of wind that caught the dust. I don't know. But I do know that while you've stood here arguing about who let him escape, he's made his way well out of here."

The guard captain swore again. "Separate and find him," he ordered. "Captain Torg, you go—"

"No, sir, thank you."

The captain stopped and stared. "What?"

Torg shook his head. "Shianan Becknam is a commander, and yet he still trains the troops for combat. Think on that. Ask anyone who's worked with him and they'll tell you he's a fearsome fighter." He rubbed blood from his face. "He knows we'll be following after him. And you want me to walk alone into whatever trap he's setting? No, sir. This is your command, but I'll take my chances with a military court before I'll take on Shianan Becknam in a real fight."

The guards exchanged glances, suddenly less willing to plunge into the growth around them. The captain clenched his fists. "I don't care if he can sprout horns, we'll find him! He's the only one who knows where the Shard is hidden. Which would you rather face, Becknam or Pairvyn ni'Ai?"

The guards shifted and fingered their weaponry.

"Spread out and look for him or his trail. And if there's a magic user about, find him, too!"

CHAPTER 59

Luca fitted the third key and twisted, and this time it slipped into the mechanism. The shackles opened and Shianan cradled his bruised and torn wrists. "We have to hurry. How far is the Shard?"

"The Shard?"

"I won't leave this land open to the Ryuven," Shianan said firmly. "And unless we return it, I have no chance of ever earning clemency. How far?"

"Two hours or so if we hurry."

"Let's go."

They chose a line parallel to the road and set a brisk pace. Luca naturally dropped behind Shianan.

"What are you doing?" Shianan demanded. "You should know by now we don't hold the usual rules. Come beside me—it will make talking easier, anyway. Who was that?"

"What?"

"Who worked the magic?"

Luca shook his head. "I don't know, Master Shianan. It surprised me as much as anyone."

"Then who?" He frowned. "Only Mage Hazelrig would have any reason...." He looked at Luca. "Did you know he would come?"

Luca shook his head quickly.

If Shianan noticed his anxiety, he gave no sign. "Let's get to the Shard."

Shianan ran unevenly, panting audibly. Luca reached into the bag slung around him and felt for an apple. "Master Shianan, take this. You need something."

"I need that Shard," he answered, but he took the apple.

Despite his beaten frame and fatigue, Shianan set a grueling pace. Finally Luca panted, "Wait—wait, this is it."

Shianan stumbled to a halt and dropped his hands to his knees, bracing himself to catch his breath. "Here?"

Luca looked at the trunk broken over a rock and the two oaks to their right. "I think so." He moved, breathing hard, until he could see the two white birches fall into alignment. The grass seemed a little less full where the two lines intersected. "Yes, it's here." Luca looked around for the digging stick he'd abandoned. When he found it, he glanced back at Shianan and saw him on the ground, bent over his knees. Luca, alarmed, started toward him. "Master Shianan?"

Shianan drowsed where he sat. He lifted his head. "Do we have it?"

"In a moment," Luca said. "Rest a moment, and I'll bring it up."

Shianan did not protest, and he lay down and did not move again. Luca returned to the buried Shard.

Uncovering it went more quickly, as the dirt was already loosened and he no longer cared to make the site appear undisturbed. "Master Shianan!" He carried it to the sleeping figure. "Here it is."

"Hm?" Shianan roused and then abruptly seized the Shard. "I want to see it." He ripped back the protective wrappings and exposed the jagged crystalline stone. He sagged with relief. "Now, let's get it back to Alham."

"But—"

"I won't let people die for lack of the Shard," Shianan said. "And if I return it, maybe there will be some lenience for me."

"No!" The word burst from Luca before he could think. "You should flee. Leave the Shard for them to find and run!"

Shianan pushed his hair back, moving his hand gingerly over his swollen face. "And how will they find it, when they don't know where to look? Should I send you to carry it to them? No. I'll take it." He swallowed. "Perhaps I can give them some story about reclaiming it from thieves. Maybe they'll even believe me."

Luca shook his head and clenched his fingers on the digging stick. "No—Master Shianan—don't do this."

Shianan struggled to his feet. "Running is futile, Luca. I know this. I'll only die panicked and exhausted."

"And in doing this you'll only die tortured and sooner!" Luca was beyond himself now, no longer thinking of his proper slave's position. "Why escape at all if you will only surrender yourself to them again?"

"I will prove I am doing this of my own will," Shianan returned sharply. He pulled the wrapping around the crystal again. "I was not forced to return the Shard—I brought it myself."

"Do you think they will allow that?" Luca grabbed for Shianan's sleeve, leaving muddy streaks. "You got away—that endangers those guards. They won't admit you escaped them. They will take you in chains again and carry back the Shard themselves."

Shianan moved toward the road with long strides. "Every person who died in Caftford died because of me, Luca. I won't be a murderer again. I will return the Shard."

Luca hurried beside him while Shianan cradled the wrapped Shard. "But—"

"But what?" demanded Shianan. "Do not presume to tell me what to do. My life is my own, unlike yours. And I see precious little else I can yet do with my life, given they will never let me hide and I will never let myself keep back the Shard, and I have received precious little help from Ewan Hazelrig in this matter."

Luca seized on this. "He might be helping you—maybe that was his magic that—"

"If he intends to help me, then where is he?" Shianan made a sharp gesture that encompassed the road and both sides.

"How could he find you?" Luca pleaded. "He might be with the soldiers by now. How would you expect him to find you here?"

Shianan rolled his eyes. "He's a mage, Luca—and not just a mage, but the White Mage of the Great Circle. He can track a charm across the countryside as easily as you can mark a fly crossing a room. If he did not even give you a trailing charm to carry, then—" He saw Luca's expression and stopped mid-sentence. "No. Luca, you did not. Tell me you didn't!"

Luca gulped. "I could not leave you. Not to this. I couldn't let them torture you when you didn't even know...."

"Luca, you stupid, stubborn...." Shianan sounded angry, furious, more than Luca had ever heard him. "It was almost the last thing I did, but I found a place where you would be safe and well-used and away from suspicion. Did you not think for a moment what you were doing?" His pace quickened as he looked ahead. "Did you think they would hesitate for a moment to rip you limb from limb if they thought you knew where the Shard was hidden?"

"Master...."

"And now you've thrown away your safe place. My final order to you, Luca, and you stupid, stubborn, recalcitrant, insubordinate...."

"Master, I only wanted—"

"You are a slave!" Shianan snarled, making Luca flinch. "It does not matter what you want! You are only to obey my orders, and I ordered you to be safely away from this!" He half-turned and shoved the Shard into Luca's chest, taking the digging stick. "Carry that."

Luca took it numbly.

Shianan faced forward again, charging up the road's incline at an angry walk. He threw an arm across Luca's chest, shoving him backward. "And get behind me."

Luca hesitated and then stumbled after him at a slave's distance. "I'm sorry, master...."

"Quiet!" snapped Shianan. "This has nothing to do with your glaring, stupid disobedience. It's only that I don't want you killed in your first fight."

Luca blinked. "Wha—"

The attack came from the side, as a swordsman leapt from cover. Shianan angled to meet him, sweeping the stick to check the strange swordsman's advance. The attacker beat once against the stick's return and then moved, trying to get inside the range of the makeshift staff. Shianan whipped the staff vertically to reverse it and drove the end into the other's midsection as he dropped low, so the swordsman's downward cut fell uselessly across the staff. He rose, stepping forward, and the rearward end of the staff swung around and crushed the swordsman's neck.

Luca almost missed the second attacker. "Behind—!"

The stick dropped from the first swordsman's neck and reversed in Shianan's hands as he spun, whipping outward to meet the incoming sword.

The stick splintered with the impact, cracking audibly. Luca gasped as the sword went through. Shianan seemed to be jarred by the collision but he let the disruption turn him, stepping forward and bringing the rear of the shortened stick into the attacker's temple even as the sword continued on its path. The man staggered, and Shianan hit him again to knock him down. Luca stared as he rammed the broken stick down to make sure he stayed. Shianan lifted it for another driving blow and shouted, "Luca!"

Luca spun and stumbled as something crashed hard into the Shard, knocking him backward. He stared in horror as the swordsman advanced, swinging the blade back toward him, and he thrust the Shard from him as he fell.

The swordsman recoiled and then fumbled to catch the Shard. Luca saw Shianan plunge the broken stick into the prone body again and start forward. The man with the Shard whirled, slashing with the sword, and ran the way they'd come.

Luca dug his fingers into the rutted road and scrambled to his feet. Shianan was a few paces behind the fleeing swordsman, wasting no breath in demands or threats. The swordsman whirled and swung one-handed toward Shianan—

Shianan's next stride ended in a lunge that took him low to the ground and far forward as he braced the broken stick with both hands. The makeshift staff caught the descending arm just above the elbow, snapping it with its own force. Shianan drove forward from his lunge and into the stunned attacker.

Someone seized Luca and twisted him to the ground, wrenching his arm behind him. He gasped as a hand slapped against his shoulder, pinning him on his knees. Other guards ran past, plunging down the incline toward Shianan and the strange attackers. "No!" he screamed.

Shianan, inside the reach of the sword, shoved the stick through the crook of the arm which cradled the Shard. The swordsman recoiled but Shianan had already wrenched the stick down and around, snapping the arm back at an unnatural angle. The swordsman pitched and screamed as the Shard dropped to the road and rolled.

The guards swarmed them. Luca tried to rise—"No!"—and was forced down again by his shoulder. He twisted his head and saw Shianan dragged backward over a guard's knee by a stick across his throat. Two other guards were wrapped about his arms, pinning him in place.

"No! He has the Shard!" Luca screamed. "He was bringing it back! Stop!"

Shianan choked against the stick. Another guard put a sword's point to his stomach.

"He found the Shard!" sobbed Luca. "Stop it!" A figure moved beside him but he could not look away. "He was bringing it back!"

Someone seized a handful of Luca's hair and twisted his head. "You're making a lot of noise," the guard captain growled. "You'd better—"

"Don't do this!" Luca begged. "He was bringing back the Shard!"

The captain frowned. "What do you mean, bringing it back?"

"They were trying to kill him," Luca sobbed, and as suddenly as that, inspiration struck him. *Perhaps I can give them some story about reclaiming it from thieves.* Luca gulped and continued, "They tried to kill him weeks ago. They lied, they had a man lie to say he saw him steal the Shard, but it was only to have you kill him since they couldn't do it themselves." Luca barely knew what he was saying—he'd planned none of this—but he plunged on recklessly. "Don't you see—"

"Captain!" One of the guards looked up from a swordsman's prone body. "This is Vagus!"

"Vagus?" repeated the captain. "But—he's not under the commander. And there was no guard assigned here." He took a step toward the still swordsman, scowled, and then turned on Luca still kneeling in the road. "Explain!"

"That is why my master couldn't tell you he was innocent." Luca's mind whirled. "He did not know if it were a single hired man or a conspiracy within the guard. He let you believe he was guilty so they would be at ease. They weren't expecting him to follow, and he could find the Shard. He was bringing it back!"

The guard captain looked from Luca to each of the three disabled swordsmen. "He was following them?"

Luca would have said anything. "He took the Shard back from them. He was bringing it back to Alham."

"Who? Who wanted to kill him?"

Torg, listening beside them, was pale and wide-eyed. Luca ignored him and stared earnestly at the guard captain. Not the king who hated his bastard son—the guards wouldn't dare to cross that. It had to be someone they did not fear, someone they already mistrusted.... "A merchant," he blurted. "One who was cheating the army when my master exposed the fraud.... You have the Shard! Please!"

The guard captain stared at him for a long moment. Luca hardly dared to breathe. Then he turned toward Shianan. The guard with the stick across his throat had loosened it, letting him breathe, but they still held him pinned firmly. The guards watched their captain, waiting.

The captain took Luca's shirt collar and dragged him forward. He stopped beside Shianan, helpless with a stick across his throat and a knee in his kidney and a sword on his gut, and pitched Luca to the ground again. "Is this true?" he demanded.

Luca looked desperately at Shianan and held his breath. If only his master would—he had seemed so determined to surrender himself, but if the guard captain believed for only a moment....

Shianan's eyes rolled to find him. "Luca," he croaked, "you stupid, obstinate, disobedient piece of Furmelle refuse." His throat worked against the stick as he drew his next breath. "I told you to stay silent on that."

Luca sagged forward on his palms, shoulders dropping with relief. The guard captain stared for an eternal moment and then rocked abruptly to life. "Get that off his neck! Let go of the man."

The guards released him as if he were heated steel, and Shianan fell awkwardly into a sitting position on the rutted road. Luca made himself stare at the ground. Shianan was supposed to be angry with him, so he should not endanger their frail lie, and there would be nothing he could offer his master at this moment, anyway. He heard Shianan cough.

"Commander," began the captain in muted awe, "you didn't— we didn't—how were we supposed to know?"

"You weren't," Shianan answered hoarsely. "I wanted the conspirators to think their plan had worked. You shouldn't have known even yet, if my idiot fool of a slave had the wits to recognize what was best for him."

Luca allowed himself the faintest of smiles as he dropped his head lower in mock contrition.

"But...." The captain was clearly disturbed. "I'm sorry, sir. I hope you'll understand...."

Shianan chuckled weakly. "Don't worry, captain. If you really believed I had taken the Shard, what you did was probably justified." He coughed again.

The captain turned. "What about the others?"

"That one's never getting up again," reported one guard, pointing to the second attacker. "Something's broke, he's dead."

"Vagus isn't breathing!" called the guard crouching beside him. "I—I don't think he's going to. His neck...."

The guard captain faced Shianan. "Commander...."

"We've got this one, sir," said the guard standing beside the third attacker. "He's got no arms, but he's living."

Luca rose, afraid their fragile reprieve might be ended. The third attacker sat rocking in the road, one arm dangling uselessly and the other cradled in his lap. The guard captain walked around Shianan to the crippled swordsman, who made a small moaning sound as he lifted his head.

"Vagus couldn't squirt in a ditch without a map and luck," the guard captain said. "I know this wasn't planned by the three of you. Who hired you?"

"I don't know his name."

The guard captain sighed and squatted to take hold of the man's twisted arm. For one instant the swordsman looked at him with wide, white-rimmed eyes. "No—"

The captain lifted the arm and rotated it. The man gasped and twitched, lifting his other arm as if to help himself but it swung limply. The captain spoke over the man's sound. "Does he pay you enough for this, too? What is his name?"

"I don't know!"

The captain half-stood, changing the angle of the arm. Luca shrank back as the man cried aloud, a sound too familiar from Furmelle and other places. "You don't know?" pressed the captain.

"He met us in a pub!" shrieked the swordsman. "The Dancing Maid! He paid us five hundred pias and promised as much again if we'd kill him!"

"Kill who?"

"Him! The commander! Please, I don't know his name!"

"And what about the Shard?"

"I don't know about—" The captain shifted and he screamed. "Oh, no, sweet Holy One, no! Please, yes, we took the Shard, it's all as you said!" He writhed but could not withdraw his torn arm. "We took it! Please, for the love of all that's—"

The captain lowered the arm but did not release it. "Where was the Shard? Where were you taking it?"

The swordsman whimpered.

The captain sighed again. "I tell you, man, he's not paying you enough—"

"It was buried," cut in Shianan. "I think these men were only to retrieve it. You'll find a hole not a quarter mile from this spot, marked by two oaks and two hemlocks."

"Birches, my lord."

"Shut up, Luca."

"Yes, master."

The captain turned back to the crippled swordsman. "And you were taking it to him again?"

"Yes!" he offered quickly, before the captain could move his arm again. "Yes, yes, at the Dancing Maid again, tomorrow night. He was going to pay us then."

"You're sure?" The captain moved.

The man wailed. Shianan's voice cut across the sound. "Captain."

The captain looked startled and released the twisted arm to drop to the ground. "Yes, sir." He stood, ignoring the man who reached for one injured arm with another and rocked with pain. "You, Holzer, make up a sling for this man's arms so we can get him back. Hollan, throw Vagus over your shoulder, and somebody put the other corpse on the slave, and—"

"No," said Shianan.

"Sir?"

"He'll be helping me."

The guard captain looked uncomfortable. "Oh. Right. Somebody else get that body, then. Commander, I—you weren't...."

Shianan shook his head. "We already dismissed that. And don't flatter yourself, it wasn't all you."

"Right, sir." The guard captain's eyes landed on Torg. "You! You help the commander, too. Trevor, come here—I want you to carry a message back."

Luca crawled forward to Shianan. "Master Shianan," he whispered, "are you injured?"

Shianan looked at him with flat incredulous eyes. "Nothing new," he said finally, as Luca squirmed. "Nothing that a strong dose of willow bark, a dozen poultices, and a week of sleep won't cure."

Torg came to crouch beside them. "Commander...."

Shianan smiled weakly. "I'm sorry about your jaw, captain."

Torg shook his head tightly. "A boyhood fantasy of yours, I'm sure. Commander—you're sure it's a merchant who wants your death?"

"Did you find someone else?"

"No. It's only...." He exhaled, looking agitated.

Shianan shifted uncomfortably. "Get me up."

CHAPTER 60

They stopped after an hour or so at a little inn beside a minor crossroad. The Two Sisters had a painted sign of dubious character, but the public room was freshly-scrubbed and the smells from the rear kitchen were delicious.

As Shianan limped upstairs, Luca turned to Torg. "My lord." This was difficult, asking a favor of a soldier, and Shianan had called Torg strict. But he could see no other option. "My lord, if you please— could you lend some coins? There's an herbalist just there, you see, and I thought I'd buy willow bark for my master."

"Good man." Torg reached into the pouch at his belt and shook out a few coins.

"Thank you, my lord!" Luca bowed and darted for the door.

The herbalist was working with a preparation, but she called a slave from chopping wood behind the shop and had him measure out the willow bark for Luca. He bought a healthy supply; his master would be wanting it for days, and Luca thought he might offer some to the crippled prisoner, if allowed. The man had tried to kill him, but he was in pain now and would not see a healer for another day, if at all. Luca had seen too many unattended injured.

Shianan was in a chair at the room's only table, his arms crossed over his torso in what was probably intended to be a casual posture but which betrayed his chill and discomfort. There was a curtain against the wall which could separate the single bed from the rest of the room, providing a lord with privacy from his servants. The landlord had provided an unoriginal stew, not elaborate, but nourishing and warm.

The landlord had water boiling, too, and Luca set the willow bark to simmer. Then he sat down with his own bowl.

"Luca." Luca almost missed Shianan's quiet voice in the low babble of the guards' conversation. "The room is going black around this chair. Help me to bed before I humiliate myself."

Luca hurriedly set his stew aside and offered a arm as Shianan pushed himself upright. Shianan put a hand on his shoulder and tossed a casual wave to the two captains. "I want sleep. You'll trust me to bed?"

"Of course," the guard captain said, anxious to assuage his

offenses. "We'll have a guard at the door for the Shard, sir, that's all. Good night, sir."

"Good night, sir," echoed Torg, looking as if he'd rather say more.

Luca drew the curtain behind them, blocking the men's conversation, as Shianan sank gratefully to the narrow bed, pale and strained. "I have willow bark," Luca offered. "That will help."

As Luca turned away, Shianan caught his arm. "Luca," he whispered. "I meant what I said. You are a stupid and obstinate slave, stubborn and disobedient, conniving and lying, and I owe you too much."

Luca felt a quick warm surge of emotion. "I...."

"You really don't know what's best for you."

Luca shook his head. "I'm not sure about that."

"Idiot," breathed Shianan, letting his head fall against the wall. "The White Mage doesn't even condone slavery, and you could have been there instead of risking torture and death here."

Mage Hazelrig is not my own friend. But Luca did not answer aloud.

Shianan's hand moved and closed on Luca's cuff. "In all truth, Luca, I owe you more than I can pay. Ask me what you will."

Luca was taken aback. "Master Shianan...."

"Whatever is not limited by law, Luca." His face was shadowed in the single candle's light. "You know I would free you if I could.... But despite my bravado at the slavers, I don't have the power. You... well, you missed your chance, Luca. But whatever I can give. We can even go to the slave market and you can woo yourself a pretty girl who'll have you." He smiled tiredly.

Luca smiled at the feeble joke, too. "I don't know that anyone would have me." He swallowed, sobering. "But there is one thing I would ask, master."

"Don't you dare speak to me as you would that Gehrn pig," Shianan warned, his head against the wall. "What is it?"

Luca's stomach clenched. What was in his mind was something slaves did not ask. "Master, please don't—don't sell me. I don't want to go to the block again, and I—I'll never do better. I want to stay here. I know a slave can't speak for his future, but I—"

"Luca." Shianan gave him an exhausted but honest smile. "I said the Vandogan could not afford your price. No one can."

Everything cold poured out of Luca in a blinding rush. He

opened his mouth, had nothing to say, and realized he was crying.

"Don't." Shianan's cheeks were damp, too. "'Soats, Luca, it's no surprise. You should know we're two of the same. We need each other."

Luca nodded, swallowing against the lump in his throat. "Thank you, Master Shianan."

Shianan exhaled. "No, Luca, thank you." He swallowed visibly himself. "Do you—you said you had willow bark?"

Luca rubbed at his face, glad of the distraction. "Yes! I'll fetch it. One moment."

He went to the pot and poured a cup, noting it was cooling. The decoction should be strong enough to be effective. "Here, Master Shianan." He watched his master move gingerly as he drank. "Do you need me to help with your clothes?"

Shianan shook his head. "I spent one night in these already. What's another?" He drew his arms close. "And I want to be warm this night. King's sweet oats, I want to be warm."

Luca slipped outside the curtain and poured a second cup. He wiped his face again with his sleeve, shoving away the last of the tears, and carried it to the crippled prisoner. "Willow bark. It will help the pain a little."

The injured man looked at him with wide eyes. "I didn't even hear," he said in quiet horror. "What did he do to you?"

Luca shook his head, embarrassed. "I'll be all right," he said. He gave the man a tentative smile. "I'll be all right."

CHAPTER 61

Ariana continued to talk as the two senior mages took rapid notes—the Ryuven city, the worsening blight on their crops, the demographic shift as the nim indentured themselves to che and sho for bread.

"Ariana," interrupted her father with blessed perception, "I think we may break for a few minutes here. I'm sure Elysia's hand is nearly as cramped as mine, and I could use a breath of fresh air as surely as you could use a space to breathe." He smiled. "I'll have Tam bring something to eat, as well. It's been some hours already since supper."

The White and Silver Mages left her father's workshop, and Ariana slumped tiredly over the table. She did not feel up to a brief walk outside, though it would probably do her good. She was not unwell; it was just difficult to consider her answers to Elysia Parma's questions while responding promptly enough that it did not seem she was filtering. Her father was careful not to press where she gave incomplete information, or to ask after other details, but the Silver Mage was a thorough woman. Ariana sighed.

"My lady? I brought tea."

"Thank you." Ariana reached numbly for the cup Tam offered her. Then she lifted her eyes and glanced at him, her hand hesitating mid-air. "Tam...."

He smiled. "Tea, my lady?"

She could not see him as the slave boy. "Tam, you...."

He set the cup on the table. "I will leave it for you, then."

"Tam—wait."

He did. "My lady?"

"Stop that." When she looked at Tam she saw both his human form and his Ryuven shape. She saw a boy of perhaps twelve, a cheerful and attentive servant, and a monster who might have professed an attraction to her. "You—you aren't a servant."

"To the contrary, my lady, that was part of the bargain your father and I made. I could not appear to be anything but a slave, if we wished to avoid drawing attention."

She sighed. "But now.... Tam, when you said—you hoped I

would see you as more than a slave boy.... Did you mean you wanted me to know you were a Ryuven? Or Pairvyn ni'Ai?"

He glanced down. "I had not thought about my rank."

She toyed with the tea cup, knowing she was fidgeting but unable to stop. "What—"

"Tam," said Hazelrig as he passed through the door, "would you bring something to eat, please? And tea looks wonderful. Bring some for us as well, if you would. Thank you."

Elysia Parma took her seat again and glanced at her notes. "Ariana, I know you must be exhausted. Thank you for answering our questions."

Ariana shook her head. "I only wish I had been able to see more. I spent so much time in a drugged sleep, I was hardly any use at all."

"You are the first human to return from the Ryuven world. I would not call your experience useless." She slid aside the sheets dark with notes and straightened a fresh page. "And now we'll have the Shard back, and perhaps with your information we can work out an end to this."

"Back?"

Her father gave Parma a quick glance, but the Silver Mage did not notice. "It was stolen a few days ago—fortunately for you! But the bastard has been arrested now, and we'll have it returned soon enough."

The bastard.... The erudite Mage Parma did not often choose coarse language, but she couldn't have meant Shianan. Ariana looked at her father, who turned to his workbench for more ink. Beside her Tam slid a plate of finely ground oat cakes onto the table. She looked at him and saw him glance quickly away. Her pulse quickened. "Who was—"

"Tam, mind the tea," her father snapped in uncharacteristic irritation. "Leave the cakes and go. Ariana, you—"

"Who stole the Shard?" Ariana looked from Mage Parma to her father. "When? What happened?"

"We have it back now," her father said firmly, and he threw the Silver Mage something very near to a warning glance. "What happened will be sorted out soon."

Ariana looked back at him. "What? Father—"

"Later. There's no urgency, you can hear about it later, and we need to get as much detail from you as soon as we can, while memory is fresh. Now, you were telling us how you met Oniwe'aru."

Ariana caught her breath and checked her answer. If her father wanted to avoid the topic, there must be a reason. He had kept secrets from her before, but always for cause—and she would be able to ask again in private, when Mage Parma had gone.

Ariana took a breath and an oat cake. Tam bowed without speaking and retreated. Ariana glanced after him, wondering, and then her father's gaze and Parma's expectancy prompted her to continue.

CHAPTER 62

Shianan's feet dragged, his bruised and knotted muscles protesting as he forced them up Alham's hills. His legs marked with bruises from kicks, his aching back and ribs, his abdomen sore from repeated punches, his face swollen and bloodied—he must look as awful as he felt. He fixed his mind on the Naziar, thinking of more blissful sleep.

Finally they entered the Naziar, and as they crossed the yard, it seemed all activity stopped and all eyes stared incessantly at him. Obviously the guards' message had spread farther than its first report. Shianan closed his eyes, knowing the path by heart. Let them think what they would. He wanted only his bed.

Instinct prodded him awake at the same instant a startled sound from Luca drew his attention. He blinked into focus and recoiled, but not quickly enough to avoid the hands that seized his arms. "Shianan Becknam," a voice blared, "you are summoned to the Court of the High Star for immediate trial."

"Now?" His swollen wrists were pressed together and shackles fitted over the bruises. "Why? Why now?"

The fresh guards who had seized him pushed past those who had escorted him to the Shard, watching with dull startlement. "You will answer the Court," one replied shortly. "Move out."

"No," protested Luca. He started to follow. "Wait—"

A guard shoved him back roughly. "On your way, slave."

"But my master—"

The guard struck Luca, sending him reeling through the watching group. "On your way, I said!"

"Leave him!" snapped Shianan.

"But I have to testify!" Luca burst, turning back. "I'm witness to when they tried to kill him!"

"Luca, no!"

"Testify?" repeated the sergeant who had announced Shianan's arrest. "You're eager for it?"

"Luca!" Shianan stepped forward, heedless of the hands which seized him. "A slave's word is not admissible unless it's—extracted."

Luca blinked in horrified understanding. "But...."

391

"Luca, don't!"

"Take the slave," the sergeant ordered. "We'll hold him until the court is ready for him." He looked at Shianan. "They're ready for you now."

They walked him briskly into the stone keep and toward the ceremonial chambers where the Court of the High Star met. He was pushed forward with jabbing fingers and blunt tips, dagger pommels, whatever was handy. No one was called before the Court of the High Star unless more or less expendable, and no one would complain if a prisoner appeared a little the worse for wear.

The labyrinth of corridors swam before him as he stumbled forward, and his tired brain could not track their path. There was no need, though; he would not need to find his way out again. He closed his burning eyes and let the guards push him around corners.

Then he heard the creak of massive doors and they drew him into a high-ceilinged chamber, ringed with padded benches and staring eyes. Shianan barely had time to note the high dais at the far end before the guards forced him to his knees. Someone shoved his head down, as if Shianan did not know himself to bow it.

"You're late, Bailaha."

The voice had a quality of icy detachment. Shianan gulped, afraid despite himself. He was not sure if he were expected to answer. "My honored lord, circumstances—"

"Silence." The voice was not interested in his circumstances. "You will have an opportunity to speak for yourself when all else is said. You will remain silent while the evidence against you is presented. My lord?"

"The Court of the High Star commences to try Commander Shianan Becknam, Count of Bailaha, who stands accused of the theft of the Shard of Elan, of treachery against the defense of the realm, and of high treason against the state."

Shianan strained his eyes to look around him. The boxed alcove where the king might sit to observe was empty.

The court officer continued. "The first evidence is the eyewitness testimony of Yergman Camb, who saw the accused prisoner carrying away the Shard."

He saw only a bundle! thought Shianan angrily, before recalling the man had in fact seen nothing at all. But perhaps in this telling, he would have seen the Shard itself in Shianan's hands.

"Yergman Camb went out," someone offered. "We waited so

long this morning, he was given permission to return home during our recess. He's been sent for, as soon as word came that the prisoner had returned."

"Will it be long?"

"No, my honored lord, I don't believe so. He lives within the fortress walls."

"Thank you. Then while the witness is brought, we shall hear other testimony. The Court requests His Highness Prince Soren to come and speak for us, if it pleases him."

Shianan's stomach clenched. He had, after all, confessed to stealing the Shard, because he had, of course, actually stolen it. And the prince's word could not be refuted.

He could not see much of the prince's approach with his head bowed, but he heard movement from one side of the room and a pair of well-made boots crossed the limited field of his vision. Soren swore an oath of truth in loyalty to the crown and stood before the court, the members of which had risen in respect to their prince. There were a few formal exchanges of phrase, typical court protocol, and then the meat of the testimony began. "Your Highness, did the accused prisoner speak of the Shard?"

"He did, my honored lord."

"Did he confess to stealing it?"

Shianan clenched his jaw.

"He did."

Shianan swallowed. He would die, then.

"Your Highness, did he indicate to you why he would commit such a crime against his king and country?"

Shianan's heart seemed to stop, and for the first time he realized he feared humiliation more than death.

"Er, he did not say much of that."

Shianan blinked, surprised by the prince's tacit answer. He exhaled gratefully, his shoulders slumping. Of course, they would not want to embarrass Ariana Hazelrig.

"But he did confess to stealing the Shard?"

"He did."

"Thank you, Your Highness. The Court has no further questions."

The boots departed, and Shianan wished suddenly that the entire process were finished, that they would simply take him out and behead him quickly.

"The Court calls Captain Refend."

The voice which swore truth and loyalty was that of the guard captain. Shianan felt a quick stab of remorse for the man, who had only hours before believed Shianan had recovered the Shard from thieves. Which he had, in a manner of speaking, though the thief had held it for only a moment.

"Captain, you heard the accused prisoner confess to the theft of the Shard?"

"I did, my honored lord, but I—"

"Please answer our questions, captain, for the moment. You took the accused prisoner to retrieve the hidden Shard?"

"That was my duty, my honored lord."

"Did he direct you to find it, demonstrating he knew its hiding place?"

"In a way, my honored lord."

"In a way? Explain."

"He told us which way to start out, and we did. But he did not dig up the Shard himself."

"We presume your men would have done the work, yes."

"No, my lord, let me explain. When we were some leagues out, we were attacked magically. A dust storm came up and blinded and choked us all. During this, the prisoner and his slave together overpowered some and escaped."

"Your prisoner escaped?"

"With the aid of magic."

Shianan pitied the captain, forced to admit his failure in his attempt to explain the innocence of a condemned man, when it would do no good.

"We followed them," the captain continued quickly, "and caught them again, when the prisoner was engaged in fighting some men. We captured him and the last of these men and found the Shard in his possession."

"In whose possession?"

"The prisoner had been fighting the other men for it. He told us he'd let himself be believed guilty so the real thieves would think themselves unsuspected and move with the Shard."

There was a moment of silence as this completely unexpected piece of testimony echoed about the oval room. Murmurs reverberated but did not carry clearly. "Did you believe him?" asked the officiating voice at last.

"I did not at first, my honored lord, but the last swordsman admitted they'd taken the Shard when I asked. Said he'd been hired by a man in a tavern to carry it back and kill the commander."

There was a ripple of surprise. Shianan wondered if he dared allow himself to hope he'd escape, somehow. Was it possible...?

"To kill him? Why would they do that?"

"They'd tried once before, it seems. It's a merchant behind it, he says, one who lost money when the swindling came out. But these particular men were given five hundred pias and more to carry the Shard and kill the commander."

Sweet Holy One, bless Luca, thought Shianan. It was such a simple story, so quick to tell, and the captain had retold it vaguely enough that it seemed the explanation came from the swordsman rather than Luca and Shianan.

The officiating lord cleared his throat over the rumble of discussion. "We still have a witness who says he saw the accused prisoner in the act of stealing the Shard. What you have told us might be a clever lie. Or not so clever, perhaps; why did the accused prisoner allow himself to be arrested and questioned if he were not guilty? If he knew the culprit, why did he not accuse him and save himself?"

"There's a reason for that, my honored lord, or at least he offered one. I can't say to whether it's fit or not. But one of the party paid to kill him, and I don't like to say this, but one was a guardsman himself. Bailaha said he didn't know how many were corrupted, and so he couldn't reveal what he knew 'til he saw who was involved."

"You say a guard was there? Can you bring him for us?"

"He's dead now, my lord, in the fight, but he was there. We carried him back. Vagus was him."

There was a pause, and Shianan found it difficult to breathe. His hands were slick with sweat, but there was no chance of slipping the shackles.

"I think," the voice came slowly, "we should hear the testimony of our eyewitness."

The guards had not yet returned with Yergman Camb, and the nobles and officials passed the waiting in exchanging theories, whispering possibilities. Shianan's knees ached on the stone floor and his neck hurt with the unmoving weight of his head and the abuse of the last few days, but he did not move. There were still two unforgiving guards on either side of him.

And then there was a flurry of movement at a door. "My

honored lord!" burst someone breathlessly. "We found Yergman Camb, but—but he's dead, my lord. His throat's slit."

Shianan caught his breath amid the gasp that filled the room. No one intervened as he lifted his head to stare at the reporting guard. "Explain!"

"It is as I said, my honored lord. We went for him and found his rooms empty. He was behind the house, dead in the alley. Someone had cut his throat."

Shianan had a sudden, horrific image of Karlm the Vandogan slashing the throat of the slave who'd failed to kill him.

The court minister stared down at Shianan, caught facing him. They blinked at one another for a moment. "The accused prisoner has been under guard," the officiating minister said slowly.

"Oh, yes," confirmed one of the men beside Shianan. "We took charge of him directly from Captain Refend's party."

"He has not left my presence since we left Alham," Refend responded, "save for a few hours yesterday after the magic attack. But that was leagues away."

"We saw Camb this morning, anyway," muttered the minister. "Perhaps the accused prisoner has an accomplice? Where is this slave you mentioned, Captain Refend?"

"We have him, my honored lord," offered a court guard quickly. "We've kept him for questioning."

Shianan tensed as two more guards dragged Luca into the oval room, throwing him to his knees before the court. Shianan watched, helpless, but Luca did not look at him.

"This is the slave which helped the accused prisoner to escape?"

"Yes, my honored lord," answered Refend.

"To help a traitor is to commit treason," pronounced the minister. "But let's excavate the truth from him. Prepare—"

"No!" Shianan's voice surprised them all, even himself.

The minister stared at him in astonishment. "No?" he repeated incredulously after a moment. "You seem to think your command carries some—"

"You needn't question him. I'll tell you everything myself. He doesn't know much."

The minister picked up a quill pen. "You are anxious that we ask him no questions?"

"It's only—he is a good servant, my lord. He has saved my life twice or thrice now. I don't want him tortured."

The minister raised an eyebrow. "You recognize the word of a slave is without honor and cannot be admitted unless extracted under torture?"

Shianan bowed his head. "He was a freeman once, my lord. Let him swear by what was dear then."

"And how came an honest freeman to be a slave? An enslaved freeman has no more honor than a bred slave. Slaves lie to be contrary."

He had to save Luca. "Then ask me. I am no slave. If my word is not good enough, ask again."

The minister smirked. "You'd rather we torture you than your slave?"

Shianan clenched his teeth, too anxious to feel shamed. "Torture is poor payment for saving my life, my lord."

"My honored lord," came another voice. "A soldier has just offered his testimony in the matter."

The minister raised his eyebrows. "Offered?"

"He was not called for this trial, my lord, but he claims he has information relevant to it."

"Perhaps he can speak to the conspiracy the accused prisoner claims existed." The minister glanced at Luca, trembling on the stone floor. "We'll interrogate the slave after. Bring in the soldier."

Shianan did not dare to turn his head. He could not antagonize the court if he wanted to bargain for Luca. What information could anyone else have? Had someone else seen him with the Shard?

"Captain?"

"Captain Torg, my honored lord," came the answer. Shianan looked up despite himself. Torg's fingers were flexing at his side but he looked resolute. "I thought it my duty to inform the court of what I myself know."

"Proceed."

"The commander spoke to me a couple of weeks ago about someone trying to kill him. It was one of the merchants come to bid for contracts, he was pretty sure, but we didn't have any idea why."

"So the accused prisoner told you, well before the Shard was stolen, he believed his life was targeted?"

"He did. He suspected a particular individual, but he had no evidence, as he'd seen the man kill the slave who'd failed to murder the commander. He knew his word wasn't enough to arrest the man."

The minister looked surprised. "And he did not report this?"

"To whom, my lord? It was only his word against the merchant's, and he supposed the man must be in the employ of someone else."

Someone pushed Shianan's head down, and he stared at the stone tiles as he listened.

"Did you see any evidence of this yourself?"

"I had no reason to disbelieve him, my honored lord. I knew the commander many years and never found him in the habit of being untruthful."

"And yet he's accused of high treason. Could he not have mentioned this to avert suspicion later?"

"I suppose he might have, my honored lord. But I took the liberty of bringing another witness for your court. With your permission, I'll bring him."

Shianan's pulse quickened. He didn't know what Torg was doing, but he didn't want another of his very few friends caught in this tangle....

"Bring them," affirmed the minister.

The doors creaked open. "Let me go!" snapped a voice. "I'll walk myself, thank you!"

Shianan knew the voice. He looked up to see the Vandogan merchant Karlm between two frowning guards. Then a heavy hand slapped his head down again, sending a spasm through his neck.

"How very crowded it is. Move the slave. And who is this man?"

"This is Karlm, a merchant of Vandoga, here to negotiate for a supply contract with our army. He is also the man whom Commander Becknam suspected of plotting his death. He has a slave as well, who may have information if Karlm is unwilling to answer."

"Everyone answers the Court of the High Star," the minister said ominously. "But why have you brought them?"

"I respectfully suggest, my honored lord, you ask Karlm why he found it necessary to send a slave to murder Commander Becknam, and why he killed that slave when she failed. As neither Becknam nor I could guess why a Vandogan would come this far to kill a commander, it might also be prudent to question Karlm regarding his masters or employers."

"Let go of me! My lord, I am a foreigner and a guest here, and I have no quarrel with your local officers. This is plainly—"

"My honored lord!" This was the voice of the White Mage, and

Shianan twitched against the hand on his head. "I regret my late arrival, but you will understand the Circle's first duty was to see to the security of the Shard. We have examined it, and it is unharmed and uncontaminated."

"Thank you, Mage Hazelrig. It is good to know we have only to punish the intent and not the actual destruction of the Shard."

"I never meant to destroy it!" Shianan burst, but his voice did little to fill the room. The guards' hands tightened and one took a handful of hair, warning him not to speak again.

"My honored lord, I wonder if we could review the case before us. We have Shianan Becknam, Count of Bailaha, a noble peer of the court, here as an accused prisoner. This man has no previous record of treason, no suspicion of any crime at all to my knowledge. From what I have heard, he has been an exemplary officer, though I admit I have little to do with the army's affairs and it may be better to ask General Septime or another on that mark."

"With all respect, what is your point, Mage Hazelrig?"

"Please let me continue, my honored lord. This man is accused by another who claims to have seen him commit a crime. But while I was not present for the preliminary hearings, I am told the eyewitness described seeing the accused carry a bundle—and I am certain we cannot convict a man on a bundle, unless we have some method of knowing what was within it. We could question this eyewitness to learn why he believed it was the Shard within this bundle, but we cannot, because he has been murdered. I suppose it might have been a random crime within our fortress walls, but I'm sure we all believe it's more likely his murder has something to do with his testimony on this matter. Bailaha could not have been the one to silence this witness. As it has been presented that someone has made one or more attempts on his life—a concern he also voiced to me, and asked assistance—I think we must consider that this accusation was a means of having this court do the work of an assassin."

"Are you arguing he's innocent?" The minister drummed his fingers. "Mage Hazelrig, the man has been accused. He must prove his innocence. That is the law, no matter what we might choose."

"I understand that, my honored lord. But I say he has begun to prove it, as far as he can. You have before you the man Bailaha accuses of attempting his murder—why not question him?"

Shianan tried to make his exhausted brain work. If he could prove Karlm had tried to kill him, then they might believe Karlm had stolen the Shard and framed Shianan in another attempt. If the man were guilty of one crime, he might as well be guilty of two—and being innocent of the Shard's theft would not save him if he were convicted of seeking to murder a king's officer. In fact, a Vandogan murdering a king's officer might be warfare of a sort even without the theft of the Shard.... Shianan could not think it through. His aching head pounded.

"The prisoner will rise!"

Shianan blinked, and for a second he did not recognize that the order was for him. The guards lifted him to his unsteady feet.

He was so tired. Why couldn't it all end?

"Commander Shianan Becknam, Count of Bailaha, do you accuse this man of plotting your murder?"

Shianan lifted his head and looked at Karlm, who stared back with an alarmed expression. He could not have expected to find himself here. "I do, my honored lord," Shianan answered, startled at his weak voice. "I myself saw him kill a slave who had failed to kill me and refused to try again. If someone will look in his guest rooms, the stain is probably yet visible; there's a lot of blood from the throat."

"And," the minister continued, "do you accuse him of stealing the Shard?"

Shianan took a deep breath. "I have no evidence, my lord," he said slowly. "But I do not even know the reason this man wanted my death."

"Then he will be asked," replied the minister. "Take him away."

Karlm lunged in the hands of his guards, struggling, but they were more than ready for him and he was dragged away.

The minister looked down at Torg. "Thank you, captain. Is there anything else on which you would like to inform the court?"

"No, my honored lord, I don't think so. Except I would wager my eyeteeth that Shianan Becknam would die before letting harm come to this kingdom. I don't believe he's capable of plotting treason, my lord. Thank you." Torg bowed and retreated without looking at the prisoner.

Shianan gulped. He had not thought to endanger anyone else. He had not dreamed that Torg would risk his own standing by defending Shianan.

"And now the slave."

"My honored lord," Shianan blurted, still standing, "all he can tell you is he was also witness to Karlm killing a slave. Since you have Karlm himself now to question, please let him go unharmed."

The minister chuckled. "You are certainly anxious to spare him."

Shianan was too exhausted to argue. "My lord...."

"My honored lord." Prince Soren's voice cut across the chamber. "If I may offer a suggestion?"

"Please, Your Highness."

"Let us not waste this court's time on a slave. Our concern is with the master. The law demands once a man is accused here, he must prove his innocence. This prisoner was once accused by Yergman Camb, but that accuser is not here for the trial. It is uncertain whether or not he could be held now on that accusation. But I heard the prisoner confess the theft, and mine is the only voice to accuse him now in this court. Let him answer that."

Shianan's heart sank. How could he refute the prince? And how could he argue against his own confession?

"Well, Bailaha? Will you answer His Highness?"

Shianan could hardly remember what he had said. It seemed years ago rather than two nights. He looked down to gain time and tried to think. "My honored lord," he began slowly. "I did answer that I had stolen the Shard."

"You wanted to see how deep the corruption went?"

He was not so tired nor so pained that he would fall into that trap. "I did not suspect His Highness—of course not. But I could not be certain who might overhear."

The minister gave him a long, surveying look, curling his lip at the sight of the battered man swaying unsteadily before him. "You must be very dedicated to your efforts," he commented dryly. "Have you anything else to say in your defense?"

"Only a little, my honored lord: the Shard has been returned and in good condition. I am told the witness claimed he saw me leaving by the eastern door of the Wheel, but in fact I left by the western door that night. Perhaps someone else saw me. His accusation is wholly a lie. I would not argue with His Highness, but his accusation is in fact only the repetition of my own words to him. I have dedicated my life to the protection of this kingdom and its people. I stand before this court accused by my own voice alone and without any witness to my crime. Judge me as you will."

He sagged as he finished his speech, utterly drained. That was all he could manage. He would live or die as they heard him.

"Then we will pass the bag."

A small drawstring bag was carried solemnly about the room. Shianan distantly heard the soft clinks as pebbles were dropped into it. The bag was returned to the minister, who dumped it with a rattle on his desk. A long moment passed while the stones were counted smoothly from one group to another.

"The accused prisoner goes free," pronounced the minister. "Release him."

The guards obeyed literally, and Shianan swayed. Free! He was not to be executed gruesomely—he could go to his own bed and sleep. He took a step forward and stumbled.

His right hand landed on a shoulder and arms caught him beneath the elbows. "Steady, Master Shianan. I'll go with you."

Shianan only nodded, and he ignored the noise of the dismissing court and calls from those around them as he let Luca lead him. He never knew how Luca found his way from the court's chamber to the yard, but it was only a few minutes before he was locking the door while Shianan tripped toward his bed. He fell across it without caring that he nearly missed.

"Is there anything I can bring you, Master Shianan?"

Shianan could not remain awake long enough to answer.

CHAPTER 63

Ariana was thinking of buying several vegetable pies and going to Ranne's bookbinding shop when a messenger came for her father. At first she thought nothing of it—notes often came for the White Mage, and of course the Shard had just been recovered—but he crumpled it into his pocket just a shade too quickly. "What is it?" she asked, wobbling on one foot to tug on a shoe.

He looked at her and for the first time in her life she could see him weighing whether to give her the truth. "The Shard is back in Alham, and I must see to it."

"Can I help?"

"No, it won't need more than a few of us, and you've earned a small reprieve from your Circle duties. Stay and try to rest a bit."

Ariana scowled. "No one ever says to try to rest unless he's hiding something. What is it?"

Her father met her eyes and then he gently cupped her cheeks. "I'll tell you when it's all sorted," he said softly. "For now—I don't want anyone asking more questions about how you came home. I don't want anyone looking for more than what they're supposing right now. Does that make sense?"

She blinked at him. "You're trying to keep me out of sight."

"Only for now."

Icy fingers slid about her heart. "Do they suspect you? Or Tam? Do they know?"

"No, no, they don't suspect. And I don't want to give them any reason to wonder. Let me answer the questions, let them take Mage Parma's word for your story, and it will be done quickly."

She understood. "But—can I at least tell Shianan Becknam I'm back?"

He smiled at her. "He already knows. And I'm sure he'll come as soon as he can."

Ariana regarded him skeptically. "You're not telling me something."

He exhaled. "Ariana...."

She held up her hands. "Fine, don't tell me. But this secret had better not last another fifteen years."

He kissed her forehead. "Be patient with me. I have been very, very frightened these past weeks, and I don't want to risk losing you again."

She made herself smile. "It's all right now, Father. Tamaryl took care of me."

He smiled, blinked several times, and kissed her forehead again. "I'll be back as soon as I can."

When he had gone, Ariana hobbled to a chair and drew on her other shoe. She glanced at her black robes and then reached for her old civilian cloak. It had a hood and wouldn't advertise her identity so blatantly.

At the Wheel she avoided the cellar stairs, taking the long way around to the Silver Mage's office. Mage Parma wasn't there, but Ariana wasn't surprised. She would be assisting in looking over the recovered Shard. Ariana knocked at the gold door, and then at the yellow, and then the orange. Someone would be here, and someone would tell her what her father feared.

It wasn't until she found the Crimson Mage that she learned it was Shianan Becknam who was accused of stealing the Shard.

Ariana flew around a corner and saw her father. She flung herself at him. "Father! Where is he? What will they do to him?"

He caught her arms and held her. "Hush, it's all right. He's been released."

She seemed to deflate, as if too much tension had run from her at once. "They should have known it was a mistake. He couldn't ever steal the Shard—he was so protective when we first brought it. It's ridiculous to suggest it." She turned accusing eyes on him. "Why didn't you tell me? I would have testified he never could have done it."

"What could you say?" He held her eyes. "You weren't here when the Shard disappeared—weren't even alive, as far as anyone else knew. What would your word be worth to them?"

"But—but I would have done something." She felt sick with useless belated worry. The Court of the High Star—and she had done nothing.

"I testified," Ewan said gently. "I saw him the night the Shard was taken, so I was able to speak for him. And it's ended now."

She swallowed. "At least they realized it was a mistake. At least they let him go. I didn't think the Court of the High Star let anyone go."

Luca heard a distant rapping and hoped dimly it had nothing to do with their door. He was wrapped warmly on his low mattress, reveling in the doing of nothing at all. The last two days and then the threat of torture before the Court had drained him, leaving his joints like water. Still, he had little ground for complaint beside his master.

The rapping continued, and Luca realized it came from the outer door. He rolled off the mattress, pushing his blankets aside, and stumbled blinking toward the door. His master did not stir, too soundly asleep to hear the knocking or Luca's movement.

Luca rubbed his sleeve across his face, hoping he looked presentable enough, and opened the door. "Yes?"

"It took you long enough."

"I'm sorry for your wait. How may I serve?"

The man who looked down at him was in a dark livery. When he moved, a wrist cuff showed beneath his sleeve. "I have been sent to summon your master."

Luca thought of Shianan lying unmoving on the bed, exactly as he had fallen. "I will be glad to give him your message."

The other slave frowned. "Do you usually delay his messages?"

"My master is not available at this time. I will—"

"You will tell him directly."

It would have been easy enough to observe Shianan had returned to his rooms and not gone out again, so a lie would not suffice. "Listen," Luca tried, hoping to touch the other slave's empathy, "my master is sleeping, and I would not wake him. Surely you understand—"

"You afraid of a cuff or a cut?" asked the slave. He tapped a badge sewn to the sleeve of his livery. "I could give you as much myself for delaying my instructions. And then he would add more for making him disobedient to his prince."

"His prince?"

The slave rolled his eyes and tapped the badge again. "His Highness wants Bailaha. He is summoned directly. His Highness says there is a personal score to settle."

Luca's stomach clenched into an icy mass. "One moment," he said, hearing his voice distant and strange. "I'll wake him."

CHAPTER 64

Shianan felt the hand on his shoulder but could not make himself respond. The hand shook him, but the rocking motion seemed far, far from his body.... He groaned a protest.

"Master Shianan, please—I don't like this, but please wake. It's the prince, he's sent for you. Do you hear?"

Shianan felt as if he were in a muddled dream. "Luca?"

"The prince has sent for you, Master Shianan. You're to go immediately."

Shianan groaned again. "You can't mean it."

"The messenger is in the office."

"King's runny oats." Shianan wished his eyes would focus. "Tell him I'll be out as soon as I've changed." He pulled painfully upright, and the room moved about him. His abused body had stiffened while he slept. "What does he want, do we know?"

Luca looked unhappy. "He says there's a personal score to settle."

Shianan didn't have the energy to curse. He flicked his eyes toward the door, and Luca went to ask the servant to wait. When he returned, Shianan was staring blearily at his feet. His boots had been removed while he slept.

Luca opened a chest and selected a clean shirt, throwing it over the lid. "What would you like?"

"Not sure it'll matter," Shianan mumbled. "If he's settling our score, I could save the washing and stay in this."

Luca did not answer, but he drew out a tunic and leggings. Shianan started to peel his bloodstained clothing off, but the first movement was arrested by a sharp spasm in his back. He froze, wincing, and Luca came to his rescue, quickly unlacing and removing the muddy clothes and guiding the fresh clothing over his arms. "Thanks," muttered Shianan. "What day is it?"

"The same, Master Shianan."

"'Soats. You should have let me sleep three days, at least." He shook his head gingerly before Luca could apologize. "No, it wasn't your fault. Fetch my boots, wherever they went, and let's see how he means to settle our account."

407

The servant in prince's livery gave a small bow to Shianan. "I am to conduct your lordship to join my master His Highness. If you will follow me?"

Shianan nodded tiredly. It had been too much to hope the court had been enough.

Luca draped a cloak over Shianan's shoulders and took his own. Shianan thought distantly he should not accompany them—he didn't want Luca involved in whatever unpleasantness would come—but he couldn't summon the effort to order him to stay. Instead he shuffled after the prince's servant.

The slave did not lead them toward the palace but across the yard to the gates. Shianan glanced at the Naziar, rising dark behind them against the late afternoon sky. The slave kept his pace slow to match Shianan's, though Shianan was embarrassed by it. He did not hurry, however. He was not anxious to meet the prince.

The Court of the High Star had released Shianan despite the prince's testimony. Soren might think himself publicly embarrassed. And if Shianan were innocent, it meant he had lied to the prince; if he had not lied, then Soren knew Shianan was the thief.

They crossed the high bridge over the river's bend, the last still water before the final tumble into the ocean. Thin ice filmed where the current was slowest, showing winter's steady creep. Shianan pulled his cloak tighter and bent his head against the wind.

And then the slave paused, and Shianan stumbled to an abrupt halt. He wondered in miserable panic if he could manage a proper bow without falling.

"Bailaha," said the prince.

Shianan bowed, not as deeply as he should, and awkwardly drew himself upright again. "Your Highness."

"Steady," cautioned Soren as Shianan wobbled. "Follow a little further?" He turned away, two more servants falling in alongside him. Shianan followed obediently, feeling Luca's eyes on him.

They turned toward a building set into the upper hill, marked with ornate gates. Shianan blinked, believing at first he had misidentified their location. "Your Highness?"

"We'll talk inside."

They passed through the gilded doors of the Kalen baths. Luca stepped closer to Shianan as they entered a lobby with a splashing fountain. The attendant leapt up, welcomed the prince warmly, and led them deep within the building. "This room, Your Highness. Your slaves can wait in the yard or the corridor. Would you—"

"I'll stay," whispered Luca.

"I'm sorry?" The host glanced toward Shianan.

Shianan swallowed. "Er, I'll be keeping him with me."

Soren nodded. "Yes, we'll keep one each. But you may send those I requested."

"Of course, Your Highness. Please, go in. You'll find the water hot and the room ready."

Shianan stepped into the private room with unsteady dread. What kind of punishment would be meted out in the baths? Was it the prince-heir after his death, after all?

The room was roughly square, with a spacious long pool full of swirling, steaming water. The rest of the room was taken with two couches fitted with jewel-toned silken sheets and a table of salts, lotions, soaps, and oils.

"Go ahead." Soren nodded toward the pool. "I don't intend to stand on ceremony tonight." He gestured to two of his three servants, who closed the door as they left.

Shianan did not move. "Your Highness, I'm afraid I don't understand."

"Were you not told?" Soren sat on a couch and removed his boot. "There is a considerable debt between us."

Shianan, standing, nodded uncomfortably.

"Your confession made things awkward, but in the end, I was hitting a bound man, and one ultimately judged innocent." Soren sighed. "I do not know how to make true amends, but I thought that after several days as you've had, a visit to the baths and a healer might be appreciated, at least."

"Your Highness...."

"Remember, I said a prince should be the first to apologize. Higher standard, and all that." He smiled. "And I have another purpose, too, but that can wait. You look as if you might drop at any moment."

Shianan hesitated. Someone at these baths had meant to kill him, once, and he could not quite bring himself to believe the prince's offer was genuine. But Luca was behind him, able to warn of danger, and Prince Soren would not need such an elaborate plot to avenge himself, and Shianan was too exhausted to keep up a wary defense. "Thank you, Your Highness."

It was embarrassing how he needed Luca's help again to ease

the clothing over his head, but Soren turned his back. Shianan moved stiffly to the pool and refused to need Luca's arm. The stone edging was deliciously warm against his hand. He tried to lower himself into the hot water but dropped as his arm failed him. But he only splashed into the bath, sending water over himself, and a wave of heat rolled through him.

Soren was already reclining at his end of the pool. "Ethan, bring soap, please," he said, his head against the warm stone border. "I forgot to take one."

The prince's servant went to the table. "What would you like, master?"

"Did they set out a mint soap? I'd like that. And bring one for Bailaha as well. He'll want something gentle, though."

Luca moved to the table and selected a bowl. The servant Ethan glanced at him but said nothing. Each delivered a soap to his master.

One normally didn't wash in a common bath, but entered a communal soak only after scrubbing properly clean. The prince was setting precedent for Shianan, washing more easily in the pool. He was grateful.

Shianan's limbs moved more easily, suspended in the mild current of the comfortably hot bath. He began to spread the milky lather over himself, moving gingerly over the cuts and abrasions that stung in the water. His face was particularly tricky; there was no feature which was not sore or swollen, and even rinsing the soap away took care.

Soren finished washing long before Shianan, and he lay floating low in the water, his head on the edge. Shianan set aside the soap and tried to copy the prince's posture, his neck twinging and grinding. He shifted several times, trying to ease himself back, and then something soft slid beneath his head. He blinked upward and saw Luca, who had folded a thick towel into a pillow. Before Shianan could speak, Luca moved away again, a perfect silent and invisible servant.

"Bailaha...."

Shianan made the effort to speak. "Your Highness?"

The prince gave a small chuckle. "Bailaha," he repeated. He lifted his head and offered a tentative grin. "We are two men in a bathhouse. Would you mind very much if I suggested we suspend formality for this evening?"

It was his place to dictate the terms of their interaction. "If you will, Your Highness."

"Then I will call you Becknam, and you will call me Laguna." Soren watched as Ethan poured two drinks from a common pitcher and offered one to his master.

Generally a royal was called by his house's name only by the very privileged or after he had been deposed. "I—my lord...."

"It's all right, Becknam. I trust you won't tell anyone of our lapse, I'm sure Ethan will keep his silence, and it's obvious you place a high confidence in your own slave."

Shianan glanced at Luca, pressed against the wall as if awaiting Ande's next order. "I do trust him. But I do not wish to be disrespectful to my prince."

Soren made a dismissive gesture which splashed water across the surface. "I hardly see how accommodating my own request could be disrespectful. How do you feel?"

"Better, my lord," answered Shianan truthfully. He took the drink from Ethan and tried it, a fruity tea enhanced with herbs or spices. He could taste willow bark and other medicines layered within the flavors; he was being doctored.

"Good. But I suppose you'll tell me you've had worse, right?" Soren chuckled.

Shianan allowed himself to laugh as he leaned against his makeshift pillow again. "Actually, no, I don't think so."

Soren sobered. "I'm sorry. I was so angry when you said you had taken it, so—I had been sure you were innocent, you see. I felt very much betrayed when you confessed."

Shianan did not know how to answer.

"I turned that anger on you, which seemed most logical, I suppose. But even if I really believed it, I was wrong."

Shianan could not allow the prince to continue apologizing. "You would not expect a criminal to suddenly offer all his secrets, my lord."

"You had suddenly offered a confession." Soren shifted. "And I broke our unwritten law that no one strikes royal blood. All my talk that we shared a father, and then I hit you like an obstreperous slave."

No one strikes...? Royal blood? Shianan cleared his throat with a sharp derisive laugh and was suddenly worried Soren had heard.

He had. "You laugh? Is my embarrassment so amusing?"

"No, no, lord."

But Soren kept his eyes on him. Did he suspect? But Shianan

could not, would not admit the king struck him, and he had to say something to answer the prince. "No, I laugh only because—because Luca once told me I was a slave to the king." He grimaced, but it was all that had come to mind. "So it was fitting, I suppose."

"Who is Luca? He certainly has an odd idea of the military."

"Luca is the trusted servant."

"Your—your slave calls you a slave?"

Shianan shifted in the water. "He is not so wrong, if you think of it. I obey my master's orders without question."

Soren's eyes narrowed, and for a moment Shianan wondered what he thought. But then he turned in the pool, bobbing in the current. "Your trusted servant has great liberty of speech." He put his back to the wall and looked at the room behind Shianan, probably eying Luca.

"I suppose some might think so." Shianan glanced toward Luca, who stared back wide-eyed in alarm. Then he abruptly realized both Shianan and Soren were looking at him and his eyes dropped to the floor. Shianan regretted frightening him. "But I can hardly complain when he is right."

Soren splashed as he moved. "Don't worry, I understand. Some might criticize Ethan, but I wouldn't trade him for ivory. He's the only one I'd trust to hear me apologize to a mere commander who escaped the Court of the High Star by the skin of his teeth."

Ethan smiled and made a small bow in the direction of the pool, and then he delivered a bowl of dampened colored salt. Soren took a handful and began to scrub himself. Shianan flinched involuntarily away. He would not be scrubbing with salt for some time.

"Ethan, would you call for the aeliptos? I think we're ready for massage."

Shianan winced. "I thank you, my lord, but I think I'll—"

"No, Becknam, I know what I'm doing. If you cannot bear it, well, I'll apologize again, but I want you to try it. This is my reparation to you." He rose from the water and wrapped a towel around himself.

Shianan wished he had the strength to move with half as much grace. Soren squeezed out his hair and lay face down on one couch. Shianan took the other, shivering despite the steamy air. Sheets settled over him. Luca was certainly earning his feed this evening.

Shianan felt much better for the soak. The door opened, admitting a wave of cool air and two slaves. Shianan turned his head to watch them bow, first to the prince and then to the two guests together.

Soren gestured toward Shianan. "Danye," he said, his voice muffled by the couch, "would you see to my friend? He's in need of a careful touch."

"Certainly, my lord."

Shianan eyed the aelipto as Danye drew back the warm silken sheets and looked down at him. There was a moment of hesitation, and then the slave ventured, "My lord, is there a span anywhere where you are not bruised?"

"They might have missed a spot, but it wasn't for lack of trying."

"Then let's try to ease that." Danye poured something into his hands and rubbed them to warm it. The scent of rosemary and other herbs came to Shianan as, despite Soren's assurance, he braced himself. This could not but hurt, and yet he could not refuse the prince.

But Danye was careful, and the first few strokes only brushed his shoulders, soothing where he'd prepared for pain. Then the slave began working the ointment into Shianan's battered body, taking extra caution where the skin had split. There were twinges where his fingers probed swollen areas, but the liquid seemed to ease the soreness.

Shianan relaxed into the couch as the slave alternately numbed the injuries and kneaded between the bruises. Exhaustion crept over him again, but it was no longer a nauseating weariness, only a desire to sink further and further into the couch and rest.

A thought came to him, and he shifted. "I beg your pardon, my lord," Danye said quickly. "Did I hurt you?"

"Nm," mumbled Shianan, and he moved his head so he could speak. "Where's Luca?"

"Here, master."

"I'll need clothes." Now that he had bathed the blood and fear-sweat from his body, he wanted fresh clothing.

"I'll bring some," Luca answered slowly, "if you would have me go now."

Luca did not trust the Kalen baths and the prince. Shianan realized he himself did trust Soren. It was the wildest scheme possible to kill Shianan by luxury, Karlm was in prison, and it was hard to distrust anyone while the slave was rubbing away the pain and aches of three days' abuse. "Go," he managed sleepily.

He only vaguely sensed Luca's departure. In a moment more,

he was deeply asleep, utterly unaware of Danye's continued treatment of the welts and bruises.

Soren turned at the aelipto's prompting and let him work the muscle tension from the rest of him. He hoped Becknam was benefiting. The man had looked truly awful when dragged before the court and only marginally less terrible tonight.

"My lord, will you turn?" A voice came from the other couch. "My lord?"

Soren waved the slave away and sat upright. Danye had a hand on Shianan's shoulder, but Shianan was completely asleep. Danye glanced to the prince, a question on his face.

Soren shook his head. "Let him sleep."

Danye nodded and wiped his hands on a small towel. Ethan gave each of the slaves a generous handful of coins and closed the door behind them.

Soren rose, stretching, and looked at the man asleep opposite him. He crossed and stood over the couch, bending to look at Shianan. The commander's face was swollen and discolored, but the resemblance was there to be seen, if Soren sought it.

He bent close, hearing Shianan's faint snores. "Little brother," he whispered, "we've ill-used you." He stooped and kissed him lightly on the temple. "I'm sorry."

He turned back and began to dress.

As Luca jogged through the twilight, returning from Shianan's rooms, a figure in a side street snapped to catch another's attention. "That's the commander's slave, ain't it?"

"I think you're right. He'll know where the man is."

"Let's follow him, then. Whistle up the others."

CHAPTER 65

Luca returned and found the prince dressing. "Your master's asleep," he warned Luca. "But come a moment. I have a question for you."

Luca's stomach clenched. He glanced at Shianan—he seemed legitimately asleep, flattened comfortably on the couch—and then approached the prince, setting Shianan's clothing aside on a low stool. He was not sure how a slave acknowledged a prince, but Shianan had knelt before the king, and a slave could certainly not do less. He went down on one knee, ignoring that it landed in a puddle.

"I see someone trained you well," the prince commented dryly, his voice modulated to avoid disturbing Shianan. "At your ease. I asked your master here for two purposes. The first was, as I said, to make amends in some poor way. The second.... Well, I suspect you may be able to answer as well as he. He has equally protested that he did and did not steal the Shard. It is my opinion he did, given his explanation of the Black Mage's disappearance and her subsequent reappearance."

Luca could not breathe. He knew?!

"Did he take the Shard?"

Faced with so blunt a question, Luca stared helplessly at the floor and panicked.

"This foreign merchant in prison now—what place has he in this? I hope he is not an innocent scapegoat for the commander."

"No!" Luca blurted. "No, my lord. The Vandogan tried—he sent a slave—he killed her, I saw it—"

"Stop! Luca, is it? Luca, calm yourself and tell me plainly."

Luca crouched lower over his knee. "I'm sorry, my lord. The Vandogan did try to kill my master, and when the slave did not succeed, we saw him kill the slave."

"You're sure?"

The horrifying scene would never leave his memory. Luca nodded emphatically.

"I see." He paused. "Luca, there's no need to cower."

Luca could not help it. He was afraid of this place and of the murder and of the royalty before him.

Soren sighed. "One of the guards said you'd volunteered to be questioned by the court. Is that true? Were you ordered to testify to his innocence?"

"I committed myself, my lord. He didn't ask."

"Why? What slave would submit to torture of his own will?"

"A grateful one, my lord. He is a good man. He did not deserve execution." He could barely hear himself.

"I agree. But I am surprised at the depth of your gratitude." Soren chuckled. "Perhaps you hoped for minimal torture. A switch instead of a scourge, or maybe they would just twist a finger?"

Luca did not smile.

Soren drew on his shirt. "One other question, for you alone," he continued. "Why did you say your master was the king's slave?"

Luca winced. He had known the moment Shianan repeated his statement it would bring trouble.

"Obviously a commander must obey the orders of the king, as a slave must obey the orders of his master," the prince said, as if to fill the silence where Luca had not answered promptly. "Is that all you meant to say?"

Luca's mind reeled. He was before Ande again, knowing no matter what he said, what answer he gave, he could not escape punishment.

"Luca?"

Or, this was not about Luca's impudent speech, he realized. This was about his master. That was no easier to answer. "My lord, that is what I meant to say."

Soren shifted. "Luca, I am asking you—"

"My master has never discussed his meetings with me," Luca blurted desperately.

Soren was quiet a long moment. Then he shrugged into his doublet, nodding toward Shianan as he tied the laces. "Take care of your master. Good night."

Luca dropped his head until his forehead touched his knee. Soren gestured to Ethan and left, still wrapping his belt.

After the door had closed, Luca got to his feet, more than a little sore himself. He looked at Shianan, sleeping soundly. He needed the sleep and more. Luca didn't want to wake him.

Luca sat tentatively on the couch the prince had abandoned. It was soft but comfortably firm. After a moment of guilty debate he let himself slide until he lay upon the sheets.

But he could not sleep so soon after his exchange with the prince. Could Prince Soren arrest Shianan again, knowing about the Shard? Why did he ask about Shianan and the king?

He looked at Shianan, snoring softly, and wondered how late they dared stay. Shianan looked comfortable, but they would probably not be welcome overnight. Luca crossed to the couch and touched his arm. "Master Shianan?"

"King's oats, stop waking me." He blinked and lifted his head slightly. "Where is...."

"His Highness has already gone," Luca said. "Let's go home."

Shianan looked at him oddly and smiled. "Did you bring my clothes?"

Ariana was the last to learn anything—Tam's identity as a Ryuven, Tamaryl's role as Pairvyn ni'Ai, Shianan's arrest for so stupid a charge as stealing the very Shard he'd brought to Alham.

But Shianan had been released, one of a bare handful of freed prisoners in the High Star's history, and she had nearly wept with relief. They were safe, Shianan and her father. No one knew about Tam. They were out of danger.

Now they had only hours before the restoration of the shield. She, Tamaryl, and her father sat together in the White Mage's workroom.

Ariana pushed a paper across the table to Tam. "What do you think of this?"

"Yet another proposed trade agreement?" Tam's eyes flicked over the page as he read and reread. "Indeed, leaping directly into central marketplaces would be very efficient. But for what?"

"What do the Ryuven have to offer us?"

Tam sighed. "Exactly. The question of generations: who would trade with a Ryuven, and for what?"

"But few believe you raid out of hunger," Ewan Hazelrig put in. "They see the raids as destructive as well as thieving, and at times battles occur with no seizure of goods at all."

"That's a function of vain glory-chasing by our idiotic *sho*," grumbled Tam.

"Regardless, I think most nowadays believe the Ryuven take the warehouse stores simply to wreak damage rather than for their own use. And the Ryuven haven't done much to alter that impression."

"But one-sided demand will lead to nothing." Tam gestured in frustration. "There's a chance Oniwe'aru will listen now, but we must find something which humans want and the Ryuven can provide. Trade requires viable demand."

Ariana sighed. "I wish you could bottle your magic. That might be useful." She drew the paper back and began doodling in the margin. She wanted to speak to Shianan, to confirm he was truly safe after the Court of the High Star. She wanted the Alham court to forget his bastard status and their suspicion. She wanted to hear Oniwe'aru's assurances he would not send Tamaryl again to pillage their farms. She wanted Tam to be safe in their world. She wanted so many things, and so few of them would be granted....

She rubbed her eyes tiredly; she would think of nothing useful soon. "I can't solve a crisis of kings tonight."

Her father looked at her with concern. "Go on to bed; you're still recovering. Tam and I will let you know if we find anything."

She did not believe they would, and neither did they, but none of them would say so. "Good night."

CHAPTER 66

Shianan gave a small wave to the attendant as they left the baths and went into the frigid air. Moonlight glistened off wet stones, and they shivered in the wind.

"Rain?" Shianan winced as ice struck his bruised cheek. "Sleet. Splendid."

Luca ducked his head against the wet, stinging wind. "I'll build up the fire when we arrive."

Shianan drew up his hood and tucked his hands beneath his arms. "And while you're doing that, I think I'll sleep. Again." He shivered and shook his cloak so that it overlapped around him. "Or, perhaps, I'll eat something and then sleep. I've only just realized I haven't had a proper meal in days. Is there anything left from the merchants?"

Luca shook his head. "No. But I'll find something."

Shianan slipped on an icy cobblestone. "The kitchen won't be open at this hour." Around them the streets were nearly empty.

"I'll go to a bakery. There will be someone preparing dough for the morning baking. They'll sell a loaf."

"Thanks." Shianan slipped again, and he adjusted his pace. Luca nodded and turned away to a cross street.

Shianan watched him go. *Let's go home*, Luca had said. It was a comfortable phrase.

Shianan looked ahead and saw a sheen of ice on the bridge. He shivered—he hated the rain, and cold rain in particular. What fortune that this freezing sleet had not come two nights before, when he was chained on the parapet, he thought acidly. He did not want to relive that night.

He glanced down, picking his footing on the slick stones, and started across the bridge. Twenty feet or so beneath him, the water moved sluggishly, pushing thin sheets of ice across its surface. The steep walls of the river's channel, cut by centuries into the stone, glistened with freezing rain. Shianan looked down the river, bright in the moonlight, and wished he were already home. He wished he'd thought to ask Luca to put a warming stone in his bed when he'd gone for fresh clothing. After his night on the walk and two days beaten and hungry, Shianan craved warmth.

Some instinct warned him to turn just as the men behind him fanned across the bridge. Two held staves and one had a sword. Shianan gulped cold air and seized initiative. He could not allow them to attack in a concerted effort.

He tore the cloak from his shoulders and snapped it toward the nearest staff, slowing the weapon long enough to lunge within its reach as it spun against his back. The attacker retreated but not quickly enough, and he did not know how to defend himself from someone within the circle of his weapon. Shianan snapped the man's head upward sharply and took the staff from him.

He whirled, expecting to see the others closing on him, but they held their ground. Shianan had one heart-pounding instant of joy in seeing them respect the distance, and then he saw the archer.

It was only a small crossbow, a thing for hunting, but it would be enough. He had not seen it at first, but it was undeniable now, raised and targeted on him. The man beside the archer held no weapon. He was the leader. And he, Shianan realized, was the merchant Jarrick Roald.

"What do you want?" Shianan growled, keeping the staff ready. The crossbow could kill, but if the bolt missed he would have a few precious seconds before the archer could reload.

Roald looked unhappily determined. "I'm sorry, commander. I liked you, I think. But you're in the way of our alliance, and you have to go."

"What alliance?" Shianan stayed still. "I even offered you the contract. What else do you want?"

"You never signed it."

"I've been busy."

Roald didn't acknowledge the grim humor. "Even with the contract, the alliance won't profit as much as when their own men were in place. You ended that, and so they decided to replace you with someone more agreeable."

"They?" Shianan repeated. "This alliance of yours?" He had to find a way to discharge that crossbow without taking the bolt himself. "Roald, think. You can't kill me without drawing attention."

Roald shook his head. "They say you have to die tonight. Karlm is in prison for your attempted murder. If you die while he's under guard, it clears him from suspicion."

"This is madness. Roald, your house will profit with the

contract I offered. You don't need to do this."

"It isn't my choice."

He should have died immediately, Shianan realized. The delay was evidence the reluctant Roald could be dissuaded. But if the archer released, even Roald's regret could not help Shianan.

As if hearing Shianan's thoughts, the remaining man with the staff moved impatiently. "Are you going to talk him to death? Do it, if you will!"

Roald looked at him sharply but said nothing. His throat worked and after a moment he began, "Then—"

"Stop!" Luca's voice shrieked from the end of the bridge. "Stop! Jarrick, don't!" Luca plunged across the slick bridge, slipping. "Jarrick, don't do this!"

Roald spun around, jaw hanging. Luca ran toward him frantically, arms pumping and flailing as he slid on the ice. "Stop!"

"Get back!" snapped the archer, turning toward the approaching slave.

Roald whipped toward him, reaching for the crossbow. "No—!"

"Don't!" shouted Shianan.

"Jarrick, don't—!"

The mechanical snap was crisply loud in the night air as the crossbow released. Luca recoiled and slipped on the ice. His momentum and the slight crest of the bridge carried him easily the arm's reach to the edge, where he clawed wide-eyed at a pillar and then slipped from sight.

"No!" screamed Jarrick and Shianan together. Shianan leapt forward, intent on reaching the archer before he could reload. The archer reached for a bolt and jammed the endcap into the track with wide eyes, knowing the danger. Shianan closed the distance and the archer made a fair attempt to block the staff with the half-loaded crossbow, but Shianan reversed it and drove the other end hard into the man's face. He wheeled and evaded a sword slash, using the staff's superior reach to ram the swordsman's abdomen. He followed by closing and hitting hard, stunning the swordsman. The remaining attacker was not closing.

Shianan did not wait to finish his attackers or even to see if they meant to continue. He bolted for the end of the bridge, already calculating. There was an old, narrow street which dropped to the level of the river, known appropriately enough as Old River Street, and from there he might be able to find Luca and pull him from the

421

stone channel before he was carried into the sea. But he had to hurry—the water was icy, Shianan was not sure if the bolt had struck him or not, and Luca might have been further injured in the fall.

"Wait!" called a frantic voice behind him. "Your lordship, wait!"

Shianan had no time for Roald. He took a corner to a street which ran downhill.

"Bailaha!"

Shianan took the next corner too fast and slipped on the ice-glazed street. He landed hard, awakening every ache and bruise he'd collected. He sucked air through his teeth and scrabbled painfully to his feet. He could hear Roald's steps echoing through the empty streets. "Wait!"

Shianan started limping downhill again. The older roads curved and dipped, darkened by leaning buildings and stinking with garbage. A couple of dogs barked from the shelter of their alley. Shianan hurried as best he could, cold air ripping at his lungs. He was taking too long. How would Luca survive the water?

Then he was within sight of the river, and he rushed to the dirty paved edge where the poor threw their trash into the water. The current here pushed debris toward the bank as the river bent upon itself. He sank painfully to his knees and peered across the moonlit river, straining his eyes. Bundles of trash and clumps of garbage tormented him. Where was Luca? Had he clung to some other part of the channel? Was he swimming somewhere, looking for a place he could climb out of the river? The sleet-iced walls would not permit that....

There! He stared at a larger dark shape in the water, not far from the bank. That was a man, certainly. He leaned forward, but the shape was beyond the reach of his staff.

The clothing and cloak bulged with trapped air, keeping him mostly afloat as he drifted with the current. But the man's face was hidden in the water as he floated unmoving.

Shianan fought down a surge of panic and reached again, straining forward as far as he could. The tip of the staff touched the ballooned cloak. He twisted and teased and toyed until the staff caught in the cloak, and he began to coax the body toward him.

It couldn't be Luca, he breathed. Sweet Holy One, let it be some poor murdered soul who was dumped in the river. Luca wasn't floating this still, he was swimming somewhere around the bend, he was fine, he was not drifting face down in an icy river....

The body reached the edge, bumping gently into the stone and paving bank, and Shianan reached down for it, seizing a handful of cloth. But he could not haul it clear of the water. He tried again and again, grunting with the effort, but the body was too heavy with water and he was too weak. He sobbed a prayer and tried again and yet again.

Someone moved beside him and another hand groped for a hold on the body. "It's Luca?" breathed Roald. "That was Luca?"

They pulled together and the limp form came reluctantly from the water. Shianan fell backward with the momentum and then scrabbled forward, helping Roald roll the body so they could see the face.

It was Luca, icy to the touch. There was no sound of his breathing, and his open eyes showed wide, dilated pupils.

Shianan was unable to move. It wasn't possible. It wasn't possible that Luca could be dead....

Roald stared mutely, dull shock over his features. Shianan fell forward and jerked at the laces of tunic and shirt, baring Luca's pale chest. He put his ear to the chest—the skin was cold, far too cold—and heard nothing.

No. Please, sweet Holy One, no.

There was a tiny whisper of sound—Shianan was not sure if he'd imagined it or if he'd heard only the pulse of his own ear. He laid his hand across Luca's throat and felt nothing. Luca did not move. Shianan remained frozen for a long count of ten, when the whisper of sound came again.

Was that a heartbeat? It was far too slow to be a heartbeat.... There was no pulse. Luca could not be living. But....

Shianan had frozen to near-death on the outpost walk. He might have died in such exposure, but he had lived.

He rocked upright and grabbed Luca with shaking hands. "Help me." His teeth chattered. "Help me carry him."

Roald looked at him with a tear-streaked face. "Who near here will hold the body until—"

"No! Help me carry him. We have to take him to the baths."

Roald stared, uncomprehending, but he obeyed. Shianan took Luca's legs, knowing he could never manage the shoulders, and staggered toward the hill. The Kalen baths were not far from the river, and the gate attendant might still be present. If he could hear their calls for help....

It was an arduous journey uphill with Luca's sodden, frigid body, but they did not pause except for the times Shianan slipped and fell to his knees, clutching Luca's ankles one-handed as he pushed himself up again. They dared not waste a moment. If that faint, faint sound had been a heartbeat, if there were a chance, they could not lose time. He prayed he was not deluding himself.

He led Roald to the Kalen baths and fell against the ornate gates. "Help," he called weakly, realizing no one would ever hear his thin, cracking voice. "Help us...."

"Hello!" shouted Roald. "Open the gates! Hurry!"

It seemed a long time until the gates opened, but the attendant hurried to grasp the limp body slumping between them. "What is it? What's—" His eyes fell on the cuffs exposed as Luca's body dangled. "A slave?"

"Never mind that," snapped Shianan. "We need him inside."

The attendant looked at Shianan, apparently recalling that despite his battered appearance, he had been invited by the prince and was probably too important a personage to irritate with questions or protests that the baths were closed. He nodded and took Luca's legs at the knees, relieving Shianan's burden.

He took them to a room near the front where the bath water steamed and they eased Luca onto the couch. Shianan began ripping feverishly at Luca's sodden clothing. "Get these off him. And we need hot drink. Lots of hot drink."

"I'll send for it." The attendant ran from the room.

Shianan glanced after him and then turned toward Roald. "Bring Captain Torg. We need him here."

Roald shook his head as he yanked a boot from Luca's lifeless leg. "I'm not leaving."

"We need Captain Torg!"

"He's my brother! I won't leave!"

Shianan had no patience for this. "Be realistic—I barely made it here. I'll never make good time. You have to go."

"I can't—"

"Go!" Shianan commanded in the voice kept for stupid, hesitant soldiers. "If you want your brother to live, bring Torg now!"

Roald hesitated, opened his mouth as if to protest, and then with a quick glance at Luca he pushed himself back from the couch. "Where do I find him?"

"His quarters are in the east end of the south barracks. Use my name to bring him. Run." The last was unnecessary, as Roald was already hurrying from the room.

Shianan turned his attention back to Luca and his numbed fingers tugged at the shirt. When it clung wetly to the frigid skin, he found a seam and ripped it loose. Luca's body moved loosely with the motion, never showing sign of life. The skin was slick and faintly blue. Shianan sagged weakly against the edge of the couch, suddenly hopeless. "Oh, Luca," he breathed. "I never asked for this kind of loyalty."

But he could not wait—if Luca were dead, there would be time enough to mourn. If there were a chance he could be recalled to life, Shianan did not have the luxury of misery. He peeled away the wet leggings and then, concentrating all his depleted strength, he gathered the limp cold body and staggered toward the bath, dropping it into the hot water. He sorted out the limbs, pressing Luca gently beneath the surface with only his face above.

"Not like that," Torg's voice instructed from the door. "Pull his arms and legs out." He came into the room with Roald tripping on his heels. "That's what I did with you, but Inuk traders told me later it's better to let the arms and legs stay cool while the body warms first. They should know. Keep his torso in the water." He moved to the side of the bath and helped. "How long was he in?"

"Ten minutes, maybe fifteen," Shianan supplied unhappily. "I'm not sure."

"Did he go under immediately?"

"I don't know! I couldn't see. I was busy fighting off assassins." Shianan threw a dark look toward Roald, whose fault this was, but the merchant was looking at the floating slave.

Torg left off feeling for a pulse and held his hand close over the slave's mouth, trying to catch a breath. He looked grim. "King's oats, sir, this is—he's not there. I don't see how he can come back from this."

Heat burst through Shianan. "We'll give him the chance! What can it hurt to try? Would you have us just watch him die?"

Torg exhaled and shook his head. "No, sir, I wouldn't. You had more breath, but you were near as frozen. What do we have warm to give him?"

"I sent for hot drink long ago," Shianan answered in frustration, "but nothing's come yet."

Torg looked at Roald. "Then go and—"

"No," Roald said firmly. "I went for you, and I'm not leaving

425

again."

Torg blinked in surprise and looked at Shianan, who gave him a quiet look of command. "I'll see what's keeping the man, then." He closed the door behind him.

Jarrick Roald looked at Shianan. "You knew," he said. "You knew who he was, and you didn't tell me."

Shianan tore his eyes from Luca. "That was not my choice."

"What?"

"He didn't want to see you."

"You kept him—"

"He didn't want to see you! Can't you understand that? He hid from you!"

Roald stared, disbelieving. "You can't—that's not true. Why would he... Why would he do that?"

Shianan turned his eyes to Luca's pale, silent form. "That's easy enough to guess. You'd thrown him away once already. Why would he risk that again?"

No sound came from Roald. Shianan was tempted to look at him, to see if his words had cut through disbelief, but it was more important to stare at the still form drifting slightly in the motion of the bath.

Luca....

Torg entered, carrying a gilded pitcher. He paused and looked worriedly at Shianan. "King's oats, sir, are you well enough to be—"

"I am not the one in greatest danger here, captain."

"Right, sir." Torg started forward again. "I have some hot water, which is better than nothing. He'll bring some tea in a bit, when he finds it, and he's bringing more wood for the brazier as well. We'll need this room baking hot."

"Water? Tea?" Roald sounded strained. "I'll buy the brandy myself, if it's a question of—"

"Do you want to kill him?" demanded Torg. "Strong drink will suck the life right out of him. He needs something hot and slow, nothing that will flush his skin." He took up a gleaming cup and poured steaming water into it. "Let's get some of this into him, if he'll swallow. Can you get his head, sir?"

Shianan took Luca's lolling head and Torg eased water over his lips and into his mouth. There was no effort to swallow, no response of any variety. Shianan looked worriedly at Torg, who swore under his breath before raising his eyes to meet his commander's. "I'm sorry, sir.

426

I don't know what to do. You at least took the tea I gave you. He's not even shivering."

A black rift opened within Shianan. "But...."

"There's not much pulse in him, if it's even there. I'm not sure, myself." He looked unhappy. "Much as I hate to say it, sir, I don't see how he can make it. I know you're fond of him, but you might be needing another slave."

Shianan pushed the thought away before it could hurt him. "Go for Mage Hazelrig. Abdil Row. Bring him here."

"Sir! I—the White Mage?"

"He'll help. He owes me a favor."

Torg hesitated. "Sir—it's a slave...."

Shianan make a sharp, frustrated gesture. "It's more complicated than that, Torg. Please, hurry. Tell Mage Hazelrig to bring what he needs for mage healing and I'll explain when he arrives."

Torg looked both doubtful and curious, but he turned obediently toward the door. Shianan stumbled backward to the couch and sank upon it, still staring at Luca. Roald remained standing, stiff and unmoving.

Luca.... Shianan swallowed against the lump in his throat. He couldn't lose this friend, whom he owed so much, who shared his secrets, who had fallen while trying to save Shianan yet again....

The attendant came with an armload of charcoal. He spent a moment building up the fire, glancing first at the still figure bobbing in the bath's current and then at the two men waiting silently, and then he retreated.

After a moment Shianan tried offering the water again. Luca did not respond as the water ran into his mouth, did not even cough when Shianan sloshed too much and it seemed it should choke him. It was as if he were dead. Perhaps he was.

Panic seized Shianan and he took Luca about the torso, half-lifting him so that his head lolled limply as Shianan pressed his ear to his chest, cold under the warm film of water. Roald started to ask a question and Shianan snapped at him impatiently, straining to listen. There! A slow, quiet slosh, what he hoped desperately might be a heartbeat.

Sweet Holy One, please—I don't ask much. Just let him live. Please, let him live. I know my wants aren't important, but I'll do anything, just please, please, let him live....

The door opened and Ewan Hazelrig entered with Torg.

Shianan leapt to his feet and stumbled unsteadily. "My lord mage! Please, if you can help him—"

Hazelrig held up a hand to interrupt him. "The captain says it's a very near thing. Let me see him." He went directly to the bath, kneeling and setting down a bag. "Captain, I'll need you opposite me to support him. I want to be able to handle him while keeping what we can in the hot water."

Torg drew off his boots before stepping into the deep bath. He moved around Luca and faced Hazelrig, bringing his arms underneath so that Luca lay silently at the surface of the water. "Like this?"

"Yes, thank you." Hazelrig pulled a jar from his bag and removed the traveling seal. He scooped out a handful of a pale blue ointment and spread it thinly across Luca's chest. "First let's see if there's any heartbeat left."

He opened his hands above the anointed skin and closed his eyes, concentrating. They watched silently, and then Hazelrig opened his eyes and stared down at Luca. For an agonizing moment Shianan thought he was going to pronounce a final hopeless end, but then he pointed. "There. Do you see?"

Shianan did not. He leaned closer, along with Roald and Torg, and after a few eternal seconds a faint flicker of pink showed beneath Hazelrig's pointing finger, over Luca's heart. It disappeared as quickly as it had come, leaving Shianan doubting whether he'd seen it at all, but Hazelrig seemed satisfied. He turned and searched for something else in his bag, and Shianan saw another brief flicker of pink marking Luca's slow, weak heartbeat. "He's alive, then? And he can be recovered?"

"He's alive, technically," confirmed Hazelrig, drawing out an amulet and examining it. "But I cannot promise we can bring him back. You can see his heart is barely beating. It's as if he's fallen dormant, like a squirrel or tortoise in winter." He set aside the amulet and withdrew another. "But we will try. I cannot work miracles, you understand, and mage healing is best for magical injury. With this—if there is anything left in him that would fight the cold and revive, I can provide the energy for it to try again. But if not... Well, we will have tried."

"I'll pay it." Roald's voice shook. "I'll pay whatever price. I know mage healing is expensive, but if it will save him, I'll pay it."

"Quiet," said Hazelrig firmly. "Let me work."

He touched the second amulet and murmured under his

breath. Shianan saw nothing change, but Hazelrig withdrew his fingers suddenly, letting the amulet dangle by a thin chain, and extended it over Luca's chest. He held it low, nearly brushing the wet skin, and moved it slowly along the length of his torso.

Roald was quivering with impatient anxiety, gnawing at a knuckle. Shianan felt a sharp pain and realized he was biting fiercely at his thumbnail. *Come on, Luca. Feel it. Fight it. Fight it, Luca, come back to us....*

And then there was a quick flickering of pink, as the feeble heartbeat fluttered worriedly, and the torso twitched once, the first movement they'd seen since pulling him from the river's icy grip. Shianan's breath caught. "Luca?"

"Not yet," cautioned Hazelrig, still moving the amulet steadily. "But he's recognized the help here. Now he needs to use it."

There was another tiny twitch, a subtle movement of the skin, and then a third. Hazelrig's face was taut as he swept the amulet over the pale body. Luca's mouth moved, making Shianan lean forward, and then his blue lips tightened into a forceful cough.

"Yes, good!" Hazelrig's words were half cheer, half encouragement.

And then Luca convulsed in the bath, coughing violently as he folded in Torg's unprepared arms. Shianan and Roald reached for him as he hacked river water and spittle, gagging with the force of his effort, his chest rattling and wheezing between ragged, painful coughs. Shianan and Roald held tightly to his shoulders, wincing with the ferocity of it.

At last the fit slowed and the muscles relaxed, as Luca coughed more sporadically. Shianan released him, thinking to let him lie in the warming water once more. Roald leaned alongside Hazelrig and then recoiled as if burned, staring in horror at the striped skin across Luca's back.

Shianan felt a quick stab of sympathetic horror and then a swell of indignant anger. When Roald turned baleful eyes on him, he shot back an accusing glare of his own. "Oh, no. Blame yourself for what's happened, not me."

"Give him something to drink," said Torg. Roald held Luca upright while Shianan sloshed hot water into his mouth and Hazelrig worked the amulet over him. This time Luca's lips moved and his throat worked as he swallowed.

"Give him more," urged Roald in a tight, odd voice, and Shianan spared a glance to note the merchant had tears running down his face. He poured more water into Luca, who drank unconsciously.

"Look." Hazelrig withdrew the amulet for a moment and they watched a tiny ripple of motion move through Luca's body. A moment later it happened again, and then his teeth chattered weakly once or twice. "He's trying to shiver."

Torg nodded enthusiastically. "That's good! He's trying to warm himself."

The pale flicker of pink came more steadily, now. Shianan stared at it, his thoughts a prayer. *Sweet Holy One....*

Hazelrig reapplied the amulet and gradually the shivering became more pronounced. The mage nodded. "Thank you, captain, you may let him down now. Do we have something hot and sweet to drink? He'll need quick energy."

"I've ordered tea," answered Torg, easing Luca back into the water. "And a place like this will have plenty of honey for it, I'll bet."

"Then pour it into him," Hazelrig said. "And keep this amulet over him for another hour yet. Beyond that he'll have little need of it, I hope, but it won't hurt to have it near." He looked over his shoulder. "My lord commander, may I speak with you privately?"

Shianan nodded automatically, his eyes on Luca. "Of course, my lord mage." He pushed himself to his feet, recalling suddenly how weary and weak he was.

Hazelrig closed the door behind them and faced Shianan in the empty corridor. "How are you, your lordship?"

"I'm sorry?"

"You've had a rough few days."

Shianan shook his head. "I'm recovering. Bruises and cuts and soreness, no more."

Hazelrig threw his arms around him, stunning Shianan. "Thank you," he whispered, his voice suddenly gruff. "You saved my daughter. Thank you." He released Shianan and looked uncomfortable. "I'm sorry. But I do not know how to express my thanks." He withdrew the unused amulet and held it out by the chain. "This is for your own hurts. I'm so sorry I could not do more to alleviate them while you were under arrest." He held up a finger, activating the magic. "It may be uncomfortable for a time, but bear with it for the best result."

Shianan accepted the amulet, his skin tingling. "Thank you, my lord mage. But I've already said—there is no need to thank me."

Hazelrig made a dismissive gesture. "The healing amulet is not for my daughter, it is for your bravery and sacrifice. I would have sent more help with Luca, had I known he would follow you."

Shianan felt a pang. "He was not supposed to follow. I thought he'd be safe with you."

"That was clever, giving him a bill of sale to remove him from reach. He should have been safe, had he stayed." He looked at Shianan narrowly. "His well-being is important to you."

Shianan, caught, swallowed and nodded. "He is—more than a slave. A friend." He exhaled and stared at the amulet warming his hand. "If the king had fathered a second bastard, it might have been Luca."

Hazelrig nodded, as if he understood. "Let me know if I can help again. And thank you again for what you've done. Come when you can."

Shianan nodded. He did not know if he would visit the mage's house. If Ariana did not ask after him, he would not use his actions to indebt her to him. But he could think about that later. Right now, he wasn't sure he could think clearly on anything.

Hazelrig seemed to recognize this. He put a hand on Shianan's shoulder. "Get some rest and use that amulet. You'll be no good to him or yourself or anyone in this condition."

Shianan nodded dully and Hazelrig left. Shianan went back into the room, heat wrapping him as he entered. Even so, Torg was building up the fire in the brazier. Shianan nodded; the room should be as warm as they could make it.

But then he saw why the captain had busied himself with a task. Jarrick Roald sat on the wood and stone edging of the bath, sobbing softly. Shianan clenched his jaw. It was fine to weep now for his brother, years after his surrender. He should have fought for him then.

Shianan limped to the couch and sat heavily. He pressed the amulet the mage had given him to his bruised abdomen. Warmth spread through him as if someone had poured heated oil over his skin, only unlike oil this penetrated and ran through his insides. After a moment it became uncomfortably warm, but he recalled Hazelrig's words and kept it in place. He closed his eyes and folded his arms across the amulet, shielding it from view of the others. The rising heat seemed it would scorch him, as every bruise and cut and contusion and welt seemed to burn. He bit off a small sound of discomfort.

431

"Sir?"

He ignored Torg. He would like to ignore everything. He was tired, so tired, and hungry, and tired, and he only wanted to see that Luca would be well and then he wanted to sleep....

"Sir! Are you all right?"

He sat up abruptly, wondering how the couch had come so near his face. "I'm fine. Where's that tea?"

CHAPTER 67

Today, Ariana wanted to see Shianan. She slid out of bed and began to dress. She would go to him today. He would be free for a time, surely—no one released from the Court of the High Star would resume his duties at next dawn—and maybe he would be glad to see her, as well.

No fresh wash water by the door, so Tam was not yet awake. She would have to rouse him as she had done for years. The thought was uncomfortable, now that she knew his true form and true nature. It seemed wrong to wake the Pairvyn ni'Ai.

What had become of the other servant? The night she'd arrived, when the house was bursting with excited mages and grateful friends and hopeful questioners, she'd seen a second servant, serving drinks and tiny pieces of Mother Harriet's pies. She'd thought it was the black-haired slave the Gehrn priest had brought. Or perhaps he wasn't the same at all, and only someone borrowed to help in the rush. She hadn't seen him since that night.

She left her room and went out to fetch her own water, not ready to face Tam. There was something there which was not yet defined, and it frightened her in a vague sort of way.

Her father was already in the kitchen, nibbling an oat cake rolled to contain the sweet berry syrup he'd added. "Good morning, darling. I'd guessed you might sleep late."

"I thought I'd pay a visit to the commander, to congratulate him on his release."

Her father shook his head. "Not this morning, I'm afraid. I was called out in the middle of the night at his lordship's request, to attend a half-dead man. He'll have his hands full this morning, and he's not well himself."

Ariana caught at the phrase. "What do you mean, not well himself?"

He sighed. "You might have guessed the guards would not be pleased with the man they thought stole the Shard. There was a raid, and—Pairvyn ni'Ai was there...."

Ariana's stomach made an unsteady little jump. "Oh. Oh, I see." Sick horror, belated but real, clawed through her. They must have been furious. They must have half-killed him. It was amazing anew they had released him at all. "Does he—I can help him...."

He smiled gently. "I've already given him a healing amulet, my girl, and there's not much more you could do. And he'll have his hands full, as I said. You should wait."

"Wait for what?" She made a frustrated gesture. "I should try to help him."

"Why?" Her father's question was odd, but his expression was odder, strangely curious for her answer.

"Because he's my friend."

"Your friend," her father repeated. He took another bite of oat cake.

"Why are you questioning this?"

"I'm only curious about my daughter's friends."

"Is this because he's the bastard? Because I'm more than half-sick of that! He's a fine man and he's doing what he can under the circumstances, and I like him. I'm in no danger associating with him, especially since he's been released from the Court of the High Star. Won't that do more to help his reputation than any number of battles?"

"It might, at that," Hazelrig mused. "Don't be angry, darling, I was only asking. I like him, too, more than you guess." He took another bite to fill his mouth.

"Then I'm going to see Shianan now."

"Shianan?"

She turned in indignant embarrassment. "He asked me to call him so!"

Her father nodded, apparently serious, but she was not quite convinced he wasn't inwardly laughing. "I'm sorry, I had not heard that. Go on, then."

But when Ariana knocked repeatedly at the commander's office door, there was no answer.

CHAPTER 68

Shianan woke, feeling twinges in his back, and then he thought of Luca and rolled over on the couch. Roald, seated against the far wall, glanced at him. "You're awake?"

Shianan sat up and looked toward the bath. "How is he?"

"Hasn't woken yet, but he's been shivering off and on. You've been asleep only a short while."

Shianan was not reassured by this. "Do we have any tea left?"

"Finished. I gave him the last of it a few minutes ago. Your captain left, something about morning duties."

The room was stifling and hot, and drops of sweat rolled down Shianan's face. The amulet Mage Hazelrig had given him was clenched in his hand, leaving marks where he'd squeezed it as he slept. He turned and looked at Luca, still in the steaming water, his head reclining on a rolled towel at the edge and his heels resting on the stone edge of one side. Thus anchored, he floated and drifted in the bath. His skin looked a normal color.

Roald cleared his throat. "Your lordship, I—I wonder.... Luca is your slave, isn't he?"

Shianan nodded silently.

"I wonder—well, if he's your slave, and you understand the situation—I want him freed."

Shianan turned back to him. "That's impossible."

"My lord! After hearing all I've told you—"

"You misunderstand. Since you failed to kill me, Luca cannot go free. It has nothing to do with my preference. Under Chrenada law, only by a specific provision in the master's death-will may a slave be freed." And any such will would have been invalidated for treason, which was why he'd falsified a sale to Mage Hazelrig instead of freeing Luca as he would have preferred.

"But...."

"It is a question of law, Roald. Especially after Furmelle.... It is prison to me if I free him."

"Then sell him to me."

"You want to purchase your brother as a slave?"

"I want to redeem him!" Roald's words came quickly, eagerly.

435

"There is no such law in our country. If I purchased him fairly, I could take him home and free him there."

Shianan looked back at Luca, unmoving but for the mild drift of the current. "And what is the price of your brother?"

That cut Roald. He looked away, his jaw clenching visibly. "I have told you, what we did was a mistake. No one regrets it more than I do."

"Really? I think Luca might."

"Because of men like you?"

"Me?" Shianan whirled on Roald. "I told you those stripes were not from me. That was a parting gift from his master before me, a man who starved and beat and choked him. And only the Holy One knows what came before that. I promised Luca, by his request, that no price could ever buy him of me, and you accuse me of what?" He clenched his fists, sweating in the sweltering room. "Don't accuse me of cruelty, Roald, not to my dearest friend. I might be many things, but I won't let Luca go for mere profit."

"As you think I did?" Roald met Shianan's eyes. "I did not know it was coming, and I don't think I believed it when I saw it. I had only just arrived home when the trader passed, dragging him—I could not even react. I was stunned. And I rushed to our father, and he explained.... I should have run after him that moment, redeemed him that night, but with what? If we'd had the money, we would not have found ourselves in such a quandary in the first place!"

"And you think to rectify that mistake now."

"If you will let me." He studied Shianan. "How long have you had him? Since Furmelle?"

Shianan shook his head. "Not nearly that long. Only weeks." He half-smiled at the other's surprise. "There were—circumstances, which demanded we know each other more quickly. Luca is a good and honorable man."

"I'm glad to hear that." He sighed. "It cannot be coincidence that brought me to you, that allowed me to find Luca with a master who wanted his welfare. Most men would have given him for dead when they pulled him breathless from the river. But you.... If you do regard him as a friend, my lord, you will give him this chance at being a freeman once more."

Shianan looked away. "Don't try to manipulate me."

"It's only—he can't remain a slave...."

"Enough," Shianan snapped. "We'll talk later." He rose stiffly from the couch. "I'm going for more tea and whatever else I can argue out of that attendant."

The mage's amulet was working. His thoughts roiled as he walked down the corridor. If Luca were awake, would he be glad of a chance to return home and be free once more?

That was ridiculous, he realized. Who would choose to remain a slave?

He found a new attendant for the morning, and curtly he explained the situation and ordered tea and whatever food could be brought. "Even rolls from the bakery. Whatever you can find."

When he opened the door, he found Roald standing over the bath, staring anxiously at Luca. "What is it?"

"He was—I thought he was waking." Roald never took his eyes from his brother.

Luca stirred and opened his eyes. He blinked toward the ceiling and at the bath in blank confusion, and then he seemed to notice them. "Jarrick?" he rasped.

"Luca!" Jarrick reached for him, heedless of the water, and pulled him close.

Luca's jaw dangled in shock as he was lifted from the water and he recoiled, pushing his brother away. "Jarrick.... You...."

Shianan was frozen, watching the brothers' reunion. It was painful seeing Luca naked, thin, and shivering before Jarrick's enthusiastic fraternal affection. Luca stumbled unsteadily and nearly went down, landing against the wall backing the bath. "Jarrick," he whispered.

"Luca!" Shianan moved nearer. "Are you all right? How are you?"

Luca's eyes turned uncertainly to him. "I—I'm...." His teeth began to chatter and he hugged himself, cold out of the steaming water. He seemed to realize he was not dressed. "What happened?"

"Luca—" began Roald.

"Sit down," ordered Shianan peremptorily, anxious that Luca not be chilled and unwilling to see Jarrick Roald embrace him again. "We'll get you something to wear shortly. You'd gone into the river and—you nearly died."

"I thought I had," murmured Luca, sinking back into the water. He curled his knees to his chest, hugging them close as he looked from Shianan to Jarrick. Water lapped at his chin.

"We thought you were dead," Jarrick Roald offered brokenly.

"And I thought—I thought you were dead. For years. I couldn't believe it when I heard your voice, when I saw you and then you fell—I couldn't believe I'd seen you only just before you died again—"

Luca's wide eyes suddenly narrowed. "You were going to kill him! Why?"

"Because we must have this market!" Roald's voice wavered between defensive and pleading. "We joined a league of merchants to help our house recover. We've done well thus far, but this is a critical point. The alliance decided to move more—aggressively in this case...."

"Aggressively?" Shianan snorted.

"You could not be allowed to stand in the way," Roald protested. "You uncovered their most profitable scheme and utterly destroyed it. If you hadn't cost them a fortune—in lost profits, and in payoffs and bribes to keep those who couldn't be sacrificed out of prison, and in preparation for the next arrangement.... If you hadn't robbed them of so much, they wouldn't have cared about you. But you exposed their richest scheme and they couldn't let you do it again—"

"It was a sloppy scheme," Luca criticized to his knees. "It should have fallen apart long ago."

"Luca! You saw it?"

Luca looked up at his brother. "Did you see their shoddy books? No one could have believed those accounts. Does that mean I have to die, too?"

"We'll never tell," Roald said hastily. "They don't know you're alive—they don't know you saw the accounts. They don't know you exposed them."

Shianan was staring at Luca, flushed with the bath's heat and conflicted emotion. But Luca met Jarrick's gaze directly, without dropping his eyes, and he had not yet used the timid tone he usually adopted before others. He might have been reluctant to meet his brother again, but it had returned him to a previous time in his life, a time when he was not afraid.

"So you won't kill me for them, but you will kill another?" Luca demanded.

Yes, Luca was his own man now that he faced his brother.

"Luca, you don't understand—I was only—we had to! I can't let us lose everything we've rebuilt. If I hadn't done it, someone else—Karlm was originally—"

"So you are willing to sacrifice one person to save your house,"

Shianan observed acidly. "Still."

Jarrick's face went red. "No! You don't understand anything!"

"I understand enough." Shianan wiped his mouth as if he'd eaten something foul.

Luca was staring at Roald. "Jarrick, you can't kill him. I won't let you. I'll go to the king myself and tell him about your alliance and the murders and—and anything else I can think of! You can't think this is justified by—"

"I wanted to save our house! I didn't want to see us on the brink again!"

"I'd rather see you all sweating for Sandis than killing!"

"I can't lose anyone else!" Jarrick stopped and took a steadying breath. "You don't understand, Luca. Father—he's changed. Since you—since you. He isn't the man he was. And I don't want to—I don't want to ever be in that position again, do you understand? I don't want to ever be pushed to that point!"

Luca glared over his wet knees, his arms wrapped about his legs but his voice steady. "If you would kill Shianan, you've already been pushed to that point."

"Enough." Shianan looked between them. "I think we can agree, no one here can kill me now. I'm aware of him, and he can't risk killing me and losing you, Luca. Yes, Roald—Luca is my legal property, and he won't be turned over to you if I die. You'll have to find another way to salvage your house than to kill me."

Roald looked as if he wanted to argue, but lacked the words or strength.

"Luca, put something on. You need warm clothes. And—" A knock at the door interrupted him. "Come!"

Luca pushed his arms below the water's surface, hiding the cuffs. A slave entered with a tray of hot drinks, fresh bread, and honey. "My lords, I was told to offer this.... We don't generally keep meals for guests, and I am to apologize—"

"Leave it, it's fine," Shianan said impatiently. "You may go." The slave blinked, set the tray on a table, and retreated. Shianan poured a generous amount of honey into one of the cups and extended it to Luca. "Drink. You need something in you."

Roald sneered. "Do you mean to prove you're a kind man, concerned for his slave?"

Shianan shot him a disgusted glare. "No, I'm just a viciously efficient utilitarian looking out for the functionality of his own property." He tore into a piece of bread, feeling the hunger of three days. "Luca, get your clothes. Let's go." He wanted away from Roald, and he didn't think he could safely or effectively evict him.

Luca drank silently and then rose from the tub, wrapping one of the fluffy towels around himself and shivering.

Roald straightened. "Becknam—my lord—what I said...."

"If you have any questions regarding your contract," Shianan said, "you may call at my office at a later time. Luca?"

Luca was holding a shredded shirt at arm's length. "Master Shianan...."

"Oh. We needed to get you in the hot water.... Just put on your tunic and cloak."

"But, this one was yours."

Shianan blinked and then sighed, feeling his face move awkwardly into a smile. "Is that so? I suppose it will need some mending. Come on, let's go."

Roald might have wanted to say something else, but he couldn't seem to find the words as he looked at Shianan. Perhaps he couldn't say it in Luca's hearing. Luca glanced over his shoulder at his brother and followed his master out the door.

CHAPTER 69

Shianan's head was resting on his arm, sliding dangerously close to the desk, when a knock at the door recalled him to wakefulness. He straightened. "Come!"

It was Mage Ewan Hazelrig who entered. "Good afternoon."

"My lord mage! Please come in."

Hazelrig smiled. "You have something which belongs to me, I think."

"What? Oh." Shianan hesitated, glancing toward the door behind which Luca slept, wrapped in blankets and warmed by a overfilled brazier. "I see."

Hazelrig raised an eyebrow. "Yes?"

"To tell the truth, I had forgotten. I have—not had a chance to think on much." He sighed. "And now I find there are too many claims on Luca."

"Oh?"

Shianan pushed a hand through his hair. "Luca was born a freeman. His brother, still a freeman, would like to purchase him. But as his family sold him into slavery so they could prosper, I am reluctant. In the meantime, I had written out a bill of sale to you."

"Which was never actually paid, and I would not hold you to half an exchange. I presume you do not really wish to sell him to me?"

"My lord mage, I do not."

"I didn't think so. I have here said bill of sale, for your disposal." He set it on the desk. "How is he?"

"Recovering. I thank you again for your help. Without that...." Shianan's voice nearly betrayed him. "Well, thank you." He swallowed against the lump in his throat. "If I owe for the mage healing...."

Hazelrig made a dismissive gesture. "Nothing. I owe you as much or more. Anyway, Ariana was working with me long before she was Black Mage, and together we produced more healing amulets than expected. A few may go missing without trouble." He hesitated. "While it isn't my concern, as my brief ownership has been rescinded, what will you do about his brother?"

Shianan gnawed at his raw thumb. "I don't know. His brother let him be sold in the first place, but Luca seemed... improved, when he

441

spoke with him. But his brother would take him to the Wakari Coast, and—and Luca is my friend. I haven't many friends. Can I let one go that far?"

"I'm afraid I cannot answer that." Hazelrig sighed. "How are you?"

"The amulet you supplied is worth gold, or maybe the Shard itself."

"You'll need to sleep, of course. That's the price of mage healing, along with slower final natural healing."

"My lord mage, I have craved sleep more than I can say even before your help."

"Then consider yourself advised to submit." Hazelrig stood. "Luca left unexpectedly, and there are some items to be collected. But there's no hurry. Send him only when he is recovered."

When the mage had gone, Shianan locked the door. He would open it to no one, he resolved, neither general nor the king himself, until he had slept his fill.

He did not hear when the Black Mage came yet again to his door and knocked a long while before giving up.

"Hello." Tam regarded Luca, shame-faced on the doorstep. "Our master is in the sitting room."

"Not quite," Hazelrig corrected from his chair. "Luca's bill of sale was revoked, so I'm not his master. Come in, Luca. You've come for the clothes and things?"

Luca nodded. "And—I'm sorry, my lord. I was a poor servant to you."

"You were useful enough when that crowd was here," Hazelrig said. "You had a prior loyalty, that is all. And considering the outcome, I see no reason to argue with it. Tam, could you see to the amulets in the workroom? I worry they're not progressing as they should."

Tam's face clouded at being excused. "I will."

Hazelrig followed Luca toward the room he'd shared with Tam for a single night, beside the kitchen. "I think I'll see if there's any pie remaining."

"My lord, if you'd like me to bring—"

"No, no, I can fetch it myself. Get your things." Hazelrig paused. "The commander mentioned your brother had come."

Luca gave him a quick, worried glance, and Hazelrig regretted his words. But Luca paused in the doorway. "Yes."

"So you'll be returning with him?" It could not be otherwise. A man who would sacrifice himself to return a daughter would not refuse to redeem a slave to his family.

Luca remained still. "I—I don't know."

Hazelrig blinked. "Are you unsure of Becknam? Or don't you want to go?"

Luca looked away. "I don't know...."

Hazelrig hadn't realized Luca might be as torn as Becknam. He glanced toward the kitchen. "Well, I'll—"

"I don't know," Luca repeated, staring at the wall. His hands clenched into fists at his side.

Hazelrig hesitated. "Why not?" he prompted gently. "Why wouldn't you go?"

"Jarrick—they let me...." Luca gulped and blurted, "If Master Shianan had been my brother, I would never have been taken!"

Hazelrig looked at Luca in quiet shock.

"I'm sorry." Luca looked down, ashamed. "I'm sorry, my lord. It's not my place to—"

"Whose place would it be, to think your thoughts? Who else should know your brother and your master as you do?" Hazelrig pitied the young man before him. "I'm sorry. I didn't mean to pry."

Luca shook his head tightly. "I shouldn't have said anything, my lord."

Hazelrig turned away. There was little he could do except be glad it was not important to save face before a slave—a fact which did nothing to cheer him. "Take your things," he said awkwardly, and he went to the kitchen.

Brothers.... Both Becknam and Luca had spoken of that. No wonder Luca had gone to his master's aid instead of remaining with Hazelrig. It was almost too bad Luca had a brother to come for him....

Nonsense. Hazelrig despised the slavery which chained men and trade. If Luca could be freed, that was of course best. But it was nearly a shame that of all the desperate enslaved in Alham, Luca would be the one to be rescued.

CHAPTER 70

Shianan walked stiffly into the training ground and dropped one of the two wooden training swords he carried, surveying the soldiers waiting. They were unnaturally quiet, and as he looked over them their eyes slid, avoiding his gaze.

So be it, then.

"Good afternoon," he announced. "I'm glad to see you all again. There was some doubt that I would be here today."

No response. They were leery of him. And rightly so.

"Does anyone recall being a part of an unscheduled training melee some days ago? In the yard? I believe there was some practice of subduing a prisoner. Was anyone there?"

No one answered. As he watched, they shuffled and shifted.

He planted the tip of the waster into the ground. "Well, then, we'll have to rely upon my memory alone. Unfortunately I was somewhat occupied at the time, but I do recall seeing Tref Plowman. Where is he? Tref Plowman, come forward."

There was a ripple of surprise, anxiety and even suppressed amusement. Then a man was pushed to the front, his face unhappy.

"Thank you." Shianan gave him a pleasant smile. "Now, I don't know if anyone noticed, but this man gave a splendid example of using his bodyweight to unbalance an opponent from the side. Did anyone see?"

Plowman looked down. "Um, commander, I'm—"

"One moment, soldier, I'm speaking." Shianan looked past the shame-faced soldier and continued speaking. "As I said, it was a splendid example. He drove directly into the subject at the best possible angle and took him to the ground. He even delivered a solid punch to the temple. Unfortunately, this brilliant example was directed toward an officer. This could be cause for the stocks and a sound strapping."

Plowman paled and glanced toward the group, probably thinking of the dozen or more others who had been with him in the attack.

Shianan smiled generously. "But it was such a good example, I hesitate to punish it. So instead, Plowman will have an individual

445

training session with me." He spun the wooden sword in his hand.

There was a general ripple of relief and then hungry anticipation. Someone snickered, and someone else hooted in laughter. Plowman did not look reassured.

Shianan planted the sword's tip again. "However, this will be a private session. The rest of you will be on a conditioning run about the fortress." The growing merriment vanished. "You'll circle the Naziar palace, then the fortress compound, and then the greater open market below the gates." The soldiers' eyes widened and there was a soft murmur of incredulity. "And I have set watchers along the route to ensure everyone makes it to each checkpoint. Anyone failing to complete the entire route tonight will repeat it tomorrow." He smiled cheerily at them. "Any questions?"

No one dared.

Shianan nodded. "On your way, then. Captain Torg will see you make it to the market fountain, to start. Move!"

They blinked at him with astonished, unhappy expressions and then the group began to shuffle toward the gates. "At a run!" snapped Shianan. "Move out!"

Satisfied they were on their way, he turned toward Tref Plowman, who hung back. "Sir," he began miserably, "I—"

"Pick up your sword, soldier."

The sword was not Plowman's best weapon, as Shianan well knew, and even with his bruises, aches, and cuts, he was more than able to best Plowman. At the end of an hour, Plowman took the twentieth "cut" to his right arm, wincing with the impact to an area surely already discolored with bruising. Shianan, panting, limped backward. "Straighten up and watch your eight, Plowman. Come again." He was hurting, too. Hazelrig's amulet was never intended to carry him through an hour of sparring.

Plowman limped forward—Shianan had not limited his attention to arms—and raised the waster. Shianan let him attack, sloppy now with weariness, and moved easily inside the wooden blade, rapping down smartly across the collarbone and shoulder. He'd pulled his blow for that one—no point to crippling the man—but by Plowman's face, there would be a matching bruise there as well. The soldier yelped. "I'm sorry, sir.."

Shianan regarded him. "You haven't quit on me yet, and you haven't groveled for mercy."

"I can't quit, or you'd beat me to pulpy jelly. And groveling—if

I thought it would help, sir, I would." He looked miserably ashamed. "I'm sorry, sir, I truly am. We had no right to do what we did."

Shianan shook his head. "I have no quarrel with your anger," he answered. "Only with the expression of it. What if the general hadn't stopped it? What if you'd killed the only man who knew where to find the Shard?" He raised his sword. "Come again, soldier. You could be running with your friends."

Plowman obeyed, this time managing to keep the exchange of swords playing for a moment before taking a solid hit to his thigh. "A soldier without a leg is a soldier without his life," Shianan said archly as the soldier staggered. "But I think you know that well enough. Put these away and be sure you go over what we've done. I want your mistakes corrected."

"Yes, sir. Thank you, sir."

A man waited to one side, leaning on a staff, and Shianan beckoned him as he limped toward his quarters. He wondered if the amulet would have any use left. "Trader?"

"Matteo, my lord. I had your message."

Shianan nodded stiffly. "I'll want you tonight, but I have very specific instructions."

Ewan Hazelrig came into the kitchen, where Tam was stacking dishes. He leaned against the door frame until Tam looked at him. "Yes?"

"You know you needn't do all that."

"Habit, I suppose." Tam thumbed a crooked dish into alignment. "And you haven't any other servant at the moment. And, it's something to occupy me." He stared at the plates.

"You could be in your own world. There must be plenty to occupy you there."

"Yes. Plenty." He paused. "Too much."

"I see. The return was not all that you hoped?"

"Oh, it was. But—there was more, too. And I... I'm not sure how I will address some of it." He gave the mage a crooked smile. "Woman problems," he confided, looking for all the world like a precocious twelve-year-old.

Hazelrig laughed at the image. "I'm sorry to hear that." He sobered. "You know it's tomorrow."

"I know." Tam stared at the wooden surface of the table. "I

wish we'd found a way to render it unnecessary."

Hazelrig sighed. "You and I spent years on that. We did not find anything to make a peace."

"But that was when I was trapped here. If we had an idea now, something I could present myself to Oniwe'aru and convince him...."

"That would be ideal," agreed Hazelrig. "But what would you do about her?"

Tam looked sharply at him. "What?"

"You couldn't court her as you are now. You'd need to conceal yourself in another form. And I don't know if you can even—comport yourself properly when you're disguised. I had wanted grandchildren, you know. Or did you intend to take her back to—"

"How," interrupted Tam unevenly, "how long have you—I was very careful—how did you know?"

Hazelrig gave him a small, sympathetic smile. "How long have you had an eye for her?"

"I don't know. I thought I respected her as your daughter, as my nominal mistress, as a friend, though she did not truly know me. And then.... I know it must seem odd to you, that I've known her as a child as much as a woman, but—well, we live longer lives, and such a view is less uncommon for us." Tam looked suddenly embarrassed. "Why am I telling all this?"

"Because I asked, and I asked because it has a bearing on my daughter."

Tam looked down. "I'm sorry. I know your daughter was never a part of any agreement."

"She was not." Hazelrig took a seat. "However, I have raised my daughter with independence and intelligence. She may choose her own way. You've seen I do not pressure her in these affairs."

"I have."

"And I am not so opposed to the idea of a Ryuven as a son. Or rather, less so than most of my peers, at least with an eye to one particular Ryuven." He smiled. "I'm not sure I'd want to see her cross into your world again, but.... None of that matters, however, unless you intend to act."

Tam's expression was wrong for his young face. "I don't know," he admitted. "She is young. I could be happy with her, and I would try to make her happy. But I would not take her to my world to stay. I have been an exile myself. If I surrendered my place again, we could stay here—but I would be an exile again, and we would have the constant fear I might be discovered." He flushed. "And there is also the question of your grandchildren, as you put it. While I may assure you that my human guise is—very functional, I do not know if we could successfully have children, and I do not know what characteristics they would bear."

Hazelrig looked thoughtful. "It would certainly shine a clearer light on my research into our histories."

"My lord mage." Tam gave him a flat look.

"What of her choice—if she would have you, and where she would prefer to live?"

"Why make things awkward if it is impossible?" Tamaryl sighed. "She knows, or she suspects, and already it has changed her. I would not lose her friendship, even if I cannot be more."

"You know Shianan Becknam would like to court her."

Tam stiffened. "Shianan Becknam may hate me and my kind, but he is a good man outside of that, I think. She could do much worse."

Hazelrig sighed. "If you have no regrets...."

"No, I will have regrets, whatever I do. But I mean to have fewer, and to leave her with none."

"You will return before tomorrow's shield-making, then?"

"I think so." He paused. "I will be sad to leave this place. There is a part of my life here, which you have made."

Hazelrig rose and put a hand on the boy's shoulder, turning him gently. "I will be sorry to see you go."

Tam sniffed, suddenly very like a twelve-year-old. "I'll go tomorrow morning, then."

CHAPTER 71

Shianan sat at his desk, staring at papers he didn't see. He did not look at the two men waiting in the corner. He had to harden himself, turn his racing pulse to ice in his veins, lest he fail in his purpose. Every selfish urge wanted to abandon the intent, and he walked a blade's-edge in doing what he must.

He would have to do it quickly, before his will gave out.

Luca entered with a gust of cold air and noted the two men against the wall. "I'm sorry if I interrupted. Would you like me to bring anything?"

Shianan shook his head, feeling as if it were made of iron. "Stay, Luca," he said hoarsely. "I need to speak with you."

"Yes?" Luca looked concerned—but not suspicious.

Shianan drove bitten nails into his palms. "Luca.... Your brother has been looking for you a long time."

"He did," Luca agreed, with a small glance toward the silent men in the corner, "until he assumed I was dead."

"He wanted to—ransom you. Redeem you."

"Redeem?"

Shianan could not read Luca's expression. Perhaps Luca himself didn't know what he felt.

Shianan might not, either. But Luca's family wanted him—*wanted* him. And somewhere deep, where he refused to probe, Shianan knew he himself would do anything....

He cleared his throat gruffly. "You're going with him."

Luca stared. "I'm going.... But—no!"

The men stirred in the corner.

Luca shook his head. "I don't want to go!"

Trader Matteo moved and took Luca's arm. "Come along."

"No!" Luca jerked away. He recoiled into the slaver's assistant behind him and spun. They moved to his arms.

Shianan started to his feet, his heart in his throat. "Luca...."

"Let go!" shrieked Luca. He tore loose and lunged toward the desk. His fingers clawed across the surface and grasped the opposite edge, his eyes inches from Shianan's. "You promised," he pleaded. "You said no one could buy me."

451

Shianan swallowed hard. "I said no one could afford your price, and that's true. But he's your own blood, Luca. He has a better claim on you than I could."

"Don't do this!"

"Luca—"

The trader's assistant reached to seize a handful of hair at Luca's forehead, peeling him back from the desk. Shianan jerked forward. "That's enough!"

The trader hesitated, holding Luca's bent arm but without applying pressure. "I'm sorry, your lordship. I remember what you said. But he's got to come with us, after all."

"Do it without harm," snapped Shianan.

Trader Matteo looked doubtfully at Luca. "Right. If he doesn't fight." He nodded to the assistant, who ran a loop of cord through the rings on Luca's cuffs, trapping them behind his back. "That will help, anyway."

"Master Shianan," breathed Luca, "I—I hardly know my brother now."

"The more reason I should let you go." Shianan bowed his head so he saw only the cluttered desk. "Be careful of him."

"As you say, lordship." The slavers started forward. Luca resisted briefly, but the assistant simply lifted the cord on his wrists and he submitted. Then they were through the door, leaving a gust of frigid wind to sweep the office.

Shianan dropped to his chair, seeing the desktop blur beneath him. He had done the right thing—he was sure of it. Luca deserved better than slavery, and he should have the opportunity to return to his family. Their friendship gave Shianan no right to keep him bound in a position where he could not but crave that friendship.... He had done the right thing, but that did not make it easy.

He dropped his head to his hands and sobbed.

Jarrick Roald took a breath, drawing courage, and then rapped at the door. Shianan Becknam had summoned him, and he hadn't dared to guess the reason. Did the commander want information on the merchant alliance? A ransom for Luca? Revenge for the attempts on his life?

"Come," came a voice through the door. Jarrick opened it and entered, warm air brushing his face. The commander was at the desk, writing. He threw down his pen and lifted his head. His eyes were rimmed red. "Jarrick Roald."

"Your lordship, I—"

"Be quiet, Roald. I have something to say to you, and I won't extend our interaction beyond strict necessity." He shoved paper and pen across the desk. "Write, quickly, the names of those who are left from the initial scheme to fleece the army. I want the names of whoever worked with Karlm in this league. I doubt his is the mind at the back of it." He tapped the paper impatiently. "Now!"

Roald's hands moved without his instruction, taking up the pen and listing six names on the page. "These are all I know. I've met only these three, but I know Karlm takes instruction from this one."

"These are all the names you know?"

Jarrick nodded.

The commander withdrew the page and leveled a finger at Jarrick. "It is only for Luca's sake that you are not this moment begging the inquisitors to hear your confession. You must know that."

Jarrick nodded.

"And it is equally for Luca's sake that you have this contract to save your house." Becknam withdrew a sealed document and nearly flung it at Jarrick. "If your house falls now, Luca's sacrifice was worthless. He deserves better than that. And he deserves a house to return to."

Jarrick blinked. "My lord?"

"I'm sending Luca with you."

Jarrick caught his breath. "My lord—thank you. I know you will—I can advance part now—"

"I am not asking for payment." Becknam's tone was dark. "Do you think you could possibly buy him? No, I am sending Luca with you only because he deserves more than slavery in a foreign land, and because I want him to return to his family and home. He's already at the caravan staging ground, waiting for you." He tapped the contract sharply. "You'd better hurry. You leave at dawn."

"Dawn?"

"You have your contract, you have your brother. You have no other business here." Becknam's narrowed eyes communicated clearly that the alliance was beyond Jarrick's concern now. "You have no reason to remain in Alham."

Jarrick swallowed. "Yes, my lord."

"Now get out of sight before I forget you're Luca's brother as well as the foot-licking scut who nearly killed him and me both."

Jarrick hesitated and then made a hasty bow. "Thank you, your lordship." Clutching the precious contract, he fled through the door.

CHAPTER 72

"Tam?" Hazelrig closed the office door against the bustle of the Wheel and pulled his white robes over his shoulders. "Tam, you haven't much time."

"I know." The boy who was not a boy straightened a casket of phlogisticated earth in the storage cabinet and turned to face Ewan, his arms folded across his chest. He looked across the room at nothing in particular. "It's hard to leave. I worked so hard to believe I would stay forever.... I never expected to return."

"But Oniwe'aru welcomed you."

"He did. And it would be foolish indeed to waste that, wouldn't it?" He took a deep breath. "Is my lady coming? I would like to bid her farewell before I go."

Ewan reached without looking to a plaque mounted with fifteen crystals, his fingers automatically brushing the one labeled *Black*. He had been White Mage a long time. He energized the stone and flicked it once, so that it rang with a whining buzz. The consonant crystal in Ariana's office would sound as well, alerting her the White Mage wanted her.

Tam twiddled awkwardly with a tray of sand on Hazelrig's table. A moment later Ariana tapped at the door and entered, already in her black robes. She saw them standing together, looking at her, and quickly closed the door. "You're going now?"

Tam nodded. "This is my final chance."

For a moment Ariana looked as if she might cry, but her jaw tightened and she swallowed visibly. She crossed the room and bent to embrace his short figure. "We'll miss you. Thank you for—for everything."

Tam held her, but not tightly, his eyes closed. "I'll miss you, my lady. I'll miss you dearly." He released her and turned to the White Mage. "And you...."

Ewan knelt and pulled the boy into his arms. "I wish there were some way. I wish I could see you again. I'm sorry I couldn't do more, my friend."

Tam smiled sadly. "You did all anyone could." He stepped back, his throat working. "If you release me here within the Wheel, with all the members of the Great Circle within a short radius...."

Ewan chuckled. "They'll all come rushing in a panic, and I'll tell them we just banished a Ryuven who tried for the Shard. You'll be safely home, and Ariana and I will be minor heroes." He hesitated. "Are you ready?"

Tam nodded. "As I ever will be."

Ewan stood and gave Tam a fond, sad look. Tam glanced at Ariana with a conflicted smile and then faced the White Mage.

"Tamaryl," said Ewan quietly.

Power swelled within the room, crackling through their robes and rustling papers on the desk. The shape of the boy Tam expanded and shredded into light, and a winged Ryuven stood in his place.

Tamaryl stepped forward, clasping Ewan close once more. "Goodbye, my lord mage. May we never meet again." He turned and faced Ariana. "My lady."

She caught his wrist. "I...."

He bent swiftly and kissed her, surprising her with both action and intensity. But it ended as quickly as it began, leaving her with the taste of him and a tingling of power on her lips. Then he pulled backward. "I love you both," he said, looking between them. "Goodbye."

The air stretched and cracked with the opening between worlds, and then Tamaryl was gone. Ariana's ears popped as she stared at where he had been.

There was a tumult outside the door. Ewan turned, raising his hands for calm, as the door flung open and mages and soldiers pushed inside. "It's all right," he called over their excited voices. "Everything's fine. He's gone now, and he did not succeed in taking the Shard."

The generalized anxiety subsided, and the crowd settled to discussing the near disaster. "Not a moment too soon for the Shield," Elysia Parma muttered. "The audacity of coming into the Wheel!"

"It will be only a few minutes, now," Ewan soothed her.

But Ariana wondered if it were too soon. She would never again see the Ryuven world, Maru, Tamaryl. She pressed her tingling lips together as they left the White Mage's office. Her father brushed away questions, protesting that the recreation of the shield took priority over discussion of a Ryuven already banished.

In the cellar, the White Mage knelt before the Shard of Elan and emptied a vial over it. Dark, viscous liquid seeped over the Shard and sank unnaturally into the crystal—Ryuven blood, against which the shield would harmonize. Then he walked to his designated position, straightening his robes. This time Ariana took her place among the Circle, and at her father's signal they began as one, carving signs from the air.

The iridescent indigo hemisphere appeared, solidified, expanded. Ariana felt a ripple of recalled terror and shoved it away; she had to concentrate on her task. It wouldn't do to stumble in her first formal charge as Black Mage, and in something so important and visible as the shield-making.

And then the shield rushed outward, running past them and over the kingdom, and the magic was finished. The mages let their arms drop, tired and drained, as a cheer went up around the room. Ariana smiled and took a step toward her father, surprised as she staggered a little. The effort had required more than she'd thought.

The White Mage smiled and nodded, exchanging comments and congratulations, as he made his way toward Ariana. "How do you feel?" he asked her, slipping an arm around her shoulders.

Tired, Ariana meant to answer, but her voice said, "I wish we hadn't."

Quickly her father pulled her close. "I know," he whispered, his voice husky. "I'll miss him, too. You can't imagine how much I came to rely upon him, and—and he was a good friend, for all that he was Pairvyn ni'Ai." He gave her a final squeeze. "I think Elysia has ordered refreshment. She must have remembered it's a difficult working." He left his arm about her shoulders and they ascended the stairs.

TO BE CONTINUED

Blood & Bond
Kin & Kind

AUTHOR'S NOTE

Please, don't anyone in our modern world rely upon our heroes' protocol for treating hypothermia! Young Shianan was lucky, but it's astonishing Luca survived. We can attribute that miracle to a strong dose of Ewan Hazelrig's fantastic magic and the overwhelming juggernaut of authorial necessity. So much physical handling might have stopped his bradycardic heart, killing him rather more permanently. And of course, Luca's resistance to such subsequent nuisances as pneumonia may be best laid to his arcane treatment; without Mage Hazelrig, he would not have fared so well.

Many good things can be learned from fiction, but there are far safer and more effective methods in our modern and mundane world for warming a hypothermic individual than a steaming bath.

GET A FREE STORY AND MORE

The website has everything from background research and inspiration to story glossaries and book club discussion guides, as well as an infrequent newsletter for events and releases. Go to **www.LauraVAB.com** to receive the prequel "Wings & War," available first only as a preorder bonus and now exclusively from my site, as well as other free stories and sneak peeks, special or advance offers, and release specials for the sequels..

Thank you for reading, and please be sure to review *Shard & Shield* at your favorite site. I read every review! and I'd love to hear from you.

CPSIA information can be obtained
at www.ICGtesting.com
Printed in the USA
LVHW031939190220
647495LV00004B/798